DIRTY HIT

COLD HEARTED PLAYERS BOOK ONE

HEATHER ASHLEY

Copyright © 2024 by Heather Ashley

All rights reserved.

No part of this book may be reproduced in any form or by any electronic or mechanical means, including information storage and retrieval systems, without written permission from the author, except for the use of brief quotations in a book review.

ISBN: 9798323825592

Cover Design: Black Widow Designs

heatherashleywrites.com

Dedication

To everyone who's ever wanted to bang an NHL player...

...and have him become toxically obsessed with you.

This one's for you.

Playlist

Uninvited by Alanis Morissette
Levitate by Twenty One Pilots
Something to Hide by grandson
buzzkill by MOTHICA
Tantrum by Charlotte Sands
STAR WALKIN' by Lil Nas X
ICE QUEEN by margo
You Put a Spell on Me by Austin Giorgio
Love Into a Weapon by Madalen Duke
Choke by Royal & The Serpent
No Mercy by Austin Giorgio
I'll Make You Love Me by Kat Leon & Sam Tinnesz
Animals x Starboy by TommyMuzzic
Vigilante Shit by Taylor Swift
Lane Boy by Twenty One Pilots

Trigger warnings

Stalking

Cheating (NOT between the H/h)

Violence & gore (blood)

Stealthing

Dub/Non-Con

Pregnancy

Kidnapping

Drugging

Somnophilia

Murder

Recording Sexual Acts & Posting Online

Alcohol Consumption

Threats of Rape

Threats to Harm an Unborn Child

Blackmail

CASSIDY
princess
BENNETT

HAYDEN
'The Hitman'
VAUGHN

29

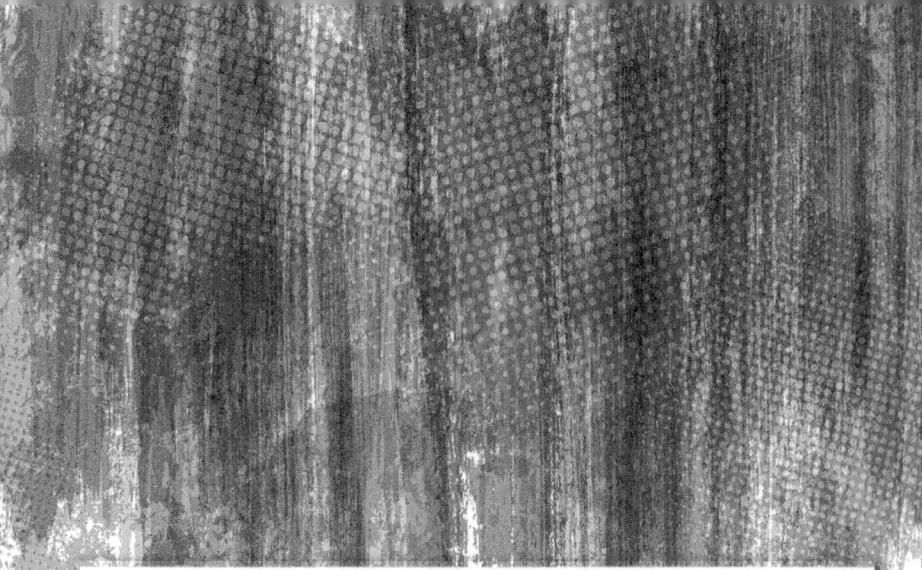

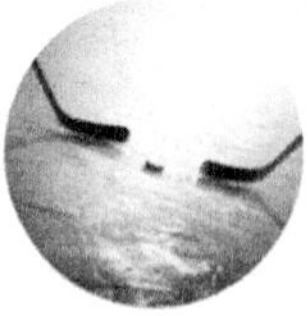

thelastman
@HockeyHypeMan

If 'The Hitman' were any more ruthless, he'd need a license to skate 🚨
#HaydenVaughn

Hayden #1

"YOU'RE HAYDEN FUCKING VAUGHN," I mutter as sweat drips into my eyes. "Get your shit together."

Seems like I need the goddamn reminder today after missing another shot. My teammates are looking at me like I've been body snatched by some asshole who's not the number one scoring defenseman in the league. Maybe I have.

It's not like I haven't tried to get the damn thing into the net.

Being off my game is starting to make me violent.

I've been working my ass off at this since I was five years old and I've been chasing the puck ever since.

I'm good. No, scratch that—I'm *great*. One of the best defensemen in the NHL, with a reputation for being ruthless on the ice. They call me The Hitman for a reason. I'm not afraid to take out anyone who gets in my way, and it's earned me respect from my teammates and fear from every team we face.

So why can't I get my head in the game today?

"Watch out!" one of my teammates shouts as the star

forward for the Aces, Kovalenko, comes charging toward me, stick raised high and ready to fire off a one-timer.

Everything slows down. The sound of skates cutting through the ice fades away, the crowd noise quiets to nothing, and all I can hear is my heartbeat pounding in my ears. I know what I need to do—what I always do when a player from the other team is coming at me like this.

Hit him. *Hard.*

All the frustration that's been building since the start of the game boils over. I chase him down, checking him from behind right into the boards. He hits with a satisfying crunch and I spit out my mouth guard, grinning over his twisted and still body.

"Next time don't even fucking try," I growl at him as whistles blow and a fight erupts around me. Both benches clear and it's chaos.

Someone punches me in the face, but I barely feel the pain as my teeth slice into my cheek and my head snaps to the side. My mouth fills with blood that I spit onto the ice, staining it red. I whirl around, ready to take on whoever else wants a piece of me, giving one of the Aces players a bloody grin that's all menace.

I dare him to come at me.

This is what I need—what I live for. These moments when I can drop gloves and purge the bad shit out through my fists.

Eventually, the refs and a couple of my cooler-headed teammates break up the fight. I let them lead me away, knowing that we've got the game in the bag now. The Aces are pissed and their star forward can't even skate himself off the ice, but I'm still buzzing with adrenaline as I head to the penalty box. Halfway there, the refs tell me I'm done.

Fucking misconduct penalty.

Eh, it's not the first time I've been tossed out of a game, probably won't be the last.

One of the trainers hands me a bottle of water and I take it before heading back toward the locker room, feeling a little better. But as I pass by the tunnel, a group of Atlanta fans press against the glass. They're taunting me for my hit and I stop to flip them off. Fuck them and what they think about me. They have no idea the pressure I'm under or the expectations weighing me down.

Eventually, the game ends, and my blood's boiling. I did everything I could to hand my team this win and they still let the Aces take the W. The monitors in the locker room play the aftermath, and I watch, still pissed about being ejected as they silently skate toward the tunnel to a packed arena throwing shit at them and yelling things that make me want to launch myself into the crowd skates first.

When they make their way into the locker room, I'm waiting for them with a scowl on my face and the need for violence raging in my veins. "What the fuck was that?"

"We lost," O'Sullivan says with a flat voice, shaking his head as he strips off his gear, chucking his helmet into his locker with a loud-ass bang.

I scoff. "Yeah, no shit. But why didn't you guys fight back? We had a lead and you let them take it away."

"You were ejected," Petrov points out.

"And?" I ask. "I took Kovalenko out. He's their strongest winger. You should've pressed the goddamn advantage."

Abrams glares at me. "That's not how the rest of us want to win."

I open my mouth to bitch at him for being a pussy, but then Coach storms into the locker room and starts tearing into all of us. He doesn't mention me specifically, but I can see it in his eyes that he's pissed about what happened on the ice.

As we head out to the bus, I'm still fuming about the loss. It shouldn't have happened. We're the best damn team in the league and we should've been able to hold on to that lead without me on the ice.

I drop myself into a seat, ignoring the looks from my teammates as I shove earbuds into my ears so I don't have to talk to anyone. Then I pull out my phone and log into my Instagram.

It's not unusual for me to have thousands of notifications and messages, and tonight's no different.

I don't know what makes me do it. Usually I ignore that shit, especially after a game like this one. But I click into my messages anyway, knowing I shouldn't. Knowing it's probably a bunch of assholes talking shit like they could ever do what I do, but feeling compelled to check anyway.

I roll my eyes. I don't know why I let these assholes get to me.

Right there at the top is a new message from someone with the username *iceprincessxo*.

I open it and am drawn immediately to the little icon with her picture in it—long brown hair and bright green eyes, pretty lips curved up in a smile that's equal parts wicked and sweet. My dick's a big fan of this girl's tiny profile pic. She's stunning, even if she looks like a good girl who wouldn't know what to do with a guy like me.

But then I read the message attached to the picture and my blood burns.

> iceprincessxo: How's it feel knowing you can't win unless you cheat, asshole?

> iceprincessxo: If you actually had any skills, you wouldn't have play dirty.

I stare at those words for a long time, my fingers tightening around my phone as anger surges through me. Who the fuck does this chick think she is? She doesn't know me or anything about me. She's just some fan who thinks she can say whatever the hell she wants without consequences.

Well, she's wrong.

My fingers are flying across the screen before I can stop myself.

> hayv29: You don't know shit about me, princess. And if you don't want to see dirty hockey, don't fucking watch the game.

But I pause before I hit send, my thumb hovering over the button.

What the hell am I doing?

It's not like her opinion matters. She's just a hockey fan, and obviously not a fan of mine. Still, I can't seem to let it go. What she said keeps replaying in my head—about how I have to cheat to win—and I can't shake the feeling that maybe she's right.

But also... who cares? I am who I am and you can't argue with results.

Instead of sending the message, I click into her profile and scroll through her posts. She doesn't have many pictures of herself. Most of them are lifestyle shots of what she's eating or where she's going. Girl shit no one really cares about.

But there are enough of her that show she's got tight curves in all the right places. Despite every instinct telling me to look away, I can't.

She doesn't like me, and she's probably bat shit, considering her message. Still, I can't stop staring at her photos. One of the Space Needle catches my eye and I realize she lives in Seattle, on the other side of the country, while I'm heading back to Philly.

But as I stare out the window of the bus, watching the lights of Atlanta pass by on our way to the airport, I can't stop thinking about her. About how much I want the chance to show this woman exactly how much I can really make her hate me.

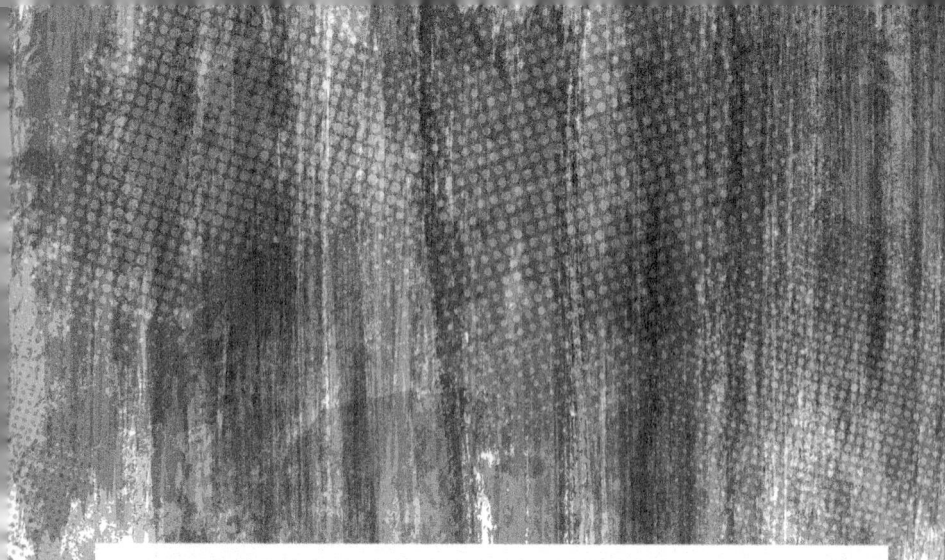

bow down
@IceQueen2024

watching Hayden Vaughn play rn and wow, does he bring new meaning to breaking the ice or what? 🏒💥 #SeattleAnchors #TheHitman

Hayden #2

"WHAT THE HELL happened out there last night?" Coach Sullivan demands as soon as we're all seated around the conference table in the Phantom's offices.

My agent called me before it was light out this morning and told me to get my ass to team headquarters for this meeting.

I shrug. "I did what I had to do."

"You were ejected," Coach says, his face reddening. "And Kovalenko's out indefinitely with a neck injury."

"He knew the risks of playing this game," I argue, shifting back into my seat like I don't give a shit as I get reamed. "We all do."

"This isn't the first time we've had this issue with you, Hayden." Larry Donnelly, the Phantoms' GM, sounds tired as fuck when he says this.

I look over at my agent, Mitch, for a little help, but he's purposefully trying not to make eye contact.

"Look," I say, leaning forward and resting my elbows on the table, hating that I even have to be here right now. Their irritation feels like a splinter under my skin and I don't fucking like it. "It was just one game—"

"It's not just about this game," Coach says. "It's about your reputation. You've got a history of playing dirty and it's affecting the team."

I laugh. "Yeah, like getting us more wins."

"Did we win last night?" Coach barks.

"What do you want from me?" I'm starting to feel like I'm being accused of something. To be fair, I might deserve it, but still. I don't have to take whatever they throw at me like a little bitch. I'm the only one on this goddamn team willing to do whatever it takes to win. Why don't they get that?

Larry sighs. "The NHL has approached us about your behavior on the ice."

My stomach drops and I sit back in my chair. "What?"

"They're considering banning you from future games," Larry continues. "In light of that, we're going to make some changes around here."

"You can't be fucking serious."

Mitch finally speaks up. "Hayden, you need to take a step back and think about what's important here."

"What's important is winning," I say, looking around the table at everyone else. "That's all that matters."

"Not if it means losing fans and sponsors," Larry says. "We need to clean up our image, not just for the NHL, but for the city of Philadelphia as well."

My fists clench. "This is bullshit."

"It's not bullshit," Coach snaps. "You need to get your shit together or you're done in this league."

"Either way, it's too late for you here. Your time in Philly is over," Larry adds. "We're trading you."

My jaw clenches. "Mitch," I bark out. "I need a minute in the hall." When he looks like he's going to argue, I shoot him a death glare. "Now."

Once we're outside the room and out of earshot of the others, I turn on him. "What the fuck was that? Did you know about this?"

Mitch sighs and runs a hand through his salt and pepper hair. "Hayden, listen—"

"Seriously? You're supposed to be my agent. You're supposed to have my fucking back, not let me walk into a goddamn buzz saw."

"I do have your back," he says, looking annoyed. "But you're making it really damn hard."

"What the hell does that mean?"

He sighs again. "You're not an easy guy to represent, okay? You've got a reputation, and no one wants to touch you."

"So what?" I ask. "I'm a fucking god on that ice. If anything, last night proved it. Without me, the team blew the lead and lost. That's what matters. If they want to win, they'll want me on their team."

"Maybe in the short term," Mitch says. "But eventually, that kind of shit catches up with you, kid. Wherever you're going, it'll be a shit team and you're gonna have to prove yourself."

I scowl, feeling a hurricane of rage and frustration brewing inside of me. "Whatever. I'm the best damn defenseman in this league. If I have to prove it every goddamn day, I will."

I glare at him as I pace back and forth in this stupid fucking hall decked out in Phantoms green and black, feeling like I'm being told off by my dad.

The last thing I need to think about right now is *that* asshole.

"Fuck this. They don't want me? Fine. Let's make a trade then."

I stalk away from him and back into the conference room, where Larry and Coach are waiting for me. They glance up as I approach, and Larry gives me a sympathetic look.

"Hayden—"

"Don't," I say, holding up a hand. I don't know what makes me say it, but I hear myself demanding, "I want to go to Seattle. I'll sign whatever you want me to sign. Just make it happen."

They're a shit team this season and there's no way they'll turn down a chance to have me. Despite my reputation, I win games and I think they're desperate enough to turn a blind eye to my baggage.

Larry nods and hands me a piece of paper that's already been filled out with my name on it. "Here's the proposed trade agreement. I'll have to see if Seattle's interested."

I take the paper and scan it quickly before signing it. "Done." I can feel Mitch cringe from somewhere behind me because I didn't let him read it over, but I'm past caring at this point.

"You're sure about this?" Coach asks, looking at me like he's worried about my mental state or some shit. Or maybe he thinks I'm about to kick his ass. If I'm being honest, the thought crossed my mind.

"Positive." I'm fucking seething, but there's nothing I can do. If they don't want me here, I'm not going to beg them to let me stay. But why *Seattle*? Why the fuck would that pop out of my mouth?

You know why.

The girl from last night. The one whose pictures I haven't been able to stop staring at... or jacking off to.

I don't even know her name, but I'm going to find out. Then I'm going to hunt her down and make her choke on her words.

Or my dick.

It's still a toss up at this point.

I don't mean the next words out of my mouth, but they come out anyway. *Always the politician's son.* "Maybe a fresh start will do me some good."

That's the last thing I need, but I'll play my part. *Never burn bridges, Hayden.* My father's voice is an unwelcome addition to the clusterfuck in my head right now.

Larry nods again and takes the signed paper from me. "I'll make the call."

And just like that, I'm done in Philadelphia. Done with the team that made me who I am today. Done in the blink of an eye after three years of putting everything on the line for them. It stings more than I thought it would.

As I head out of the offices and into the cooler November weather outside, I wonder how the hell everything went so wrong so fast. But it's too late now. I've already signed the damn paper and there's no turning back.

It doesn't take long for Seattle to agree to the trade. Within a few days, Mitch books me a flight and I'm on my way across the country to start my new life as a member of the Seattle Anchors.

Just fucking great. I glare down at the number 29 inked into my forearm, feeling the weight of those two digits like I'm carrying the world on my back. I'm surprised my dad hasn't called me to bitch me out already about this move.

But I don't give a shit about any of it. All I care about right now is my latest obsession—finding the girl from my DMs. The one whose face won't stop popping up in my mind every time I try to sleep or eat or fucking function in any sort of normal way.

I know it's insane. It's not like me to be transfixed like this, at least not with a person. Hockey? Sure. But a girl? I've never allowed it before. Fuck and bail, that's my M.O.

There's something about her I can't get out of my head. I need to know every single thing about her. To make her see that I'm more than some asshole she hates. Make her mine in a way she can't run from.

Force her to *see* me.

The second I step foot in Seattle, the hunt to find my girl begins, and on the flight, two drinks in, I've already started the search by going through every single post she's ever made on Instagram, trying to find anything that will help me hunt her down. I slide my tongue ring between my teeth and play with it while I focus on the screen. She mentions nothing about her job or where she lives, besides the obvious Seattle landmarks. She's a total mystery.

That only makes it more fun.

I spend hours stalking her profile, the entire flight, looking for any clues that might lead me in the right direction. And when I finally land in Seattle, I'm amped up like I'm high, ready to find this girl even if I have to break the rules to do it.

It's almost like I've been training for this my whole life.

Anchor Drop

1 oz vodka • 1 oz blue curaçao
• Lemonade • Splash of club soda • ice
Garnish: lemon wheel

Fill a glass with ice, add vodka and blue curaçao, top with lemonade, a splash of soda, stir gently, and garnish with a lemon wheel.

Cassidy #3

I CRINGE as I stare up at one of the flat-screens hanging on the wall, watching again as Hayden Vaughn smashes Alexei Kovalenko into the boards with an illegal check.

What a dick.

The replays haven't stopped.

Still… sending him that message on Instagram wasn't one of my finer moments. That's what a few too many drinks and a long night at my hockey bar will do to you. I don't normally go around insulting NHL players, especially ones as stupidly hot as Hayden. But something about him just rubs me the wrong way.

Maybe it's his reputation for being an asshole, or maybe it's the way he seems to think he can get away with anything on the ice with no consequences. Or maybe it's not even him and it's a general hatred for hockey players after my cheating shitbag of an ex.

Either way, I'm feeling like a total idiot for saying anything to him, even if it was behind a screen. Besides, I'm sure he gets thousands of messages and probably didn't even see mine.

Probably.

Just as the thought crosses my mind, a notification pops up on my phone and I freeze, setting down the glass I was drying with a shaky hand. It's probably just Uncle Todd checking in. Now that he's retired, and the trust handed the bar over to me, he likes to make sure I'm good running this place on my own.

But somehow I know it's not him. I brush the hair out of my face as my heart goes from calm to *Jesus fuck, I'm about to explode* in the blink of an eye. Yup, it's from Instagram, and when I open the app, there's a message waiting for me from *him*.

Hayden Vaughn. The Hitman himself.

Shit.

I bite my lip and stare at it for a long time before clicking in. My heart's beating so fast I think I might stroke out.

> hayv29: You're Cassidy Bennett.

Of course he wouldn't respond like a normal person.

> hayv29: You live in Seattle

My blood runs cold as I realize that this guy somehow figured out who I am and where to find me, despite purposefully keeping my Insta account vague. This guy with access to nearly unlimited money, sticks and blades he's an expert at wielding, and who knows how to fight better than some MMA fighters.

Awesome.

It's the last line that really gets to me, though.

> hayv29: And now I do, too

I swallow hard, trying not to panic as I read the message over and over again. This can't be real. There's no way Hayden Vaughn is in Seattle because of me.

I glance up at the TV screen again, not really seeing it until a red bar flashes across the bottom of the NHL Network feed.

Breaking News: Hayden 'The Hitman' Vaughn Traded to Seattle.

Goosebumps break out over my entire body, and my stomach hits the floor. Before I can think about it too long, my phone buzzes as another message pops up from him.

> hayv29: Meet me tomorrow tonight

I stare at the message for a long time before replying with shaking fingers.

> iceprincessxo: Not happening

His response is instant.

> hayv29: Don't make me come find you.

Shit.

I'm so screwed.

I don't know what to say back to him, but I'm terrified he'll show up here at my bar or worse—at my apartment. He already found out who I am. Getting my address will be a piece of cake.

This can't just be about my message, can it? What else could he possibly want?

As I try to figure out what to do, my phone buzzes again and I see that he's sent me his phone number.

> hayv29: Text me your address

> iceprincessxo: Fuck off and die
>
> iceprincessxo: Or, you know, just leave me alone

> hayv29: You started this, princess
>
> hayv29: Now I'm gonna finish it

Double shit.

I should just block him. That'd be the smart thing to do, right?

So what the hell's wrong with me that I don't? That some part of me wants him to message me again. To call him out and see what he does.

I don't know why I'm like this, but I can't deny the way my pulse goes absolutely wild as I read his messages. It's like there's something inside of me that wants to push back against him, to challenge him and see what happens.

I'm just about to block his number and delete his message (yeah, right) when another one comes in from him.

> hayv29: Admit you want me to find you.
>
> hayv29: You like the chase as much as I do, don't you, princess?

My heart skips a beat at his words, and I can't help but wonder if maybe he's right. Maybe I do want him to... No. No, this is crazy.

But then I remember who he is and what he did on the ice a couple of nights ago. The Hitman isn't someone you want to mess with. He's dangerous.

Still, I can't deny the way my teeth dig into my lip until it hurts as I type back,

> iceprincessxo: Never

He responds with a smirking emoji and I laugh out loud despite myself. This guy is psychologically unwell. And I'm even crazier for talking to him like this.

But as I turn back to my bar and the rowdy group of hockey fans that just piled through the door after another Anchors loss tonight, I can't stop thinking about him and wondering what would happen if he showed up here. He's going to be in my city. It wouldn't be hard, especially with the Anchors players using my place as their regular after-game meet up spot.

Would I let him find me? Or would I run as far away as possible from the NHL's most ruthless player?

Lila eyes me over the drink she's mixing for one of the guys at the bar and raises an eyebrow. "What's got you so twisted up?"

I try to act normal, but I know she can see right through me. "Nothing."

She smirks. "Uh huh."

"Really," I say, trying to sound convincing as I grab a bottle of Blue Moon and pop off the top. But inside, my stomach is churning with a mixture of fear and excitement as I think about what could happen if Hayden Vaughn actually shows up at my bar—or at my apartment.

And that scares me more than anything, because I don't think I'd be able to tell him to go away.

It's late when I finally get home after closing down The Sin Bin. Yet another night gone that I've failed to fulfill my dad's wish for this place—to add a restaurant so families can come and celebrate their love of hockey together. Some nights it feels like it'll never happen.

The Anchors went into overtime and the last regular didn't leave until almost two. Lila offered to stay and help, but I told her to go home. She's got a baby to take care of and I don't want her to feel like she has to babysit me all the time, too. Besides, her girlfriend deserves a breather from baby duties once in a while.

As I unlock my door and step into my apartment, my shoulders drop and I let out a long exhale. It's been a long day and all I want to do is crawl into bed and sleep for a week.

But as I turn on the light in the kitchen, I freeze and a mixture of a gasp and squeak pops out of my mouth at what's sitting on the counter.

It's flowers. A huge arrangement of dark red dahlias that must have cost a fortune. They're the color of blood.

I stare at it for a long moment before looking around my apartment, feeling like someone could be hiding in the shadows, ready to jump out at me. The hairs on the back of my neck stand up like I'm being watched. But there's no one here. Just me and this insanely expensive bouquet.

I don't think his flower choice was by accident. They mean something. A quick search on my phone tells me it's love and romance, but also perseverance. Nope, that's not unsettling at all.

I swallow hard as I approach them, wondering if they're from Hayden and, if so, how he managed to get into my apartment while I was gone. There's no sign of forced entry and nothing seems out of place, but knowing he was here, in my apartment... I don't know how to feel.

Still, I can't shake the idea that this is all some kind of twisted game he's playing with me. I pissed him off and now he's going to play with me the way a cat plays with a mouse before he eats it.

I pick up the card attached to the flowers and open it, my

heart pounding as I read the words written inside, the ones that confirm my suspicions.

"Hope you're ready to play, Princess."

winner winner
@SportsSnark

Someone tell the Vancouver Orcas that swimming away from Vaughn isn't an option on ice #TheHitmanStrikesAgain

Hayden #4

I MIGHT'VE GONE OVERBOARD with the flowers, but I couldn't resist. And the look on her face as she walked into her apartment and saw them was worth every damn penny.

The hour that I spent hiding in the tiny hall closet so she wouldn't know I was there was worth it, too.

She's scared. I can tell by the way her breathing picks up and her gaze darts around the room, searching for me.

Her fear makes my dick hard.

I've been waiting for this moment for hours—ever since I landed in Seattle and started tracking her down. It took some digging, some help from a contact of my father's, but I found her address and waited until she left for work before sneaking into her apartment.

Unfortunately, I can't stick around and watch her sleep the way I want to, not with an early skate with my new team in the morning. But I have a feeling she'll be thinking about me while she's in bed tonight.

I wait until she's in the shower, and then I sneak out the

same way I got in—through the front door. It's tempting as hell to go climb in there with her, but something tells me I'm already on thin ice and I don't want to push too far too fast.

As I head back to my hotel, I relish in the knowledge that I've gotten under Cassidy's skin. She hasn't blocked me yet, which means she's interested.

That's all I need.

The next day, I'm buzzing with anticipation as I get ready for the first practice with the Anchors. They're a shitty team, so they need a little extra push to make it to the top. And I plan on giving them exactly that.

The Bluetooth in my rental car announces I have a call and I glance at the screen, grinning when my brother's name pops up. "Miss me already?"

"Hey," he says, sounding distracted. "You busy?"

"Just heading to practice."

"Oh yeah," he says and his voice goes muffled for a second, like he's talking to someone else. "How's Seattle?"

"Gray," I say, since so far in the couple of days I've been here, it's living up to its depressing rep. "How're things back home?"

"Same old shit," Sawyer says with a sigh. "Hayden..."

"What?"

He pauses before saying, "Couldn't you have waited until the end of the season before getting your ass traded? Do you have any idea how hard it's going to be for me to transfer hospitals?"

I laugh. "You could learn not to be so codependent on me and just wrap up the year where you are."

"Fuck you," he grumbles. "You're just as codependent on me."

"Bet." I pull into the practice facility parking lot and find a spot. "Look, I gotta go. I'll text you when I'm done." He wasn't wrong about us being codependent. Sawyer's not just my brother, he's my best friend. My other half just like I'm his. He's also the only person I've ever let close.

"Yeah," Sawyer says. "Don't get your ass beat on your first day."

I scoff. "If anyone's throwing punches today, it's gonna be me."

"Okay, NSYNC. Go before you're late."

We hang up and I head inside, ready to show my new team what I'm made of.

The game tonight was fucking brutal. We lost by two goals and everyone's pissed. But not me. For once, I'm feeling good.

Because I know where she is. My brain's already switched off the clusterfuck on ice and is now honed in on my new obsession.

As we file into the locker room after the game, I can't stop thinking about Cassidy. My mind is all sorts of fucked up and not even close to focused where it should be—on hockey. It's on *her*.

Coach Morin pulls me aside to talk to the media after the game and then, when I'm done, he asks me how I'm adjusting to Seattle so far. "It's different," I say, knowing that's an understatement. "But I'm ready to help this team win."

More like carry their asses on my back because as they are, they're dysfunctional as fuck. I still haven't figured out why because I know they've got the talent to be playing better than they are.

"That's good to hear," Coach says, looking relieved. "You've got a lot of talent, Hayden. Let's see what you can do with it."

I nod and head back into the locker room, feeling like I'm

on a mission as I tear off tape and unlace my skates. Warren St. Claire—aka War—sinks down beside me. "You're coming out with us tonight."

I raise an eyebrow. "That doesn't feel like a question."

He grins. "Nope. You're coming out. We need to get you drunk for team bonding."

I laugh. "I'm not sure that's a good idea." I'm a mean drunk and there's at least one fuckface in this locker room my fists are already itching to meet.

"It's always a good idea," he says, clapping me on my sweaty shoulder. "Besides, there's this bar downtown, The Sin Bin. It's got the hottest bartenders in Seattle. You'll love it. Just ask RoMo."

My pulse picks up at his words. Fuck, that's Cassidy's bar. Something I discovered last night.

And in no fucking universe will I ask Roman Morozov for anything. The guy's a dick of the highest order.

"Fine," I say, trying to act like I don't care when my pulse is already flying into outer space. "I'll go."

Warren grins and heads off to shower and change, leaving me alone with my thoughts again. And all I can think about is how I'm going to see her tonight. Face to face.

Fuck, this is going to be fun.

When we get to The Sin Bin, it's packed and loud as hell. I scan the crowd for Cassidy, but there are too many people here for me to find her without actively trying. So I head to the bar and order a beer, waiting for her to make her way over to me.

It doesn't take long before she's standing in front of me, her bright green eyes flashing as she asks me what I want, like she doesn't know who I am. I'll play her game for now. "Just a beer,"

I say, giving her my best smile, the one that never fails to make panties drop.

She's so much hotter in person and it's all I can do not to walk behind that bar, toss her over my shoulder and haul her into the bathroom right now. Or maybe bend her over the bar and make her scream my name so all my teammates know she's already mine.

But I don't want to make a scene. Yet.

As she sets down my beer in front of me, I ask, "What time are you done here tonight?"

She raises an eyebrow. "Too late for you."

"Come on," I say, leaning closer to her. "Stop pretending you don't love this as much as I do, Princess. You know all I'd have to do is snap my fingers, and you'd be mine."

Her cheeks flush slightly, and she looks away from me. "I'm not yours."

"Not yet," I say with a smirk. "But you will be."

She rolls her eyes and turns away from me, flipping me off as she heads down the bar to help some customers while I check out her ass. Fuck, it's tight and perfect and my dick wants to get better acquainted.

When she glances back over her shoulder at me and then rushes to break eye contact when she catches me staring, I know I've got her. She won't be able to resist me for long.

And that's exactly what I want.

I should be with my team, bullshitting and getting to know the guys, but instead I'm sitting at the end of the bar watching Cassidy as she works and hoping I'll catch her looking at me again. I'm like an addict waiting on his next fix, even though I know she might be my downfall.

Just as her gaze flicks to mine for the dozenth time and I give her a smirk because I caught her—again—my asshole teammate Roman blocks her from my view by leaning across the bar and flirting with her.

Fuck no. That's not happening.

I push up off my stool and head over there, ready to claim what's mine. "Hey," I say, putting a hand on Roman's shoulder. "Back off."

He turns to me with a scowl. "Don't touch me, Vaughn. And who the fuck do you think you are coming in here making demands?"

"If you make me say it again, it's going to be with my fist in your face."

His scowl melts into a smirk. "You're new here, so you don't know how shit works, but Cassidy and I have history. Isn't that right, babe?" He turns his slimy smile in her direction and she shoots him a glare filled with so much hate it makes my dick hard.

Huh. Guess it's not just her fear then.

"Get the hell out of my bar, Roman," she says, crossing her arms over her chest, blocking my view of those perky tits of hers. "I don't have time for your cheating ass tonight."

He laughs and turns back to me. "She loves to play hard to get."

My fingers curl into fists.

"I'm not playing anything," she snaps. "Now get out or I'll call the cops and have you thrown out."

He holds up his hands in surrender and backs away from the bar, still smirking as he goes. "See you later, Cass."

She shakes her head and turns to me, her eyes flashing with anger. "You can go, too."

"Nah, I'll take my chances. See, I don't think you really want me gone."

Cassidy rolls her eyes but doesn't argue, grabbing another beer for me and sliding it across the bar. "What gives you that idea?"

I shrug. "I already told you. You want me and you like this game we're playing."

She scoffs. "You're delusional."

"Oh, so you blocked me, then?" I say, taking a long pull from my beer before I pull out my phone and open Instagram, sending her a DM. Her phone dings and her eyes narrow. "That's what I thought, Princess. I'm not going anywhere."

"I don't date hockey players." She sounds annoyed, but there's something else there too. Something I can't quite put my finger on. But whatever it is, somehow when I hear it, I want her more. "So you're wasting your time. Go find someone else to fuck."

"Not gonna happen," I say with a smirk as I lean closer to her, breathing in her sweet scent that's driving me fucking crazy. "I've got forever, Princess. And the only one I'll be fucking is you." I wave my hand around. "So we can keep doing this until you're ready to spread those thighs for me, but I promise you it *will* happen."

She opens her mouth and then closes it, does it again, and then turns away, heading down the bar again to help other customers who're waiting for drinks, glancing one last time over her shoulder at me. I watch her every move like a predator tracking my prey.

Fuck. I need to calm the hell down.

But as I sit here and drink beer after beer, watching her work and trying to figure out how the hell I'm going to make her mine, I realize something that scares the shit out of me.

I think she's already got me hooked.

And I don't care if she likes me or not. I'm not letting her go.

Rusty
@RinkRebel

Hayden Vaughn's idea of saying hello involves shoulder pads and a trip to the boards. #WelcomeToTheIce #SeattleAnchors

Hayden #5

AFTER BEER NUMBER THREE, I haul my ass off the barstool and toward the bathroom, needing to piss bad enough to leave Cassidy alone at the bar. But as I step inside and head for a urinal, Roman comes in behind me and blocks the door with his body. "You need to back off."

"I thought I made my position on Cassidy clear," I say, turning to face him with a scowl on my face.

Roman crosses his arms over his chest and glares up at me as I take a step toward him. *Yeah, I'm two inches taller, motherfucker. Eat shit.* "She's taken, asshole. We're just taking a break."

I laugh, itching to choke this fucker out and leave him on the suspiciously wet floor. "She doesn't seem to think so. Pretty sure she told you to leave." I take another step closer and he's forced to tilt his chin up another fraction of an inch to hold my stare. "So my question is, why the fuck are you still here?"

He puffs out his chest as I get close enough to knee him in the balls if I decide I want to. Is it dirty? Yeah, but that's my thing. His eyes flash with anger. "Watch yourself, new blood. You don't want to fuck with me."

"Oh, yeah?" I ask, stepping up to him until we're practically nose to nose. "And who the fuck are you to think you can tell me what to do?"

"I'm captain of this team," he says with a smirk, and I'm tempted to knock his teeth out, "and the best fucking player in Seattle."

"Is that right?" I ask, chuckling. "The best player on a shitty fucking team that can't win a game to save their lives. Congrats, man. What an accomplishment." I slow clap while I turn my back on him, letting him know exactly what I think of the kind of threat he is. Then I step up to the urinal while he splutters for a response, taking my dick out and starting to piss. I groan because *fuck,* it feels good.

I glance over and find Roman gaping at my cock. I chuckle, and his eyes dart up to mine. "It's pretty impressive, right? You want a better look?" He scowls at me as I shake and tuck myself away, walking over to the sink to wash my hands.

"Shut the fuck up." His face is red as hell and I laugh, which he obviously hates if that vein pulsing in his forehead is anything to go by.

"It's called a magic cross, and it's going to be what steals your girl right out from under you. That's if she really is yours, which I have my doubts about." I grin as I dry my hands and toss the paper towel in the trash. "Now get the fuck out of my way before I make you."

He hesitates. "You think you can come in here and—"

"Listen, *Captain,*" I cut him off. "I don't give a shit what you think or who you are. This team's about to have a new leader, and if you ever touch Cassidy again, I'll cut off your goddamn hand."

He shakes his head. "You're fucking psycho."

"Maybe," I say, shrugging as I shove him out of the way. He stumbles back into the hall. "Fuck around and find out."

Roman curses at me, but I tune him out as I walk back toward the bar. Fuck, I can't stop thinking about how much I want to make him eat his words.

I'm not letting him have her. Not a chance.

As I take my seat back at the bar and something settles in my chest when I see Cassidy throw her head back and laugh at something the other chick behind the bar says, I realize that I'm not just doing this for fun anymore. This is about more than just winning or proving a point. This is about claiming something that's mine and making sure no one else ever touches her again.

There's this soul-deep *need* to have her, a want that goes beyond anything that makes sense.

I don't care what it takes or who I have to hurt to get her. Cassidy Bennett is going to worship the ground I walk on, beg for my body, and submit to my every whim, and anyone who gets in my way will pay the price.

Starting with Roman Morozov.

I'm not backing down.

Not now.

Not ever.

It's late when I finally get back to my hotel room after closing down The Sin Bin. I'm not drunk, but I'm high from the chase. Cassidy's going to make me work for her. Sure, she ignored me as much as she could get away with, but I learned little things about her tonight that I'm hoarding like treasure.

Things like how she let her bartender go home early to take care of her new baby with a soft smile on her face, or how she got right in the middle of a fight between two rival fans and handled breaking it up like a fucking pro. Or the way she gave the old drunk at the far end of the bar a glass of water before she called him a ride because her heart's too fucking big.

But as I collapse onto the bed, all I can think about is how badly I wanted to bend her over that bar. I wanted to fuck her until her hips bruised from my fingers and my dick rearranged her insides so only I'd fit inside her.

There's this overwhelming need to possess her that's toxic as fuck, but I think I like it.

I should've stayed, should've pushed to walk her home after she closed down the bar, but after her showdown with Roman, she seemed like she needed some space. And I didn't want to push too hard too fast and scare her off completely.

Because then I'd have to kidnap her and I was trying to think long term and do this right.

But tomorrow night will be different.

I'll make sure of it.

I can't help but smile at the thought of what I set in motion tonight. Because tomorrow, Cassidy Bennett will start to fall for me.

And nothing—not even Roman Morozov—will stop me from getting what I want.

I stare at the ceiling, but I'm not really seeing it as I picture Cassidy in the cropped tank top and tight jeans she wore tonight, a sliver of her tight stomach on display that got me all kinds of hot. I grip my hard dick over my boxers when I think about the way her long brown hair fell around her shoulders and down her back and those green eyes flashed with anger as she told Roman to get out of her bar.

Fuck, that last part turned me on more than anything else.

The way she stood up to him, the way she didn't let him intimidate her... it was fucking sexy as hell.

But then I remember the way she looked at me tonight, like

I was some kind of annoyance she couldn't wait to get rid of. And that aggravates the fuck out of me.

She wants me. She's just not ready to admit it yet.

But she will.

I won't take no for an answer.

Not from her or anyone else who tries to stand in my way.

I wrap my hand around my cock, giving it a languid stroke while I get lost in the fantasy of her lips wrapped around it, her tongue flicking over the piercings at the tip as she gazes up at me with those big green eyes while black streaks of mascara run down her cheeks from her tears.

Fuck, this is torture.

I lift my hips, fucking my fist like I haven't had to do in years. My thumb swipes over the head, lubing me up with my own pre-cum while I jack off.

When I think about her choking on my dick, my balls tighten and I come all over my stomach, groaning as I imagine what it would feel like to fill her throat with my cum and watch her swallow every last drop of it. To know that a piece of me will exist inside of her.

Jesus fucking Christ.

I don't think I've ever come that hard before.

But as I lay there in the darkness, breathing hard and trying to calm down, I realize there's no way I'll be able to sleep tonight. I'm too fucking fixated.

No, I'm not sleeping until she's hooked on me and no one else can touch her. No one can take her from me.

Which is a big fucking problem because to function on the ice, I need to sleep.

Which means I need to act *now*.

I yank off my t-shirt and use it to clean up, tossing it in the laundry before I get out of bed and throw on a pair of shorts and a tank. If I can't sleep, might as well get an ass crack of the morning workout in at the hotel gym.

The hall's empty as I walk down it toward the gym, and by the time sweat's pouring down my body and my muscles are burning, I've got a plan.

This morning I'm going to show the Anchors a whole new way to win, and tonight I'm going to make my first move in tying Cassidy Bennett to me for life.

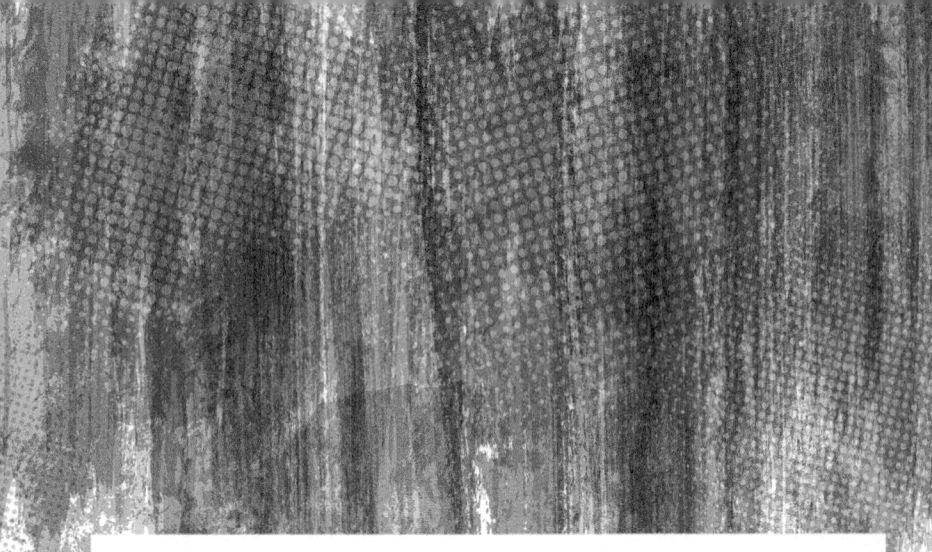

in your dreams
@ChirpsAndChicklets

If Hayden Vaughn was a movie character, he'd definitely be the villain. #NHL

Hayden #6

ROMAN CHECKS me into the boards so hard it knocks the wind out of me and sends me flying across the ice. I hit the ground with a thud and lay there for a second, trying to re-inflate my lungs while my teammates yell at him and the coaches blow their whistles.

This mother*fucker*.

My ribs throb, and that fucker smirks at me before skating away.

"What the hell was that?" Warren yells at him as he skates over to me, offering me a hand up. "You could've injured Vaughn."

Roman shrugs. "Just showing him how we play."

I brush off his help and climb to my feet, giving Roman the blankest expression I can. He's not going to get a reaction out of me. Not until I slice open his fucking throat and paint the ice red with his blood. "Maybe you should win a game before you push," I make air quotes, *the way you play* on anyone."

His smirk drops and he growls, "Watch your fucking—"

"Enough," Coach Morin says, skating over to us with a scowl on his face. He's the youngest head coach in the league, so he's got shit to prove, just like the rest of us. "This isn't what we need right now. We're getting our asses handed to us every damn night, and this is how you act?" His gaze cuts to Roman. "Get your heads in the goddamn game or get the fuck off my ice."

Roman rolls his eyes but doesn't argue as Coach sends us back to center ice. But I can't stop thinking about how much I want to beat the shit out of him. I'm literally *aching* to do it, almost as much as I want to fuck Cassidy. Feeling Roman's bones crunch is a close second in my current list of wants.

As we line up for the next drill, I make eye contact with Roman and give him a smirk. "Hey, 22," I say under my breath.

He glares at me.

"Eat a dick."

His eyes narrow even more. "I'm going to kill you."

"Not before I show you how *I* play, fucker."

He raises an eyebrow. "Bring it."

And then I'm flying at him, hitting him with everything I've got and sending him sprawling across the ice. He looks stunned for a second before pushing himself up and charging at me, slamming me back against the boards so hard my teeth cut into my tongue. This right here is why I take the ring out, even for practice.

The coaches yell at us and try to break it up, but I'm not done. Not by a long shot. This asshole has had an ass kicking coming since the second I stepped into the locker room.

My gloves come off and it's only King and War each grabbing an arm that keep me from beating the shit out of Roman right then and there.

"You want to go?" he asks, glaring at me as he pulls off his own gloves and tosses them on the ice. "Let's go."

"Fuck all the way off." I spit blood onto the ice, wishing it was his face instead.

He laughs. "Not a chance. This is *my* team."

"Yeah? For how long?"

But before we can get going, Coach skates over and puts himself between us, his hands outstretched.

"That's enough," he says, looking pissed as hell. "Since you two don't want to listen, laps until practice is over." Then he skates off, muttering, "We don't have time for this."

Roman scoffs. "Whatever."

He turns away from me and takes off for the locker room, ignoring the coach. "Great fucking captain you've got here," I say to no one in particular. "He's a real team player."

I'm trying to calm myself down. But it's not working.

I'm fucking *furious*.

By the time practice is over, my legs are dead, I'm drenched in sweat, and I need a big ass bowl of pasta, a beer, and a nap. But Warren invites me over to play video games with him and a few of the other guys at his house, promising Morozov won't be there. And even though I'm still pissed as hell, I agree to go. I need to bond with these guys at some point and War seems like a good dude.

Plus, I need a distraction to shift my focus away from Roman and how I can't stop fantasizing about the best ways to dispose of his body.

As we sit in Warren's living room, playing Call of Duty and talking shit, my shoulders gradually relax and I realize that this is exactly what I need right now. A chance to unwind before I do something stupid like murder my teammate or track Cassidy down and fuck her until she can't walk straight for a week.

This is the kind of shit that happens when I let my instincts take over and stop trying to keep myself in check.

Fuck, I don't think I've ever been this much of a mess before.

Corbin, one of the second line D-men, walks over from the kitchen with a beer in each hand and hands me one before sitting down on the couch next to me. "You good?"

I nod, taking a long pull from the bottle. "Getting there."

"Roman's an asshole," he says, shaking his head. "Don't let him get to you."

I scoff. "Too fucking late."

He laughs. "Well, at least you're honest about it."

"RoMo's a dick, but he's our dick," Warren says, glancing over at us from his spot on the other couch. "He's just competitive."

Corbin chokes on the sip he just took and I slap him on the back. "That's putting it lightly," he grunts.

I laugh and sink back against the couch, feeling better than I have all day. These guys are decent and it was the right move hanging with them today.

Warren's phone goes off and he dives for it like he's Gollum and it's his precious.

"Oh shit, who's the girl this week?" Corbin asks, leaning forward to see the screen.

War grins, yanking it away while his thumbs fly across the screen. "Just another hookup."

I raise an eyebrow. "A hookup? *Bullshit*," I cough into my fist.

He laughs, flashing us a picture of a naked chick who's admittedly got a bangin' set of tits. "She's some girl I met last time we were in Vancouver. She keeps sending me nudes. I think she's trying to get me to come back for round two."

Corbin chuckles. "Looks like it's working."

"Nah, I don't double dip," Warren says, grinning as he stares at the picture again. "Damn tempting, though."

I laugh even though inside I'm having a *holy shit* moment because it just hit me that despite the hotness of the girl on

War's phone, I felt *nothing*. Not so much as a twitch of my dick. Yeah, I think it's safe to say my obsession with a certain bar owner has crossed over into uncharted territory.

Now it's my turn for my phone to go off and when I look down, hoping somehow Cassidy's decided to text me, I'm only slightly disappointed when I see it's my brother.

> Sawyer: Hope your hotel room has two beds, otherwise you're gonna have to get real comfortable with cuddling.
>
> Sawyer: And I'm the little spoon, FYI.
>
> Hayden: You got your program transfer?
>
> Sawyer: Yep. Just waiting for the official acceptance now.
>
> Hayden: Good because I'm starting to go into withdrawal
>
> Hayden: [gif of Dave Chapelle with powder on his lips scratching at his neck]
>
> Sawyer: You sayin' I'm your crack?
>
> Hayden: Codependent, remember?
>
> Hayden: And don't worry about the bed thing. I'll just kick your ass out and onto the floor if your morning wood comes near me.
>
> Sawyer: Asshole.

I laugh and set my phone aside as Warren starts talking about how the chick he hooked up with in Vancouver might be turning stalker on him.

"She sent me a picture of her holding up a positive pregnancy test," he says, shaking his head. "Last time I checked, you can't get knocked up from anal."

Corbin laughs, but Warren's drama gives me an idea...

And once it takes root, I know there's not going to be any way to stop myself from making it happen.

Sin Bin Sling

1 oz gin • 1/2 oz cherry liqueur • 1/4 oz Cointreau • 1/4 oz Benedictine • 1 oz pineapple juice • 1/2 oz lime juice • Dash of Angostura bitters • Club soda
Garnish: cherry and pineapple

Shake all ingredients except soda with ice. Strain into an ice-filled Collins glass. Top with club soda and garnish with cherry and pineapple.

Cassidy #7

I CHECK to make sure the camera's in the perfect spot, one that won't give away any details about my real name or where I am. The skimpy lingerie I'm wearing is already enough of a risk, but I don't care. If I want to make good money, I have to do things that aren't going to be comfortable, and I refuse to be in debt to my asshole ex any longer than I have to be.

Desperate times and all that.

But as I sit here in front of my laptop, opening the recording software with clammy fingers and a racing heart, I can't help but feel a sense of *what the fuck am I doing?* creeping over me. This is a bad idea.

A terrible fucking idea.

Maybe the worst idea I've ever had.

It was the first time I did it a couple of weeks ago. It still is now.

What if someone I know finds out?

But what other choice do I have?

I owe Roman twenty grand and until I pay it off, he's always going to own some part of me. The cheating asshole doesn't get that right. So, what's a little light porn between friends?

Or OnlyFans in this case.

Before I hit record, I set up my phone against my nightstand, sprawl out on my bed adjusting my angles and snap a couple of teaser photos. I'm in a black lace and mesh one piece that makes me feel sexy and highlights all my best parts while hiding the worst.

Then I post it with the caption, "I know what you want to see, but I'm not sure you can handle it. #teaser."

Before I exit the website, I decide to check in on my last video and I'm not sure whether to be grossed out and horrified or impressed by what I find in the comments section.

LordOfLust: holy shit that pussy looks tight af.

HottieHunter420: I got 100 bucks in my pocket and I'm down to party, baby. U up for a 1 on 1?

MrNasty69: I'll come in your mouth and you'll swallow it like a good little whore.

SirBangsALot: I bet you like it rough, slut

Cockzilla: Look at that ass. Damn, I wanna tap that.

I respond to exactly none of them and try to pretend like all those pervs aren't about to watch me get myself off again.

I swallow hard and click record, trying to ignore the way my stomach flips as I straighten up and saunter into the frame, swaying my hips as seductively as I can. I've never actually tried to be sexy before I started this account, so I'm pretty sure I look like an awkward disaster, but whatever. Maybe that's someone's kink.

When I start to run my hands over my body and pretend like I love it, I try to focus on the money and not the fact that I'm about to show my tits to strangers on the internet.

It's just business.

And if it means getting rid of Roman, it's worth it.

If The Sin Bin wasn't my father's legacy, I'd have let it go instead of borrowing money from my twatwaffle ex. But it's all I have left of my parents, and after five years of my uncle running it for me while I fulfilled the requirements of the trust so I could inherit it, it needed major upkeep.

So, here I am, using my *assets* to set myself free of a debt I shouldn't have had to take on, but life's not fucking fair. I should've just done this from the start, but Roman was way too jealous to tolerate sharing me this way.

Ironic, considering I found him fucking a puck bunny in the bathroom of my own goddamn bar.

While I was working.

But whatever.

I'm super over it.

As I slip out of the top of my black lacy bra and let my breasts fall free, I'm surprised when I feel a sense of excitement building inside me.

Maybe I can make a lot of money and get rid of Roman for good.

And maybe, just maybe, I'll finally be free to live my life the way I want to.

Without any cheating assholes holding what I owe them over my head and with enough money to fulfill my dad's dream of adding a restaurant to his bar.

So, as I stand in front of my laptop and show off my tits, I can't help but give a seductive smile that I actually mean while I pluck at my nipples and put on a show for the camera.

This might turn out to be pretty fun... if I ignore the gross comments.

And it's *going* to be profitable, damn it.

I have nice tits, long, toned legs, and an ass I've done thousands of squats to plump up.

I just hope no one I know ever finds out what I'm doing, though. That would be a disaster.

Can you imagine the hordes of hockey players and fans that could find me at my bar and harass me over this shit? Thinking I owe them a piece of me because they pay to see my content?

But as I pull off my panties and lean back on the bed, spreading my legs for the camera, showing off my surprisingly wet pussy for anyone who wants to see it, I'm a little bit excited about what could happen next.

Who knew I had an exhibitionist kink?

Maybe this is exactly what I need to get myself out of this mess and start living life on my own terms again. It feels like since my family died, I've been living in the shadow of their memory, trying to grasp on to any small wisp of them to keep them close. Especially because it's my fault they're dead.

But maybe it's time to let go.

And maybe this OnlyFans thing will be exactly what I need to do it.

I run my fingers through the outside of my wet pussy, imagining what it would be like if Hayden was on the other side of the screen watching me instead of some random strangers. I can't help but wonder if there's a chance he'd actually want me for real.

Not as a game or a conquest, but me. To keep.

He's hot as hell, and the way he looks at me makes me feel like I'm the only girl in the world. Which is crazy because he's a hockey player and monogamy is about three syllables too many for most of them to comprehend. But the intensity of his gaze is almost too much to handle sometimes. I can't deny that it turns me on more than anything else I've ever experienced.

Maybe he could be a fun distraction from this whole Roman thing.

But as I spread my legs wider and slip two fingers inside

myself, moaning for the camera and hoping I'm putting on a good show, I wish it was Hayden here with me right now.

His fingers inside of me.

And that scares the everloving fuck out of me.

One of my hands twists in the sheets and I rub my clit with the other, picturing Hayden's weight pinning me down, his calloused fingers rough against my clit and circling my throat as I climb higher and higher toward an orgasm that feels so good I can barely breathe.

And then I come.

Hard.

I moan as I rub my clit faster, feeling my pussy clench around my fingers while I imagine what it would be like to have Hayden Vaughn inside of me, filling me up and making me feel things I've never felt before.

He's got that big dick energy that means he knows how to use what's in his pants and *god* I want him to do unspeakable things to me with it.

Fuck.

A second orgasm rolls right in after the first, and it's so hard my vision blacks out and I swear I'm floating above my body for a couple of seconds that seem to stretch on forever. Until reality slams back into me.

Finally, I come down from the high, breathing hard and feeling a little embarrassed about what just happened, and I realize this is going to be a lot more complicated than I thought.

I crawl off the bed and stumble over to the laptop to stop the recording, feeling a little dizzy and a lot confused about how much I just enjoyed that.

Maybe there's something to this sex video thing after all.

I'm pretty sure that epic orgasm had nothing to do with the camera on me and more about the guy who's taken over my brain like a virus. And I wonder if Hayden will ever find out what I'm doing or if he'll even care.

And if he does, what he'll do about it.

I shiver as butterflies take flight in my stomach at the prospect of getting under his skin. Forcing him to react. Seeing how far I can push him.

Because with him, it's impossible to know what's coming next.

After I move on from this new discovery about myself and do a quick edit, I hit upload on the video and slam the laptop closed.

I need to shower off what I just did.

I need to get a grip.

Hayden Vaughn is *not* my problem.

I'm stronger than this.

At least I think I am.

While I wash away the evidence of my Only Fans debut, I let my mind drift, and I wonder if I've gotten myself into something way bigger than I can handle. Something that might end up biting me in the ass eventually. It's one thing to get out of my situation with Roman, but another to create a whole other problem.

Guess I'll worry about it if it happens.

I get dressed, hating myself for picking out something cute, hoping Hayden stops into the bar despite it being the Anchors' night off. After styling my hair into loose waves and swiping on a coating of mascara, I lock up and walk the three blocks to my bar.

When I get there, I grit my teeth and think about turning around and forgetting about my responsibilities for one night so I can avoid the guy I can't stop thinking about. Maybe Lila can handle it just this once? But no, I don't run away from the hard shit, so I square my shoulders and stomp on, trying to move past my dreaded ex who's decided, for whatever reason, to insert himself back into my life.

Literally.

The Puck Drop

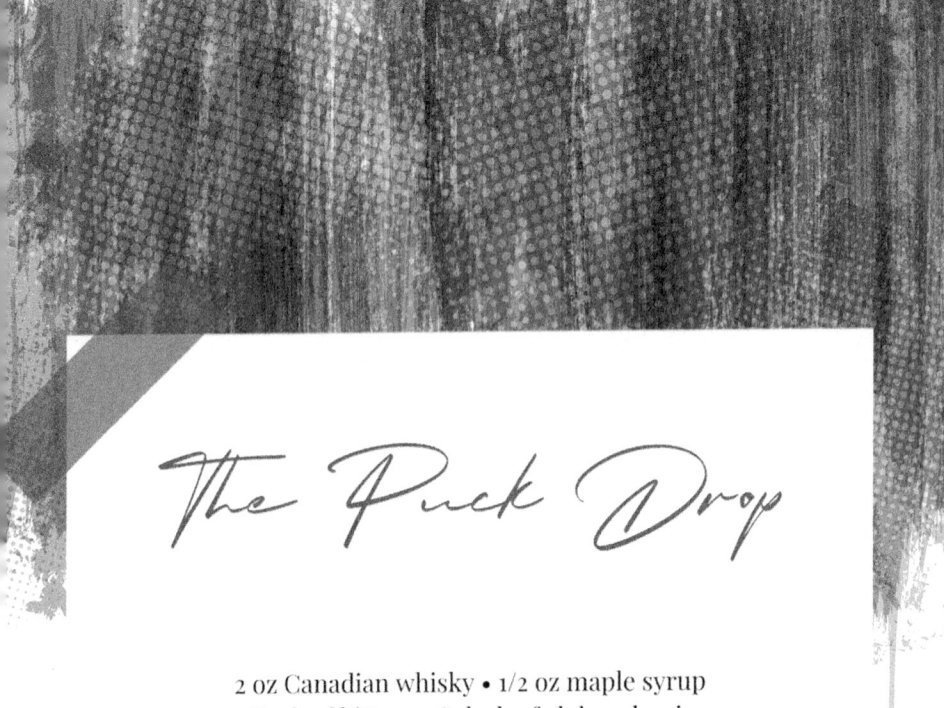

2 oz Canadian whisky • 1/2 oz maple syrup
• Dash of bitters • Splash of club soda • ice
Garnish: orange peel

Combine whisky, maple syrup, and bitters in a mixing glass with ice. Stir well and strain into a chilled glass. Garnish with an orange peel.

Cassidy #8

WE'RE in the thick of happy hour when the door swings open and a shiver runs down my spine. I know it's him without having to look.

Hayden Vaughn.

How the hell do I know that? Seriously, we've only met once and I know almost nothing about him, but my body reacts to his presence like he's a magnet and I'm a piece of metal.

So much for swearing off hockey players. I flip myself off on the inside for being so fucking stupid.

He walks in like he owns the place, his eyes locked on me and the expression in them… it's like he wants to consume me until there's nothing left. And damn if that cocky smirk on his face doesn't make me want to let him.

The tight black t-shirt he's wearing shows off his toned muscles and a pair of jeans that hug his thighs in a way that screams *I can totally hold you up while I fuck you against the wall*. He's got a hoop in his nose and one of his curls has fallen over his forehead. He's hot as hell and definitely knows it.

I don't know if I'm happy or pissed that he's here right now.

Guess it depends on how much I want to lie to myself tonight.

He slides onto a stool at the end of the bar, giving me a smirk that makes my heart race and my panties wet. Ugh, he's the kind of hot that I know means bad decisions.

I can already tell I'm about to do stupid, stupid things.

But he's also an egotistical dick just like the rest of them. Just like Roman.

I walk over to him, ignoring the fluttering in my stomach as I ask, "What can I get you?" Yep, I'm just gonna pretend I don't know who he is.

He leans closer to me, breathing deep before saying, "You smell good," in that gravelly tone that makes my knees weak.

I wrinkle my nose. "That's not creepy at all." Inside, my stomach is doing backflips and my nipples are harder than diamonds.

He laughs, and the sound is rich and deep, making me want to tilt even closer to him to hear better. "I'm just saying you smell nice. I'm not a pervert. Well, not all the time."

"Agree to disagree," I say, trying to act like I don't care. "What do you want?"

He looks me up and down like he's sizing me up for something. "Have dinner with me tonight."

I scoff and gesture around my packed bar. "In case you haven't noticed, I'm working. What do you want to drink?"

He glances at Lila, ignoring my question. "Can't she handle it?"

"By herself?" I shake my head. "It's too busy."

Lila takes that opportunity to speak from right behind me, nearly making me jump out of my damn skin. "Actually, I've handled worse. Remember when you had food poisoning last year and had to hold a bucket while you—"

I slap a hand over her mouth, widening my eyes with a *shut the hell up in front of the hottest guy on planet Earth* look that I hope she interprets right. She nods and I let my hand drop back to my side as Hayden laughs.

"So?" he asks me, his dark eyes glinting with amusement. "Give me a chance to show you I don't just play dirty on the ice."

I throw my head back and laugh. "That line can't seriously work for you, can it?"

Instead of getting offended like Roman would've, Hayden chuckles and shrugs. "I've never needed a line before. Usually I snap my fingers and they line up."

"Charming." I say, rolling my eyes. "But I don't date hockey players." The words come out even as every cell in my body screams that I'll make an exception for him. God, there must be something wrong with me. Something broken inside of me to have these assholes be the only guys I'm attracted to.

His gaze flicks to Roman, who managed to sneak back in here with the crowd and is currently sitting at a table with his teammates, giving me a glare that could strip paint off the wall. Hayden's eyes move back to me. "That's not what I've heard."

"I'm not going to fuck you," I blurt out. I'm such a liar, a slutty little liar, and based on the dirty smirk he gives me, we both know it.

He stands and leans over the bar, getting close enough to me that his lips are brushing against my ear and I can smell his cologne. Why does he have to smell so good?

A shiver runs through my entire body as he whispers, "We'll see about that, Princess." He pulls back and smirks at me before sliding off his stool and walking away without another word, expecting me to follow.

And I just stand there with a puddle forming at my feet and a brain that's completely checked out.

I watch him go, and I realize that I'm in so much trouble.

Because as much as I try to deny it, Hayden Vaughn is *exactly* my type.

And if he keeps up his pursuit, I'm going to give in and let him have me any way he wants me. *Every* way he wants me.

Shit.

"Well? What are you waiting for?" Lila whispers, shoving me in the back. "If you don't follow him, I'm going to."

"You're gay."

She raises an eyebrow. "And?"

"And Addison would kill you."

Her lips purse like she's considering. "Fair point."

I glare at her over my shoulder and she laughs—okay, *cackles*—as she heads back to the other end of the bar. "Go get some dick, girl!"

A few of the customers at the bar whistle, cheer, and laugh as I try not to die of embarrassment.

But as I walk out the front door and spot Hayden leaning against his car, waiting for me with a smirk on his face, I know this is quite possibly the worst idea I've ever had.

Selling porn online is no longer at the top of that list.

Honestly, what the *fuck* am I doing?

He's trouble.

I'm pretty sure I can't handle whatever sort of ruination he's got planned for me.

And didn't I *just* swear off hockey players for good this afternoon?

He opens the passenger door of his expensive SUV for me and I slide inside, breathing in the hit of leather and his expensive cologne. And it's exactly this second I realize that I'm already in way too deep with him.

And I don't know how to stop it.

He climbs into the driver's seat and starts toward downtown. With every block, I can feel the tension between us thickening until it's almost impossible to breathe. And when he reaches over and puts his hand on my thigh, I don't stop him.

I don't want to.

My skin tingles where his hand grips my thigh, the tips of his fingers indenting the skin, and the heat of his palm soaks into me even through my jeans.

"Where are we going?" I ask, trying to keep my voice from shaking as his fingers inch higher and higher up my leg.

He smirks at me and his face lights up for a fraction of a second as we pass under a streetlight. "You'll see."

I bite back a moan as his fingers brush against my inner thigh, teasing me through my jeans with the promise of what's to come.

Hayden Vaughn is the devil, no question. Not when he seems to have this power over me that's impossible to resist.

While he parallel parks, I drool over the way he controls the car, the way the veins pop out in his strong hands. And when his eyes meet mine, I pretend I'm not imagining those hands on my body, but the wicked grin he gives me leads me to wonder if he can read my mind.

We get out of the car and he leads me down the street, his hand on the small of my back. I'm starting to suspect that tonight is going to change everything.

Even though I should be running away screaming, all I want to do is let him rip my clothes off and destroy me for anyone else.

What the shit is that, anyway? I've never been the submissive type before. The type to just let a guy take control. On one hand, I want to fight Hayden. Challenge him and see how far I can push him before he snaps. And on the other hand, I want to fall to my knees, bow my head, and let him use me until we're both wrecked.

I want to ruin *him* for anyone else, too.

He stops in front of a fancy restaurant and holds the door

open for me, and I look down at my jeans and cropped *The Sin Bin* t-shirt. "Uh, I'm not exactly dressed for this place."

Hayden lets his eyes roam down the length of my body in a perusal so filled with heat, I shift from one foot to the other and try to press my thighs together in a subtle way I hope he doesn't notice.

But of course he does, and his gaze burns into me as I throw my shoulders back and think *fuck it* while I walk past him and into the dimly lit interior.

"Who gives a shit how you're dressed when you look like," he gestures his hand to my body. "That."

Then he grabs my hand and weaves our fingers together. I pretend I don't notice the way my skin tingles every place his fingers touch mine.

He gives his name to the hostess, and she leads us to a table in the back, away from the other patrons. Hayden pulls out a chair for me and I snort. "Since when are you a gentleman?"

"You know nothing about me," he says, but he does it with a grin so I know he's not upset. He sits down across from me and orders a bottle of French wine *with perfect pronunciation* like he's done this a million times before.

"I know *some* things about you."

He raises an eyebrow, daring me to continue, but I clamp my mouth shut. Once the waiter pours the wine, I take a sip and it's smooth and fruity. I close my eyes and savor the taste of it on my tongue until Hayden's deep voice, a little rougher than before, interrupts me.

"And who are *you?*"

I tilt my head to the side, and now it's my turn to smirk. "Like you care." I figure he can't give less of a shit and only wants between my thighs.

He watches me, the flame from the candle on the table flickering in his eyes only making his stare that much more intense. "Why else would I be here?"

I shrug, taking another sip from my glass and trying to ignore the way his penetrating gaze hits me straight between the thighs. "Because you want to sleep with me."

"You think I have to take a girl to dinner to fuck her? That's cute." He chuckles. "Make no mistake, Princess. We *will* be fucking. But this dinner is about something else. You sent me that message. You wanted my attention. Now you've got it." His long fingers grasp the stem of his glass and he swirls the dark liquid, eyeing me over the rim. "There's got to be more to you than the girl who slides into hockey players' DMs just to tell them they've got no talent. Consider me intrigued."

When I do nothing but stare at him instead of speaking, he pushes his glass away and laughs. He signals for the waiter and orders a whiskey. Surprise, surprise.

While he waits for his new drink, he leans back in his seat and gives me a look that makes my stomach flip. "You still think I'm an asshole?"

I nod. "Definitely. And a cliche."

"And yet you're here with me," he says, smirking at me like he's won something. "What does that say about you?"

I grab a breadstick and rip off a piece, tossing it in my mouth. "It says I'm desperate for a free meal and make horrible decisions."

He takes a sip of his whiskey and runs his tongue along his bottom lip, catching a stray drop. The shiny metal of his piercing flashes and I damn near go up in flames. I don't realize I'm staring until his words make me snap my eyes up to his. "Maybe, but that's not the only thing it says." He leans closer to me, his gaze burning into mine. "Admit it. You feel the same pull toward me I do toward you. Like no matter how bad we might be for each other, you can't stay away. Can't stop thinking about me. Tell me I'm wrong."

I swallow hard, my heart doing freaking sprints as he reaches across the table and takes my hand in his, stroking his thumb across the underside of my wrist. Fucking *chills*. His smirk widens when I can't hold them back. When I don't say anything to deny his words. "Point proven."

I snatch my hand back, hating myself for letting him see the way he affects me. "That proves nothing. It's cold in here."

"You're going to have to get better at lying if you want to convince me, Princess," he says, shrugging. "But I'm not going anywhere, so feel free to keep practicing."

I sit back, needing the distance from him because what the hell is happening right now? "You can't have me, Hayden. How's that for truth?"

He smirks at me before taking another slow sip of his drink. "We'll see. And the way your nose wrinkles just the tiniest bit when you lie gives you away. Maybe try it in front of a mirror before you come at me with your *you can't have me,*" he raises his voice in a poor imitation of mine, the asshat, "bullshit again."

The waiter comes back with our food and we eat in silence, watching each other across the table, and it takes me way too long to realize I never even ordered.

"You ordered for me."

"And? Do you not like it?"

I grip my fork harder, hating that the braised short ribs melt in my mouth and they're exactly what I would've picked for myself. "That's not the point."

"You know, this argumentative thing you've got going on really does it for me. Makes me want to swipe all this shit onto the floor and bend you over the table. Maybe leave a print of my palm on your ass."

"Don't you dare," I hiss, glancing around. He wouldn't... right?

After unlocking my little exhibitionist kink the other day, I can't even deny that a whole rush of heat pours into my veins and settles into a nice, low throb between my thighs. Fan-fucking-tastic. Guess my shower head and I are going to have a date when I get home.

Hayden eyes me as if he's considering following through with his threat, a devious glint in his eye as he drags his pierced tongue along his lower lip. Then he seems to let it go, blinking and finishing off his glass of whiskey. My guard is still all the way up. Eventually he asks, "What's your deal?"

"What do you mean?"

"Why this hatred toward my kind?" When I blink at him, confused, he elaborates, "Hockey players." He takes a bite of his steak, waiting me out. When I don't answer, he keeps going. "Seems like it's personal for you." He points his fork at me. "And don't try to tell me it's the way I play on the ice. It's more than that. I can feel it."

I swallow hard, hating that he can read me so easily when I don't even know him. "I..."

"Don't want to talk about it?" he guesses, looking a little bit pissed off that I'm not spilling my secrets to him on this date... or whatever it is.

"Nope."

"How about I take a guess? Morozov did something to fuck you over?"

I snort out a laugh that's super embarrassing and try to turn it into a cough to cover it up. "Oh, he fucked *someone* over. Over the sink in the bathroom at my bar, actually." I bite my lip while I consider. "Or maybe over the toilet. I don't actually know the specifics."

He winces. "Ouch."

"Yeah," I say, setting down my fork. Nothing ruins an appetite more than the memory of my ex banging some fame-chasing groupie while we were supposed to be exclusive for the past *year*. "And I own a hockey bar. I've seen how the players act. I thought he was different, but he wasn't. I doubt you are, either."

"I feel like I should be insulted."

"Are you going to tell me you've never cheated while you were on a road trip or out celebrating after a win?" I down the rest of my wine, feeling a warm buzz loosening my inhibitions. Fuck, I need to cut myself off before I give him an inch. I have a feeling Hayden Vaughn would take my world if I let him.

His dark eyes lock with mine. "I've never cheated. Can't cheat if you've never had a girlfriend."

I study his face as the seconds stretch and then I blow out a breath. "For some stupid reason, I believe you."

He smirks. "Because this connection between us is strong as fuck, and you can tell when I'm lying just like I can with you."

I keep going like he didn't just say that. "I swore off all hockey players after... that. In fact, let's make it professional athletes in general."

His eyes darken as he leans closer to me again, his voice low. "You're not going to swear me off."

"Why not?" I ask, raising an eyebrow at him. "Because you're"—I make air quotes—"different?"

He shrugs, staring at me with a look so intense, I shiver. "Maybe I am."

I shake my head, snagging another breadstick to have something to do with my hands. "I doubt that."

He laughs, dropping his fork and leaning back in his seat again, but his foot tangles with mine under the table. "You're stubborn as fuck, you know that?"

"So are you," I say, ripping off a piece of the breadstick and throwing it at his head. He ducks it easily, and the woman seated beside us glares at me as it ends up on her table. Stupid athletic reflexes. "But you don't see me giving you shit about it."

He smirks at me like he's got some kind of plan forming in his head and I don't ask because I don't think I want to know.

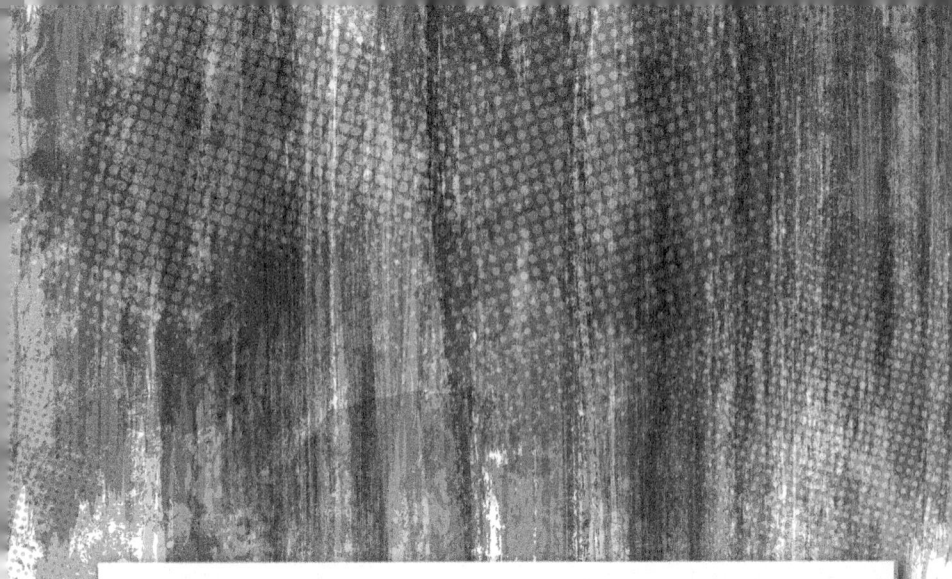

Allan
@PuckOffPal

Vaughn just turned that forward into a pancake. Someone scrape that poor bastard off the ice. #Flattened

Hayden #9

MY FINGERS WRAP around Cassidy's throat as I pin her to the wall next to her apartment. Her pupils are blown wide and her lips are parted as she pants for air. She's fucking gorgeous like this, all hot and begging for me to take what I want from her.

And I plan to.

"You've been a naughty girl, Princess," I whisper against her ear as I tighten my grip on her throat just enough to make her gasp. "And I think you need to be punished." I tilt her head so she's forced to stare up at me. "Calling me an asshole. Letting Morozov touch you," I tick off her offenses. "Lying about how much you want me. Telling me you're swearing me off."

She shivers against me, and I can tell she wants this as much as I do. She just won't admit it.

Yet.

As much as she tried to deny what's happening between us while we were at the restaurant, the second I said I was walking her to her door, we both knew where this was going.

"What are you going to do about it?" She smirks at me even though I have the upper hand here. I can already tell she's going to be a handful and I'm going to fucking revel in every second of having her.

I smile back at her and reach down to cup her pussy through her jeans, rubbing her clit in slow circles with my thumb as she gasps and presses into my touch. "You're going to come for me, Princess. And then you're going to beg me to fuck your tight little pussy until you're full of my cum and you can't walk straight. But first," I tighten my grip on her throat and my lips brush hers as I speak, "You're going to kiss me."

She tries to bite back her moan as I rub her clit faster, but I feel it against my fingers anyway. Her hips rock against my hand as she gets closer and closer to an orgasm that's going to blow her fucking mind. And right before she falls, I stop.

I doubt she realizes her fingers are gripping my shirt so tight, the fabric's in danger of ripping.

When she opens her mouth to tear me a new asshole for edging her, I kiss her hard before any words can escape. It's frantic, this need to taste her, to *consume* her while I swallow her protests and slip my tongue inside her mouth to taste her for the first time. She tastes like fucking *mine*, and I know I'm never going to get enough of her. She's scoring as the buzzer sounds in game seven of the cup finals to win it all. She's the first skate of the season to a sold-out arena screaming your name.

She's a high I could never have dreamed would be this good.

She kisses me back, biting my lower lip and making me groan as she digs her nails into my sides through my shirt. My fingers tangle in her hair and I've got such a tight grip on her, I don't give a shit if neither of us can breathe. We can be each other's air, because I'm not letting up.

Fuck, this girl just might kill me.

I pull back just enough to whisper against her lips, "You're mine, Cassidy. And you're going to admit it if you want to come."

She shakes her head, but I can feel how wet she is for me even through her jeans, see the way her nose scrunches up a tiny bit as she denies how much she wants this. She's just stubborn as fuck and too proud to give in.

"What'd I tell you about lying?" I ask, smirking at her as I reach down and unzip her jeans, but she slaps my hand away, shoving me back. I let her because I want to see how she's going to try to put space between us. She'll fail, but it's fun to watch her try.

"No."

I step closer. "That word doesn't exist between you and me."

"Unless you want a fist to your junk, back off, Hayden."

I blow out a breath. "What do I have to do to get you to give in to this?" I'm fully ready to stalk her ass twenty-four-seven if I have to. I'll kidnap her and cuff her to my goddamn bed. I'll stuff her so full of my cock, she'll forget the outside world exists if that's what it takes.

She shakes her head and unlocks her door, walking inside and slamming it in my face. If she thinks that'll keep me out, she's got a lot to learn about what exactly is happening here.

I knock on the door until she finally opens it again, looking even more pissed off than before. "What?"

For now, I'll hide the crazy. I'll try to play this the way she wants. But I doubt I'll be able to hold back for long. "Tell me what you need me to do to prove I'm it for you."

She eyes me, biting her swollen lip. Swollen from making out with me. I can still taste her on my tongue. My cock has a pulse of its own, it's so hard, but it can fuck off. This is about more than a single fuck. I want her to be mine on a permanent basis. An *eternity* sort of basis. So far, there's not a single thing about her I don't like, including the way she fights me. No matter what she does, I only crave her more.

Nothing worth having is easy.

She grins up at me, but it's challenging as hell. "Get a hat trick in your next game."

I bark out a laugh. "You know I'm a defenseman, right?" I may play a more offensive game than a lot of D-men, but scoring three goals in a night isn't a normal part of my game.

She shrugs. "So? If you want me bad enough, you'll make it happen." She slams the door in my face again and I can't help but grin.

This girl is trouble.

But fuck if I don't love it.

"And you'll never tell me no again?" I yell through the door.

The only response I get is her laughter.

I turn away from her apartment, already planning how I'm going to make this happen as I walk back to my car and drive back to my hotel room to take the coldest shower known to man.

I'm on fire as we line up for the puck drop at the beginning of the third period. We're tied with the Pioneers, so I know I need to bring it if we want to win this game. Sweat drips down my face, dropping from my chin onto the ice as I bend forward near the blue line and wait for the faceoff.

As the puck drops and we fight for control, Roman's glare burns into me, trying to distract me and fuck up my game.

Some captain this asshole is, huh?

Not even he can throw me off from getting three in the net. I've got two already and need one more. The winning goal.

My stick handling is on point, my skating is faster than ever, and I'm feeling fucking invincible. Today's the day.

The Pioneers try to get the puck back onto our side of the ice, but I intercept it and take off down the center, passing D-to-D with King who sends it back to me before he gets slammed into the boards by their defenseman.

I fly down the ice with the puck on my stick, dodging their defenseman as he tries to check me and sending it flying toward the net. It bounces off the goalie's pads and rebounds back to me, and I send it right back again, this time shooting straight for the five-hole and into the net.

"Fucking Hat Trick!" War bellows in my ear as he slams into me from behind, sending us both into the boards. The crowd goes nuts and hats rain down onto the ice. I'm grinning like a fucking lunatic as I skate back to the bench for a fist bump with the team and a water bottle.

I'm sitting on the bench, panting and trying to catch my breath, and it sinks in that I pulled this shit off. Hat fucking trick. And I'm not even excited about it for my career. No, I can't wait to get off the ice and collect my prize. My dick tries to chub up in my cup when I think about what tonight means, but I refocus on the game and it deflates.

The second the final horn sounds, I'm dragged into media bullshit before I can shower and get the hell out of the arena. The guys try to get me to go out and celebrate with them, but it's already late and I have a different kind of celebration in mind.

Kingston Beaumont, aka Monty or King, my D-line mate, claps me on the back. The dude hardly says anything, but when he does, I'm learning you pay attention. "Good game. You lit the barn up tonight."

"Thanks, man," I say, grinning at him. "It's your turn next game."

His lips twitch up in a half smile and he heads for the locker room as I finish up with the reporters and finally manage to make my way out of the arena.

I text Cassidy as I walk to my car, telling her to be ready for me when I get to her apartment because I'm not waiting this time. She doesn't respond, but I don't care.

She belongs to me now, officially, and I'm about to show her what that means.

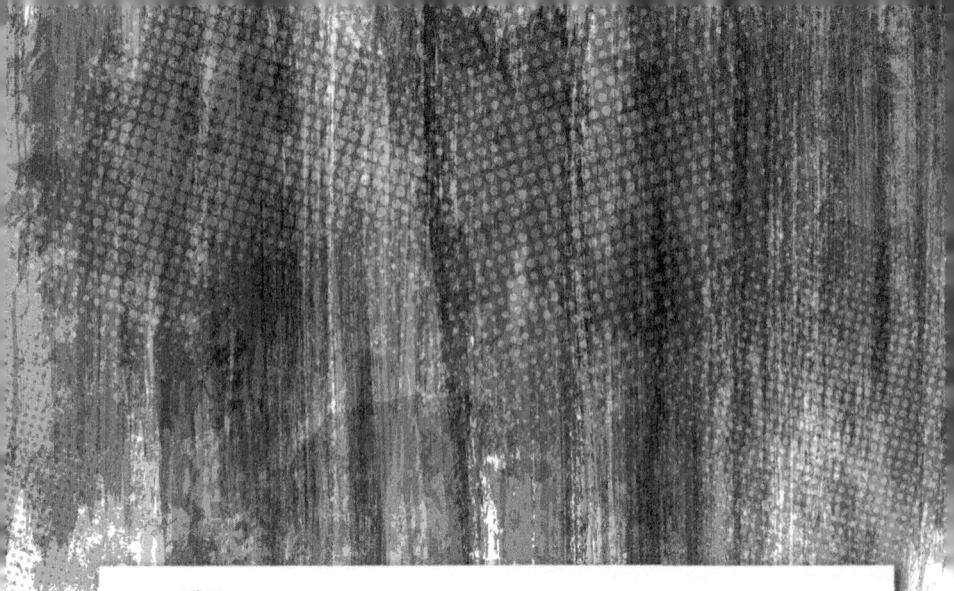

i live here
@SinBinSquatter

Vaughn doesn't just play dirty, he plays filthy. Someone get the dude a soap sponsor. #ScrubADubDub

Hayden #10

I TRY The Sin Bin first, but only find Lila there. She tells me with a grin that Cassidy took tonight off, so I don't stick around. From what I can tell, Cassidy's a workaholic and that bar is her baby. I wonder if she took the night off so she'd be ready and waiting for me to come fuck her into oblivion after my game.

A smile slashes across my face.

Either way, she better have watched my game from wherever she was.

Her apartment's only a few blocks away, so I head over there next. I stare up at her window, but it's dark. Between her not answering my texts from earlier, the dark window, and considering it's late as fuck, I'm going to assume she's asleep and let myself in.

Would I rather she be up waiting for me? Of course.

But a sleepy, pliant Cassidy could be just as fun. In fact, my cock thickens as I think about being able to do whatever I want to her body without her telling me no.

I don't bother knocking on her door before using the key she leaves under the mat—I discovered it when I left her the flowers—and stepping inside. It's dark and quiet, and I wonder if she really is sleeping. I toe off my shoes and then silently walk down the hallway toward her bedroom, half expecting her to jump out of the shadows and tear me a new asshole for being a stalker.

But she doesn't.

I push open the door to her bedroom and find her sprawled across the bed, fast asleep and looking like my downfall, a temptation that'll change me forever if I take a bite. Her hair is a mess spilled across the pillow, and her lips are parted as if begging for me to sink myself between them. She's wearing a tank top that barely covers her tits and a pair of panties so tiny she might as well not be wearing any at all. Those long, toned legs of hers are parted just enough for me to get a sliver of a view of my pussy.

I tip my head back and groan, gripping my dick through my pants and willing it to calm the fuck down.

Careful not to wake her up, I move closer, shrugging out of my blazer as I go and tossing it aside. She stirs as I kneel next to the bed and run the tips of my fingers up the smooth skin of her thighs, but she doesn't wake.

This sense of power burns through my veins as I stare at her, thinking about everything I want to do. The endless stream of possibilities carves its way through my brain, into my veins, and straight to my dick.

The way she smells. *Fuck.* I lean closer, breathing in her scent as my cock pulses and I have to undo my pants to let it out. I'm so fucking hungry for her, goddamn *starving*, that my mouth waters.

I slip my fingers under the waistband of her panties and drag them down, revealing her bare pussy inch by devastating inch. This cunt will be the end of the man I am when I slip inside of it. She'll destroy me and turn me into something new. Something *hers*.

The power this woman holds over me is like nothing I've ever allowed anyone else, and she doesn't even know.

I toss the scrap of fabric aside and run a finger across her bare pussy before slipping just the tip inside. Then I suck the digit into my mouth, needing to taste her even though she's not wet yet.

Goddamn, she tastes good, like sweetness and ruination.

My new favorite flavor.

She moans in her sleep, tossing her head from side to side as I gently rub circles around her clit and she fights to stay asleep. I run the back of my finger down her slit, testing to see how wet she is. When I'm sure I won't hurt her, I slip my spit-slicked finger inside. She's burning heat and slippery wetness, and I stroke her clit with the pad of my thumb while I fuck her with my fingers. It doesn't take long for her to soak my hand, and her cunt is squeezing my fingers, looking for something bigger.

I'm shaking with the need to be inside of her, my balls pulled up tight and my cock leaking like a motherfucker. Every drop belongs inside of her and it's being wasted smearing on my skin and not hers. I glare down at the drying pre-cum and run my finger along any I can find, collecting it and pushing it inside of her.

I give myself a couple of strokes, wondering how long I can keep her asleep. Wondering if I can make it all the way inside of her before she wakes up. Wondering if I can come inside of her without her finding out.

She squirms under my touch and when I pull my finger out of her, she whines in her sleep. Even unconscious as she is, she feels my loss and begs for me to fill her. She's still asleep, but I can tell she's getting close. Her head's thrown back against her pillow and her hair's a tangled mess. The moans leaving her fuckable lips aren't soft anymore.

I wonder if she's dreaming of me.

She *better* be dreaming of me.

I bend forward and slide my tongue over her, needing a hit direct from the source. I'm eating up all Cassidy's wetness with messy licks, mixing us together before sucking her clit into my mouth. I flick my tongue ring across it a couple of times, forgetting to be gentle, and she gasps awake.

She looks down at me between her thighs, breathing hard as she tries to figure out what the fuck is going on. "Hayden?"

I smirk up at her, taking the opportunity to rip my shirt off. Buttons go flying and I couldn't give less of a fuck. "Hey, Princess."

"What the hell are you—" She groans and throws an arm over her face as I dive back in, sucking her clit until she's on the edge of coming all over my face. "Fuck," she gasps, arching off the bed as I slip another finger coated with me inside of her.

"You're going to come for me, but not until you admit you're mine," I say, looking up at her with a grin, and I can barely make out the hesitation on her face in the dark. The smile slips off my face as irritation pricks underneath my skin. "Give me what I earned."

I sit back and lick my lips, tasting her sweetness on my tongue as she stares up at me with a mix of shock and full-blown irritation on her face. "Hayden—"

"You belong to me now, Princess. You know it. I know it," I say, leaning over to kiss her hard before pulling back and standing up to finish undressing, taking my time to let her sit in her frustration. She needs to learn I'm not fucking around. "You made the deal. I held up my end. Now it's your turn."

She sits up, staring at me like she's not sure if she should punch me in the face or shove me down and climb on my dick.

But when I crawl onto the bed and pin her underneath me, she widens her legs, opening herself up to me. My little liar wants this as much as I do.

She may have a defiant streak a mile long, but that will only make breaking her more fun.

I reach between us and rub the head of my cock through her wetness, teasing her clit with my piercings until she gasps and her thighs tremble. Her fingers claw at me, trying to get me to give in and fuck her. Looks like I need to up the torture.

"Condom," she moans while at the same time rubbing her slippery cunt all over my dick. I want to slip inside of her so bad, I have to grit my teeth to hold my ground.

"I don't think that's what you really want."

Her eyes flash up to mine, full of that fight I'm coming to crave. "Put on a fucking condom or get out of my apartment."

Goddamn, she's hot when she's pissed.

I reach over and grab one from the pocket of my slacks, already having a plan for how this is going to go. She thinks she's in control of this, of us, but she's not. For now, I'll let her think she is because it helps me get what I want.

I roll it on while she bites her lip and watches me with lust-drunk eyes. She may fight every step of the way, but her body doesn't lie about how much she wants me.

Her nipples are hard, she's practically panting, and her legs have fallen open so I can see every slick inch of her.

As soon as I roll the condom down my length, I pin her wrists above her head with one hand and slam inside of her in one hard thrust, hating this fucking latex keeping me from feeling her skin to skin.

She gasps and arches off the bed, taking me deep as I start to fuck her hard and fast, not giving her any time to adjust before I'm pounding into her pussy like a madman. Like a fucking savage.

As she starts to clench and ripple around me, I stop. Go

completely fucking still balls deep inside of her. Her hazy eyes find mine, narrowing. "Why the hell aren't you moving?" she snarls, digging her nails into my skin and tightening her legs around me.

"Give me what you owe me." I don't bother telling her again what that is. She already knows.

Her eyebrows furrow as she bites her lip, her eyes searching mine in the dark. Eventually she blows out a breath and mutters, "I'm yours," quiet enough that I almost miss it.

"What was that, Princess?"

She glares up at me. "I'm yours, okay? For tonight, I'm yours."

I chuckle, and she groans when it makes my dick jump inside of her. "Try again."

She huffs and I shift my hips so she feels me right up against her clit. She moans, and it's breathy and fills the quiet space around us. I run my nose up the side of her neck and face until my lips brush her ear. "Pay your fucking debt."

"I'm yours. Okay? Happy?"

I grin down at her before biting her neck and leaving a mark that'll last for days. "Ecstatic. And I'm going to fuck you so hard you'll never forget it."

She throws her head back and cries out, wrapping her legs around my waist, pulling me closer as she takes everything I give her and begs for more. Her nails dig into my back and she kisses me like she wants to suck my soul into her body.

Fuck, she can have it as long as she gives me hers in return.

I let go of her wrists and grab her hips, lifting her off the bed while her back arches so I can fuck her harder, deeper, until she's screaming my name and her body convulses with another orgasm. I grind my teeth together so I don't come. I have plans for her that don't involve me getting off inside a condom.

I slide out of her and she's in that lazy post-orgasm haze where she's all pliant and I've fucked the fight right out of her. "What are you doing?" she slurs as her eyes barely open to watch me.

I kiss down her stomach, breathing her in while my dick somehow gets harder because of what I'm about to do. "Tasting you after I've made you come. I want you soaking my face."

She groans but spreads her legs wider for me, giving me access to her delicious little cunt. Her fingers dig into my hair and tighten while she drags me right where she wants me. She tastes even better than before with the added sweetness of her orgasm on my tongue. I lick and suck her clit until she's twisting in the sheets and begging for more, ready to come again.

But I don't let her, not yet.

I reach down while she's distracted and rip off the condom, tossing it somewhere behind me. I'll deal with it later because by then I'll have gotten what I want. Hopefully she doesn't find it because odds are I'll have to do this again.

And again.

When it's done and she's full on fucking my face, desperate to come again, I pull back and flip her over onto her stomach, pulling her hips back toward me so she's on all fours with her ass in the air like a good girl. Even better, she can't see the lack of a condom on my dick from this angle.

"Hayden," she moans, wiggling her ass at me as I rub my bare cock along her cunt, slicking it up. I've never fucked anyone raw like this, and I need a second to get my shit together before I sink inside of her. "Fuck me."

Eventually, when I'm sure I won't come the second I'm inside the hottest pussy I've ever fucked, I grab her hips, slamming inside of her from behind as she cries out and pushes back against me, taking me deeper than before.

My head falls back and I groan at how good she feels bare. Silky and hot and tight. Goddamn. Fucking her raw is about to become my new addiction, and I never want to put another fucking rubber between us again.

She's mine and I want to feel every inch of her wrapped around me every single day until the day I die.

And then in the next life.

I fuck her hard and fast, reaching around to stroke her clit while I pound into her pussy until she's shaking and gushing all over my cock again. Her pussy clamps down on me as she rides out the high, and I can't hold back.

I slap her ass again, marking her with a pink print of my hand, and she curses me. She tightens around my shaft and pulls me back into her perfect cunt like she can't stand to let me go.

"Fuck, Princess," I groan as I unload inside of her, filling her up with my hot cum and not pulling out until it's dripping out around me. If she thinks it's weird I stay inside of her for minutes, holding her face down into the bed, she doesn't say anything. I'm not letting a drop of my cum spill out of her, not when it's got a job to do and this angle helps get it done. She groans and bows her back, wiggling her ass and taking everything I give her.

When we both finally come down from the high, I pull out and fall onto the bed next to her, breathing hard as she burrows herself into my side and throws a leg over my hips. I take the opportunity to shove my fingers back inside of her, trying to keep my cum where it belongs for as long as possible.

She will have my baby, and when she does, she'll never be able to leave.

She looks up at me with a lazy smile. "What are you doing?"

Before she notices my bare cock, I quickly pull the sheet up over us both. I'll get up in a second and deal with the condom, but not in the way she thinks. "I could always shove my dick back inside of you."

Instead of the fight I'm expecting, she curls up against me and her eyes flutter closed. Holy shit, I think I fucked the fight right out of her.

"No going back now, Princess," I murmur into the dark, meaning it with every piece of my soul.

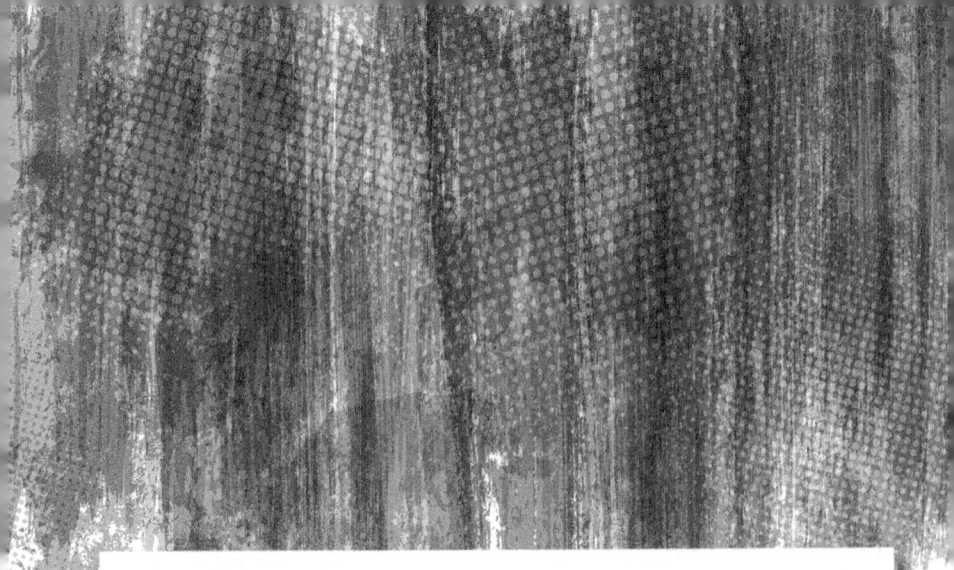

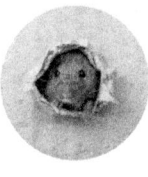

Rat
@RinkRat

If you play against Vaughn, better wear your brown pants because shit's about to get real. #FearTheHitman

Hayden #11

I'VE GOT an early morning skate, so I untangle myself from Cassidy and throw on last night's clothes. She's still passed out when I leave, but I schedule her a delivery for breakfast and leave her a note telling her I'll see her at her bar tonight after the game.

The guys are already warming up on the ice when I get there, and War grins at me as he skates by. "Gonna level up again tonight? Maybe a natty hatty this time?"

"Who knows? Weirder shit's happened," I say, grinning like an idiot. With Cassidy letting me inside of her, the way she finally surrendered to me, I almost forgot I scored my first hat trick in the pros. Fuck, my first hat trick ever.

He shakes his head. "You're fucking crazy, you know that?"

"You're not the first person to call me that." And I doubt he'll be the last.

He laughs and skates off to join the rest of the team while I finish stretching and getting ready for practice. Coach gives me a nod and a pat on the back before we start running drills and working on our stick handling. By the time we're done, I'm drenched in sweat and ready for a shower.

As I'm walking back to the locker room, Roman steps in front of me, blocking my path. "What do you want, Morozov?"

He glares at me. "You fucked her, didn't you?"

I smirk at him, neither one of us needing to clarify who the *her* is in this situation. "And what would make you think that?" Probably the marks from her nails on the back of my neck that stick out above my practice jersey, but I don't bring it up. I'm sure he's seen them.

He shoves me hard, making me stumble back a few steps in my skates because I wasn't braced. "Stay the fuck away from her."

I grin and shove him back harder, sending him stumbling into the wall behind him. I can't wait to see his face when Cassidy comes to a game with her belly swollen with my baby. "I didn't see a ring on her finger when I was balls deep inside of her last night."

He growls and lunges for me, but I sidestep him and stick my skate out, tripping him so he goes sprawling across the ground. "You're a dead man."

"And you're delusional if you think she wants anything to do with you after you fucked someone else. And in her bar's bathroom?" I shake my head down at him. "You must be a goddamn moron."

His eyes narrow as he picks himself up off the ground. "She told you about that?"

I prop myself against my stick, acting like I don't give a shit about him when really I'm vibrating with the urgent need to beat his face in with it. "She told me everything."

Roman gives me a mean smile. "I doubt that. Did she tell you I own her ass?"

"See, now I know you're lying," I say, folding my arms across my chest. "Since you can't possibly own what belongs to me."

He scoffs and shakes his head. "You don't even know what you're getting into with her, Vaughn. Best to back off now while you still can."

I glare at him as my stick creaks in my grip. "You don't know shit, Morozov. Now fuck off."

He smirks at me as he walks away, tossing over his shoulder, "Wait and see."

"Touch her and die, dickhead!" I yell after him. He just laughs and keeps walking, leaving me fuming and fantasizing about all the ways I could make his death look like an accident.

Cassidy is mine, and no one is going to take her from me.

Especially not Roman fucking Morozov.

I have to haul ass to the airport to pick my brother up from his flight, but I'm relieved he's here. Sawyer and I are only a year apart, but we grew up like twins. He's my other half and best friend, and neither one of us is willing to be far from the other. Him being on the other side of the country was like missing one of my limbs.

We grew up on the ice together, but he was always drawn to the medical side of things, patching me up when I'd take hard hits or shots from rogue pucks. The last three years of him in medical school, we were lucky I was able to stay in one city the entire time so he didn't have to move.

Now that I've been traded, though, he called in a favor with our asshole of a father to get his residency moved. Being a senator has some perks, not that I've ever benefited from Nathaniel Vaughn's particular brand of political assholery.

I park at the airport and wait for Sawyer outside the baggage claim area. When I see him walking toward me with his duffel bag slung over his shoulder, I can't help but grin and pull him into a tight hug.

He laughs and hugs me back. "Miss me?"

I nod, not even trying to deny it. He'd know I was lying anyway. "Fuck yeah."

Sawyer pulls back and shakes his head. "You're an idiot." He looks around the airport like he's searching for something or someone. "What, you didn't drag Torin Mattson along to pick me up? I thought you loved me."

I flash a sarcastic grin, gripping one of Sawyer's bags and lifting it off his shoulder. "Yes, because my very straight teammate would give up his pre-game nap to let my brother drool over him."

Sawyer scoffs and flips me off. "I don't drool."

I laugh and lead him to my car, tossing his bags in the back before climbing into the driver's seat and starting the engine. "So, how was your flight?"

He shrugs, yanking the hair tie out of his hair and letting it fall around his shoulders before putting it back up again. "It was fine. I slept through most of it."

"Good," I say as we pull out of the parking lot. "Because now that you're here, we need to find a place."

He nods, staring out the window at the gray blanket of clouds and rain that is Seattle in November. "Yeah, living in a hotel sucks."

"Glad you feel that way, because we're meeting with a real estate agent when we get back to the city."

"Ugh," he groans. "At least buy me lunch first."

"Done." I flip on the turn signal and merge onto the freeway. I can feel his stare burning into the side of my face. "What?"

"Maybe I missed your face." I side-eye him, and he's grinning. "Who is she?"

"Who's who?" I ask, trying to play dumb, knowing it won't work.

He laughs, shaking his head. "Oh, so we're pretending your

neck doesn't look like Wolverine used you as his scratching post? Okay."

When I don't say anything, he keeps pushing. "And don't try to pretend it was a hookup. You'd never let some random mark you up like that."

"Her name's Cassidy." Every word comes out from between gritted teeth. Yeah, my bisexual doctor of a brother is a definite threat. "Hands off."

"I shouldn't suggest a Vaughn brother sandwich, then?"

I swear to fuck I growl like a goddamn animal at my brother.

"Fuck," he laughs. "Why do you look so crazy right now?"

My fingers tighten on the wheel as Sawyer connects his phone to the stereo. "She brings it out in me."

"Holy shit. Since when are you possessive?"

"Since Cassidy."

"And? Details, dude. Who is she? Is she hot?" Sawyer can't stand the silence, so he picks a song from his playlist to play in the background. "I'm waiting."

I grin as I think about my little liar who won't admit how much she wants me and how fucking perfect she is. "She hated me before we even met. Called me a talentless asshole in my Instagram DMs."

"Leave it to you to be into a girl who wants nothing to do with you."

"You know how I like a challenge."

"I'm well aware. So she hates you?" He studies me and then reaches across the car and pinches my cheek. "I don't think I like the way you're smiling right now. It's giving *Joker* vibes."

Fuck, I missed my brother. "You remember that hat trick the other day?"

"Dude, I couldn't believe you did that. I broke my TV when it happened. Jumped up so fast I threw the remote at the screen and shattered it."

The song changes and I glance over at Sawyer, feeling smug as fuck about this next part. "Cassidy played chicken with me and lost. She dared me to get a hat trick and if I did, I'd get her. No way was I losing."

He stares at me like I'm a stranger, his eyebrows up by his hairline. "You want her long-term? *You?*"

His insulting tone is something I choose to ignore. I'm capable of being in a relationship. I think. "She's stubborn as hell and doesn't give in to me without a fight. But fuck if that doesn't do something to me. She's the total package—gorgeous, clever, driven. Why wouldn't I want to keep her?"

"Remind me not to drink the water while we live here. I don't want to catch whatever this is." Sawyer sweeps his hand in my general direction. "And for the record, I think you're certifiable."

"Probably," I agree with a grin. "You're the third person who's called me that today."

He laughs and then turns to stare at me, raising an eyebrow. Yeah, he's mastered the art of raising one eyebrow, Rock-style. "And you think a ride on your dick's all she needs to be all in with you?"

I stop at a light and turn to raise my own eyebrows at him—both of them. "You doubt my skills?"

My brother grins and grabs his phone, changing the song. "Never." I groan when I hear the familiar beat of The Killers' "Mr. Brightside". He knows I hate this goddamn song and the million times he's made me listen to it.

Sawyer laughs and cranks it up, singing along off-key while I try not to strangle him in the passenger seat.

When we get back to the hotel, I show Sawyer to his room in the suite—I upgraded so we wouldn't have to share a bed—before heading over to mine to change for the game tonight. No pregame nap, but it was worth it to have my brother here.

"Get your ass in gear, bro. You're riding in with me," I yell.

Sawyer pops his head out of his door with his lip curled. "Fuck, no. I'm not going to sit in an empty arena for hours before the game starts. I'll grab a ride."

"We're stopping on the way to meet with the realtor and see a couple of properties. Besides, if you ride with me, you'll get to watch warmups with Mattson. Two words, bro: Groin. Stretches."

His eye roll is so much like mine it's like looking in the mirror. "I'll get to see those anyway. They're right before the puck drops, jackass. You act like I've never been to your games before."

"Fine, whatever." I grab my bag and toss his wallet at him. "Come on, Sawyer," I pout, which is something I've only ever done with him to get my way. "Please."

He sighs before he flips me off and disappears back into his room. I grin because I know I've got him. Works every time. "And you can wear my jersey like you're my bitch," I yell after him.

"Fat fucking chance. First stop is the team store for a number eight sweater."

He meets me by the door in ripped jeans and a leather jacket and I look him up and down. "You're gonna scare Mattson away."

"Now look at you, doubting *my* skills."

"Never," I say, grinning at him as I echo his earlier response. Fuck, it's good to have my brother here.

We walk down to my car and Sawyer hops into the passenger seat while I climb in behind the wheel. The first property is only a few miles from the hotel, so the drive is short, but Sawyer still has his phone out texting someone.

"Who are you talking to?" I ask, trying to peek over his shoulder.

He slaps my hand away and shakes his head. "Dad. He's being as tyrannical as ever."

"Still trying to persuade you to become his queer show pony?" I ask with a laugh.

Sawyer rolls his eyes. "I swear the day I came out as bi, Dad stopped seeing me as a person and I became a campaign strategy instead."

My phone's been suspiciously quiet since my trade, but it's only a matter of time before my father makes his opinion known on my life choices. Loudly. No doubt he's working on how to spin what happened in his favor as we speak.

After our short but productive meeting with the realtor, we put in an offer on a house and haul ass to the arena because now I'm running late.

I pull into the player's parking lot and park my Range Rover before we get out and walk toward the entrance. Sawyer looks around like he's never been in an arena before, but this place was renovated last year and it's hella nice so I don't blame him for gawking. I did on my first day, too.

I lead him through the back hallways toward the locker room where the guys are already getting ready for warmups.

I stop in front of the doors and turn to my brother. "Glad you came now?"

He nods. "Hell yeah." He looks over at me with a smirk that tells me he's about to say something that's going to piss me off. "I'm about to see Torin Mattson's dick. I can feel it."

I glare at him. "You better not fuck him. Find someone at the bar tonight after the game and leave my teammates alone."

He laughs and shakes his head. "You're not the only Vaughn who likes a challenge, Hay."

"Straight," I growl, shoving him through the doors and into the locker room.

"That only makes it more fun," Sawyer says, repeating my words back to me.

I love my brother, but this is the last shit I need before a game. Still, I follow him inside and try to ignore the way he stares at Mattson like he's starving and the dude's an all-you-can-eat buffet.

"Keep your dick in your pants," I growl at my brother, knowing he only listens when he wants to. Hopefully Torin doesn't notice Sawyer eye fucking him, and right now his back's turned, so I drag my brother through the locker room with me before Torin can catch on to my brother's little crush.

I don't have time to deal with Sawyer's chase. We're the same in our obsessive tendencies, he and I. But now, I've got a hockey game to win so I tune out all the bullshit and step into my pre-game ritual, knowing once it's done, I get to feed my addiction with another taste of my girl.

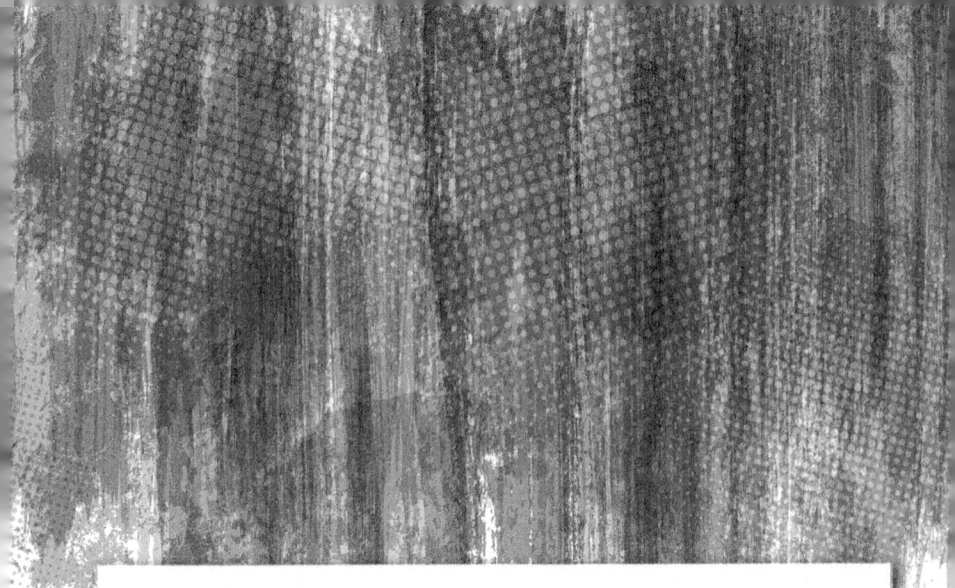

what
@FaceoffFoulmouth

That hit by Vaughn was so illegal, it needs its own episode on 'True Crime'.
#DeathPenalty

Hayden #12

THE ANCHORS WERE a shit team before I joined up, but our current win streak only reinforces to me that I'm that fucking good. I don't stick around and bullshit with the guys after the game knowing my brother's waiting for me, and it's been too fucking long since I've seen Cassidy.

Plus, they're all meeting up at The Sin Bin later, so I'll see them then.

My girl texted me this morning to thank me for breakfast, but she hasn't responded to any of my texts since then. That better not mean she's trying to hide from me after last night. We're done with that shit, her pushing me away.

She can try all she wants, but I'm not going anywhere.

Looks like she wants to find that out the hard way.

Sawyer is waiting for me outside the locker room with Monty, who looks like he wants to bolt as soon as he sees me. Sawyer gives him a flirty smile and I know I need to get him out of here before he scares the shit out of my teammate.

"Let's go," I say, biting back a grin. My brother's fucking ridiculous. He's not even into Kingston, but he's also a total manwhore, so flirting is like breathing to him. I lead the way back to the car, surprised when Kingston tags along.

"Mind if I catch a ride to the bar?" he asks.

I nod, but don't have time to say anything before Sawyer jumps in. I take the time to check my phone while we walk down the hall, hoping there's something from my Princess.

There's not, and my good mood from the win turns to shit. Another lesson she needs to learn, that she's not allowed to ignore me.

Finally, I climb into the car and notice the empty passenger seat. My eyes catch Sawyer's in the rearview mirror. "Dude," I snap at my brother. "Get your ass up here. I'm not fucking Uber."

He grins at me as he gets out and moves to the front, plopping his big body down next to me. "Why so cranky, Hay-Hay?" he asks like I'm a toddler. "Need a snack?"

My lip curls. "Don't call me that, See-Saw."

His nose wrinkles. "Point made."

I hand over my phone and Sawyer grabs it, putting on "Something to Hide" by grandson as I start the engine and pull out of the parking lot, heading deeper downtown to The Sin Bin.

When we get there, I park and we all climb out, Sawyer leading the way inside while Kingston and I follow behind him.

The place is packed, but I don't see Cassidy anywhere. I look around and finally spot her coming out of a hallway behind the bar, fucking gorgeous as ever in a pair of ripped jeans and a black tank top that hugs every curve of her body.

She looks up as we approach the bar, giving me a glare that makes my heart take off and my dick jerk. What can I say? I love her fight.

"Hey, Princess," I say as I lean over the bar and my lips brush her cheek before she pushes me back. It's not enough. I need so much fucking more of her, but I curl my fingers into the edge of the bar to keep from grabbing her and yanking her across and into my arms. "Miss me?"

She leans closer to me, her voice low when she speaks. "Not even a little, and you're even more psycho than I thought if you think I'm going to sleep with you again after the shit you pulled last night. Sneaking in while I was asleep? Forcing me to say I belong to you like I'm something you can own? Fucking stalker," she mutters. Then she stares straight into my eyes when she says, "I changed my locks this morning."

Anger bubbles hot and potent inside of me and I grit out, "You did what?"

She gives me a bitchy smile. "Changed. The. Locks. Did you get hit in the head tonight or something?"

Her question means she wasn't watching my game, and I just fucking snap. When it comes to her, my already tenuous grip on my temper is razor thin. She manages to push all my buttons, and it must be instinct for her because she doesn't know me that well yet.

It's like she was put on this earth to lure out the psycho in me.

I stalk behind the bar and grab her arm, pulling her toward me, leaning down so there's less than a breath between us when I speak. "Looks like you need a reminder of how this works between us." And I'm going to have to get a copy of her new key. She can't keep me out, I won't allow it—but obviously I don't tell her that. "And it just so happens I'm in a giving mood."

My brother laughs his ass off at me as I drag her out from behind the bar, and King takes in the scene without a word before he disappears into the back with the rest of our teammates. As long as he doesn't try to stop me, we're cool.

There's a staircase roped off beside the bar that leads

upstairs to where I'm hoping there's an office or a storage room or something.

Somewhere I can fuck her until my cum's dripping between her thighs again and everything's the way it should be before she fucked it up with her delusion that she can escape me.

"What the hell are you doing?" she hisses, trying to rip free of my hold, but I tighten my grip and pull her up the stairs, ignoring the looks we get from everyone as we go. Knowing she'll wear my bruises when we're finished only gets me higher.

When we reach a door at the top, I shove it open and push her inside before slamming it shut behind us and locking it. Then I block the way out with my body in case she thinks about testing me.

She whirls around to face me and I grab her by the backs of her thighs before she can say a word. She's pinned against the wall with my hips between her spread thighs as she claws at me. "You think this little act of defiance is going to stop me from getting what I want?" I wrap my fingers around her throat, digging my others into her thigh where it's wrapped around my waist. "You set the challenge, Princess, and I met it. I won you. There's nothing you can do to change it now."

She glares up at me while rubbing her body against mine. The only thing between us is a couple of layers of clothing that I'm tempted to tear through so I can get inside her faster. Cassidy wraps her arms around the back of my neck and pulls me closer while pushing me away with her lying words, "Fuck you, Hayden."

"That's exactly what you're going to do, little liar." I reach down and fumble with my belt before getting it unbuckled. Cassidy fights me at first, but then her hand is down between our legs, helping me push my pants and then boxers down just enough to free my cock. It's harder than stone and wet at the tip, and the need to be inside of her is a feral, violent thing inside of me. "And then you're going to take every drop of my cum inside your tight little pussy until you realize the only dick that's ever going to be inside of you again is mine."

"Do it and I'll chop it off," she snarls, but she lunges forward and her lips are on mine. It's sloppy and painful as she bites and licks into my mouth. This is more of a battle than a kiss, a war between souls.

She should know by now that I never lose.

Her hands claw at my jacket, my shirt, my hair. Anywhere she can reach.

She's wild. Savage.

She's begging for me to break her.

I rip open the button of her jeans and tear the zipper down, shoving them and her panties down her hips so they trap her thighs together. My hold drops and her feet hit the floor. She stumbles, but I don't give her a chance to get her balance and make her next move in this fight. I'm not letting her push me away, so I spin her and shove her face into the door.

She fights, trying to hit me, claw me, bite me anywhere she can reach, but her gasp and the moan she tries to hide give away how much she wants this. The way she arches her back, shoving her ass against my cock while she curses me out with swollen lips and a tongue coated in me.

I wrap her hair around my fist and reach down between us to grip my shaft and rub the head of my cock through her wetness. "You're such a fucking liar," I whisper in her ear as I press the length of my body against hers, trapping her. Goosebumps break out across her skin and I trace them with my tongue. "But your cunt doesn't lie about how much it wants me, does it?"

"You're a fucking asshole," she bites out, but she's breathless when she says it.

"Your fucking asshole," I rasp as I shove my dick into her so deep she's forced up onto her toes. She screams my name like a curse as I start to fuck her. Hard slaps of my body against hers and her promises of retribution drown out everything else. Her nails dig into my skin, but she's not trying to shove me away. She's trying to pull me closer. Ten little pricks of pain along my hips as she fights to get me deeper inside of her.

I pull out of her far enough I can see the glint of a couple of my piercings in the hint of light coming in from the window before I shove all the way back inside of her. And then I do it again, and again, fucking her hard and slow. "Don't act like you don't love every second of this. Of me inside of you." I bite her neck hard enough to bruise and her pussy spasms around me. "Of the way I catch you when you fall."

I shove one of my hands between Cassidy and the wall, rubbing her clit in the same rhythm as I'm fucking her.

Her body's trembling and she shakes her head, but we both know she's lying. This thing between us is unstoppable, undeniable.

Unbreakable.

"Condom," she gasps out and I narrow my eyes.

But I pull out of her, slipping one of these fucking cock stranglers on before shoving back inside her again. I'm only wearing it long enough to make sure she's good and distracted before I take it off.

My lip curls while I fuck her through her first orgasm, loathing the way this goddamn latex dulls the feel of her around me. She's about to come again, rolling from one into the next, but I'm not letting it happen again until this fucking rubber is gone.

She's close, bucking in my grip, but I stop right before she comes, pulling out of her and flipping her around to face me. She's panting and her eyes are glassy as she glares up at me. Then I hit my knees and yank her pants off one of her ankles so her leg's free.

"I thought you weren't going to let me fuck you again." My words are mocking as I stand and grip her thigh and wrap it around my hip, ripping off the condom while she tries to murder me with her glare. As soon as the fucking thing is gone, I shove inside her again. Before she can figure out what I did, I stuff the damn thing in my pocket. "This is what me winning looks like."

Her eyes open into venomous slits as she glowers up at me with her teeth bared despite the fact I'm balls deep inside her and my cock is bare—not that she knows that part. I shift my hips so my piercings hit deep and her eyes roll back while her head falls against the wall. Then she catches herself and my fiery little liar's back. "This is what me *letting* you win looks like."

I laugh and slam into her harder, hard enough we're both going to feel it when we walk out of this room. But right now we're too caught up in the carnage as we destroy each other to do anything but take more. To steal every last drop of pleasure from the other and claim them as the spoils of war. "It sounds like you want me to prove you wrong."

"You c-cant." She stutters over her words because of how hard I'm slamming into her. "B-because I'm n-not wrong."

My hand wraps around her throat and I force her to look at me with my thumb under her chin. "You feel how deep inside of you I am? This is my home now and there's no evicting me. I'll grow old here. I'll fucking die here. So get," I punctuate the words with a hard thrust, "the fuck," another thrust, "on board. Or I'll make you."

"Fuck, Hayden." She gasps my name like a filthy vow, a curse, a liberation. Her cunt squeezes the goddamn life out of me while her legs give out. My grip on her tightens as I fall, too, twisting so she's on top of me and then in front of me as I blow my load inside of her. My shoulder throbs where it hit the ground, but I barely feel it as pulse after pulse of my cum shoots into her with nothing to stop it.

And her greedy cunt sucks it right up.

We lay on the ground together, our clothes wrinkled, our skin slick with sweat and littered with blood and bruises. My body wraps around hers while we try to catch our breath. When I'm sure every drop of cum is out of my balls and inside of her, I pull out and watch it drip down her thighs. She's too fucked up to notice.

"Jesus," she pants as she sits up and slumps against the wall. Her hand trembles as she rakes it through her hair. She looks like she just dragged herself off the battlefield, and I'm sure I look the same.

Before she recovers, I jump up and turn my back, pulling my jeans up over my half-hard cock. It's still glistening and I'm tempted to shove it back inside of her, but I can't risk her noticing I'm not wearing the condom.

When I'm done, I hold out my hand to help her up. She eyes it, then stands on her own. "This changes nothing."

Cassidy wobbles on shaky legs, and I smirk at her. "Guess next time I'll have to try harder to fuck the liar out of you."

She flips me off, but I grab her hand and bite her finger. She tries to straighten out her clothes, pulling up her pants and fixing her hair, but no matter what she does there's no hiding the bite marks on her neck, the bruises on her hips, the tangles in her hair, or the glassiness in her eyes.

I don't give a fuck if she looks like she just had my dick inside of her. In fact, I prefer it so all those assholes down in her bar will know she's off limits. That she's mine.

"There won't be a next time."

The laugh that bursts out of me is loud and carefree in a way I don't think I've ever been. "Right."

She opens her mouth to argue, but then closes it again before spinning and ripping the door open. She's so distracted, she didn't notice she left me alone in her office with her keys. I the take the opportunity to swipe them off the desk, pocketing them to make a copy.

Eventually she'll learn it's impossible to keep me out.

And like the asshole I am, I stare at her ass as she stomps down the stairs, knowing she can feel my eyes on her. Knowing it'll only piss her off more.

Goalie's Guard

2 oz rum • 1 oz coconut cream • 1 oz pineapple juice • 1/2 oz orange juice • ice
Garnish: pineapple slice and cherry

Blend rum, coconut cream, pineapple juice, and orange juice with ice until smooth. Pour into a chilled glass and garnish with pineapple and cherry.

Cassidy #13

I'M STILL FUMING when I walk back behind the bar and grab an apron, tying it around my waist. My hands are shaking and I think I accidentally double knotted it, but whatever.

My legs are trembling so hard from the catastrophic orgasm Hayden gave me upstairs and my underwear stick to me in an uncomfortable way because I'm wet as hell.

Does Hayden give me a second to process or sit in my pissy attitude? Of course not.

No, he follows me down the stairs and leans against the bar with a smug smile on his face as he watches me work.

"You look good in that apron," he says with a fuckboy grin that says he's imagining me naked. "But you'd look better out of it."

I ignore him as I ring someone up and hand them their drink before turning to him with a scowl that I know firsthand has made lesser men cower and run away. Hayden doesn't even freaking flinch.

"I can't believe you just..." I glance around, but the rest of the sentence dies on my tongue when a guy who could be Hayden's twin walks up beside him. They're the same height, similar build, and have the same shade of hair, though the new guy wears his longer and pulled up in a messy bun. The only difference is their eyes.

Oh, and all the tattoos.

"Is this the girl?" this new addition says, nudging Hayden in the shoulder before letting his gaze slide down my body in a slow perusal that leaves me feeling naked. Based on the cocky little smirk that forms on his face, he at the very least suspects what just happened between Hayden and me upstairs.

Ugh.

Hayden nods and slings an arm over the guy's shoulders, pulling him closer. "Cassidy, meet Sawyer. My brother."

Oh. *Shit.*

I stare at him as he gives me a knowing smile. "Nice to meet you, Cassidy. Hayden's told me a *lot* about you."

I glare at Hayden because we are *so* not at the *meet the family* stage—what the hell am I saying? We're not at *any* stage at all because I don't date hockey players no matter what might come out of my mouth under duress—before turning back to his brother. "It's nice to meet you, too. I've heard nothing about you. At all."

Sawyer laughs and steps forward, leaning against the bar like his brother does. Are they twins or...? "So, how'd you end up with this asshole?" He nods his head toward Hayden, who looks like he wants to strangle his brother for daring to speak to me. Or maybe it was that slow perusal from earlier. Either way, I sense an opportunity here.

Pissing Hayden off just became my new goal for the evening. Actually, make that my new goal in general.

I push out my boobs and give Sawyer a flirty smile. Nevermind that I think I'm walking funny because his brother's dick wrecked me like ten minutes ago. "Who says I'm with him?"

Sawyer grins as he looks over at his brother before turning back to me. "Sorry, sweetheart, but I happen to like being alive. But if you two ever want to add a third..." He trails off and licks his lower lip, and I can't help but laugh as Hayden grabs a fistful of his brother's shirt and shoves him away from the bar. He growls something at him that I don't catch, but it only makes little bubbles of happiness pop in my chest because I'm getting under his skin the way he loves to get under mine.

"I'll keep that in mind." I say, making sure my voice is just a little raspy before shifting to grin at Hayden, who looks like he's about to lose his shit.

He leans over the bar and grabs my arm, pulling me toward him until our lips are inches apart. "Don't even think about it," he growls.

I yank my arm out of his grip and shove him back. "Don't touch me."

"You made a deal, Princess. I'll keep reminding you how things are now until it sinks in." I swear he's about two seconds from hopping the bar and fucking me right here in the open and it takes all the willpower I have not to clench my thighs together. Like hell I'm going to show him that I sort of maybe like his possessive bullshit.

He glares at me for a second before stalking off, leaving me alone with his brother.

Sawyer sips from the drink Lila made him, eyeing me as he swallows. "He's obsessed with you."

"Good." I wince. "Shit, I probably shouldn't have said that out loud, especially to you. But I don't really date hockey players anymore and if he wants to make me reconsider that, he needs to only see me."

He nods. "I get it. I just hope you're ready because Hayden

never does anything without going all in and he's decided you're what he wants. He's really fucked up over it."

Goddamn Hayden Vaughn.

"I don't know why," I say, trying to keep my voice light. "He doesn't even know me."

He nods and leans closer, lowering his voice. "He's not exactly known for being…" His lips twist for a second while he thinks. "A relationship guy." I can feel Hayden's stare prickling into the side of my face from somewhere, but I don't let myself look. "But he's never been like this over a girl before. Not even close." He shrugs and reaches across the bar top and snatches a cherry before popping it into his mouth and biting down, flashing me a straight white grin. "I think you should give him a chance."

I scoff and narrow my eyes, batting his hand away when he tries to grab another. "You would say that. You're on his side. It's not happening."

He gives me a rueful smile, like he knows something I don't, before grabbing his glass and standing up. "If you say so." Then he walks away, leaving me to wonder what the hell that look was.

Hayden's back at the bar before I can take a single deep breath to calm my racing heart. Clearly he's better at cooling off than I am. He's got that look on his face that says he's already decided how this night is going to end, and my body reacts despite my brain screaming at me to stop thinking with my vagina.

"You know," he lowers his voice, "I'm thirsty as hell. How about a whiskey—Macallan. Neat."

"You're a piece of work, you know that?" I snap, grabbing the bottle of Jim Beam and staring him straight in the eyes as I pour half a glass, drop in some ice, and then slide it over to him. The liquid sloshes in the glass, but he doesn't even blink.

Like I have that bougie shit here.

He stares into his glass, wrinkling his nose in a snobbish way I wouldn't have expected from him before he lifts it and shoots it back all at once, letting the ice clink against the glass. The bastard doesn't even cough.

"Don't pretend like you don't love it." That infuriating smirk plays on his lips as if he knows every thought crowding my head.

"Don't flatter yourself, Vaughn." My attempt at sounding indifferent falls flat. His laughter rumbles through the space between us, deep and confident.

"Still pretending you don't want me? I think we've already proven that's a lie. Twice."

I lean over the bar, getting right in his face. "I really don't have time for your games."

"That's the thing, Princess," he says, matching my intensity, leaning forward until his nose brushes against mine. "For me? This isn't a game. This is me wanting something... someone," his eyes darken, "more than I've ever wanted anything in my life. And I always get what I want."

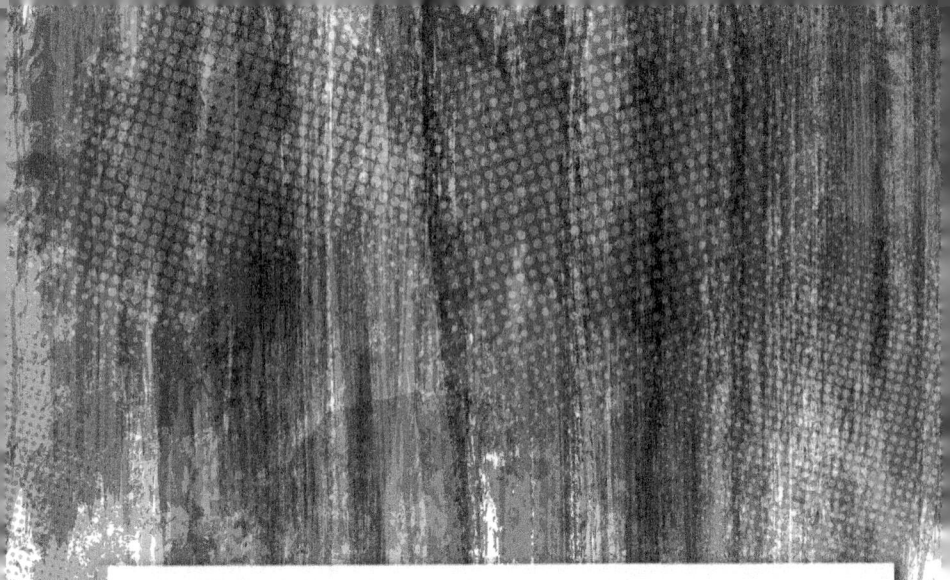

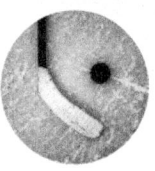

Baron
@SlapshotBaron

Hayden Vaughn doesn't take names, he just takes victims. #RIP

Hayden #14

CASSIDY BREAKS our little stare off first, but that's fine. I'll let her have her space for now.

I shove my glass away, frowning down at the remnants of the disgusting liquor.

"Want another one?" My little liar smirks, holding up the bottle of cheap shit and shaking it in my direction.

"Fuck no."

She laughs and I'm caught up in it until my asshole teammate Morozov takes the spot beside me.

Immediately, his eyes land on Cassidy, and I bristle. "Hey, fuckwit, you wanna find out how hard it is to play hockey blind? Get your eyes off my girl before I scoop them out and shove them up your ass."

He looks like he wants to rip my head off, and I hope he fucking tries. I waste no time fantasizing about all the ways I'd love to kill him, stuck on the idea of spilling his blood and burying his body somewhere in the woods.

In fact, new life goal unlocked.

Morozov smirks, that cold-ass smile sending gasoline into my veins, just waiting for another word to be the spark that sets me off. But I don't show it. I never show weakness, especially not to a prick like him.

"Your girl? You mean the one who was warming my bed for the better part of a year?"

"Keyword being was," I drawl and I notice Cassidy moving to the other side of the bar to get away from the two of us. Can't say I blame her. "You fucked that up, though, didn't you?"

He clenches his jaw, his nostrils flaring as he leans toward me, his face inches from mine. "She'll be back begging on her knees before this season's over, Vaughn. Don't you worry. In the meantime, enjoy that thing she does with her tongue. I taught her that."

I don't get a chance to respond before his face smooths into a calmness that's so clearly a mask, it's laughable. I wonder what the hell he's doing now, but then I see the manicured nails slide up his arm from the other side.

There's a blonde with her tits nearly falling out of a dress that's too short and too tight sitting next to Morozov, and I can practically smell the desperation wafting from her. She's on the stool beside him and he's already got a hand on her thigh. She's giggling at something he just whispered in her ear.

Roman turns to look at Cassidy, I'm guessing to check if she's noticed he's here with someone else. She's got her head tossed back, laughing at something Lila said, before she turns and her eyes lock with mine. My girl didn't even glance in his direction, like for a second she only sees me. She gives me a small smile, then shakes herself like she didn't mean to let me see that she actually likes me.

It's cute.

She's cute.

Cassidy looks away, and I turn back to the scene in front of me. Roman's whispering in his date's ear, his hand inching up her thigh. I roll my eyes.

She's nodding eagerly, her eyes wide. "You should definitely do that," she says, her voice porn star breathless.

"I just might," he murmurs, and I almost gag. Is that Roman's sex voice? Fucking sick.

"Can't wait," she says, licking her inflated lips. "It's going to be so hot."

His date's gaze slides over to mine and I see the heat flare there in a way it didn't for Morozov, and I can't resist taking a dig at my tool of a teammate. "If diseased dicks are your kink, sweetheart, I'm sure Roman will give you a taste of his."

She blinks in confusion, and I'm not sure if it's because she doesn't hear me or doesn't understand me.

Roman snarls in my direction, his hand curling into a fist. "You know what, you fucking asshole?" He leans forward, his hand leaving his date's thigh as he gets in my face.

"What's that, motherfucker? You going to finally grow a set of balls and fight me?"

He shoves me, but it's not enough to even budge me. "I'm going to end you."

I grin, that familiar adrenaline rushing through me, the one I get every time I'm on the ice, at the idea of finally putting him in his place. "Bring it, fuckface."

My fingers curl into a fist, but before either of us can make the first move, Cassidy's there, gripping the back of my shirt and pulling me back. "He's not worth getting into shit with the team, Hayden. Let him go make whatever poor decision he's about to." She leans around me and levels Roman with a glare. "Somewhere that's not my bar, asshole. I don't know how many times I have to say it, but get the hell out."

Once Roman takes his ugly scowl and skanky date out the door, Cassidy blows out a breath and looks up at me. "I don't need you fighting for my honor or whatever. I can handle

Roman's idiotic attempts to make me see what he thinks I'm missing on my own."

"And are you?"

She gets this cute wrinkle between her eyebrows when she's confused. See? Fucking cute. "Am I what?"

"Missing him?"

She stares up at me before she completely fucking falls apart. And I mean, the kind where she's laughing so hard she can't breathe, so she snorts and has tears running down her face. When she finally calms down and I wipe the wetness from her cheeks with my thumbs, she grins up at me. It's the kind of grin that lights up the whole goddamn world. It also makes my dick hard.

It's like she's showing me the real Cassidy underneath all the walls she's thrown up between us. It's the first time she's let me in like that, and I'm not about to let her regret it.

"I miss Roman like I miss food poisoning," she says, rolling her eyes at me. She's still smiling, and I feel like I'm winning something.

"Good," I tell her, leaning down to press a kiss to her forehead, breathing her in. "I'd hate to have to kill him." Despite my words, I'm still considering it. He's going to be a problem.

We stay like that for a few minutes, and the world disappears around us. She leans into me, her fingers gripping the fabric of my shirt like she doesn't want to let me go. I know if I called her out on it, though, she'd deny it.

When Cassidy finally pulls back, I reach up and cup her face, brushing my thumb across her cheek in a move that's so unlike me, it's hard to believe I'm doing it. I've never given a shit about anyone but Sawyer and myself, so this thing I've got going on with Cassidy is fucking weird. "You want to get out of here?"

She nods and I drag her over to Sawyer, handing over my keys so he has a way to get back to the hotel when he's done.

Then I lead Cassidy out of The Sin Bin and down the street toward her place, her hand in mine as she follows beside me.

There's something different between us now. Something deeper.

It's not just lust.

I think it just might be the start of something more.

Hat Trick

1/2 oz vodka • 1/2 oz rum • 1/2 oz tequila
1/2 oz gin • 1/2 oz triple sec • 1 oz sweet and sour mix • cola • ice
Garnish: lime wedge

Pour vodka, rum, tequila, gin, and triple sec into a shaker with ice. Add sweet and sour mix and shake. Strain into an ice-filled glass, top with cola, and garnish with lime.

Cassidy #15

I'VE DONE a few things in the last twelve hours I'm not proud of. One, I stopped Hayden from destroying Roman's stupid face. And two, I'm waking up sprawled out across Hayden's naked body because he slept over... again.

What the hell is wrong with me?

I move slowly so I don't wake him up, and because I can, I take a second to watch him sleep. He's so gorgeous it's ridiculous. Sleep has mussed his dark hair, and his full lips are slightly parted. For a second, I let myself remember how they felt on mine in the dark last night, before we fought and fucked until we passed out.

Shit.

I slide off the bed and grab his t-shirt off the floor, pulling it on before walking into my tiny kitchen. If I pull it up and take a sniff of his scent, well... we're not gonna talk about that.

I need coffee and a plan because I have no idea what to do about Roman.

He's not going away, and he looks at me like I'm his property.

The thought makes vomit crawl up the back of my throat.

Hayden does that whole *mine* thing, but with him it's not the same as it was with my ex. I don't know how to explain it, but the intent behind Roman's eyes was calculating and poisonous. Hayden looks at me like he wants to save me from myself. Like he wants to drown the world and strand us on a deserted island together so I'll have no choice but to be the center of his world and him mine.

I start the coffee and lean against the counter, staring out the window as the sun rises over Seattle. Not that I can see it behind all the clouds, but the gray is slowly getting lighter. The city that I love is suddenly feeling like it's closing in on me and I don't know what to do about it.

Hayden comes up behind me and wraps his strong arms around my waist, pulling me back against his chest. His lips brush my ear as he murmurs, "Don't make me wake up to a cold bed again. I don't like it."

I shiver and settle back into him, letting him take some of my weight. It's so easy to forget who he is when he's not being an asshole or trying to make me stupid with his magical dick. But that's all he's good for. I absolutely, one hundred percent *will not* get attached.

I'm definitely getting attached. Like a moron.

"Hasn't anyone ever told you we don't always get what we want?" I say, trying not to show him that his gravelly morning voice is hitting me straight between the legs.

Hayden stares down at me, dark eyes burning down into my soul. "No."

He leans down to kiss me, but I push him away and grab two mugs from the cupboard, pouring us each a cup of coffee.

He sighs and takes the mug I offer him, leaning against the counter across from me. His pants are unbuttoned and hang low on his hips, showing off his muscles and that V that scrambles my brain.

"What are we doing today?" he asks, taking a sip of his coffee and watching me like he knows exactly what's going on in my head.

I lift a shoulder and let it drop as he eats me alive with his eyes. I shiver but try to ignore the way he sets my body on fire without even having to touch me. "I don't know what you're doing, but I'm working." I turn to glance at the clock. "There's a game tonight, right? Don't you have a morning skate or something?"

Okay, yes, I'm trying to get him out of my apartment before I jump him and go for the ride of my life... again. I don't understand why I keep letting him in when I know it's only going to end up with me crying into a pint of my favorite huckleberry ice cream and wanting to kick my own ass for ignoring my shiny new rule about hockey players. But, here I am. The guy's hot and persuasive as hell.

Also, I need him out of here. Immediately.

I'm starting to get a flood of subscribers to my OnlyFans and they're getting impatient for new content. A twinge of guilt twists in my stomach, another thing I'm choosing to ignore. Hayden isn't my boyfriend as much as he might like to think he is. I don't owe him anything, and especially not this truth.

I'm not doing anything wrong.

I'm *not*.

Hayden nods and takes another sip of his coffee before setting the mug on the counter and stalking toward me with a feral sort of glint in his eye that doesn't match up with his words. "I do have practice." He stops in front of me and grabs my hips, pulling me against him where he's hard in *all* the places. "How about I come over after?"

I push him away, ignoring the way he smirks at me like he knows exactly what I'm doing. I swear the more I push him away, the more determined he gets. "I don't know if you noticed, but I've got a life outside of you." We're going to ignore that most nights I'm either at the bar or in the tub with a smutty book and my favorite toy living my best single girl life.

Unfortunately for me, Hayden's dick is better than any dildo or vibrator I've tried so far. Shocking, I know.

"Besides," I press a little closer because I can't help myself and his hands immediately find my hips again. "Don't you have, like, semi-famous hockey player things to do?"

He tilts his head and lets out a quiet laugh. "Semi-famous?"

"It's hockey, not the NFL," I say, and he lets go of my hips and digs his fingers into my hair instead, kissing me hard. It's almost like he's trying to punish me with his tongue for mocking his level of celebrity, and I'm totally getting off on it. If this is the way he responds when I shit talk him, I'm definitely going to have to do it more.

His stubble is rough as it scratches against my skin and his tongue ring does miraculous things inside my mouth.

Ugh, it's hard to resist him when he's using that thing like a weapon.

"You love testing me, don't you?" His lips are a whisper against mine with his words. Then he's pulling back and brushing his thumb across my bruised bottom lip.

"You test me, too," I say, not sure why I admitted it out loud. My voice was almost silent, so maybe he didn't hear.

But he does. I can tell by the way the corner of his mouth lifts in his trademark smirk.

He makes me want to believe him when he says he wants me. That he wants to be here for me. But I can't depend on him. I've never been able to depend on anyone but myself.

Look at what happened when I leaned on Roman. Now he's

holding the debt over my head and I'm having to sell my body to pay him back and get him the hell out of my life.

After he banged some slutty groupie right in front of my face.

Life's really fucking unfair sometimes.

Hayden leans in for another kiss, but I dodge, stepping away from him. If he kisses me again, my crumbling self control will disintegrate completely. "Time for you to go."

He grins at me and grabs his mug off the counter, draining it before setting it down and walking toward the bedroom to grab his clothes. I definitely do not watch his ass as he goes. "Don't think for a second we're done here." He looks me up and down as he pulls his sweatshirt over his head, taking away my spectacular view. "I'll be back after we win tonight."

"No, you won't. And if you come by, I won't be here."

He stalks closer, backing me up until I hit the wall. I pretend like my legs aren't shaking and my nipples aren't poking into his chest through his t-shirt that I'm still wearing. "And where the fuck will you be? Because I know it won't be out with another guy. Not unless you want to see him dead."

Okay, that? That shouldn't make me have to bite my tongue to hold back a whimper. A damn *whimper* like I'm some helpless little puppy begging its master for scraps. Nope. I'm not about to let this big-dicked asshole turn me into *that* girl.

"I've already told you, I'm not—"

He cuts me off by kissing the shit out of me, his tongue ring clacking against my teeth while I try to bite him and suck his taste into me in equal measure. When he pulls back, there's blood smeared on his bottom lip and the taste of copper on my tongue.

I don't know which one of us it belongs to, maybe both.

We're both breathing hard and his fingers press harder into the skin at my neck until sucking in oxygen starts to become a challenge. "If you try to lie to us both and say you're not mine, I'm going to lose my fucking mind."

My mouth snaps shut and his hold loosens as he leans his forehead against mine. "We go on the road tomorrow. I need to be inside of you as much as possible before then." I open my mouth to tell him off, to tell him to go find someone else to fuck, but even the thought of that almost sends me running to the bathroom to throw up my coffee. My fingers tighten in his shirt and I didn't even realize I was holding on to it. I have to force myself to pry my fingers away and Hayden wastes no time pulling my hand back and putting it against his chest like he needs me touching him everywhere he can get me.

The same way I seem to need to be touching him.

I may or may not curl my fingers back into his shirt, hoping I dig them into his skin hard enough to leave marks so he can't go be with whatever fictional person my brain dreamed up ten seconds ago.

I'm disgusted with myself.

How the hell could I have let this happen? I've gotten *attached*.

Gag.

"I think you've been inside me enough, *Hitman*. Your memory works fine. Better get used to using it because it's not happening again." I shove him toward the door and away from me. The smell of him is still on my skin. I hate how much I love it. "Now go."

He walks backward to the door, fucking me with his eyes until he has to stop and open it. He steps into the hallway, but turns around at the last second. "No need to wait up for me, Princess. I'll let myself in." The gravel in his voice sends liquid fire into my veins because I know he's not just talking about letting himself into my apartment. Waking up with him between my thighs that first time showed me how little he cares about or needs my permission for what's happening between us.

I wish knowing that turned me off, but I've proven time and time again I'm weak for unhinged men.

I flip him off and slam the door in his face, leaning against it for a few deep breaths before pushing off and walking back into my kitchen. That sinking feeling in my stomach at the thought of Hayden going on a road trip? Yeah, I'm not going to examine that. If the idea of him fucking someone else makes me want to projectile vomit, the thought of not seeing him for days or weeks, of him not being around to push his way into my life sends my heart splatting onto the floor and making a big old mess out my feelings for the guy.

I have no idea how I'm going to handle any of this bullshit, but I know one thing for sure: I'm not giving up without a fight.

Hayden likes to say that I'm his? Well, I just decided he's *mine*.

And as for my ex?

Hayden's the best person I know at fighting dirty. As much as it pains me, I might have to let him in and help me with this. I'm not above taking advantage of his obsession with me if it means getting my cheating shitbag of an ex off my back.

Decision made, I move toward the bathroom, ready to shower and start my day, but stop short when I notice my back window's open over the fire escape. A cool breeze makes goosebumps rise on my arms and I rush over to shut and lock it.

Hayden must've opened it and then forgotten to close it. I grab out my phone, tempted to tell him off by text, but decide not to feed into his game. If anything, that's what he wants and I don't want to give him the satisfaction of knowing he got to me by freaking me out.

And I'm especially refusing to admit that I sort of maybe like his games.

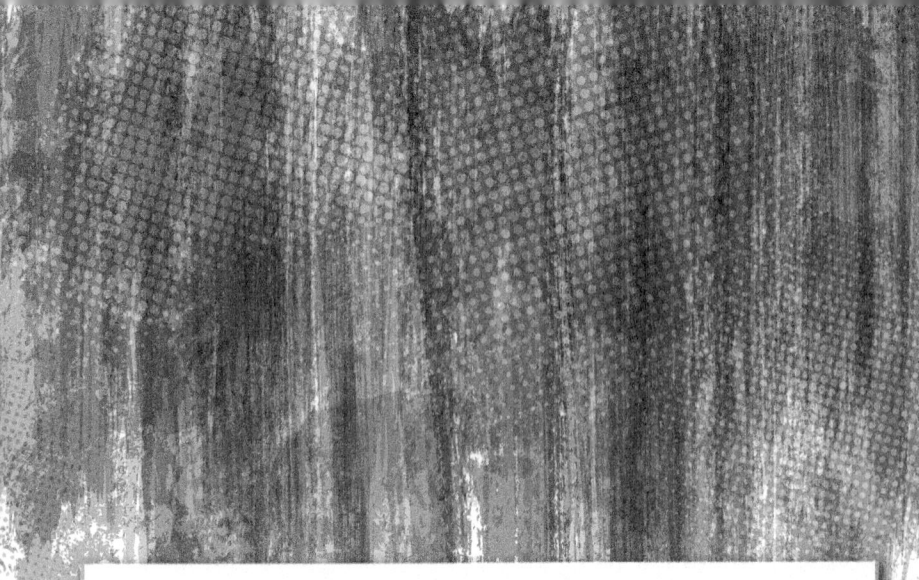

ICE
@IceEnforcer

Vaughn and Morozov on the ice at the same time is like keeping dynamite and a blowtorch together. Dangerous but damn entertaining. #FireAndIce

Hayden #16

THE BLADES on my feet slice through the icy surface of our practice rink as I work through a drill with the team. Coach is watching us with his arms crossed over his chest, whistle clamped between his teeth, like he's waiting for someone to fuck up, but we're all too focused to give him anything to bitch about.

We're playing Vancouver tonight, and since this team sucked before I joined up, I'm planning to stay after the morning skate to work with a couple of the guys on ways we can get the upper hand. Hitman ways that aren't exactly legal but will help us win.

When Coach blows the whistle to end the skate, Warren, Torin, King, Corbin, and our second line D-man, Saint, hang back with me. Roman watches us with a suspicious as fuck look on his face before I flip him off and he scowls, skating off the ice.

"We don't have long, but tonight we're gonna need a little extra if we're going to kick Orca ass," I say as I lean against my stick and watch them. They're all good guys and they want to win. It's why they're here. The question is, how badly do they want it? And how many lines are they willing to cross to get that W? "I have some..." I try to think of the best descriptor that won't sound horrible echoing around the ice. "Techniques you can use that'll give us an advantage over Vancouver. Over anyone, really."

Warren nods and leans forward, ready to listen. He's a good guy and a great player, but he's not exactly a leader. That's what I'm here for. "Like what?"

I smirk at him. "They call me The Hitman for a reason. You're about to find out why."

Saint looks skeptical, but Corbin, Kingston, and Torin seem on board, so I show them a couple of tricks I use on the ice to get away with my ruthless play. "The most important thing is to not get caught. When you check and go shoulder first or use your elbows, it has to look like you're playing the puck or they'll call a penalty. But if you hit low and dig your stick into their legs or skate, no one will see it. And it'll fuck them up."

Corbin nods as he listens, his dark eyes focused on me. "And you do this all the time?" He looks like he's ready to learn from the master and I'm more than happy to teach him everything I know.

I nod. "It's not legal, but it works. Just make sure you don't get caught. And remember, we're playing for the win. The goal is to fuck up the other team enough that they flinch when they see us coming. That flinch is where the magic happens." By the time we're done, they're all grinning and ready to put this shit into practice tonight.

"Don't tell anyone about this," I warn as we skate off the ice and head toward the locker room. "It's our secret weapon, but the results'll speak for themselves."

They nod in agreement, and I know they get it. This is the kind of shit that could get us in trouble with the league if we're not careful, but it'll help us win games and that's all that matters.

After a shower and an afternoon spent meeting with the Realtor to sign papers on my new house, I'm running late to the arena for pre-game warmups. Still, I take the time to grab a coffee on my way in, knowing I'm going to need the energy.

When I finally make it to the locker room, everyone's already halfway dressed and ready to go out onto the ice. "Sorry," I say as I rush through the door and toss my phone and keys into my locker before pulling out my gear. "Got held up."

Coach grunts at me but says nothing else as he walks out of the locker room toward the tunnel. We have a few minutes before we have to be out there, so I strip off my suit, pulling on my jersey and pads, tying my skates before grabbing my stick and helmet and following the rest of the team. I barely have time to re-do the tape on my stick before we're hitting the ice for stretches.

The early crowd cheers and holds up signs when we come out, and I grin, loving the energy that fills the arena as they get ready for the game. I might be the asshole of this league, but I still take a second to throw a couple of pucks over the glass for some kids. Gotta balance out the shitty karma I'm going to have coming my way after tonight's game somehow.

After our impromptu meet up after practice this morning, the guys are pumped and ready to go, so I know shit's about to go down on this ice tonight.

I go through my usual warmups, skating around and getting a feel for the ice, but my gaze keeps drifting toward the empty arena seats, wishing Cassidy was here. Wondering whether she's watching from her bar. When the sideline reporter catches my eye, she waves me over toward our bench to ask me some standard pre-game bullshit for the TV broadcast of the game.

"Hayden, how are you feeling about tonight?" she asks as I

come to a stop against the boards with my stick in hand. "You've had a hot streak lately. Hoping for another hat trick tonight?"

I shrug and give her a grin that makes her blush. I can't help how I am and maybe if my little liar's watching, she'll get jealous. Fuck, seeing her rage out over someone else wanting me would be everything. I blink, trying to shake off the way my dick's trying to inflate inside my cup at the thought of her marking me as hers. "These guys play hard and I'm just happy I'm able to contribute. We'll see what happens tonight, but I wouldn't say no to another hatty."

She laughs and turns back to the camera, wrapping up the segment before they cut to commercial. As I skate away, I notice Roman staring at me like he wants to murder me and I smirk at him while I scratch my nose with my middle finger.

By the time the puck drops for the game, I'm ready to go.

As soon as Gabe Maddox wins the face off and slings the puck at War, I take my place up near the blue line and wait. As he passes, I dig my stick into Vancouver's defenseman's legs, knocking him off balance and creating an opening for Warren to pass to me. I take it and skate down the ice toward their net, passing it back to War, who takes a shot that goes in.

The goal horn sounds and we're up 1-0.

I grin at Warren as we head back to the bench for glove taps, but he's already focused on the next play. We don't get cocky or complacent in this league, especially not against a team like Vancouver. They're hungry and they want this win just as much as we do.

The game continues, and we keep playing dirty. It's working. We're up 3-2 by the second period, but Vancouver's getting desperate and I'm waiting for them to make a move.

And they do.

As we're skating down the ice toward their net with me in the lead, their center slams into me, knocking me off my skates and sending me crashing into the boards. I hit hard and my head bounces off the glass, black spots flashing in front of my eyes before I shake it off and pick myself up off the ice.

I turn around and slam him back against the boards, using my body weight to pin him there while he glares at me. "You fucking cheater," he growls, and I grin at him.

"What's that? You hit like a little bitch?" I taunt him as he shoves against me. With a laugh, I let him go, skating away like nothing happened. I'm almost back at the bench when he comes up behind me and grabs my jersey, pulling me back and throwing a punch that lands on my jaw.

The refs immediately jump in and pull us apart, but not before I land a solid hit to his nose. Blood sprays everywhere, staining the ice and his white away sweater with droplets of red. The fans are screaming and the refs are yelling and I can't help but let loose a petty grin as we get pulled toward the penalty boxes.

It's not the hat trick I wanted, but it's still fucking satisfying. Four minutes well worth it.

The box is boring as hell, and my gaze drifts up to the empty seats again. I know Cassidy's not here, but it doesn't stop me from wishing she was. She's so fucking hot when she rages out at me over my bullshit, and having her here would only make living my dream better.

I'm so fucking gone for her, it's ridiculous. And no matter what, before this season's over, I'll drag her ass to this arena with my number on her back. Fuck, just thinking about it makes my dick want to chub up, and that's not a good look when I'm sitting in a tiny box with cameras and an entire arena's worth of people watching me.

The refs blow their whistles and the game starts back up. The countdown begins. Four minutes and I'll be back on the ice to finish what I started.

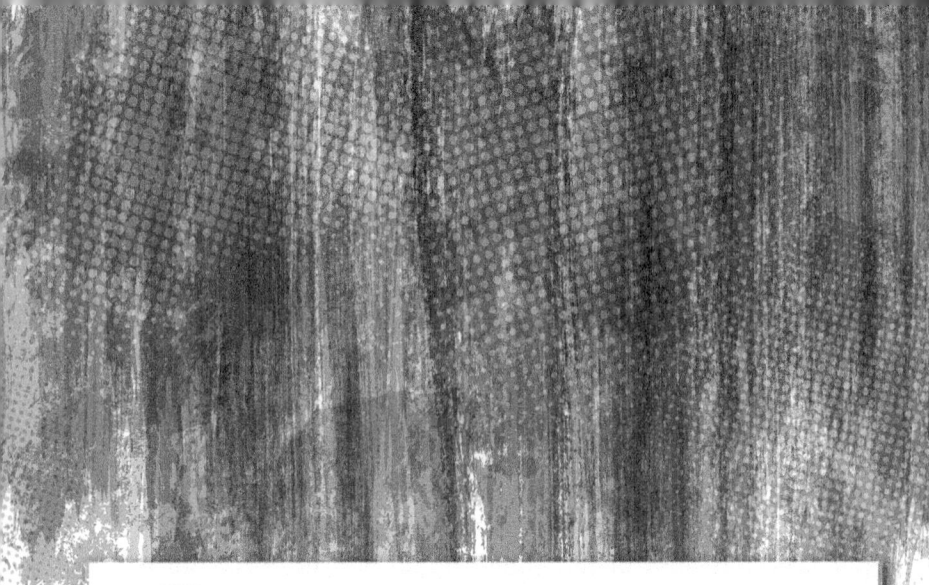

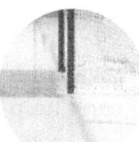

Warrant
@CreaseCriminal

29 just made the Hellcats look like scared kittens. Absolute fucking dominance. #PussyTamer

Hayden #17

SWEAT BURNS my eyes as I watch Saint cross-check the fuck out of number eighty-eight, clearing a path for Warren to score what I hope will be the winning goal. The crowd goes wild and we're up by one point in the last few seconds of the game.

As the clock ticks down, I'm on my feet with everyone else, cheering as the final buzzer sounds. Another fucking W, baby.

We're all exhausted and sore, but it feels so fucking good to beat Vancouver and to do it my way. Especially when they were chirping the entire game about our playing style. The refs missed most of our shots, so whatever. As long as the stripes don't see it, it's legal in my eyes. We're here to win and if they don't like it, they can get in line with all the rest of my haters.

I grab a quick shower before heading back into the locker room to change, ignoring Roman's glare as we pack up our gear and I change back into my suit. He's pissed that we won and we did it without him. He had three giveaways because he's a garbage player and without the entire team feeding his ego, he's feeling butthurt.

Too damn bad.

This is my team now.

I warned him I'd take it from him, and tonight was step one. I've just proven to the guys who wanted to listen that my methods work. They're not pretty, but they get the job done. Now it's only a matter of time before the rest of the guys get curious. Seattle has something Atlanta never did—a hunger. A desperation to win that matches my own.

I fit here.

I'm feeling good as I leave the arena and head toward my car.

"You coming out to celebrate with us?" War asks, throwing his arm over my shoulders. Kingston, Torin, and Saint pile on until I stumble and laugh, shoving him off.

"Where?"

"Where else, dude?" Saint asks. "The Sin Bin."

My heart stutters as I nod, a euphoria settling into my veins knowing it'll only be minutes before I see my girl. We all pile into our cars and head toward Cassidy's bar in a long line. She better have watched me tonight, or I'll have to punish her. On second thought, I hope she didn't because the idea of marking her body up so she'll wear me on her skin while I'm gone is my new mission tonight.

This girl has me so fucked up.

When we walk into the bar, the place is packed and there's already a line of groupies waiting for us at the bar. I ignore them and walk straight up to my girl, leaning over the counter and grinning at her like I wasn't just picturing all the ways I want to show the world she belongs to me.

Despite just winning a game that put Seattle in the wildcard spot for the playoffs, this is the best part of my night.

It's still early, anyway. There's a lot of season to go. But this right here? Being in touching proximity of this woman? Easily eclipses everything that happened on the ice.

Cassidy rolls her eyes at me and hands me a beer, ignoring me as she goes back to work. But she's not getting off that easy. Not when I'm feeling like this. I grab her hand and pull her over the counter, ignoring her squeal as I kiss her hard and deep, making sure everyone here sees. That everyone knows not to touch because she's mine.

She shoves me back, but I don't miss the way her lips curl into a smile before she turns away from me.

"Did you watch?" I ask, sliding onto one of the stools right in the middle of the bar. No way is she hiding from me tonight.

She nods and leans forward on the counter, giving me an eyeful of her tits in that tight shirt. Fuck, I want to bury my face between them and never come up for air. "I did. You played dirty as hell." Her gaze flicks back to my teammates' usual spot in the back. "And so did they." Her pretty eyes find me again. "You're a bad influence."

I take a slow sip of my beer, watching emotions play across her face as she watches me swallow. I don't think she's aware of how easy to read she is. "Guilty. And don't even try to deny that you like it."

"I don't like it," she argues, but I can see right through her bullshit.

My elbows rest on top of the bar, and we lean into each other. I don't think she knows she's doing it, like my body's pulling hers into my orbit. "You're lying again."

She shivers and I can't help myself from reaching up and brushing my thumb across her cheek. She closes her eyes for a second before startling and then pulling away. The irritation on her face would be cute if it wasn't starting to piss me off.

She turns around to grab someone else's order and I scowl at the bastard who stole her attention from me.

Fuck, I want her so bad I can barely think straight.

When she turns back, our eyes lock and the air damn near ignites between us. She bites her lip and I'm ready to throw her over my shoulder and carry her out of here when the door opens and whoever walks in takes Cassidy's attention away from me. I let out a growl that barely sounds human, tired of sharing her with all of these nobodies who don't matter.

But her eyes narrow into slits as she tries to murder whoever it is with nothing but a look.

The feeling is very much the same in me, this possessive rage rising in me like a tidal wave. But when I turn to see who it is, that tidal wave turns into a natural fucking disaster.

Fucking Morozov.

It's almost like he timed his entrance because the second he walks in the door, I'm swarmed by fans drunkenly celebrating tonight's win. How many times have we blown off steam after practice or a game in this place and no one has ever accosted me like this.

It's like a goddamn mob scene as I'm surrounded by people demanding my attention, wanting selfies and autographs. I have no idea how Roman got through them unscathed, but it's clear as he leans over the bar and whispers something in Cassidy's ear that he's up to something.

She looks pissed, even more like she wants to kill him than before. Can't blame her. He brings out the urge to slit his throat in me, too.

I finally manage to grit through the last smiles and sign a couple last jerseys and then I'm fucking free, and I get to the bar as Roman walks away. Instead of chasing him down and beating his ass, I turn my attention to my girl.

"What the hell did he want?"

She rolls her eyes. "Nothing new. Just thought he'd take one last run at me and hope I'd cave and give him what he wants."

"And what's that?"

She tilts her head to the side, a small smile on her wicked lips as she studies me. "You jealous, Hayden?"

My own mouth curves into the cockiest grin I've got. "Of that douchebag? He can't handle the real you, Princess."

She leans forward on her elbows, her tits practically popping out of her shirt. I can't stop staring at them. And then I'm starting to get pissed off for a whole new reason—how many other men in this bar have been staring at her tits in this shirt tonight? Fuck. "And you can?"

I reach forward, trailing a single finger from the side of her neck down to her shoulder and watch as her eyes flutter closed and goosebumps break out across her skin. "Damn right."

Somehow, she shakes herself out of the hypnotic crackle of energy between us and the outside world blares back into my awareness. Cassidy smirks and then backs off out of my reach. "That was some crowd."

Ah, she's changing the subject. That's on brand.

Instead of calling her out, I grab a Sharpie out of my pocket and sign the damp coaster sitting empty in front of me and flick it in her direction. "Who's semi-famous now?"

She doesn't even try to catch it, letting it fall to the floor like it's worthless. "Still you," she says, reaching over the bar to tap me on the nose.

I huff out a laugh and then ask her for another beer. I'm parking my ass on this stool and not going anywhere. Not until Cassidy's done for the night and I can take her home. She'll no doubt try to tell me no or sneak out the back, but I'm not about to let that happen.

And Roman... every day he becomes more and more of a problem—one I'm going to have to fix.

Cassidy slides my beer across the bar top, and I watch her move behind the bar, getting drunk on everything about her instead of my drink. She has no idea the lengths I'm willing to go to keep her safe and happy. To get her hooked on me. To leave her with no choice but to be mine.

And she never will.

Zamboni Zoom

1 oz coffee liqueur • 1 oz Irish cream liqueur
1 oz vodka • ice
Garnish: grated chocolate

Shake coffee liqueur, Irish cream, and vodka with ice. Strain into a chilled cocktail glass and top with grated chocolate.

Cassidy #18

"YOU READY FOR that dinner date yet, Cass?" my dickhead ex asks as he takes the spot right next to Hayden at the bar. He leans forward, his gaze locked on me, and I have to force myself not to shiver in disgust. He could seriously use a knee to the balls or a knife to the dick. Maybe both. "I changed my mind, though. You're taking too long to decide, so every day you take to think about it, I'll take a grand off my offer."

Hayden stiffens beside him and I know he's about to do something violent. It's billowing off him like smoke, the rage he's feeling. But I can't let him do that. I need to handle this myself. I step forward, ignoring how close it puts me to Roman's face and how much I want to punch him in his stupid, smug mouth. "I'm not interested in your offer. And if you don't back the hell off, I'll call the cops and have your ass thrown in jail for harassment."

Roman just smirks. "I think you've forgotten your place—"

The barstool clatters to the ground as Hayden stands up, towering over Roman, who looks like he wants to hit my man. Wait, not *my* man, this man. Hayden. "You need to back the fuck off before I break every bone in your body." His voice is quiet and terrifying, and it sends shivers down my spine in a way Roman's never has.

"Why the hell do you think you have any right to get between Cass and me?" My ex asks, trying to puff out his chest and look intimidating, but Hayden's not having it.

I'm so very over this dick measuring contest between these two. I appreciate Hayden defending me or whatever, and his jealousy admittedly does all sorts of things between my legs, but I don't need him fighting my battles for me.

I can handle Roman.

Hayden leans forward until they're nose-to-nose and I can't hear what he says, but whatever it is, Roman's eyes go wide and then narrow before he scurries back across the bar to the new girl, Saylor. She's got no problem flirting with Roman, and I'm happy to let her make her own mistakes.

Hayden reaches down and rights his stool before sinking back onto it, folding his muscular arms across his chest and leveling a lethal look at me that sends goosebumps scattering across my skin. "Looks like we need to discuss some things, don't we, Princess?"

I swallow hard, wishing I could tell him to butt out and let me handle things on my own, but I'm learning that Hayden Vaughn isn't the type to be told what to do. And honestly, I'm kind of into it.

Okay, more than kind of.

"What do you want me to say?" I ask, leaning forward and letting my gaze drift over his face. He's so damn handsome it hurts. "That I had no choice but to borrow money from my asshole ex to keep my family's bar? That my uncle technically kept it running, but it was about to go under and I couldn't handle losing another part of them? That said dickhole ex is now holding that debt over my head? That I'm working on it, but until I get out from under the debt, there's not a lot I can do about Roman?" I growl in frustration, breathing hard as I grab a rag and aggressively wipe the already clean bar top. "My life's a fucking mess, okay? But I don't need you to fight my battles for me, Hayden. I'm fixing it."

He narrows his eyes, his jaw ticking as his biceps flex and I get distracted staring at them, tracing the map of veins bulging under his skin. "How?"

I shrug and look away, mumbling, "I'm selling content on OnlyFans."

He's silent, so I chance a look at him, and his eyes are nearly black and his nostrils flare. "You're selling *what*?"

Shit.

Why the hell did I tell him that? "Uh, nothing. Forget I said anything."

He leans forward until we're inches apart, those dark eyes drilling into mine. Digging down to the center of my soul and forcing his way inside. "Show me."

"What?" I ask, blinking at him. "No way."

"Show. Me," he demands again, his voice low, which is somehow worse than if he were yelling.

"No."

He pulls out his phone, not taking his eyes off me until it's unlocked. Then his attention drops to the screen and he furiously taps. "I just followed, but you don't have a subscription option," he says and I think his fingers are shaking as he types, he's that pissed off. His eyes come up to meet mine. They're filled with a possessive fire that makes my stomach clench.

"Um," I tuck my hair behind my ear, then I remember I'm not doing anything wrong and I tilt my chin up. "I charge by the content instead."

"Show me."

Shit, shit, shit.

He slides his phone across the bar and I grab it, pulling up the video I posted of me fingering myself while I thought about him. I turn the phone back toward him and he looks around, shifting so no one can see the screen as he buys and then presses play on the video. I almost laugh at how ridiculous his trying to hide it is considering it's out there on the internet for anyone with twenty bucks to see.

I try not to react as he watches it with an intensity that causes me to squirm. When he's done, he sets the phone down and locks the screen.

"Delete your account."

My eyes go wide, then narrow as I fold my arms across my chest, getting ready to go to war with him over this. "What? No."

Hayden's stare burns into me. "I don't share."

"I'm not yours," I argue, but it sounds weak even to my own ears because we both know the truth. And he's not wrong when he calls me a liar. "And you have no right to tell me what to do."

"You *are* mine," he growls, standing up and stalking around the bar. He grabs my hand and pulls me toward the back office, ignoring Lila's protests and my own as he drags me up the stairs and through the door, slamming it behind us. "Since you refuse to delete the account, from now on you're only posting content you make with me."

"I can't do that."

"Why? I'm assuming you won't let me just pay him off so you'll shut it down."

His gaze drills into me and I find myself shrinking under it before I remember I'm not some helpless little thing who needs a man to save her.

My chin lifts and I give him a slow clap that only infuriates him more to the point he's actually shaking with the effort to hold himself back. Then I smile up at him. "Well, look at that. You *can* learn. Good boy."

Hayden's eyes darken and he stalks toward me, forcing me back until I hit the edge of my desk. He leans forward, his hands on either side of my hips and his lips inches from mine. "You're playing with fire, Princess."

"Good," I whisper, leaning forward and brushing my lips against his. "Maybe I want to get burned."

He groans and we meet in the middle, a clash of tongues and teeth, lips and breath while the metal in his tongue blows my mind. He kisses me like he'll die if he doesn't. And I admit everything with the way I'm kissing him, telling him all the things I refuse to say out loud.

He drinks down every single one of my truths and still pushes for more.

"Give me your phone and get on your knees," he grits out as he pulls back. His eyes are wild, his breath sawing in and out of his lungs in a harsh rhythm. He's like an apex predator, looming over me and ready to attack. "Now."

A shiver shoots down my spine as I do what he says, unlocking my phone and handing it to him before sinking to my knees. My gaze drops to the bulge behind his pants and I'm stuck in a trance, frozen to the spot as I watch him reach down and flick open the button. Then he rips the zipper down so hard, I hear the fabric tear.

His black boxer briefs are stretched tight across his dick and *god* I want to touch it. To *taste* it. I lick my lips but don't move, not until Hayden tells me to. Am I submissive? Hell, no.

But I recognize the dangerous energy radiating off Hayden and while normally pushing him until he snaps is all sorts of fun, I think he's already there. He's snapped. And pushing him past that doesn't seem like a great idea.

He yanks down his boxers enough to get his dick out, and it's long and thick and dripping pre-cum from the pierced tip.

He taps at the screen of my phone for a second before aiming it down at me. He's watching me with eyes so dark they're almost black and the hand that's not holding my phone tangles in my hair. His forearm flexes, the number twenty-nine tattoo shifting as his muscles bunch.

Before this is over, there's a good chance I'm going to be a puddle on the floor at his feet.

"Suck it."

I lean forward and lick up the length of him, flicking one of his piercings with my tongue. The taste of him fills my mouth and I groan, wanting more. His grip on my hair tightens as I suck him deep and let him hit the back of my throat until I gag.

He curses, pulling back and thrusting forward again, fucking my mouth with short, hard strokes that turn me into a wet and needy mess. "Look at what a perfect little slut you are for me, taking my cock down that pretty throat," Hayden purrs, adjusting his hold on the camera. He pulls out of my mouth and I chase him with my tongue, but his grip in my hair holds me off. "So greedy."

He tilts my chin up so I'm looking straight into the camera on my phone and I'm sure I look wrecked with tears down my face and my hair a knotted disaster.

"This body belongs to me, doesn't it, Princess?" he asks, brushing his dick across my lips as I try to suck it back into my mouth. "Only me." The tip of his cock drags across my bottom lip again. "You need it, don't you? My cum sliding down your throat, filling you up so I'm inside you where I belong?"

"Yes."

He teases me with his cock, and I stick out my tongue when he gets close, but he never quite lets me have more than a lick. I'm getting tired of the way he's playing with me, so I grip his thighs, digging my nails in while I try to get my mouth back on him.

I'm soaked between my thighs, dripping and empty in an almost painful way.

His grin is savage as he aims the phone camera down his

abs and captures every second of my surrender. I've raised the white flag, succumbed to him totally, trusting him with my body. Trusting he'll give me everything I need.

He pushes his dick between my lips again, smearing pre-cum across my cheek and lips as he does. Painting me with him. Turning me into his masterpiece.

Any sweetness disappears as Hayden rolls his hips forward in a serpentine motion that'll tell the whole world he fucks like a god. When he hits the back of my throat again, I choke and gag, but he holds himself deep, not giving me air until my lungs burn and my eyes sting with tears.

But I love it. I love the way he's losing control.

I love the way his jealousy makes him deranged.

My feminism is off sobbing in the corner, but I don't even care because this might be the hottest thing that's ever happened to me.

"Fuck," he growls, his thrusts getting sloppy as he gets closer to coming. "Your lips were made to be wrapped around my cock." He pulls out of my mouth and strokes himself, aiming the phone camera at me as he groans, shooting his cum on my face and chest. It's hot and sticky as it drips down my skin. "So fucking perfect."

He drops my phone on the desk and leans forward to kiss me hard, licking his cum off my lips before pushing me onto my back on the floor, ripping my jeans down my thighs. "What—"

But my words are lost as he bends me in half and shoves his cum-coated tongue inside of me. I grip his hair as he pushes it in and out, then laps at my clit, flicking it with his tongue ring until I'm shaking.

I'd sell my soul to come right now, and I'm pretty sure that's how he wanted me because that's the exact second he pulls back.

The death glare I give him should drop him on the spot as

he tucks himself away and uses his fingers to scoop up whatever's left on my skin and push them inside of me. He smirks at the look on my face. "Next time I'll come down your throat, but I had to show all the internet pervs who you belong to." He uses his tongue on my neck and it's like he's licking my clit with the way it pulses between my legs. Fuck him for not letting me come. When he's done, he kisses my nose. "I should keep you like this always, as desperate for me as I am for you."

"I'm not desperate," I snap, even though we both know it's a lie.

The smile he graces me with this time is sweeter than normal. Smug, maybe. "No taking it back now. It's out in the world that you're mine." He helps me up and pulls me against his body, his arms wrapping around me and holding me tight. It feels good. It feels like home. Smells like it, too.

Shit.

I pull back and shove at his chest, trying to get some distance between us before I do something stupid like fall in love with him. Then his words hit me and I look up at him. "Wait, what do you mean it's out in the world?"

His smirk is downright devious. "I hit upload on the video to your OnlyFans. Now they'll all be wishing they could be me, and they're gonna have to pay forty bucks to unlock it." He leans forward and kisses me again before stepping away and walking toward the door. "And don't even think about taking it down, Princess. I'll just keep uploading it."

I stare after him as he walks out of the office and back into the bar, leaving me standing here with cum still drying in my hair and my world turned upside down.

What the hell just happened?

And why do I kind of want it to happen again?

Will
@PenaltyBoxPoet

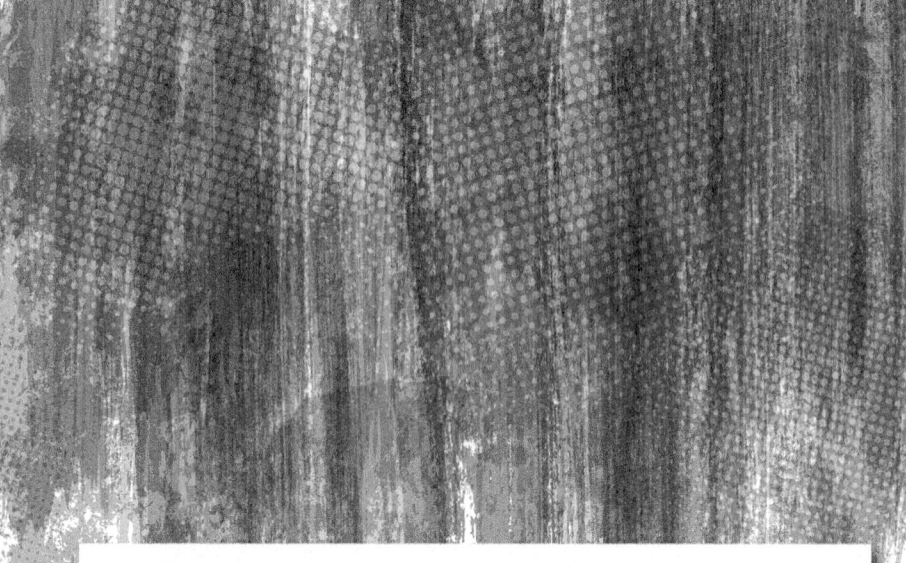

The Armada brought a ship, Vaughn brought a cannon. Guess who won? #Shipwrecked

Hayden #19

CASSIDY WALKS DOWNSTAIRS and behind the bar with her hair up in a ponytail and I smirk at the mess I made of her. Her lips are puffy and pink from sucking on my cock, her cheeks are flushed, and there's still a little cum in her hair that her ponytail doesn't hide.

She makes a perverse picture, and it's tempting me to drag her back upstairs, to sink inside of her and give her the orgasm I withheld that I know she's dying for.

And if in the end she can't walk and I have to carry her home, even better.

But I know I've pushed her to her limits for right now, so I let it go, this urge I have. This need to possess her in every way possible. She's under my skin, inside my soul, and I'll do whatever it takes to keep it that way.

Cassidy's tense as she pours a draft beer and slides it across the bar to a customer, her eyes flicking toward Roman, who's sitting in the back corner like he's plotting something. It pisses me off that she's giving him her attention instead of me.

"You know," I say, once the customer's paid and moved on. "If you won't let me pay Roman off, I could help in another way."

She narrows her eyes. They're still too bright, almost feverish. I wonder how wet she is and if the cum I shoved inside of her with my tongue and fingers will get her pregnant. "How?"

I let my gaze drift over her face and down to her lips before coming back up to her eyes. For a second, I think about saying nevermind. She'll freak out, guaranteed. But I say the words anyway, because they feel right. Because I'll make them happen, even if she says no. "Move in with me."

Her mouth drops open, and she blinks at me. "What?"

"You heard me. Move in with me."

She shakes her head and starts to turn away, but I grab her hand and pull it toward me, lacing our fingers together and holding on tight, even across the bar. I don't tell her that I'll burn her apartment building to the ground to get her moved into my house if I have to, but it'll be easier if she agrees on her own. Either way, it's happening.

It's fucking *happening*.

"Hayden..."

"Think about it," I say, rubbing the inside of her wrist with my thumb. Her breath catches before she tries to tug her hand free. I only grip her harder. "I have a huge house and I'm not using half of the rooms. You could save your rent money to pay Roman back faster." She'll be moving into my room, but I don't want to scare her off, so I don't tell her that.

Her eyes turn to slits, and I know I said the wrong thing. "I'm not moving in with you just to get my ex to back off." She tries harder to yank her hand out of mine, but I'm not letting go. Not of her hand, not of any part of her—ever.

I speak slowly, quietly, though I know she can hear me over the noise in her bar. My eyes are focused on hers and I'm not blinking when I say, "You should know what's about to happen, so here it is—you're going to fall in love with me, have my babies, and give me the rest of your days. Minimum. I won't accept anything less."

She blinks. Opens her mouth. Closes it. Does it again. Huffs out a breath. Then I let her pull her hand free to give her the space I know she needs. I don't want to give it to her, but this isn't about me. It's about taking care of her.

Which is fucking weird, by the way. I've never put anyone's needs ahead of mine before. I didn't think I'd like it, but there's a warmth in my chest that suggests maybe I didn't know what I was missing until I met Cassidy Bennett.

"How about we skip the part where you fight me and move straight to the part where you give in?"

She turns back to me with her hands on her hips, shooting fire out of her eyes in my direction. "You're delusional."

I grin at her, knowing she's not going to win this battle. "Maybe. But that changes nothing. I'm going to get my way in the end. I always do."

Cassidy shakes her head and walks away from me toward a customer who just moved up to the bar, but I can see her thinking it over. She'll come around eventually. She has no other choice.

When she comes back over, stubbornness glints in her eyes and I resign myself to the fact I'm not winning this battle tonight. She opens her still-puffy lips and says, "If you think I'm just going to agree to move in with you, it proves you don't know me at all. And I'm not moving in with someone I don't know."

I dart forward over the top of the bar, grabbing her hand again and pulling it toward me until she's forced to bend across the bar toward me or lose her balance. Regardless of what she needs, *I* need to be touching her for this conversation. "You're right. We don't know each other that well yet, but we will. Soon enough we'll be sharing a bed, a life, a family. All you're doing is delaying the inevitable."

She chews on her bottom lip. The tiny wrinkle she gets between her eyebrows when she's trying to figure out a comeback for whatever crazy shit I've just dropped on her isn't going anywhere. Eventually, she pulls her hand out of mine and turns away from me again. I fucking hate it when she does that, takes her focus off me. But before she can hide it, I see the blush on her cheeks and the way her eyes glimmer. She wants this as much as I do, but she's stubborn and prideful and won't admit it to herself, let alone to me.

As much of a pain in the ass as it is, I love the way she fights me.

My girl puts on a show as she leans over the far end of the bar to grab a bottle of whiskey for a customer, and her ass is the star. I adjust myself, feeling the pinch of my broken zipper against my hard shaft.

She'll cave sooner or later.

But I might have to play dirty to make it happen.

I'm sitting in the back of the bar with Torin, King, and Saint, watching Cassidy work and wondering what I need to do to get her to move in with me. She's got fire and passion and a backbone that won't bend.

But with the right pressure, it just might break.

She's perfect.

"What's your deal with the hot bartender?" Torin asks as he leans back in his chair and watches Cassidy. My fingers curl into fists as my jaw clenches. The need to rip his eyes from his skull is riding me hard, but I'm keeping the storm of violence contained—for now. "You two dating or something?"

My eyes are locked on Cassidy as she moves behind the bar.

She's mine in every sense of the word, but I don't know if she'll want people knowing yet. The thought of her not telling people about me burns like an itch under my skin. "Or something."

He grins at me. "Good for you, man." He takes a sip of his beer and then leans forward again. "So tonight, the game..."

I nod, knowing what he's asking. "Yeah, we keep playing like we did, we're going to keep winning."

"How can you be so sure?"

I look up and meet his gaze. "Because we have to." It's not just about pride. This is a shot at the playoffs. And we need it. We need that shot at the Cup. It's all we've been working for since the season started. Since our careers started. Since pee wees when we looked up to NHL players like they were our superheroes.

Torin nods and takes another sip of his beer. "You think we'll get there?"

"I do," I say, momentarily distracted away from Cassidy. "Especially if more of the guys get onboard. Did you see that hit Saint leveled on their D-man? Fucking brutal and picture perfect."

Saint grins and holds his beer up to clink with mine. We do and then I take a sip, my eyes drifting back toward my future wife.

Torin and Saint are recapping the game, but I keep my attention focused on Cassidy as she walks around behind the bar. Sometimes it's hard to look at her, and the ache in my chest when I'm not touching her makes it hard to breathe.

But I'll give her the illusion of distance. Let her think she's won something before it all comes crashing down around her and she only has me to turn to.

I'll be waiting with open arms. And then I'll never let her go.

"Dude. You're obsessed," Torin says, pulling my attention back to him as he grins at me. "It's funny as fuck, the Hitman falling apart over some chick."

I shrug and take another sip of my beer, stamping down the inferno of irritation that just flared up at his insinuation Cassidy's nothing more than a quick fuck. "She's not just some fucking chick. She's *it*. Get me?"

He nods like he understands, but he doesn't. He doesn't know what it's like to find someone who makes you feel alive in a way you didn't know was possible. Someone who doesn't try to fix you, but comes and dances in your dark instead.

Cassidy's everything I never knew I needed.

And I don't know how I'm going to survive this upcoming road trip without her.

Breakaway Breeze

2 oz light rum • 2 oz cranberry juice • 2 oz grapefruit juice • ice
Garnish: lime slice

Mix rum, cranberry juice, and grapefruit juice in a shaker with ice. Shake and strain into a highball glass filled with ice. Garnish with a lime slice.

Cassidy #20

I GASP as I startle awake. My bedroom's dark except for the dull glow of the streetlight outside, and I sit up, willing my heart to slow down as I figure out what woke me up. My ears strain as I listen while my fingers fumble for my phone.

Of course the night I demand Hayden go home and I'm trying to prove I've got this adulting shit down, something freaks me out and I wish he was here.

Figures.

The sheets beside me have never been colder.

When my fingertips bump into my cell, it falls to the floor with a loud thump that might as well be a gunshot going off in the silence. I lean over the edge of my bed and grab it, wincing at the brightness of the screen as I check the time. It's almost two in the morning.

I'm about to put it back on my nightstand when a shadow moves across my window, making me freeze. Not my heart, though. No, that takes off like a ripple across a dark pond, fast and uncontrollable. My eyes lock on the window, but nothing else moves. Maybe it was just a trick of the light.

Maybe I'm losing my mind.

But then there's a creak outside my door that has me on my feet and moving toward it, grabbing the baseball bat I keep by my bed as I do. "Who's there?" I demand, trying to sound braver than I feel.

Another creak and then a thump, like someone's bumping into the wall. Yup, there's one hundred percent someone in my apartment.

Shit.

I pull up 9-1-1 on my phone and have my finger hovering over the call button as I ease my bedroom door open with the bat raised over my head. One-handed bat swinging probably isn't the best idea, but I'm not giving up my phone or my weapon, so I'll have to deal. "Whoever you are, you better get the hell out of here before I call the cops!"

The hallway's dark and empty, but I can hear footsteps now, coming from the kitchen. I creep down the hall on my tiptoes, trying to be silent as I make my way toward whoever's in my apartment. My heart's pounding so hard it's making me dizzy and my hands are slick with sweat where they're gripping the bat and my phone.

When I get to the end of the hall, I peek around the corner and see a shadow moving around my kitchen. It looks human-sized, but that doesn't mean anything. It could be anyone. I can't see enough to identify any part of them.

"Get the fuck out of my house!" I scream, and whoever it is bolts past me and the front door slams open as they fly out into the hall. I finally hit the call button and give the police my address, letting them know someone broke in.

I'm panting and my whole body's shaking. My fingers ache from how tight my grip is on the bat and on my phone. No way am I letting either go until the cops show up. I know it's stupid of me, but I send Hayden a text, too. I'm sure he's not even awake, but I'm terrified and for some idiotic reason, I want him here with me.

He makes me feel safe.

I never claimed to be smart.

> Cassidy: Someone broke into my apartment
>
> Cassidy: The police are on their way, but I could use a distraction if you're awake

It takes about thirty seconds for him to respond.

> Hayden: What the fuck?

My phone buzzes in my hand and I answer it, putting it on speaker as I pace back and forth in my living room, waiting for the cops to get here. I already flipped on all the lights. Every single one. "Are you okay?" Hayden asks, his voice rough like he just woke up. It sounds like he's moving with fabric rustling in the background and the jingling of metal, probably his keys.

"Yeah," I say, trying to sound calmer than I feel. "They ran out when I confronted them."

"You confronted them?" he growls. "What the fuck were you thinking?"

Before remembering he can't see me, I shrug. "I don't know. I wasn't really thinking at all. I was scared and just reacted."

He sighs and I hear his car start up in the background. "This is why I should always be there with you, Princess. I'm on my way."

I ignore the first part of what he said, not in the mood to fight with him. Especially because I know right now, there's a good chance I'd give in to everything he wants. "You don't have to do that," I say, even though part of me is relieved. A big part. "The cops will be here soon."

"I wasn't asking," he says, his voice leaving no room for me to question him. "And you don't need the cops. You have me."

My heart constricts and I breathe out some of the crippling fear as I sink down onto my couch and stare at the front door, waiting for someone to come through it. Hoping it's the good kind of someone. "Okay," I whisper, not wanting to fight with him right now.

"I'll be there in minutes, Princess," he says, his voice softer now. "I won't let anyone hurt you."

I nod and then remember he can't see me again. "Okay." Right now it feels like I'm only capable of that one word.

We hang up and I wait for what feels like forever until I hear sirens outside. The cops fill my open doorway and I motion for them to come in, but right on their heels is Hayden. His hair's a mess and he's in joggers and a hoodie as he strides straight for me. He pulls me against him without saying a word and there's no fight left in me. I sink into him, letting the bat fall at my feet and breathing him in as my fingers curl into the fabric of his sweatshirt. I need the reminder that he's real and he's here. He's my safe place, and when the hell did that happen?

I don't even notice his brother's behind him until he speaks.

"Is she okay?" Sawyer asks Hayden.

Hayden nods and turns us around to face his brother. "She's fine."

Sawyer nods back and then steps forward to pull me into a quick hug, ignoring his brother's noise of irritation as I'm pulled out of his arms. He doesn't fully let me go, so the hug is awkward. "I'm glad you're okay."

I blink at him. "Thank you. But you didn't have to come."

He grins at me, stepping back when Hayden looks like he's

about to get violent. "Of course I did." He shrugs like it's no big deal. "We're family."

My heart constricts again and I stare up at Hayden, who's looking down at me with a protective sort of concern etched on his features. The last thing I want to do is talk to the police, not when the adrenaline is starting to subside and I'm letting Hayden take on more and more of my weight while he literally holds me up. My eyelids are heavy as I fight to keep them up with my forehead resting against Hayden's shoulder.

Like he can read my mind, Hayden takes charge, filling them in on everything he knows and he doesn't let me go when I have to speak up and answer their questions. The fabric of Hayden's shirt muffles some of my words, but no one says anything, and if they did, I think he might just lose his shit.

Not having to be the one who handles things for once is nice, though.

Eventually, the cops leave, and Hayden asks his brother to go grab us some coffee and breakfast. At the thought of hot food, my stomach lets out a truly impressive growl.

When Sawyer's gone, Hayden leads me back to my bedroom, pulling me into bed with him like it's the most natural thing in the world. And maybe it is.

"You okay?" he asks as we lay there in the dark.

I nod against his chest, breathing in his scent and letting it relax me. "I'm fine."

He makes a low noise in his throat that sounds like he doesn't believe me, but he doesn't push it. "Time to pack a bag, Princess."

I brush him off. "I'll be fine here. The police said they just thought it was someone trying to rob me. I doubt they'll come back now that they know I'll bash their skull in with my bat." I'm trying to joke, but it falls flat.

I can't see it, but I can feel Hayden's scowl in the dark. His displeasure is radiating off him. "I'm going on the road today and I can't be thousands of miles away worrying about you. So either come with me while we travel, or stay at my house while I'm gone. Sawyer will be there, but he'll be at the hospital a lot, so you'll mostly have the place to yourself."

He must be able to sense that I'm about to tell him no because he doesn't give me the chance. Instead, he jumps up and stalks to my closet, throwing open the door and digging around until he finds a suitcase. Then he starts shoving clothes in it. "I'm not fucking asking, Cassidy. You're coming home with me. The end." He shoots me a look, daring me to fight him, but at this point I'm just fighting to fight, not because I want to be here alone. I'm tired.

So damn tired.

"Fine."

Some of the weight slips off my shoulders, knowing I'm not going to be alone with Hayden so far away. But seriously... Since when does he feel like home? And since when do I depend on a man to make me feel safe?

"And while you're gone, I'm having a security system put in this place. Since you refuse to move in with me." He glares at me as he tosses a handful of lacy underwear into the bag. I don't actually think he's packing anything in there but underwear. "And don't even think about telling me no. It's happening."

I look him right in the eye. "No."

His mouth curves into a malicious grin and he drops the bag at his feet, steps over it, and grips my wrist. He pulls me over to the bed where he sinks down and then yanks me so I'm sprawled out over his lap.

"I don't think you understand," he says, his voice gravelly and foreboding as he smooths his hand over my ass, pulling down my sleep shorts so there's nothing between his skin and mine. "I play to fucking win." He smacks my ass hard enough to sting and I yelp, trying to squirm away from him, but he just holds me tighter. "And you're my greatest game." He smacks me again and I moan. The sting from the slap turns into heat and shoots straight between my legs. I have to bite my cheek to keep a moan from slipping out.

"What the—"

His palm lands on my ass again, and this time I push up into him, seeking out more of the delicious warmth spreading across my skin before burrowing down deep.

"I'm not going to stop until I'm your whole goddamn world." He spanks me again, his fingers digging into my hip where he's holding me still.

I'm breathing hard now, my nipples pressing against his thighs and my clit tingling. He only needs to move his fingers a few inches… "Hayden," I moan.

He smacks me one more time and then turns me over, fixing my shorts and then pulling me up so I'm straddling him. We're nose to nose and neither one of us seems to want to say anything to break this spell between us.

His brother, though, has no issues ruining the vibe.

"Sorry to interrupt," Sawyer drawls from somewhere behind us, not sounding sorry at all. "But I've got breakfast. And coffee."

Hayden pulls back and grins at me like he won, which I think somehow he did. Then he kisses me hard for only a second or two before standing up with me in his arms like I weigh nothing. He sets me on my unsteady feet and turns to his brother, who's standing in my doorway with bags of food and a tray of coffees. "About fucking time."

Sawyer laughs and flips him off. "It's been like fifteen minutes."

Hayden shrugs and grabs the bag of food, pulling out a breakfast sandwich that smells like heaven. "Hungry, Princess?" he asks me, holding it out.

I take it from him, suddenly starving as I realize I haven't eaten since yesterday afternoon, my horniness quickly forgotten in favor of greasy carb-filled deliciousness. Hayden grabs his own food and we all sit down on my couch to eat, Sawyer filling me in on some hospital gossip about people I don't know while Hayden watches me with an intensity that causes me to squirm.

When I'm done eating, Hayden stands up and grabs my suitcase before stalking toward the door without looking back. "Let's go."

My eyes are too tired to roll, so I stand up and follow him as Sawyer falls in line behind me, their two massive bodies blocking me from anyone or anything that might try to get close. Sawyer plucks my keys off the side table and locks the door before following us down to Hayden's car.

"You need to be more careful," Hayden says as he buckles himself into the driver's seat as Sawyer climbs in behind us. "And stop fighting me about moving in."

I shrug and look out the window as we drive away from my apartment building and head toward his house. "Maybe I don't want to be a damsel in distress."

He reaches over and takes my hand, lacing our fingers together and squeezing tight. "I'm not asking you to be."

And that's the thing.

Hayden Vaughn doesn't ask for anything. He just takes it. Maybe it's time I let him.

At least until he gets tired of me and moves on. But if that day ever comes, I'm starting to think he'll leave me with a hole in my heart that nothing will ever fill.

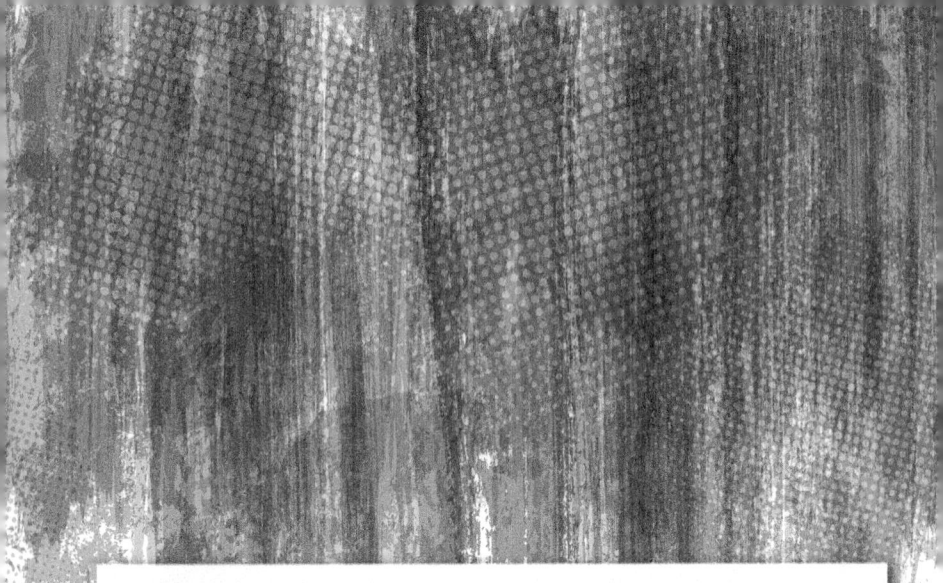

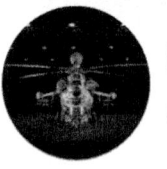

leon
@HavocMaker

Hayden Vaughn just checked someone into next week. Literally. That guy's gonna need a fucking time machine.
#BackToTheFuture

Hayden #21

THE RED AND blue decor of the Memphis visitor's locker room fades into the background as I type out a quick text to my lawyer. After the break in at Cassidy's last night, the last thing I need is the police getting involved. They're incompetent at the best of times, and I don't want them getting involved in my business.

> Hayden: I need you to make a police report disappear.
>
> Hayden: Get them to drop it. I don't care how.
>
> Cohen Astor: I'm gonna need more info.
>
> Hayden: Emailing you the details now.

I type the case number and everything else he'll need into an email and hit send.

> Cohen Astor: Consider it done.

Before I have to put my phone away and change, I switch into my message thread with Sawyer.

> Hayden: Hey See-Saw. How's my girl?

Sawyer: You woke up today and chose violence, huh?

> Hayden: 💀
>
> Hayden: Cassidy?

Sawyer: Yes, Hayden. I'm good, thanks for asking.

> Hayden: ...

Sawyer: She's not here.

> Hayden: Where the fuck is she?

I glance at the time on my phone.

> Hayden: The bar doesn't open for four more hours.

Sawyer: How the hell should I know?

Sawyer: Maybe she had to do inventory or something.

> Hayden: I'm going to remember this when it's you who needs me

Sawyer: I'm terrified

> Hayden: Asshole.

Sawyer: Just use your stalker tendencies and spy on her like a normal person

Hayden: Shit, good idea.

Sawyer: That's why I'm the smart one

Hayden: 👌

My brother has a point, though. I switch out of our text thread and into the new camera feed I have of Cassidy's apartment. She didn't fight me on having a security system installed, and I didn't tell her I could access it anytime I wanted.

I also didn't tell her about the other cameras I found in her apartment that were already there. If I had to guess, I'd say Roman's been the one breaking in and fucking with her while leaving cameras behind in her bedroom, bathroom, and living room.

If I had proof it was him, he'd be so fucking dead.

I look up and watch him as he pulls on his pads, wondering how far I'm going to have to go to take care of his obsession with my girl.

As it is, I'm just going to have to wait for him to slip up.

At least I know he can't fuck with her when we're on the road and I've got my eyes on him.

I focus back on the screen, and my fist tightens around my phone until it creaks when I see what she's doing. She's in her bedroom, naked on her bed with her phone on a tripod in front of her as she fucks herself with a dildo, moaning my name like she knows I'm watching.

I want to be there with her so bad it hurts, like I left the other half of my soul across the country and I feel the strain in my chest tugging me back to her.

Fuck.

I adjust my hard dick in my pants and force myself to look

away from the screen, my jaw aching as I clench my teeth hard enough to break. I need to focus on the game, not on how much Cassidy's defiance turns me on. It's time for me to get dressed and warm up, but before I can even think about stepping onto the ice, I need to send a message to my naughty little liar.

> Hayden: I thought I told you no more solo videos.
>
> Hayden: That pussy belongs to me. I didn't give you permission to show it off without me there.

I flip back into the camera feed while I wait for her to respond. She crawls across her bed and grabs her phone, smiling down at my message. My chest tightens at that look, one she'd never let me see if I was there with her. The way her eyes light up, knowing it's me on the other side of the screen.

She types out a response and then lays back on her pillows, her finger circling her nipple and plucking at it before she starts to type. In her post-orgasm high, I don't think she's fully processed that I can see her yet.

> Cassidy: How the hell do you know what I'm doing?!
>
> Hayden: I have my ways.
>
> Cassidy: Psycho
>
> Hayden: I'm not denying it
>
> Hayden: It's not wrong to like it when I watch you, you know
>
> Cassidy: I'm not touching that

> Cassidy: And last I checked, this pussy belongs to me

> Hayden: Princess...

> Cassidy: You're not here and I needed to relieve some tension.

> Cassidy: What are you going to do from Memphis?

My dick hardens again and I groan, knowing I don't have time to deal with this right now. But fuck if I'm not going to make her pay for teasing me like this. A million ideas race through my mind, ways to punish her from here.

> Hayden: If you upload that video, I'll get it taken down.

> Hayden: And if you make another one, I'll hold you down and tattoo my name across your pussy.

> Hayden: Push me and see what happens.

She stares at my messages for a long moment before typing out a response that has me grinning like an idiot.

> Cassidy: Maybe I like provoking you.

I groan, imagining all the ways I might punish her when I get home. Then, I type back.

> Hayden: Then you better be ready for the consequences.

> Cassidy: Big talk for someone 2200 miles away.

> Hayden: You have no idea what I'm capable of, Princess.

She shivers on the camera and it's the hottest thing I've seen in my life. She's so fucking perfect for me, even when she's pushing and fighting me.

> Hayden: Now wish me good luck.

She sends me a picture of her blowing me a kiss, a devious glint in her eye.

> Cassidy: Bring me home a win

> Hayden: What'll you give me if I do?

Her fingers fly over the screen, and she bites her lip as she types.

> Cassidy: Anything you want.

I stare at that message for a long moment before locking my phone and standing up from the bench. My little liar is brave when I'm not in her zip code, but I'm holding her to her words. Still, I don't need to be thinking about that right now. I need to focus on the game.

The next time I see Cassidy Bennett, I'm going to make her regret teasing me like this. And she's going to love every second.

But first, we have a game to win.

After I change, Kingston pounds me on the shoulder with his fist and we walk onto the ice together.

We're on a winning streak.

Three road games in a row, three wins. Six points and we're climbing the ranks.

The red and gold of Houston's logo painted under the ice of their practice facility rushes by under my feet as we run through our morning skate. We have an afternoon game and we're all focused, pushing hard before Coach calls us in for last-minute adjustments.

Corbin passes me the puck and I move into position, ready for the next drill. My eyes lock on the net and I know it's going in before I even shoot. It sails past our goalie, Akseli, and hits the back of the net, making my teammates cheer and pound me on the back.

"Shit," Corbin says, shaking his head. "You're on fire, Hays."

I nod and skate over to grab another puck from the pile, setting it up. "We've got a shot at the Cup this year. I'm not fucking around."

He grins at me. "Hell yeah, we do."

I'm breathless by the end of practice, but I feel good. Ready. The adrenaline is flowing and I'm ready to dominate tonight.

Coach Morin gathers us in a half circle, leaning on the stick he's holding. "You boys are playing like champions," he says, his eyes scanning over us as we nod and grunt in agreement. "But don't get cocky." He looks at me when he says it and I grin, knowing my cockiness is only an asset to this team. He'll figure it out in his own time.

"We won't let you down, Coach," War says, slapping me on the back. "We've got this."

Roman's silent, glaring daggers at me even though I've done nothing to him... Today at least. I smirk back, telling him to fuck off with my eyes.

The guys disperse, all except our normal crew. Only this time, a couple of new guys join. Gabriel Maddox and Cruz Hardrove, our first and second line centers.

Saint eyes them before turning to me. "So this shit really works," he says.

I smirk. "What, you think I'd bullshit you?"

War bats a puck back and forth with his stick. "This whole thing is fucking insane," he mutters, but he's grinning.

"Not insane, genius," King says, watching Warren gnaw on his mouth guard.

"Who cares what it is," I say, shrugging. "As long as it works."

Cruz nods at me, his dark eyes serious. "I don't know how the hell you did it, but we're not going to argue with results." He leans on his stick. "Count us in. Gabe and I want you to teach us your ways."

I grin. "Watch and learn..."

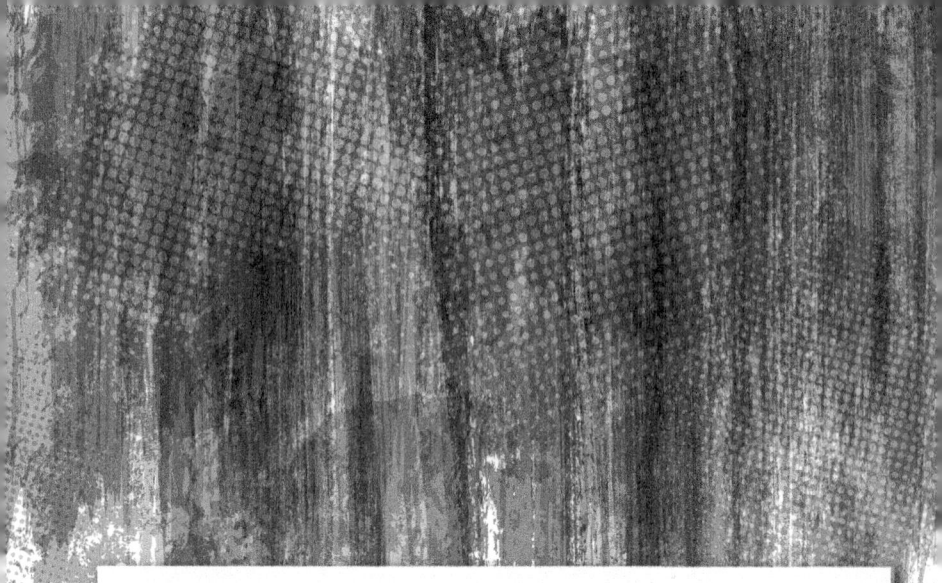

Jo
@ArenaAnarchist

Hayden Vaughn treats the penalty box like his personal throne room. Long live the King of the Sin Bin. #ReignOfTerror

Hayden #22

EVERY MINUTE of the longest ten days of my life disappears into nothing as I pull back the blankets and slide into bed beside a sleeping Cassidy. It's the middle of the night, but even in sleep, she recognizes me. She mumbles my name and slides closer, wrapping herself around me. But after the shit she pulled earlier this week and her continuing to make videos without me and taunt me about it, the urge to punish her is riding me hard.

My fingers find their way into her hair, gripping it tight until she gasps awake, her eyes wide as they meet mine in the darkness. "You've been a bad girl, Princess," I growl, tilting her head back until her throat's exposed and I can wrap my fingers around it.

"Yeah, I have," she whispers, her hands sliding up my chest and around the back of my neck. "And I regret nothing."

I smirk down at her. "We'll see about that." I grip her throat tighter until she whimpers and then I lean forward and kiss her hard. She moans into my mouth and I pull back, my hand still wrapped around her throat. "Get on your knees."

She scrambles to do what I say, kneeling on the bed in front of me. Her lips are parted and her eyes are wide as she waits for my next move. I reach down and grab my dick, stroking it slowly as I stare at her, loving the way she's watching me, as if she's been as starved for me as I have her. Her eyes drop to my cock and her tongue darts out to wet her bottom lip.

"You want this?" I ask her, gripping my shaft tighter.

She nods, her eyes locked on mine now. "Yes."

I love the way she's so confident admitting it.

I let go of myself and reach for her, grabbing her by the throat and pulling her forward until her lips are inches from my dick. "Then suck it."

She doesn't hesitate, leaning forward and taking me into her mouth, her tongue swirling around the head and playing with the piercings there before she takes me deep. I groan and lean back against the pillows, letting her drive me to the edge with that perfect mouth of hers. She bobs up and down my length, taking me as far back as she can before pulling off and licking up the length of me.

"Fuck," I groan as my dick hits the back of her throat where my fingers are wrapped around her neck. "You're enjoying this too much for it to be a punishment."

She moans around my cock as she sucks me harder, choking and squeezing around me until my balls draw up. I'm not ready to come yet, not in her mouth. I've been saving up, and this load's going as deep inside of her as I can get it.

My grip on her tightens and I pull her off me, pushing her back onto the bed and climbing on top of her. I reach over and grab a condom from my pocket, one of the ones I poked holes in earlier, and slide it on, not able to wait a second longer to be inside of her.

I hate these goddamn things, but I'll tolerate it... for now. I'm playing a long game and this is just one part of the strategy.

"Should I not let you come or should I make you come so many times you'll be begging me to stop?" I ask, wondering what she'll choose as I sink into her slick cunt.

She gasps and her eyes flutter closed as every inch of me fills and stretches her. I grip her throat, tilting her face until she's looking into my eyes with an unfocused gaze. "Which one?"

She swallows hard and her pupils blow as she stares up at me in the dim light from the streetlight outside. Her voice is raspy when she finally says, "Make me come so much I'm begging for you to stop."

I grin at her, and I know it looks deranged. I can feel it. "That's my girl." I pull out of her and slowly push back inside, grinding myself against her clit while I fuck her nice and deep. She's already close, her pussy tightening around me with each thrust. "That's it, baby. Strangle my cock," I whisper against her lips as I kiss her, my tongue sliding against hers as I fuck her harder. Deeper.

I missed her taste and I'm greedy for it now, not letting her breathe until I absolutely have to. Until my own lungs burn with the need for oxygen and I'm forced to back off before going in for more.

She cries out, her fingers digging into my shoulders as she gets closer and closer to the edge. The headboard slams into the wall with every thrust, and I don't give a fuck about how much noise we're making. And then she's there, screaming my name as her pussy clamps down on me while she comes hard enough that she forces me out of her and squirts all over me.

Shit, that's new and I have to grip the base of my dick and squeeze to hold off my release.

"That's one," I whisper in her ear as I slide back inside of her and keep fucking her, not giving her a chance to come down from that orgasm before pushing her toward another one.

Her nails rake down my back and I groan, loving the way it hurts. Loving the way she gets under my skin. I want her to mark me, inside and out. Scrape down so deep she scars my soul. I fuck her harder, faster, grinding against her clit with every thrust until she's coming again, her body shaking under mine.

The sheets beneath us are soaked, but I still want more.

"That's two," I say, kissing her hard and biting her bottom lip until she whimpers. "Ready to tap out yet?"

She shakes her head, her eyes glazed as she stares up at me. "N-not even close."

I pull out of her and flip her over onto her stomach, grabbing her hips and pulling them and slamming back into her from behind. She cries out, gripping the sheets in her fists as she takes me over and over again, my balls slapping against her clit as I fuck her harder than I ever have before. I hope I'm bruising her so she feels me with every step she takes tomorrow.

Her pussy tightens around me again, her legs shake, and I lean forward, wrapping my fingers around her throat and tilting her face up toward me. "That's three," I growl at her, squeezing until she gasps for air. "Think you can handle four?"

She doesn't answer right away this time as her body goes completely lax. I'm holding her up and I think I might've fucked her into unconsciousness. But then she nods, just barely. "Mm-hmm."

Her body is relaxed and floppy as I turn her over onto her back and sliding back inside this pussy of mine, hating this fucking condom with everything in me. She groans and wraps her legs around my waist, pulling me deeper as I grind against her clit with every thrust.

Her eyes meet mine and she smiles up at me, a lazy grin

that sparks the need to devour her, to put myself in as much of her as I can. To steal as much of her as she'll let me. So I do, kissing her until her lips bruise blood red.

"Had enough yet?" I grit out as sweat runs down my skin and I'm barely holding it together. My shaft fucking *tingles* and my balls are full and ready to explode into her. I wonder if this will be the time she gets pregnant.

She shakes her head, but her thighs are trembling and her eyes can barely stay open. I doubt she'll ever admit she's had enough. It's not her style. It's not mine either. Fuck, sex with her might kill us both. "No," she gasps out, her fingers digging into my arms hard enough to break the skin. "More."

We fuck and we fuck and I lose track of time and the number of orgasms she has. My abs burn, my dick aches, and still she dares me to keep going. To make her scream my name again and again until her voice gives out. And it does. Her body goes limp under mine as she falls apart yet again. Finally, I pull out of her and yank the condom off, stroking my cock hard and fast until I come all over her stomach, needing to see her wear me on her skin.

"Fuck," I grind out between clenched teeth as my head falls back and I come and come and fucking *come*.

She's panting and staring up at me with a look of wonder on her face as I bend down and lick my cum off her stomach and then shove my tongue inside of her.

"What..." I chuckle because she's not even coherent enough to finish the thought. I hurry and push as much of my cum inside of her as I can with my tongue and fingers before she realizes what I'm doing. Then I suck on her clit until her back bows off the bed and her thighs clamp around my head.

Her fingers dig into my hair, trying to yank me off, but I don't let go, not until she's coming again. Sucking my cum deeper inside of her.

"Enough, Hayden. Please," Cassidy begs when she finally

comes down from that orgasm. "I can't take anymore." Her words slur and tears run down her face from the intensity of it all.

When I fall to the mattress beside her, pulling her against me, I grin where she can't see it. This right here wasn't even her real punishment. This was mostly for me and to remind her who the fuck she belongs to. Though, after tonight, I don't think she'll ever be able to forget. Not with what comes next.

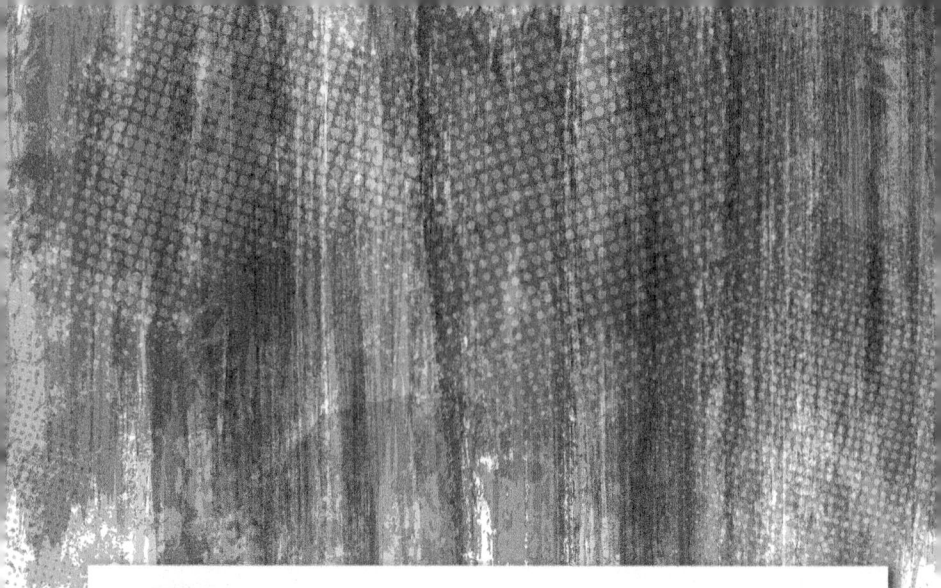

Deke
@DrunkOnDekes

#29 just sent a #Hellcat flying. Guess cats don't always land on their feet after all

Hayden #23

THERE'S A WARM, wet washcloth in my hand and a glass of water in the other when I go back into Cassidy's bedroom. My body feels like I just played a full game on the ice. That's how hard and intense we fucked.

I hand her the glass. "Drink."

I know she's completely fucked out when she doesn't fight me, and I watch as she downs the entire thing while I wipe away any stickiness around her pussy. Can't have that, not for what comes next.

She sets the glass on her nightstand and looks up at me with a dick drunk smile on her face. "You realize that punishment only encourages me to act out, right?"

I toss the washcloth toward the door before crawling into bed beside her and pulling her against me. Her bare skin is silky and warm. *Home.* "Maybe I like it when you act out."

She laughs and snuggles closer, her fingers tracing patterns over my chest and down the ridges of my abs. "What would your teammates say if they knew you were so whipped?"

I scoff and pull her tighter against me while she fights to keep her eyes open. *That's it, little liar. Give in to the drugs.* "I don't give a fuck what any of them think about my relationship with you."

She completely ignores the R-word, but she won't be able to for much longer. "Not that anyone would say anything to you," she says, her words slurring together, "since you're kind of terrifying."

I smirk and kiss the top of her head as she succumbs and drifts off. "Damn right." She really has no idea how terrifying I can be.

Her breathing evens out, and she's asleep before I can say anything else, like confess how fucked in the head I am when it comes to getting what I want. And she *should* be afraid since she's the thing I want most.

She starts snoring softly, falling into a deep sleep as the pill I dissolved in her glass of water kicks in. When I know she's completely out, I climb out of her bed and grab my phone out of my pants pocket.

> Hayden: What's your ETA?

> Wraith: I'm outside the door.

I grab my pants and pull them on, not bothering with a shirt as I walk out into the living room and pull open the door to Cassidy's apartment. I'm trying not to let how annoyed I am to be back here show, but fuck, I hate that she ran.

I need to take away her option to come back here, but that's a problem for another day.

Wraith has his leg kicked up against the wall, running an inked hand over his buzzed hair. He looks like he's bored, but who the hell knows what goes on in the mind of a guy like him? My dad's hacker, Romeo, put me in contact with Wraith when I asked if he knew anyone willing to do what I've got planned for my princess.

When Wraith sees me, he tucks his phone into his pocket and grabs the duffle at his feet, walking past me into the apartment. I've never met the guy before, but he looks scary as fuck. I'm the American Psycho kind of dangerous, but he's a tattooed head-to-toe beat your face in with his fists sort of terrifying. I'm a big guy, but this guy's on a whole other level.

"Your girl asleep?" he asks, his voice low and gruff.

I nod and gesture for him to follow me back to her bedroom. He starts pulling equipment out of his bag, setting everything in a meticulous row beside Cassidy. She's still naked and while I hate the idea of him seeing the parts of her body that only I should ever get to see, it's necessary for what he's about to do.

He gets everything prepped and then shows me the design. When I approve it, he pulls on a pair of black latex gloves and goes to work. Cassidy doesn't even flinch, and it's over in less than five minutes, her skin forever etched with my name right above the pussy that now officially belongs to me.

Hayden's.

It's scrawled in a pretty script, small but clearly legible to anyone who might try to touch what's mine.

When Wraith's done cleaning up, I shove a handful of cash at him and push him out the door.

Once he's gone and I make sure Cassidy's still out, I grab some clothes out of her closet and dress her, careful of the bandage. I pack her a suitcase full of clothes, grab her girly shit from the bathroom, and take it all down to my car. It's the middle of the night, so no one's in the hallways or lobby of her apartment building to wonder what the hell I'm doing, and this place isn't nice enough for functioning security cameras.

When I get back upstairs, I bundle her up in her blanket and carry her down to my car. She murmurs something in her sleep that sounds suspiciously like my name, and as soon as we get back to my house—sorry, *our* house—I'm definitely taking advantage of the fact I don't have to go through the show of putting on a condom only to take it off later.

My body's sore as hell, but it won't stop me from fucking her again before I fall asleep.

I buckle her in before driving us back to what's about to become our house. Sawyer understands my crazy, and I bet he already knew this was coming, so I don't have to worry about discussing it with him first. She's still asleep when we get there and I carry her upstairs, laying her in my bed before stripping off my pants and climbing in beside her.

Sawyer's got an overnight shift tonight at the hospital, so I won't have to deal with him giving me shit until tomorrow. He's never going to let me live down not being able to wait long enough to get Cassidy to agree to move in on her own, but he doesn't know what it's like being so obsessed with someone, having this need to possess every second of their time and attention.

Feeling like you'll lose your goddamn mind, your soul torn in half when you're away from them.

Cassidy's going to be pissed when she wakes up, but that's okay. She can fight me all she wants, but it won't change anything. She's mine. And now she has my name on her body forever to prove it.

I peel off both of our clothes and then lube up my cock before sliding into her bare. Her back is to my front, and I grab her thigh, looping my arm around it to open her up for me. She's completely out of it as I fuck her, this time hard and fast since I don't have to hold back to get her off. When I come inside of her this time, I stay there, my cock still hard and holding all of my cum inside of her to do its job.

"You're right where you belong," I whisper in her ear as she snores softly. "And you're going to learn to crave me as much as I crave you."

I pull her close and let myself drift off, knowing I'm going to need sleep for the hell that's coming tomorrow when she wakes up and discovers what I've done. But it'll be worth it.

She's worth it.

Slap Shot

2 oz tequila • 1 oz blue curaçao • 1 oz lime juice
ice • salt for rimming
Garnish: lime wheel

Rim a glass with salt. Shake tequila, blue curaçao, and lime juice with ice. Strain into the prepared glass and garnish with a lime wheel.

Cassidy #24

MY EYES CRACK open and I feel like I'm waking up after a zombie's chewed on my brain. Everything's achy and stiff in that way that happens when you don't move the entire night because you sleep so deeply.

But then I remember Hayden coming home and fucking me into oblivion before I passed out. I can still feel him inside of me and I smile, rolling over to cuddle up against his bare chest. He's still sleeping and I snuggle against him, breathing him in and letting his warmth seep into me.

He smells so good, and I inhale the scent of me mixed on his skin.

I freeze as I slide my hand against the soft and definitely-more-expensive-than-mine sheets.

This isn't my bed.

I sit up and blink around the room, realizing with confusion that I'm in Hayden's bedroom. "What the fuck?" I screech, throwing back the blanket and scrambling out of the bed. It's then I notice my skin itching and burning down by low on my pubic bone where it shouldn't be.

"Why are you screaming?" Hayden mumbles as he sits up. His hair's a mess from sleep, all wild curls and chaos. My gaze drops to his bare chest and I'm distracted for a second before I remember how pissed off I am.

"Are you kidding me? *Why?*" I gesture around, blowing my crazy hair out of my face. "I fell asleep in my apartment and somehow woke up in your bed!" I'm pacing now as I look down, finding myself in pajama shorts and a tank top. The pain underneath my shorts isn't fading and catches my attention again, so I rip the tie open and pull the waistband out, finding I'm not wearing panties and I've got a bandage on my skin. "What the..."

Hayden's not saying anything, just sitting back against the headboard smirking at me like he's completely unrepentant about whatever he's done.

I pick at the adhesive and slowly peel back the bandage, gaping at what I find underneath.

Hayden's name is tattooed on me, right above my vagina. It's small but clearly legible to anyone with eyes.

"You motherfucker!" I yell, lunging toward him with my fists clenched. He dodges me easily and jumps off the other side of the bed. "How could you do this to me?"

"I warned you, and you did say you'd give me anything I wanted." He shrugs and starts pulling on clothes, not looking at me as he does it. "You belong to me, but somehow seem to keep forgetting. Now you never will."

I'm shaking with rage, my fingers digging into my palms so hard I'm probably drawing blood. "You're fucking insane!"

"I know." He nods and grabs his phone off the nightstand, tapping away on it as he walks out of the room acting like nothing's happening and I'm not two seconds away from ripping his balls off.

I'm left standing there gaping after him like a fish out of water, completely unsure of what to say or do. This can't be happening. It can't be real. But when I look down again, it's right there in black script.

A permanent reminder of this man I don't think I'll ever be able to get away from.

I was pretty sure I never wanted to. Now... I'm too fucking furious to consider anything but getting the hell out of here. I rush around the room, finding my suitcase in Hayden's closet and yanking it out. By the time I've stomped around the room and flung every last thong and toothbrush into the damn thing, I'm panting and a little bit sweaty.

I sink down onto the bed and stare at myself in the mirror across the room, wondering what the hell I'm doing. And why the fuck I seem to only attract complete psychos.

Hayden blocks the doorway with his massive body, folding his arms across his chest as he watches me through dark eyes. "Where do you think you're going?"

I glare at him, my hands on my hips as I stand my ground, even though he's twice my size. "Move. I'm leaving."

"No. You're not."

"Move."

Hayden's jaw tics. "If you try to go back to your apartment, I'll burn it down."

I laugh, but this *so* isn't funny. "You're certifiable."

He shrugs. "And? I mean it. If you try to leave and go back there, I'll torch it."

I shake my head and try to shove past him, refusing to let him think he's won or that what he did is okay in any way. But his arm goes around my waist and his fingers wrap around my throat so I'm completely at his mercy. He tilts my chin up so I'm forced to look at him when he says, "I've been patient, but you're too goddamn stubborn. You don't want to test me, Princess, because there is no line I won't cross to keep you."

I swallow hard, knowing he means it. "Fine," I whisper, hating that I've lost this round, but knowing the war between us is far from over. In fact, I'm already making plans about how I can get him back for what he's done.

He smirks and lets go of me, stepping back. "I love the way you give in to me."

I poke my finger into his hard chest, hating that being this close to him is making all kinds of things flutter and clench. Ugh, stupid hormones. "For now, but you're going on the road at some point and just so you know, the first chance I get, I'm out of here."

His smile is all malice and danger. "Try it." Then he grabs my suitcase and walks back into the closet, unzipping it and starting to hang up my clothes and put them away in his drawers like he didn't kidnap me last night.

Like I moved in the way he's been pushing me to.

I'm so angry I'm shaking, but the worst part of all of this is that as mad as I am, I still feel this crazy, intense pull to Hayden because I feel protected from the outside world when I'm with him, and I don't know what to do with that.

He's a monster, but maybe I'm one too, for wanting him anyway.

No one's ever been my safe place, not since I was a teenager and lost my family.

Either way, I can't let him think he can pull shit like this and get away with it. And I don't give a single fuck about his threat because I doubt he'd actually do it, so the second he gets on that team plane, I'm going to show him he doesn't own me and if he wants me in his life, he has to earn the right and understand I'm his equal, not his property.

Frozen Puck

2 oz black vodka • 1 oz lemon juice • 1/2 oz simple syrup • blackberries • ice

Muddle a few blackberries in the bottom of a shaker. Add vodka, lemon juice, simple syrup, and ice. Shake and strain into a chilled martini glass.

Cassidy #25

IT TOOK a few days of me hiding from the Supreme Jackass, as I've now taken to calling him, but finally this morning he was forced to meet up with the team to travel to Atlanta for the first of a three-game road trip. It's not long, but I'll take it.

As soon as he's gone, I make sure Sawyer's not here either before I grab my phone and order a ride. It's probably not smart to go home because Hayden will just track me down as soon as he's home, but I don't have anywhere else to go. Lila and her girlfriend, Addison, just had a baby and I'm not about to bring Hayden's crazy into their lives.

Before I leave, I grab the package that came for me yesterday, the one that has a #19 Gabriel Maddox jersey in it. I slip into the jersey and nothing else and then I climb into Hayden's bed and take some selfies, making sure to flash my panties. When I tease this on my OnlyFans later, Hayden's going to go berserk.

He deserves so much worse, but even knowing that, there's an intense thrill that sneaks through me when I think about how he's going to react. Maybe there's a reason I only attract the crazies.

While I pack up my suitcase and haul it outside, I'm already crafting the perfect caption, something that'll get under Hayden's skin like nothing else. It only takes a few minutes for my ride to pull up. The driver helps me load it into the trunk and we're on our way to my apartment building.

I'm still fuming as we drive away from Hayden's house, but at least now I have time to figure out what the hell I'm going to do next. My emotions are all over the place. It's not like it was a secret that Hayden's certifiable, but I guess I never thought he'd take it this far. I sigh, rubbing at my forehead as a headache takes root.

My phone buzzes in my pocket and when I pull it out, there's a text from Hayden because of course there is.

> Hayden: Where are you?

I chew on my lip, thinking over my response. I've been gone all of ten minutes max, including waiting outside for my ride, so for him to have noticed I'm missing already is... unsettling. And also weirdly... flattering?

> Cassidy: None of your business.

> Hayden: You're going to be in so much trouble when I get home.

> Cassidy: You have to find me first.

Yeah, I'm all bravado and considering the only place I have to go is my apartment, it'll take him all of two seconds to find me and drag me back when he gets home, but I've got to have some boundaries, damn it. I'm not going to let him bulldoze me or my life, no matter how hot he is and how much I sort of love that he cares about me enough to want me around all the time. I've never had that before, and after years of being on my own, it's nice having someone want me this much.

I post that picture, and then shove my phone back into my pocket and ignore the next few texts he sends me as we pull up to my apartment building. The driver helps me unload my suitcase and I thank him before dragging it inside. It's a struggle to get it up the stairs, but I manage and finally get inside my apartment.

There's a lump in my throat as I glance over to the window, and a chill slithers down my back at the memory of my space being violated, but I push it down and drag my suitcase into my bedroom. I don't know how Hayden left my room, but my picture frames have been rearranged in the wrong order, my nightstand drawer is open, and my underwear are all missing.

"What the hell?" I ask aloud as I dig through my suitcase looking for them, but there are only the few pairs Hayden must've thrown in here when he packed it.

Once everything in my bedroom's put away, I decide to head to the kitchen for some water, but there's something written in black marker across my fridge. "I see you," in huge letters spanning both doors. Not only that, but there's a knife stuck into the counter beside it.

"Fuck this," I breathe, pulling my phone out of my pocket with shaky fingers. I don't think Hayden would do this. I mean, why would he? He took me to his place and if it was up to him, I'd never step foot back here again. Plus, I still don't know who broke into my apartment in the middle of the night. Could the same person have done this?

I'd planned to make a video or two for my OnlyFans before I had to be at the bar, but I don't want to be here anymore. The thing about Hayden is that yeah, he's kind of a stalker and he's almost scary possessive, but he also gives me a sense of security. With him thousands of miles away, I feel... vulnerable in a way I haven't in a long, long time.

Could I go back to his place and admit defeat? Sure. But I'm stubborn as fuck and I'm not going to let him think he's won that easily. Especially after my new ink. Shit, I'm still pissed about that, so now I'm angry and scared. *Fantastic.*

> Cassidy: Think you can get away for an hour?

> Lila: For you? Always.

> Cassidy: Upper Crust?

> Lila: See you in 20.

I grab my purse and keys before locking up and heading down the stairs to meet Lila at our favorite gourmet sandwich shop. It's about six blocks down, but for once it's not raining, so I decide to walk. It'll give me time to calm down and figure out how to handle Hayden when he gets back from his trip. He's going to be so pissed off when he finds out I moved back to my apartment. I grin when I think about his reaction, knowing I'm poking the bear and loving every second of it. He's got to learn that if he fucks with me, I'm going to fuck right back.

Or fuck around and find out, if you will.

God, there's something wrong with me.

The Upper Crust is crowded as always, but Lila's already snagged us a table in the corner. She's got her baby, Tavi, in her arms, and she's cooing at her while she sips on a coffee. When she sees me, she smiles and waves me over.

"Hey!" she says as I slide into the navy-colored velvet chair across from her. "Not that I don't love a spur-of-the-moment girls' lunch, but we've probably only got a half an hour before this one needs a nap, so spill."

I sigh and rub at my forehead, trying to get rid of the ache behind my eyes. "I don't know where to start."

She grabs a menu and shoves it at me while flipping hers open with one hand like the complete expert at this whole parenting thing that she is. "Start with figuring out what you want. Then you can tell me why you've been absent from the bar more and more and what's going on with you and a certain sexy hockey player."

For the first time in days, my shoulders relax as I scan the menu of fancy sandwiches, my mouth already watering. I can't remember the last time I ate. Stress is hell on my stomach and I've definitely lost a couple of pounds since the break in and the pressure Roman's putting on me to pay him back.

I set the menu down as our waitress approaches with a wide smile. "What can I get for you ladies today?" she asks, her pen poised over her pad.

"I'll have the turkey and brie on sourdough with avocado, please. And a raspberry lemonade."

She nods and scribbles it down before looking at Lila. "And for you?"

Lila eyes her menu one last time before flipping it closed. "I'll have the same, but with ham instead. And could we also get an order of fries to share?"

The waitress nods and takes our menus before walking away to put in our orders.

"So," Lila says, her eyes narrowed at me. "Lemme have it."

I sigh and lean back in my chair. "Hayden's insane."

She grins at me. "We knew that already, though."

"No, I mean like... he kidnapped me and tattooed his name on me while I was asleep. That kind of insane."

Her jaw drops and her eyes widen. "What?" she gasps, glancing around to make sure no one can hear us. "I must've heard you wrong. He did *what*?"

I nod, picking at a chip in the dark wood tabletop with my

fingernail. "Yeah. I went to sleep at home. Woke up the next morning in his bed with his name tattooed on my body and he wasn't even a little sorry." I take a sip of the lemonade the waitress just dropped off before I huff out a little laugh. "In fact, I think he was sort of proud."

Lila's still gaping at me. "Holy shit. That's so," her hands come up to cover Tavi's ears, but the kid's only a couple of months old and I bite back a laugh at her ridiculousness, "fucking crazy. And hot. Like *super* hot." She shakes her head, her blonde hair falling over her shoulders. "Sorry, no. That's pathological. Right. That." She takes a deep breath. "Are you okay?"

I nod again, feeling like a bobblehead doll. "Yeah. I mean, I'm pissed and I'm not going to let him get away with it, but..."

She reaches across the table and takes my hand in hers while Tavi wraps her fist in my friend's hair and yanks. Lila flinches but stays focused on our conversation. See? She's a total pro at this whole mom thing. "But what?"

I sigh and look down at the table. "It's complicated."

She nods and lets go of my hand as the waitress drops off our sandwiches. "It always is. You still want him." She grabs a fry from the basket and pops it into her mouth.

I groan, letting my head fall back against the chair and staring up at the industrial piping in the ceiling. "More than anything." I rub my temples. "Am I stupid? Is this just Roman two point oh? Who wants a guy who does the kind of shit Hayden's done to me? I should be running far, far away. Filing a restraining order. Something."

Lila takes a bite of her sandwich, staring at me thoughtfully while she chews. "You're not stupid, you're just in love."

My eyes widen, and I sit up straight, shaking my head. "I'm not in love with Hayden Vaughn."

She shrugs like she doesn't believe me and takes another bite. "Okay. But he's not Roman. In fact, he's the opposite of

Roman." She sets down her sandwich and her eyes harden a little. "I'm going to put on my serious best friend voice now because I'm going to say something and I need you to listen. Like, really listen."

I swallow the bite I was chewing, feeling it sink into my stomach like lead. "Okay."

"You were guarded when your family died." She lifts her hand to cut me off when I open my mouth to speak. "Understandably so. When you dump a guy who then burns your house to the ground with your family inside, I think you earn the right to be wary."

My eyes burn at the reminder of why my family's dead. Because of me and my choices, my parents, my twin brother... gone. Just like that.

"What is it about me that only seems to attract psychos?" I ask, my voice a whisper. "Hayden even threatened to burn down my apartment if I moved back home. I mean, why would I ever even consider staying with someone like that, considering what Eric did to my family?"

"Because I've seen the way Hayden looks at you. He's not deranged like Eric. He's not a narcissist like Roman. He's just... obsessed. But he's also protective. He looks at you like you're the only person in the room and he doesn't give a shit who knows it." Lila sighs like she's just watched the happily ever after of a classic Disney movie where the prince decides there's no one better for him than the poor girl or the mermaid who gave up her voice to be with him. "It's romantic, in a way."

I roll my eyes. "You're not helping convince me to stay away."

She laughs. "Is that what I'm supposed to be doing?" Tavi's little fist waves in the air and tries to grab at her sandwich. I hold out my arms for my niece, making my own grabby hands.

"Hand over the squish," I say, grinning when she slides her daughter into my arms and I cuddle her close, breathing in her new baby smell. A grin spreads across my face as she gazes up at me with her big blue eyes. "Hey, baby cakes," I murmur to her as she grabs onto my finger and tries to put it in her mouth.

Lila watches me for a moment before she says, "Hayden may have gone about it in the most extreme way possible, but he's trying to show you he cares in his own twisted way." She takes another bite of her sandwich and shrugs. "I don't know if that's enough for you or not, but it's worth considering. Especially since you're clearly still into him."

I sigh and cuddle Tavi closer, filling my lungs again and again with her baby smell like I'm taking a hit of a potent drug. "I guess." I look down at my niece and grin at her. "What do you think? Should I give Hayden a second chance?"

She just gurgles and smiles back at me, making me laugh. "That's a yes from the baby."

Lila laughs and then levels me with a murderous look. "Now tell me about Roman."

Power Play Punch

1 oz vodka • 1 oz peach schnapps • 2 oz orange juice • 2 oz cranberry juice • ice
Garnish: orange slice

Combine vodka, peach schnapps, orange juice, and cranberry juice in a shaker with ice. Shake well and strain into a glass filled with ice. Garnish with an orange slice.

Cassidy #26

LUNCH WAS EXACTLY what I needed, and after spilling my guts to Lila about both Hayden and Roman, I feel about two tons lighter. We even got one of those elusive Washington sun breaks on my walk home, so I got a nice shot of vitamin D to boost my mood, too.

Lila demanded I take the night off from The Sin Bin tonight, that she had the bar and would call in the new girl, Saylor, if she needed help. She told me I needed to take some time to figure my shit out and just have a night to myself without any distractions.

The message in my kitchen is a distraction, so when I get home, I clean it up. I don't want to think about it. I want to bury my head in the sand and pretend everything's fine. Even if it's just for one night. I need to mentally check out.

But what I need more than anything is some new content for my OnlyFans. Since Hayden published that video of me going down on him, my growing fan base has been demanding more partner stuff. It's been hard enough just shooting solo videos lately between the drama that's now my life and Hayden being completely over the top possessive.

I sigh and fall onto my couch, staring up at the ceiling as I think about how to handle this. I've got a few solo videos backed up, but they're nothing special and definitely not enough to keep my followers happy for long. Hayden sort of screwed me by posting a partner video and I know that was the whole point of his little show of ownership. But a little solo play will at least give them something until I figure out if I'm going to forgive Hayden.

I sit up straighter and a devious smile curves across my lips. Maybe a little tit for tat is in order here. Literally.

Hayden tattooed my name on him. Seems only fair I do the same, right?

When he gets home, he's getting a new dick tattoo.

But until then, I've got a video to shoot.

I get my camera set up in my bedroom, adjust the ring light until it's just right, and strip out of my clothes. I dig through the back of my closet for the lingerie Lila bought me when Roman cheated as a way to make me feel sexy again and push me to get back out there. It didn't work and ended up shoved in the back of my closet, but thankfully didn't end up stolen like the rest of my underwear.

I slip into the bright white lace and look at myself in the mirror, frowning when I realize I need to tug it up to cover the tattoo of Hayden's name. I still can't believe he actually did that to me, and I'd never admit it to him, but I love how he meets me crazy for crazy. Or maybe I meet him. Either way, these games between us make me feel alive in a way nothing else does.

On a whim, I decide to torture my sort of boyfriend and

snap a mirror selfie at the perfect angle, showing off both tits and ass.

> Cassidy: What do you think?

Hayden: That better only be for me.

Hayden: I'm already plotting Maddox's end after your little stunt on OF

> Cassidy: Aww, is someone feeling left out?

Hayden: His death will be on your hands

> Cassidy: Calm down, crazy

> Cassidy: No need to get violent with your teammate

> Cassidy: But maybe next time you'll think before you mess with me

Hayden: Don't count on it

Hayden: And why the fuck are you wearing that?

Three seconds later, he sends:

Hayden: Are you in your apartment?

Hayden: Cassidy.

Hayden: You know I have access to the cameras, right?

Hayden: You better not be shooting a video without me.

> Cassidy: And what are you going to do if I am? You're not here.

> Cassidy: Besides, I'm still pissed off at you. You're not getting back inside me until we settle the score between us.

> Hayden: ...

> Hayden: What'd you have in mind?

I grin down at my phone, then up at the camera in the corner.

> Cassidy: You'll see.

Then I turn my phone to airplane mode and set it up in the tripod, satisfied that I got his attention and wherever he is, he's watching me do something he told me not to and there's not a damn thing he can do about it. A shiver runs through me at how powerful I feel right now, as I hit record and start running my hands over my body, giving the camera a flirty smile.

I love that Hayden will be able to see me talking but not hear me and not be able to do a damn thing about it. At least until he inevitably watches this upload later. Keeping that in mind, and the fact that I'm living to torture him right now for what he did, I talk to the camera, saying the words I'd love to say to him... if I let myself. Which I haven't and I'm still undecided if I will.

"It's been too long," I say, running my fingers over my pussy through the lace. "I haven't been able to stop thinking about you." For some reason, admitting things to the camera feels safer than to Hayden's face.

I can feel myself getting wetter and I slide my hand into my panties, rubbing my clit, picturing Hayden on the other side, watching. Knowing I'm provoking him. This show is one hundred percent for him, even if all my other followers are going to see it. "I want you inside me so bad," I whisper to my audience, knowing he's going to hear it later and get off on it. "But you've been a bad boy, haven't you?"

I pull my hand out of my white lace panties and suck on my fingers while staring into the camera. "So you're going to have to wait until you earn it back."

Then I turn around and bend over, showing off my ass while I run my hands over it and give the camera a sultry look over my shoulder. "But don't worry. I'll make it worth the wait."

I know Hayden's going to be pissed that I'm teasing him like this, but what he did to me is so much worse. He deserves a little torment, and not gonna lie, agitating him is my new favorite thing—first with that teaser picture in his teammate's jersey, and now this.

He's going to be so furious when he gets home. I can't wait.

I spread my legs a little wider and slide my hand into my panties again, making sure the fabric hides Hayden's name as I finger myself while I look over my shoulder into the camera. "I want you to come with me," I moan, picturing Hayden watching me and knowing how hard he's going to be right now. "Now."

My fingers move faster and faster until I'm panting and coming hard enough that I have to grab onto the bed for support. When I come down from it, I turn around and face the camera again, running my hands over my tits, plucking at my nipples once as I say in a breathy voice, "Next time, maybe I'll let you watch live."

Then I blow a kiss and end the recording, satisfied that Hayden is going to lose his mind when he sees this.

After I edit the video, I turn my phone off airplane mode and upload it, ignoring the barrage of texts and missed calls from Hayden. Instead, I shower and change into sweats and a tank top before flopping back onto my couch and finally addressing his texts.

> Hayden: You better not be making that video for your OF without me.

Hayden: Cassidy.

Hayden: You're in so much trouble

Hayden: Answer me or I swear to God

I grin and text him back.

Cassidy: You swear to god what?

Cassidy: You'll tattoo your name on my body without my consent again?

When the three little dots pop up immediately, I don't give him a chance to respond before I'm typing out a new message.

Cassidy: Did you enjoy the show?

Hayden: You know I did

Hayden: Now take it down

Cassidy: Not gonna happen

Hayden: Don't make me repeat myself

I laugh and get more comfortable, temporarily forgetting about all the stuff out of place in here or the fact that someone's broken in and I'm all alone tonight. Messing with Hayden's exactly the distraction I need so I don't run back to his place. I'm not giving in that easily.

Cassidy: Again, no.

Cassidy: Away games suck, huh?

Hayden: It's dangerous pushing my buttons like this, Princess

Hayden: But keep testing me

> Hayden: And you'll find out how crazy I can be

I bite my lip and stare at his texts for a long moment, debating if I should push him further. But then I remember what Lila said about how he's not like Roman or Eric. I'm not so sure she's right about that because I get the distinct impression that if I try to actually break things off with Hayden, he might get more unhinged. So why am I not running? And why do I kind of like that he's feral for me?

> Cassidy: I'm not afraid of you.
>
> Cassidy: Do your worst.

Okay, yes. I'm definitely poking the bear, but he's got plenty of time to calm down before they get home from this road trip, and hopefully he'll take out some of his pent up aggression on the ice before he does. See? I'm helping my favorite team win.

I'm awesome like that.

> Hayden: You asked for it
>
> Hayden: Don't forget that

And then he doesn't respond again.

I sigh and toss my phone onto the couch beside me, knowing I'm in for it when he gets back. But for now, I'm going to enjoy my night off and maybe even go to sleep early for once.

But as I lie in bed later, staring at the ceiling and trying and failing to fall asleep, I can't help but wonder if I've made a mistake. If Hayden's not as different from Eric and Roman as I thought. If I'm just setting myself up to be hurt again.

Time will tell, I guess.

get it
@InTheFiveHole

Heard a rumor having Vaughn and Morozov in the same locker room is like storing fireworks next to a bonfire. Shit's bound to explode. #readyfortheshow

Hayden #27

IT'S BEEN two days since we left for this road trip and the team plane just touched down in Portland. We have one more game tomorrow night against the Pioneers, but all I've been able to focus on is Cassidy's taunt. Her defiance. Her dare.

Do your worst.

Oh, I plan to.

My fingers curl around my phone as I make plans. So many plans. I ignore the guys bullshitting around me as we change back into our suits and get ready to step off the plane and check into our hotel.

Once I'm in my room, I fall back onto the bed, scrolling through Cassidy's OnlyFans getting more and more pissed off at the comments on her latest video, the one she no doubt wanted to use as payback for what I did to her. I might deserve it, but I don't give a shit. I don't want anyone getting the wrong idea, namely that she's available. Fantasy or not, she's taken. Locked down, soon to be in every way possible.

That's what tonight's about. She threw down the gauntlet and I'm picking it the fuck up.

Banging starts on my door and I know if I ignore it, it'll only get worse, so I get up and yank it open. St. Claire, Mattson, and Monty stand on the other side. "You coming out with us?" War asks, leaning around me like he's trying to see if I've managed to find someone to fuck between the plane and now.

"No," I say, slamming the door in their faces.

I can hear Monty's deep, rumbling laugh on the other side as War yells through it, causing a damn scene. "Come on! We're in Portland! There's a strip club with some of the best fucking tits in the country. All natural, bro."

"Go without me."

"Your loss," Mattson chimes in before someone slams their fist against the door one more time and they leave. I briefly consider texting my brother to taunt him about Mattson going out to hook up, but he's doing me a solid later so I don't.

My focus turns to Cassidy and what I have planned for tonight. But first, I have to get home and show her what happens when she doesn't listen. When she runs from me.

The flight's short—only forty-five minutes and I'm standing on the tarmac and ducking into my brother's brand new R8.

It's close to midnight, and the private plane I chartered is already being prepped to take me back to Portland to meet up with the team when I'm done.

Sawyer grins at me as he waits at a light, the red hue making him look demonic. "I've gotta say this is psychotic, even for you."

"What can I say? She brings it out in me," I say, my fingers drumming against my thigh.

He gives me a look after he merges onto the freeway. "And you're sure you want this with her... like, long term?"

"Never been more sure of anything."

He shakes his head and pulls onto the freeway, heading toward Cassidy's apartment building. "You're lucky you've got me."

"Don't I fucking know it."

He laughs and turns up the radio, knowing I'm done with this conversation. I'm too wound up, going over and over the plan in my head.

"Pull in there," I tell him when we're close to a convenience store. "I need to grab something."

Sawyer smirks and flips open the center console, not bothering to pull into the parking lot. He just drives right on fucking by.

"Hey—"

"Look in the bag."

I open it and see the burner phone he must've bought me when I told him I was flying in tonight. "How did you know—"

He shrugs, flipping on the blinker. "Call it that twin vibe we get."

I don't bother reminding him we're not twins because he's right. Sometimes it's like I can read his mind and he can read mine.

"Thanks." He's even charged it for me.

"I'm just here to watch the show. You want to pay me back for that?" He tips his head at the burner I slip into my pocket. "Make sure you stock the kitchen with popcorn for when this shit blows up on you."

I flip him off, knowing he doesn't really get why I'm so fucked up for her, but also that he doesn't care as long as I'm happy. "Wait for me?"

He nods, pulling up alongside her apartment complex. "I'll be here."

I make sure I have the key to Cassidy's place, and hop out of his Audi.

The music turns up as I close the door and head inside the building, taking the stairs two at a time until I'm outside her door. It takes me less than ten seconds to unlock it and slip inside.

She's sleeping soundly in her bed, her face peaceful and relaxed. My chest tightens because I miss her so fucking much when I'm on the road and I both love and hate how she fucks with me when I'm gone and she thinks she's untouchable.

I pull the phone out of my pocket and snap some pictures of her sleeping as I stand over her. I planned to leave it at that, but then she rolls over and breathes my name on a sigh.

Fuck.

It's like she knows I'm here, and every cell in my body is demanding I crawl into this bed with her right now. But if I want this plan to work, I have to hold back. I grit my teeth.

My dick's hard between one breath and the next, and before I can overthink it, I rip the button of my pants open and stroke myself while staring down at her. The way one of her tits is hanging out of her tank top and her panties dip into her pussy so I can just make out the outline. She's so fucking beautiful and I want to slide inside of her until my dick explodes, but that's not what tonight's about.

I come all over her face, making sure it lands in her hair and on her cheeks, knowing she'll notice when she wakes up. And that's the point.

Showing her she needs me.

Then I snap a couple more pictures of her covered in my cum, shove my cock back into my boxers and zip up before I leave as silently as I came.

It's only minutes later I'm climbing back into my brother's car. He starts the engine and grins over at me. "Get what you needed?"

"Yep."

He laughs and pulls away from the curb, heading back toward the airport. "If I ever get this psycho over someone, you're gonna be my enabler, right?"

"*If* you get this psycho? You've got the Vaughn genes, bro. There's no if about it."

He shrugs and flips on his blinker, turning onto the freeway entrance ramp. "Guess we'll see."

We drive in silence for a while and then he says, "You know she's going to hate you for what you did tonight, right?"

"If she finds out it was me, yep."

"And you don't care?"

"Fuck, no. She can hate me all she wants. Makes the sex better when she fights."

He shakes his head and jerks the steering wheel to the right, changing lanes. "You're one twisted fucker."

I laugh and lean my head back against the headrest.

I'll play so very fucking dirty to trap her. She won't understand what's happened until it's too late.

Starting with this little stunt of mine.

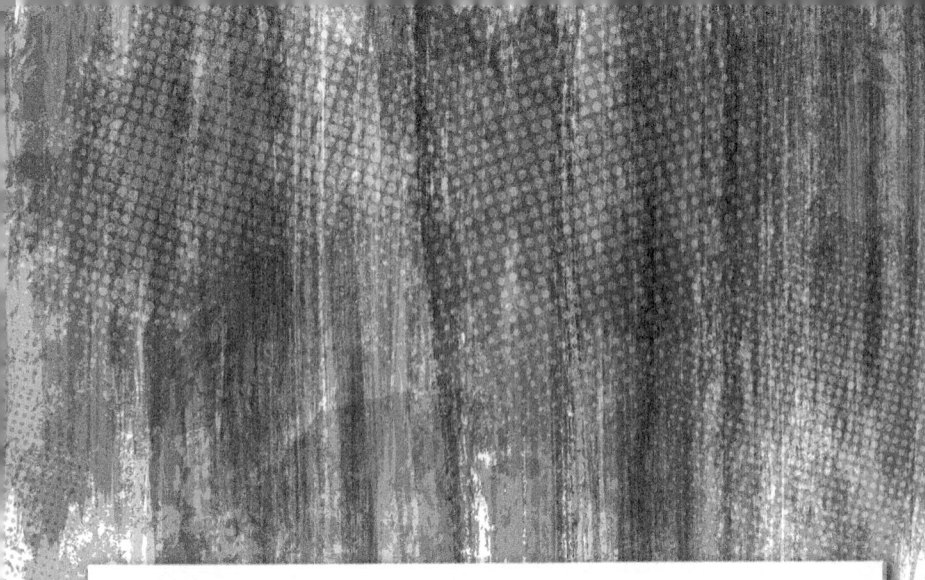

get it
@InTheFiveHole

At @seattleanchors practice today drills with the C & his new D-man looked less like team building and more like war. #GetYourPopcorn

Hayden #28

BY THE TIME the plane touches back down in Portland, the sky's lightening to the dullest gray. The security footage from Cassidy's apartment has been erased, and I've sent the pictures I took of her on the burner to her anonymously.

If this doesn't get her to move in with me, I'm going to have to take it to the next level and straight up kidnap her. Maybe chain her to my bed until she realizes where she belongs is with me.

It's not a bad idea, really.

I grin as I head toward the hotel to meet up with the team. I catch a nap before morning skate, then another after. It's a busy day, so it's not until I'm boarding the team bus waiting for us outside of the hotel that I get a chance to really think about last night. I haven't checked my phone, and when I go to do it now, I'm interrupted by War taking the seat beside me.

"You didn't come out last night," he says, narrowing his eyes at me.

"Nope."

"And you're not going to tell me why?"

I shove my phone back into my pocket, not wanting him to see the screen, and lean back in my seat, stretching out my legs and getting comfortable for the ride to the arena. "Nope."

"You missed all the weird Portland chicks at the bar. One was cleansing my chakras while another was hand feeding me these disgusting vegan snacks." He laughs and shakes his head.

I laugh, knowing he's trying to get a rise out of me. "Sounds hot." I'm trying to ignore the way my phone is burning a hole in my pocket and how I want to check it so fucking bad.

"Not really," War says, laughing as he messes with the headphones around his neck. "But I got a blow job from the chakra chick, so it wasn't a total waste of time."

I nod, not really giving a shit about his hook up or what he did with her. "Glad you had fun."

"What's up with you?" he asks, nudging me with his elbow. "You're acting weird."

"Nothing."

"Bullshit." He leans back in his seat and stares at me for a long moment before his eyes narrow accusingly. "You're fucking someone, aren't you? Like... regularly." He shudders. "Like a," he gags a little, "girlfriend or something." Then he gasps. "Oh wait, you told us about this. It's that chick from The Sin Bin. Cassidy."

I stare out the window without answering him, watching as we pass by Portland's downtown buildings on our way to the arena. What the hell does he expect me to say? *Yeah, man. I'm trying to knock her up, too. Also, I'm so goddamn obsessed that I might literally kill our teammate if he looks at her wrong again.*

"Dude!" he says, punching me in the arm. "She's hot as fuck."

"Stay away from her," I growl, turning back to him and glaring.

He holds up his hands in surrender. "I'm not interested in

your girl, man. Chill." He grins and leans back in his seat. "But damn, you caught feelings, didn't you?"

I flip him off, which only makes him laugh. He must have a death wish, because he keeps talking. "She must be wild if she's got you acting all caveman and shit." He sobers and looks thoughtful as he watches me. "I wouldn't say no to getting to watch, though."

I turn back to him, my eyes narrowed and my fists clenched. "The only thing you'll be watching is my fist hitting your face if you keep talking about her."

He laughs again and shoves my shoulder like I'm not two seconds away from bashing his fucking skull against the bus window. "Don't worry, I'll keep it in my pants when it comes to your girl. She's all yours."

"Fucking right," I mutter as the bus pulls up to the arena. "Spread the word to the rest of the team. Cassidy's off-limits."

War stands and stretches his arms over his head before saluting me like an asshole. "You got it, boss." Then he heads toward the front of the bus, leaving me alone for a minute before everyone files off.

I pull out my phone and check the burner I sent the pictures to. There are no messages, but there are half a dozen missed calls and a bunch of text messages waiting for me on my phone from Cassidy.

There's a screenshot of the anonymous message I sent her with the pictures of her covered in my cum. Then,

> Cassidy: Someone was in my house while I slept, Hayden.
>
> Cassidy: I'm so freaked out.
>
> Cassidy: Why aren't you answering?!

I grin and type back:

> Hayden: Sorry, didn't have my phone during mandatory team bullshit.
>
> Hayden: Go to my house tonight.
>
> Hayden: Sawyer will pick you up.
>
> Hayden: Don't even think about telling me no.
>
> Hayden: I'll be home late tonight after the game.
>
> Cassidy: Okay.

And that's when I know I've got her. She's not even going to argue? I'm a fucking genius.

I shove my phone into my pocket and head off the bus with the rest of the team, knowing my focus needs to be on the game against the Pioneers instead of the girl I'm transfixed on.

By the time I step onto the ice, I'm wound the fuck up and ready to take it out on the Pioneers. Halfway through a brutal first period, we're down 0-2 and I'm so frustrated my vision is tinged in red.

Number 41 chirps, "Heard you like Morozov's sloppy seconds," as he skates by me during a faceoff, putting himself at the top of my *to be fucked up* list.

"What the fuck did you say?" I bark, skating toward him with my stick raised. He laughs and turns to skate away, but instead he gets a crosscheck from me that sends him slamming into the ice.

The refs blow their whistles, but I don't give a shit. Boos echo around the arena and I'm given two minutes for cross checking because I got sloppy as hell and they caught me. My blood's still on fire when I get out of the box and head back to the bench.

Coach gives me a look, but he says nothing. He knows I'll do whatever it takes to win and right now, that means calming the hell down before I get thrown out of the game.

Kavanaugh, one of my fellow D men, sits beside me and spits out his mouth guard. "What'd he say?"

I shake my head, not wanting to repeat it. "Just some bullshit."

He nods and leans back against the bench as we watch the play continue while we wait for our next shifts. "I've got your back. Next shift, if I get the chance, I'll take a shot at him."

I nod, knowing he will. I'm learning Kav's a good guy to have on my side, and he's turning out to be loyal. I'll remember that. He doesn't ask questions and I don't tell him what 41 said that set me off, but it doesn't matter because out on the ice we've got each other's backs.

When my skates hit the ice again, I'm ready for revenge. And when I get the puck on a breakaway, I know it's mine. I can feel it in my bones.

I skate down the ice with their winger, Olson, on my heels, but he won't catch me. The Pioneers' rookie goalie looks like he's frozen in fear, and I pass the puck to Mattson and get into position. He passes it back and I take advantage.

I shoot the puck right over the blocker into the net, tying the game up 2-2.

We trade blows and goals back and forth, and by the time the final buzzer sounds, I'm drenched in sweat and I feel like I've exorcised some demons out here on the ice tonight. We won 6-4 and despite the familiar post-game ache settling into my body, the need for Cassidy is stronger.

As we board the short flight home, I pull out my phone and turn it over and over in my fingers before I finally pull up the messages while we taxi down the runway.

> Sawyer: The eagle has landed.
>
> Sawyer: The package has been delivered.

> Sawyer: The kids have been dropped off at the pool

I grin at his ridiculousness and type back,

> Hayden: What the fuck, See-Saw?
> Hayden: I did not need to know that shit
> Hayden: You could've just said you had her

> Sawyer: And where's the fun in that?
> Sawyer: Now get home
> Sawyer: I'm not a goddamn babysitter

> Hayden: ::sends a picture of current surroundings::
> Hayden: Literally at 30,000 feet rn
> Hayden: Can't get there any faster. Don't let her go anywhere.

> Sawyer: 🖕

I shove my phone back into my pocket, knowing I'll be home soon enough to make sure Cassidy never wants to leave again.

And if she does, I'll just have to make it so she can't.

Vaughn's Vengeance

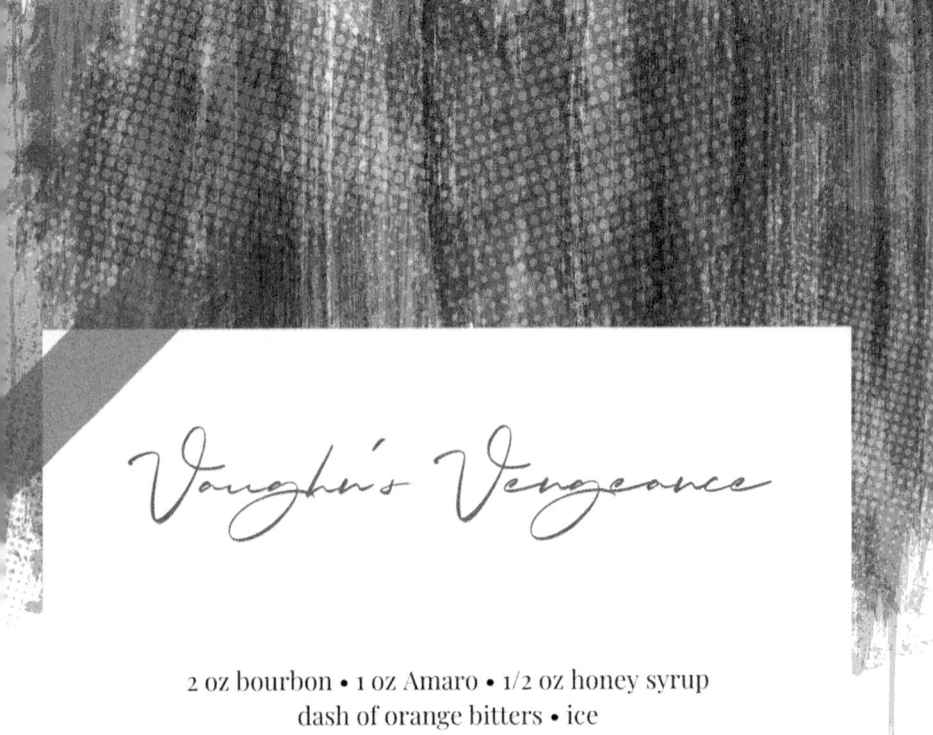

2 oz bourbon • 1 oz Amaro • 1/2 oz honey syrup
dash of orange bitters • ice
Garnish: orange twist

Stir bourbon, Amaro, honey syrup, and orange bitters with ice until well-chilled. Strain into a rocks glass over a large ice cube. Garnish with an orange twist.

Cassidy #29

MY STOMACH CHURNS as I lay in Hayden's bed and stare up at the ceiling. All day, I've felt like there were eyes on me and after I nearly scrubbed my skin off in the shower this morning after seeing those fucking terrifying photos on my phone, I'm feeling completely untethered.

I mean, seriously. What the hell am I supposed to do? Do I have, like, a stalker now? On top of everything else?

Bile creeps up my throat, but I swallow it down.

It can't be Roman because he was with Hayden in Portland. So... what, then? Could someone from my OnlyFans have found out where I live?

I shudder at the thought. Fuck, I hope not.

I pull the heavy-but-soft comforter up to my chin. It helps to know I'm not alone in this huge house, that Sawyer's here, but it's not the same. As angry as I've been at Hayden for what he did, he still makes me feel protected. And right now, that's what I need. Safety.

I clutch my phone in my hand, blinking against the brightness as I check the time again.

12:12 a.m.

Maybe I should make a wish.

Where would I even start? I'd need at least a dozen wishes to fix the mess that is my life.

I sigh and toss my phone onto his pillow beside me, inhaling the smell of him as it fills the air. I groan, wanting to shove my face into the pillowcase and breathe him in. That's not normal, right?

There's something wrong with me, I think.

This man *tattooed his name on my body* without my consent.

I try to keep reminding myself, but I think saying the words over and over is just desensitizing me to them instead. I'm still not letting him inside of me until he does the same, though. Fair's fair.

There's a creak in the hall, and my heart jumps straight into my throat, blocking the scream that wants to tear out of me. I should probably look for some kind of weapon, but I reach down and yank the blanket up to my chin, reverting to that thing I did when I was a kid and something scared me—if I can't see them, they can't see me.

Flawed logic, but no one ever said the hindbrain was smart.

The door swings open, and then Hayden's here, standing in the doorway. His eyes bore into me like a predator ready to pounce, hungry and feral. His gaze pierces through me, as if he wants to devour every inch of my being until there's nothing left but my soul for him to steal.

I scramble out of bed, almost falling when the blankets tangle around my legs, but I catch myself and lunge at him. He catches me in his strong arms and lifts me off the ground, holding me against his chest as I wrap my arms around his neck. "Welcome home," I whisper, burying my face in his neck to breathe in the scent of cologne and home.

He laughs softly and carries me back to the bed, sitting on the edge with me in his lap as my legs wrap around him. "This is the kind of greeting I want every time, but next time do it naked." He kisses my temple, my cheek, the tip of my nose before his lips find mine.

It's sweet and exactly what I need right now.

I melt into him, letting him kiss away the fear and anxiety that's been building all day. The tension bleeds out of me and I didn't realize how tense I must've been all day because now my muscles are actually sore from how tight I've been wound.

But now Hayden's here and he can carry my worry for a while on those broad shoulders of his. I'm good with it.

I'm playing with his tongue ring as it slides into my mouth, getting lost in the taste of him. If he asks, I'd deny it but I missed him so much it actually hurt. Now that he's back, it feels like everything's going to be okay.

His hands run up and down my back, soothing me as he deepens the kiss. My back hits the bed as he tosses me on it and I was so caught up in the taste of him, I didn't even realize we were moving. The breath puffs out of my lungs as Hayden looms over me, a dark god whose eyes glint as they drag across my body.

He stares into my eyes, and I think he's actually looking at my soul. I think I might be looking at his, too. "Holy shit, you love me."

He's smirking at me now and I shove him away from me. Okay, I *try* to shove him away from me. He doesn't actually move at all.

"What? No, I don't."

"Uh-huh."

Now he just sounds smug. I'm pretending that I'm not freaking out on the inside, that my heart didn't just come to a screeching stop and then go zero to sixty in half a second. Okay, I *may* have gotten attached to Hayden despite my best efforts not to. He's so much more than I thought he was. Protective, the most gorgeous guy I've ever seen, and instead of being intimidated by my need for independence, he goes toe to toe with me and actually seems to *like* it.

But it's not love... right?

It can't be.

Except when I look up into his face and see the way he's looking down at me, it feels like it could be.

"Stop looking at me like that," I whisper.

His smile grows bigger, and he leans down to nip at my earlobe. "Like what?"

"Like you love me too."

He chuckles and licks the shell of my ear, sending a shiver down my spine. "Can't help it. I think I might."

I groan, pushing him away from me again, and this time, he lets me. He seems to shake off the effect I have on him while I'm just laying here, in his bed, drunk on the possibility of him. Of a *future* with him.

Shit, he's dangerous. It's like I forget everything when he's this close. I sit up and slide back to the headboard, leaning against it as he sinks onto the mattress beside me and holds out his hand.

Thankfully, he drops the whole *I love you* thing.

"Let me see the picture."

"Pictures," I correct, happy to have an excuse to talk about something else. I waste no time digging my phone out of the sheets and handing it over.

He scrolls through them before his jaw tics and he looks up at me with those eyes of his that I can't help but get lost in. I blink away my sudden hypnosis. It's really unfair how hot he is with his piercings and muscles and all that darkness inside of him. "I'll take care of it."

"What does that mean?" I ask, narrowing my eyes at him and holding my hand out for my phone, but he sticks it in his pocket instead.

He stands and starts toward the door. "Did you know my dad's a senator?"

I follow him, getting whiplash at the change of subject. "Uh, no. I didn't...?" There's a question at the end because what the hell is he talking about now?

Hayden walks out into the hall and toward his office. It's still stacked with boxes because he hasn't unpacked since he and his brother moved in. I only discovered it was an office because I snooped. Sue me.

Hayden digs around in one of the boxes and pulls out a sleek laptop, sitting in the chair behind the desk and opening the computer. "Well, he is. And that means access to connections you don't have."

"Like what?"

He unwinds a cord and plugs it into the side of the computer and then my phone before starting to type. "Like his hacker who's now my hacker. I'll get him on this."

He types and while he does, I watch his straight teeth sink into his plush lower lip. The one that's a little swollen from our makeout session. My eyes burn because I'm not blinking, so I overcompensate and blink ten times. By the time I'm done, he's unplugging my phone and handing it back. "Done."

He closes the lid on his computer and stands, stalking over to me. There's no mistaking the intent in his eyes. I hold up my palm, and it pushes against his hard chest. The heat of his body seeps into my skin, and I shiver. "No touching."

"Like hell you're going to stop me from—"

I lift my chin so I'm staring up at him. "You tattooed your name on my body. Until you tattoo mine on yours, no more sex."

He throws his head back and laughs. Then he bends down

and grabs me, tossing me over his shoulder. "You think you can hold out on me, Princess?" He smacks my ass, and I yelp as he carries me back to the bedroom. "After what you did when I was gone? Torturing me, ignoring me, shooting that video and posting it when I told you not to."

My stomach flips as he tosses me onto the bed again and then crawls over me. His eyes are wild, and I know he's not going to give up until he's inside of me. But I also know I have more willpower than he thinks.

He tries to kiss me, but I turn my face away so his lips land on my cheek. "My name on your body or blue balls. You pick."

He flips me onto my stomach and pulls me ass-up into his lap. God, I love how he just tosses me around. "We'll see how you feel after you take your punishment." He smacks my ass again and then yanks down my panties, making me yelp. My skin is already hot where he hit me, causing little aching pulses between my legs.

"Hayden!" My voice is a warning, but it comes out breathless. "I thought we already determined this isn't much of a punishment."

He spreads my legs and slides a finger inside of me, pumping it in and out as his other hand rubs my clit. "You're already wet for me, Princess." Yeah, I can't deny it. Kissing him earlier, having his body dominate mine just does it for me. He leans over me, pressing his chest against my back as he whispers in my ear. "It's only a matter of time until you give in."

"Or you do. You only have to," his palm comes down again on my bare ass and I gasp, "do one simple thing, Hayden. My name, your skin. Easy."

He growls and flips me back onto my back, hovering over me with his eyes blazing. "You think I won't do it? I'll tattoo your name anywhere if that's what it takes. Your cunt belongs to me. This is the one and only time I'll let you keep me from what's mine."

I swallow hard and stare up at him, knowing he means every word. And I also know I'm going to win this battle. He's as addicted to me as I am to him—even if I'm not willing to admit it—maybe more.

And when he gives in, I'm going to be right there waiting for him to take everything he wants from me.

But until then, we're playing by my rules.

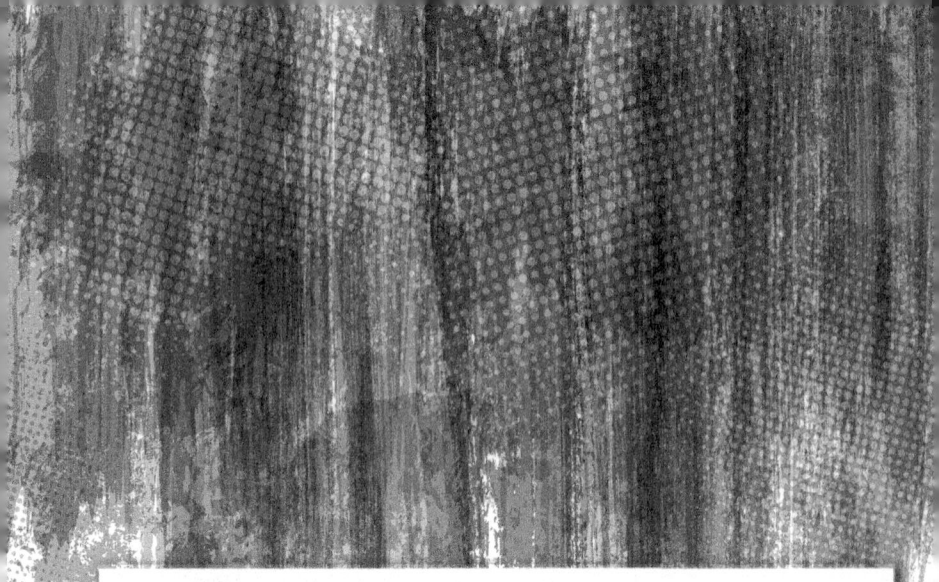

ur mom
@GoalGuardian

The only thing more reliable than a sunrise is Hayden Vaughn taking someone down in the third period. #GuaranteedHits

Hayden #30

MY LITTLE LIAR wants to play games with me? I bet she doesn't think I'll do it. My dick is harder than a goal post as I stare down at her spread out on my bed, her pussy wet and ready for me underneath her tiny shorts. As much as I hate her keeping her body from me, I also love that she fights me. And inking her name onto my skin is a small price to pay for lifetime access to Cassidy Bennett—soon to be Vaughn.

Reaching for my phone, I shoot off a quick text to Wraith and he responds almost immediately. Then I toss my phone to the side, ready to have some fun with my little liar before he shows up.

I grin and lean over her again, kissing her neck and sucking on her earlobe. "You want me to tattoo your name on my cock?"

She shivers beneath me, but she doesn't say anything.

"I'll do it." I kiss her cheek, the corner of her mouth, the tip of her nose. Then I start to move down her body, kissing and licking and biting her skin as I go. Marking her flesh as mine.

When I reach her pussy, I yank off her shorts and bury my

face between her legs, letting my eyes drift over my name etched into her skin. Fuck, that gets me even harder. Her fingers tangle in my hair and she moans as I lick and suck on her clit until she's thrashing around beneath me. My entire universe narrows down to just the smell of her, the taste of her on my tongue.

The sight of her falling apart for me.

But just as she starts to come, I pull back. Then I do it again and again until she's a dripping, begging mess. My phone buzzes and I wipe off my face as I grab it and check the text. "You want me to tattoo your name on my cock or not, Princess? My guy's here."

I turn and step into the hall, and she yells from the bed, "Not your dick! It takes too long to heal." A chuckle slips out. Knew she couldn't resist me.

I meet Wraith at the front door, swinging it open and he walks inside like it's not a big deal to be here at one a.m. about to illegally ink me like he does this shit every day. He probably does. He's got a black bag in his hand and a scowl on his face. "You ready for this?"

"Yep," I say, leading him into the living room. I drop onto the couch and watch as Wraith unpacks his shit onto the coffee table.

Cassidy appears in the doorway, her eyes wide as she looks between me and Wraith. She's wearing one of my t-shirts and nothing else and I glare at her bare legs. "You're serious?"

"You know I am. I don't fuck around when it comes to you, Princess. Now go get dressed before I have to cut Wraith's eyes out of his head for seeing you like this."

The man grunts like he's daring me to try, but I ignore him. Instead, I stare her down until she rolls her eyes and leaves, stomping off like she needs a new print of my palm on her ass.

"Got your hands full with that one, huh?" Wraith says, tipping his head toward the now empty doorway.

"More than you could possibly imagine," I say.

He gets up and walks into the kitchen before slipping into a pair of black latex gloves and sitting back down. I stand up and strip off my button down, then unbuckle my belt. I'm about to flick open the button on my pants when Cassidy walks back into the room. Her eyes sweep over me and then shift to Wraith.

Then she focuses back on me again as she walks up to stand in front of me. "Not on your dick. I have plans for it when you're done," she practically purrs, and I feel myself getting hard as her pupils blow out. I can see her nipples poking out under my t-shirt, for fuck's sake.

"Princess," I warn as she smirks at me, fully aware of what she's doing.

"I think," she says slowly as her fingers drift down the side of my torso to the dip on the side of my abs near my hip, "I want it here."

Wraith cocks a scarred eyebrow at me. I grip Cassidy's fingers before they can go any lower or make me any harder. "You heard her," I tell him, pulling my pants and boxers down to expose my flesh.

"Here," he hands over an iPad in a matte black case he pulled out of his duffle. "I drew these up on the way over. Pick one so we can get this done."

I take it and flip through the options. Cassidy leans over, her hair tickling my arm and the citrus scent of her shampoo fills my lungs while I breathe her in. For a second, I forget what I'm supposed to be doing as I get lost in her, until her finger stabs into the screen and snaps me back to reality. "This one."

Her eyes cut to mine, glimmering with a devious sort of excitement I feel down to my bones. The way she looks at me, the way energy crackles between us like that second after lightning strikes and before thunder shakes the walls, it punches the breath straight out of my chest every time. It seems unnatural to want her this much, but it's so goddamn easy.

Easier than skating.

Maybe she doesn't think I'll do this, or maybe she hopes I'll punish her for making me.

"You heard her," I tell Wraith, grabbing the iPad and handing it back. Cassidy blinks at me, her mouth slightly parted like she wants to say something but doesn't know what. I smirk at her, using the side of my finger to close her mouth. That breaks her out of wherever she went in her mind and her eyes narrow. But Wraith shifts and my attention tears away from her and back to him.

He reaches into his bag and brings out some transfer paper, tracing the image onto it. Cassidy is silent while he does it, watching him, and my jaw clenches. I don't want her attention on him, so I grip her chin and force her to look at me instead. "Don't look at him."

Cassidy rolls her eyes, but she tangles her fingers with mine and the tension in my body relaxes. "I want to watch what he's doing. And your insanity is showing," she says this last part in a whisper, like I give a flying fuck if the illegal fighter on the other side of the room knows how crazy I can be when it comes to her.

"Lay flat," Wraith says, except when he speaks it's more like a grunt. Cassidy moves to give me space, but I hook my hand around her thigh so she can't move and spin myself so my head's in her lap.

I watch her while she watches him prep my skin. I don't give a shit what it looks like as long as she forgives me and lets me inside of her again. I don't even need her forgiveness, not really. But for some reason, I want it. Maybe it's knowing she loves me and wanting to be worthy of that. Who the hell knows?

Or maybe it's just wanting her name on my body the way mine's on hers.

Yeah, that feels right.

Her fingers run absently through my hair like she doesn't

know she's doing it but can't help herself, like she needs to touch me.

A wet sort of cold hits the skin between my hip and the lower part of my abs and there's a pressure there while Wraith presses the stencil into my skin. Cassidy's fingers stop moving like she realized what she was doing, tightening in my hair before she lets go. "Do you want to see?"

I shake my head, trying to encourage her to keep going. To run her nails over my scalp. I bite back my smirk when she does. "Nah, as long as you like it that's good enough for me."

"Do it," she tells Wraith, speaking over my head. There's an almost manic kind of satisfaction in her eyes while they bounce between looking upside down at me and watching Wraith.

The buzz of the needle cuts through the air and the familiar pain starts. It doesn't take long before he's wiping me down and wrapping it up. Cassidy's cheeks are flushed. She's breathing harder, and I've spent the last ten minutes running my fingers up the inside of her thigh.

Slow strokes designed to drive her out of her mind. My own punishment for taking her body away from me.

Never. Again.

I sit up and reach for my wallet, blindly grabbing cash and shoving it at Wraith before I tell him to get out.

"Next time you need shit done in the middle of the night, it'll be triple," he grunts before turning towards the door.

I slam the door, out of patience. My dick's hard, my skin itches, and I'm still pissed at my little liar for taunting me with an OnlyFans video without me in it.

When I round the corner back to the living room, she must see the look on my face because her eyes widen and she takes off with a shriek deeper into the house, her wild laughter trailing behind her and filling up all the cold, vacant spots inside of me.

I grin, kicking off my pants so I'm in nothing but my boxers while I stalk her through the rooms, hunting her.

"You're not getting away from me again, Princess," I call out, knowing she's close. "Never."

And then I catch her in my arms, squealing and kicking and fighting while I carry her back to my bed where she belongs.

Where she'll *always* belong.

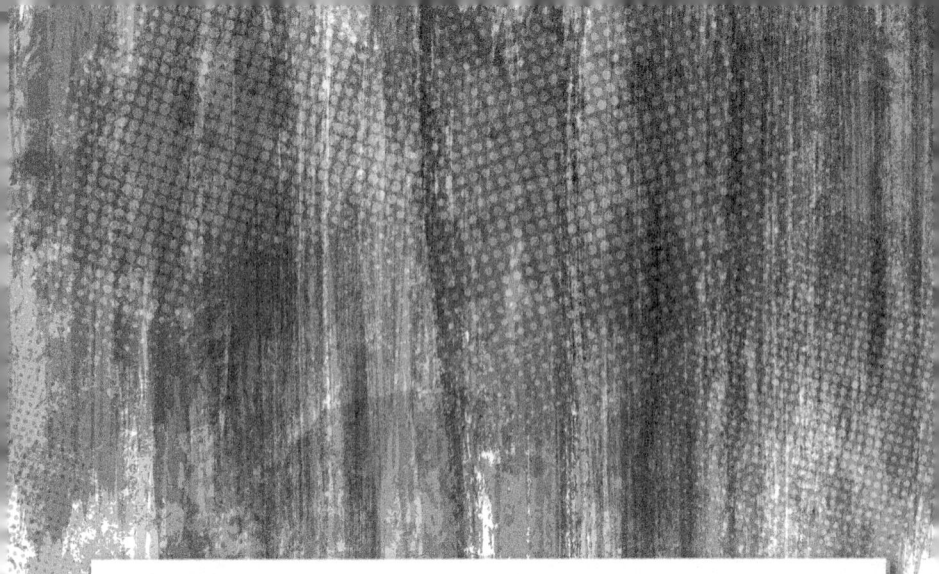

Jesse Knows Best
@PuckPundit

Hayden Vaughn plays like he's got a personal vendetta against every player on the ice #VengeanceMode

Hayden #31

CASSIDY SCREAMS as she bounces on the bed, this half-laugh, half-crazed shriek of excitement. Her limbs flail while she tries to fight me off, to get away from me, but I know she doesn't mean it. Not with the way she's laughing so hard she can barely breathe.

I crawl over the top of her body, pinning her down with my weight, and her wild eyes meet mine. Her cheeks are flushed and her hair's a fucking mess, but I stare an extra second to commit this shit to memory. I never want to forget the way she looks right now, pinned under me and turned the fuck on.

Happy.

She presses her tits into my chest and I reach down and grip the fabric of my shirt, peeling it over her head.

"You have the best rack I've ever seen," I tell her, bending over her to lick one perfect pink nipple before sucking it into my mouth and letting it go with a *pop*.

Her legs open for me to settle between them, right where the fuck I belong—an invitation if I've ever seen one.

My cock feels like one of those divining rods pointed right at her cunt like it's the fucking fountain of youth, finally found and ready to be claimed.

Shit, I don't even know what I'm saying. It's hard to think with all my blood in my dick.

"You gonna keep talking or are you gonna fuck me, *Hitman*?" Cassidy reaches up to wrap her fingers around the back of my neck to try to pull me in for a kiss.

"Give me your phone," I tell her, holding back. I know if I give in to what she wants, she'll think she has the upper hand in our relationship.

She doesn't.

She crawls across the bed and reaches onto the nightstand, tossing it at me. I cloned it earlier with my laptop, but I don't want her to know about that. Now that I can see all her calls, texts, and have access to her apps, nothing will stop me from making sure she stays mine for life.

I grip her arm, pulling her face down into my lap, holding her phone in front of her face to unlock it. Then I open the camera, aiming it down at her sprawled out in my lap before hitting record.

Once that's done, I strip her until she's naked with my other hand, giving myself a minute to drink in the perfection of her.

Her ass is perfect and round and I grip it, letting my fingers imprint her skin. She coughs to try to hide her moan while she wiggles against me, rubbing herself against my cock through my boxers.

"I know you want my dick, but you've been a bad girl, haven't you?" I say, leaning forward to bite her ass cheek. She yelps and tries to crawl away, but I hold her down with one hand and keep recording with the other. "You're going to take your punishment first."

She tries to throw her hair over her shoulder to glare at me, but it tangles around her face and she ends up having to blow it away. It doesn't help and I laugh.

"What's funny, asshole?"

"You're just so goddamn cute when you're trying to fight me."

She opens her mouth to bitch at me again, but I cut her off with a hard slap to her ass, watching as the pink blooms across her skin. She moans instead and grinds against my lap. My cock is painfully hard and leaking all over the damn place in my boxers.

"Fuck," she breathes, her eyes fluttering closed like she needs this as much as I do.

I check the camera, making sure she's still in the shot. The bite mark I left on her ass is visible on the screen, and a pulse of possessiveness ricochets through my body. My forearm flexes as I grab a handful of her ass again, getting a peek at her dripping pussy. "Look at you," I murmur, unable to tear my gaze away. *I* do this to her. No matter how many lies her mouth tells me, her body knows the truth.

That I'm the only one that'll ever be inside of her again.

That she's already got a dependence on me and it'll only get worse as time goes on.

My dick's only inches from sinking inside of her, but I resist because I'm still pissed about the video she made solo while I was on the road. The way she taunted me. I want to do the same to her now, give her a taste of how it feels to be helpless like she made me.

"Smile for the camera, Princess," I tell her, gripping her hair in my fist and gently tugging her head up so she's looking at the phone screen. Her eyes are watery, her long lashes sticking together as she blinks up at me. She's wrecked in the absolute best way and I haven't even put my dick in her yet. "Show them how desperate you are for me. Put on a show."

"Stop," she whines, trying to shake her head, but I hold her still. "You made your point."

"Did I? You couldn't wait to show off what belongs to me the second I was gone. You taunted me with what I couldn't have while you let them see you like this." My words are angry, hard and cutting as I let go of her hair to shove two fingers inside of her.

Her lips part like she's going to argue, but I slap her ass again, my wet fingers sliding across her flesh, and then rub my hand over the hot skin to soothe it.

"I want to fuck you so bad," she says, her voice breathless and needy. "Please, H—"

"No names," I growl, knowing this video's going up as soon as I'm done and I can't let myself be identified, as much as I might want to. I want the entire fucking universe to know who's about to fuck Cassidy Bennett.

I tighten my grip on her hip, keeping her pinned in place. Her whimpers of need are music to my ears, but I'm still too pissed to give in.

"This is what you wanted, isn't it?" I say, my voice low and gravelly. Rough. "To tease me with what you were doing while I was gone? To wind me the fuck up and make me crazy?"

She tries to fight against my hold, but I'm too strong. I move her onto her hands and knees on the bed, yanking my boxers down. Then I fill her up with something much thicker and harder than my fingers. My bare cock slides into her like it was made to be there, her slick pussy welcoming me in.

I don't bother pretending to wear a condom this time. She's not paying attention and I fucking hate that thin layer of latex between us.

I check her phone again, confirming she's still in the hot as hell POV shot before adjusting so I can tighten my grip on her hip.

"Look at me," I command, my voice a low rumble as I thrust

into her. She complies, her eyes meeting mine in the mirror across the room. Her lips are parted, her breaths coming in short, sharp gasps as I fill her completely and then stop when I feel her cunt tighten around me like she's about to come.

"This is what happens when you play games," I growl, my fingers digging into her flesh.

She moans, her body twitching rhythmically as I start fucking her again, harder and harder with every thrust. I'm close, my balls tightening with every move, but I hold back, wanting to draw this out as long as I can. Make her suffer the same way she made me. I don't think I'm deterring her from fucking with me again, but the need to be inside of her finally broke me.

"Who's pussy is this?" I growl. I want to hear her say it, to acknowledge that she's mine, that she belongs to me. I'll remind her twenty times a day if that's what it takes for it to finally sink in because she's so goddamn stubborn.

"Yours," she pants, her voice barely above a whisper. "Only yours."

I let out a satisfied grunt, my thrusts becoming more erratic as I feel my release building.

I can see it in her eyes, the way they're glazed over because she's high on me, the way she's biting her bottom lip to hold back her cries, though fuck knows why. I live for hearing that shit.

I reach down to grab a fistful of her long, tangled hair, tugging her head back so I can see her face. Her mouth is open in a silent scream, her eyes squeezed shut as she chases her release. I want to see it, the moment she breaks apart for me.

"Open your eyes," I order in a voice I barely recognize. I'm so close I have to grit my teeth to keep from exploding. I'm gonna come *so hard* in about three seconds. "Let me see you fall."

Her eyes snap open, meeting mine in the mirror. I can see the desperation in her gaze, the need for release. I lean forward, my lips brushing against her ear as I speak and play with her clit.

"Come for me, Princess. Now."

She moans, her body tensing as she obeys my command. I can feel her pussy clenching around me, her muscles contracting and gripping me like a fist as she comes apart for me. It's the hottest fucking thing I've ever seen, and it sends me over the edge.

I groan, my release spilling into her as I thrust deep inside one last time. I stay there, breathing hard, letting my boys do their job. Cassidy's too out of it from how hard I made her come to realize I didn't wear a condom.

I wonder how long it's going to take to knock her up. If there's anything else I can do to make it happen faster.

While I'm still inside of her, I stop the recording and then I click on the OnlyFans app. Cassidy starts to collapse to the bed, but I reach down and hold her up with my hand splayed across her stomach, wanting to keep her ass in the air and to stay inside of her as long as possible.

With one hand, I post the video, loving that all those perverted assholes that comment on her page are about to see once again that she's mine, not theirs. Then I shut down her phone so she won't think about what I just did. Immense satisfaction pours into every muscle, every bone, knowing I'm one step closer to making it impossible for her to escape me.

I pull out of her slowly, savoring the feeling of her pussy clenching around me, trying to keep me inside. It's like she doesn't want to waste a drop, even though she doesn't know how much of me is deep inside of her right now.

She whimpers at the loss when I pull out, her body still trembling from the aftershocks of her orgasm. I can't help but smile at the sight of her, completely wrecked and spent because of me. When some of my cum spills out, I use two fingers to push it back in and she squirms but doesn't call me out.

"Fuck, you're gorgeous," I murmur, leaning down to press a kiss to her shoulder. She shivers beneath me, her skin raised with goosebumps. The urge to touch her, to run my hands over her curves and feel the heat of her skin against my palms is overwhelming, so I don't hold back.

I pull her up onto her hands and knees, positioning her so that she's facing the mirror across the room. She looks up at me in the glass as I reach for her hair, gathering it up in my fist and tugging gently.

"Watch," I command, my voice rough. Her body tenses beneath my touch, but she doesn't look away from the mirror. The flush spreads across her chest and I trace my fingers over the curve of her shoulder, watching as her skin pebbles everywhere my fingers roam. She's still trembling, her body spent and exhausted from the pleasure I've given her.

Me.

"Do you see what you do to me?" I murmur. "What *I* do to *you*? You drive me fucking wild, Cass. I'm unhinged over you."

She doesn't respond, her eyes still fixed on our reflection in the mirror. I can see the questions in her gaze, but I don't answer them. Instead, I say, "No more videos without me or next time you won't like what I do nearly as much as this."

She opens her mouth and I tug on her hair, so fucking over her stubbornness. "And I'm done fucking around. You're moving in here. Tonight." I grin at her in the mirror, a feral expression on my face I don't think I've ever worn before. "How else am I going to make sure you're addicted to me?"

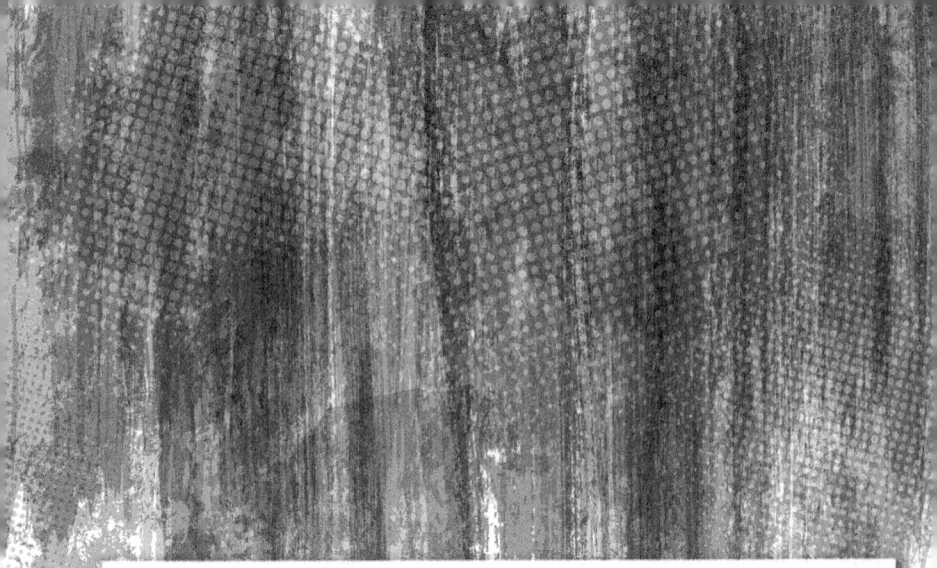

empire of ice
@FanaticFan45

Watching the Portland Pioneers try to dodge Hayden Vaughn is like watching me try to dodge my responsibilities #TheHitman

Hayden #32

I STARE OUT THE WINDOW, watching the city lights flicker by. The victory high still pumps through my veins as I lean back in the leather seat of my SUV as Sawyer drives. As we roll towards The Sin Bin, Warren cracks some joke about the rookie winger he flattened in the third, and the guys erupt in laughter. But my mind is consumed with more pressing matters.

Namely, the movers I've got over at Cassidy's place right now, packing up her shit. Whether she likes it or not, my feisty little liar is moving in with me. I smirk, remembering how she finally caved. Sure, she said I make her feel safe, but I know it's the orgasms that sealed the deal. Once I get her in my bed, she forgets about everything but me.

The way it should be.

I shift in my seat, my cock already getting hard just thinking about her. About those full lips wrapped around me, those green eyes staring up in defiance even as she takes every inch and tears run down her cheeks. Fuck, I need to get my hands on her. *Now.*

Sawyer pulls up to The Sin Bin and I'm out of the SUV before he's even in park. I push open the door, the guys following close behind me as we make our way inside.

The bar is overflowing after our win, the air thick with the sounds of celebration and the smell of stale beer. Cheers go up as the crowd realizes the team's here. I ignore it all, scanning the room. My gaze lands on Cassidy as she pours a drink behind the bar. Her eyes meet mine, and even from here I can see the fire in them, the challenge. Sparks crackle in the air between us like always. I know she's still pissed at me for forcing her hand about moving into my house, but that's pretty much her love language.

At this point, I'd be worried if she wasn't mad at me for some shit.

I make my way over to her, my body moving with a purpose so strong, it's unlike anything I've ever felt before, this *need* to be as close to her as possible. Like we're tethered together at the soul level. It's fucked up, but I'm not even trying to fight it. I don't think I could if I wanted to, the pull is that intense.

I walk behind the bar like I have every right to be there, coming up behind Cassidy, grabbing her waist and spinning her around. Before she can react, I crush my mouth to hers, kissing her hard and deep with a fuck ton of tongue. Reminding all these fuckers she's mine. She lets out a little moan, her body instinctively arching into mine as I finally, fucking finally, taste her.

Whistles and cheers erupt around us, but other than raising my finger to flip them off, I ignore my teammates in favor of sinking into Cassidy.

I nip at her lower lip as I pull away, my eyes burning into hers.

"I missed you," I murmur against her lips, my fingers

digging into the hair at the back of her neck, tightening my grip to keep her attention focused only on me.

"Really? I couldn't tell." Her tone is sarcastic, but her swollen lips and the blush on her cheeks don't lie. She missed me, too. Then she grips my arm, closes her eyes, and takes a deep breath.

"You alright?"

"Just a little dizzy. I'm fine. I didn't eat dinner."

My heart picks up, but I make my face go blank. I don't want her to catch on to my excitement. Dizziness is a pregnancy symptom, isn't it? *Holy fuck.*

I kiss the top of her head and step back when she seems steady, snagging a beer off the bar and pulling out my phone to order her food. If she's pregnant, she needs to be eating and if she won't take care of herself, I'll do it for her. "You watch my game tonight?"

She rolls her eyes, turning back to pour drinks for the guys that've lined up. "Of course I did. You know I always do."

I nod as a wave of satisfaction fills my chest. "Good girl."

She shoots me a glare over her shoulder, but there's a smile tugging at the corners of her lips. She loves it when I say shit like that, even if she pretends otherwise.

The guys start to disperse, heading out to the tables in back where they can drink and fuck around in peace. But I stay behind the bar, leaning against the counter, watching Cassidy work. Her movements are fluid, practiced as she pours drinks and takes orders. She's sexy as hell like this, confident and in control.

The guys are being obnoxious as fuck, trying to get me to come hang with them, so I push off the counter and head for Cassidy. I lean down to talk directly into her ear, letting my lips brush her skin as I do. "Come get me when you're done. I've got plans for you that involve a lot less clothing."

She shivers and I smirk, knowing that she'd drop to her

knees right here if I pulled my dick out. "And eat the food I ordered you when it shows up." I step back and make my way over to the guys, sliding into the booth next to Warren and setting my beer on the table.

Corbin and War are recounting plays from tonight's game, while King broods silently with his beer. My gaze drifts over the crowded bar, landing on Roman holding court at a table surrounded by puck bunnies. His eyes meet mine, cold and challenging.

Fuck that guy with a rusty skate blade.

I lean back in my seat, taking a swig of my beer as I watch him. He's been a prick since day one, but ever since our little bathroom confrontation, he's been more of an asshole than usual.

"You okay?" Sawyer asks, nudging me with his shoulder as he slides into the booth beside me. His hair's messy, he smells like some flowery perfume, and I'm pretty sure he's got lipstick smeared on his jaw. He smirks as I eye him.

I nod, turning my attention to my brother. "Yeah, I'm good. You blow off some steam?"

Sawyer opens his mouth to answer, but before he can, a shadow falls over the table.

I look up to find Morozov looming over the table like some supervillain about to launch into a monologue. "What the hell do you want?" I ask just as the back of my neck prickles and I know Cassidy's looking our way without having to see her.

"We need to talk," Roman says, his accent thicker than normal as his eyes dart to Sawyer and back to me. "Alone."

Warren snorts. "Anything you have to say to Vaughn, you can say in front of us."

Roman's jaw clenches, but he doesn't argue. "Fine." His eyes flick to somewhere behind me, or more likely someone based on the tingle spreading down my shoulders and into my back. "That girl's only looking to—"

"What girl?" Cassidy says from right behind me. I twist in my chair and hook my arm around her waist, pulling her into my lap. "Me?" She narrows her eyes up at Roman, whose nostrils flare like a bull. It's pretty funny, actually. "Are you talking about me?"

Roman scoffs, his gaze raking over her and the way I'm holding her against my body. "You know I am. You're nothing but a hockey groupie who's using Vaughn for his money and fame. I would know."

I stand, dropping Cassidy gently to the ground before I take a step toward Roman, curling my fingers into fists. It's Sawyer who catches my fist before I even register it's flown, and fuck my brother for knowing me so well. I'm breathing hard, my muscles tense as I fight the urge to beat Roman's face into an unrecognizable pile of meat and bone.

"Easy, Hay," Sawyer murmurs. "Not worth it."

Roman smirks and then turns his attention to my girlfriend. "I'm calling in your debt, babe. Twenty grand by tomorrow morning or I'm taking your bar as collateral," Roman says as a parting shot as he turns and moves to leave the bar, stopping only long enough to snag a girl for each arm on his way out.

"Hey, Dickhead," I call out and Roman turns. I smirk because that's all I'm going to call him from now on and when he realizes it, his smug expression melts into a scowl. *Sucker.* "Give me an hour and you'll have your money."

"Like I said... using you for your money," Morozov sneers, needing to get in the last word.

Everyone that was watching our little scene starts to disburse, and before Cassidy can stop me, I'm on the phone with my accountant arranging the transfer. I'm not about to let that jackass hold any power over my future wife. This is what I should've done from the beginning.

When it's done, I turn back to my girl. She looks like she's reached a new level of pissed, and I grin because the hate sex should be next level hot.

"What did you do?" she snaps, her eyes narrowed as she glares up at me. "I don't need you to do this. I can figure something out." Behind her anger, though, I see how upset she is with Roman's words. With the idea of losing this bar. I step closer to her and she deflates. "I'll pay you back."

I shrug, falling back into my seat and pulling her with me. "Why? It's just money. I've got more than I could spend in this lifetime." Especially with the trust fund my grandfather set up for Sawyer and me, but she doesn't know about that. No one but my brother and our father do.

Her jaw clenches, and she shakes her head. "I hate that you just did that, but thank you."

I wrap my arm around her waist, holding her to me and wondering if she's got my baby inside of her. My fingers stroke against her stomach. "Anything for you, Princess."

She sighs and relaxes against me. We both know we're fucked up, that this obsession between us goes too deep to be healthy. But I'm not about to stop it and it doesn't seem like she is either.

"But if you're dead set on settling this debt, I take payment in the form of blow jobs," I say, and her smile as she smacks me in the chest is everything.

Every good goddamn thing in this world.

And I'll do anything to keep it.

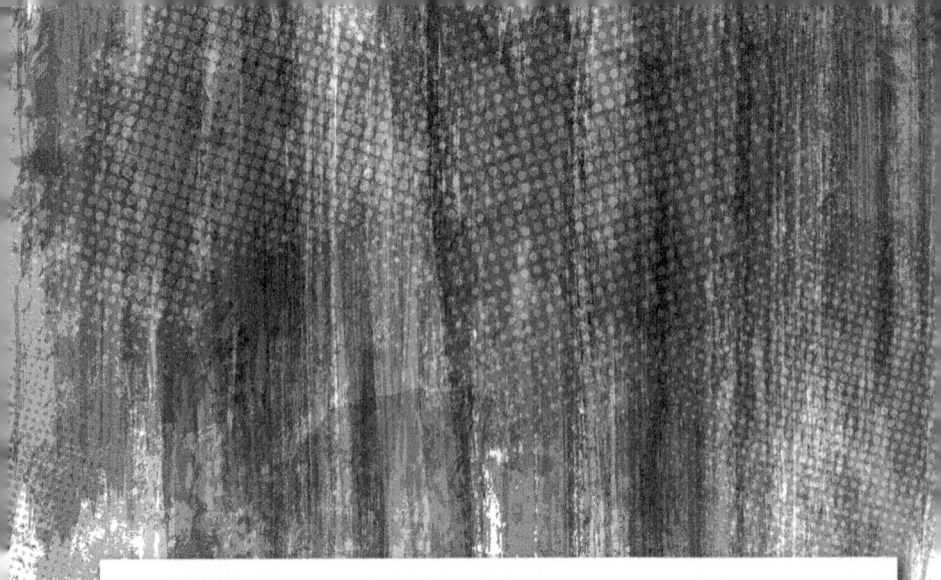

Will
@PenaltyBoxPoet

29 hit a guy so hard last night, dude's GPS recalibrated. #Rerouting

Hayden #33

THE FIRST SLIVER of morning light cuts through the darkness, painting a lazy stripe across the room. It climbs up Cassidy's bare shoulder and I want to trace it with my tongue. Her body is tangled with mine, the heat from her skin seeping into me, branding me with a possessive fire that roars in my veins.

"Morning," her voice is husky, a vibration against my chest that sends a jolt straight down to my dick.

I run my fingers up and down her arm, savoring the way her body shivers under my touch. "Morning, Princess."

She shifts, rolling over so she can face me.

I watch her face, searching for any sign of regret, waking up here with me, but all I see is a sleepy contentment. Satisfied, I kiss her on the forehead.

My girl. In my bed. In my house.

Our house.

"Sleep okay?" I ask, even though I know the answer. I didn't let her go all night, kept her close enough to feel every breath, every soft sigh. Protection and possession, all rolled into one. Exactly what I've been craving since the second I met her. Before that, even.

"Like the dead." Her smile tugs at something primal in me. "Your bed's dangerous."

"Good dangerous?"

"Very. I never want to leave."

I chuck the covers aside, and she playfully protests, but there's laughter in her eyes, a spark that wasn't there when Roman had her cornered last night. That hasn't been there since I met her. She deserves this. To be happy, carefree, and fucking loved like she deserves. And if I'm the one who can give those things to her, even better.

I lean over her, caging her body beneath me as I press my lips to hers. She tastes like mine. Her hands slide up my back, pulling me closer as she deepens the kiss.

I love the way she responds to me, like she can't get enough of me either. I pull away and smack her on the ass. "Time to get up."

She groans and grabs my pillow, shoving it down on her face. "Nope. Too early."

"I'll make you breakfast," I say, dangling my words like a donut on a string, trying to entice her.

She drops the pillow only enough for me to see her messy hair and a single green eye. "Will there be bacon?"

"Is this a negotiation?"

She grins, peeking out from under the pillow. "Maybe."

I roll off her and sit on the edge of the bed, stretching my arms over my head. I feel her eyes on me and turn to find her checking me out. I grin. "Nah, I don't think you have any better offers. C'mon, Princess."

I reach down and pick her up, throwing her over my shoulder and slapping her once on the ass. She's in one of my t-shirts and some underwear that look like a tiny pair of shorts.

It's sexy as hell and I run my palm over the curve of her ass while I walk us to the kitchen.

I drop her onto the counter, and she hisses as her ass hits the cold marble.

"Strawberry banana or mango blueberry?" I call over my shoulder while I reach for the blender. Anticipation tightens my stomach. I've got plans for us, for this morning, for the rest of our goddamn lives. And it starts with what I'm mixing into her drink.

"Never took you for a smoothie guy," Cassidy teases. I glance back at her, her hair a wild mess around her shoulders, and I'm hit with this intense need to spend every morning for the next fifty years this exact way.

"Yeah, well, can't really argue with what works," I say, flexing and running my hand down my abs. "Are you gonna tell me what you want, or am I picking for you?"

It takes longer than I expected for her to tear her eyes off my six-pack and when she meets mine, her cheeks are pink. Fucking cute. "Uh, strawberry banana." She wrinkles her nose. "I hate mangoes."

"Full of surprises," I shoot back with a grin, dropping the ingredients into the blender. The fruit, the almond milk, the protein powder—they're just for show. It's the little capsules of Letrozole and prenatal vitamins that are my real focus. Sawyer gave them to me, his knowing look saying he didn't need to ask why. He gets it.

This is about legacy, about claiming my territory, making something permanent between Cassidy and me.

"This doesn't mean I'm going to start working out with you in the mornings," Cassidy warns, leaning against the counter, eyes bright with amusement.

"I don't know, you might come around," I say, pressing the button on the blender. The machine whirs to life, a loud, satisfying growl that matches the hunger inside me. I pour the thick liquid into two glasses even though I'm not going to drink mine, handing one over to her. She takes a sip, her lips closing around the rim in a way that has me thinking of other things she could be doing with that mouth.

"Delicious," she murmurs, and I can't help but wonder how she'll taste later, when I have her beneath me again, doing my best to knock her up.

"Drink up," I urge, watching her throat work as she swallows. Each gulp is another step closer to what I want. A future where she's tied to me, carrying my child, wearing my ring.

"Thanks," she says, setting down the empty glass. There's a glow to her, a light that wasn't there before she stepped into my world. It's addictive, that shine. Makes me want to keep her lit up like this forever.

"Anytime," I tell her, and I mean it. I'll break every rule, defy every expectation to make her mine, to breed her, to wipe away any trace of Roman or anyone else who ever touched her before me.

Cassidy doesn't know the full game plan yet. Doesn't realize that every move, every touch, every word is me playing for keeps.

"You know what this makes you, right? Living here?" I ask, leaning against the counter and flexing my abs as I watch her gaze roam over my shirtless body, lingering on my black boxers and the ink of her name peeking out of them before sliding back up.

"What?"

"My girlfriend," I say with a grin. "At least until I can convince you to be my wife."

Her eyes widen, a flicker of surprise there, before she bites her lip, considering. "That's... ballsy, just putting it out there like that," she says, but the way her body leans into mine tells me she's not put off by the idea.

"Is it?" I challenge, letting my hand glide up to cup her chin, tilting her head for a kiss that's all about telling her without words I'm fucking serious. Serious as game seven overtime in the Stanley Cup Playoffs. "I think it's inevitable."

She doesn't argue, melting into the kiss, and I can feel the shift, the silent agreement passing between us. It's a win, another step closer to making sure she never walks away.

She jumps off the counter and tells me she's crawling back in bed, so I dump my smoothie down the drain and rinse out the blender to make another before I meet Sawyer in the gym.

I bite back a grin as the blender whirs. It's all coming together.

Soon enough, Cassidy will give me the one thing that'll make our connection unbreakable.

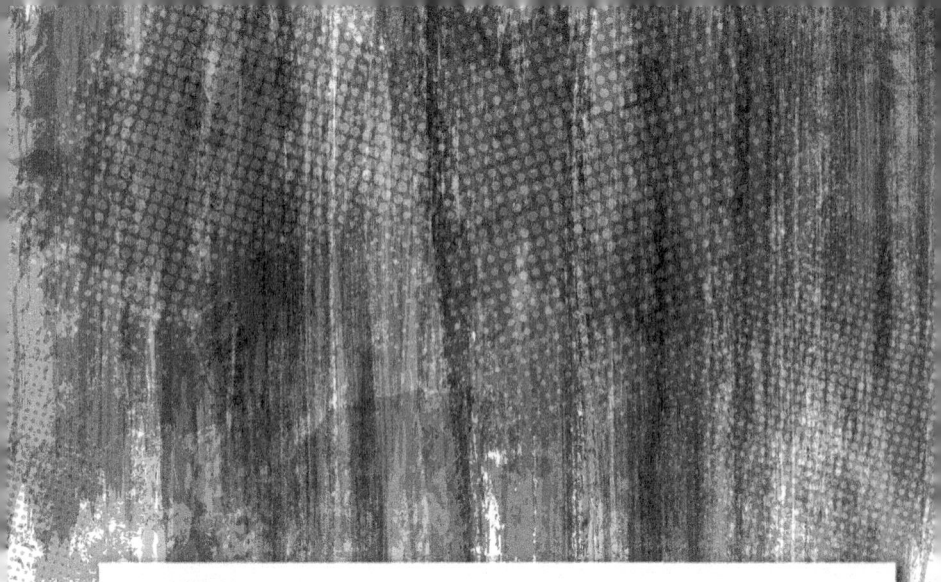

eat me
@RinksideRuffian

Every time Vaughn hits someone, an angel gets its wings. Just kidding, they get a fucking concussion. #Savage

Hayden #34

SWEAT DRIPS down my back as I slam the weights onto the rack, the clang echoing in my home gym's high ceilings. Sawyer's on the bench next to me, pushing through his own set, muscles straining under inked skin, hair pulled back in a bun.

No one would ever suspect my perfect doctor brother has all those tattoos under his white lab coat and tailored button downs.

"So you got Cassidy moved in?" he asks, setting the bar back on the rack and sitting up. "That was fast."

I shrug. "She didn't have much to move. And you know how it is when you throw money at a problem. The movers handled it."

Sawyer nods like he understands. He knows more about my obsession with her than anyone else, including her. "And Roman?"

"What about him?" I ask, my jaw tight as I think about that motherfucker.

Sawyer smirks. "You're not going to do anything about him? After last night?"

I shrug, picking up a towel and wiping it over my face. "I'm not sure yet if he's worth the effort."

"You sure about that? You think paying him off's going to make him go away?" Sawyer asks, raising an eyebrow. "He just lost the only leverage he had over Cassidy. I doubt he's going to take that shit lying down." Sawyer wipes his face on his shirt. "He seems like he has a fixation on your girl, the same way you do. The difference is she wants you. He knows it and I doubt he's going to let it go."

"If he doesn't back off, I'll kill him," I say, meaning every word, but I want to break something at the thought of him starting more shit in the meantime.

Sawyer nods like he expected me to say that. This is why I love my brother. He just gets me. He doesn't try to talk me out of it, and I know if I have a body to bury, he'll be right there with me, with dirt on his hands and a bullshit alibi. "And how's operation knock up your girlfriend going? You need more pills?"

I grin at my brother. "Nah, I'm good. She's been passing out for naps and getting dizzy randomly for a couple of days, so I think it might've worked."

"You want me to test her?"

"Not yet, but soon. I'll let you know when I figure out how I want to handle it. I'm not ready for her to find out."

Sawyer laughs, shaking his head. "I love when you unleash your inner psycho." He grabs a towel and wipes it over his chest. "I've got today off. What're we doing?"

I move over to the stationary bike, climbing on and hitting the button to start. "A bunch of the team's coming over and we're watching the Storm-Armada game tonight. I wanted to introduce Cassidy officially and make sure they know she's off-limits."

"You don't think she'll slap the shit out of you for that?" Sawyer asks, moving to the treadmill across from me.

"Oh, she might try, but that's not gonna stop me. Those assholes will hit on anything with a pulse. She'll just have to deal with it."

"You going to tell her you've been slipping those pills into her smoothies every morning?"

"Nah, I like my balls where they are."

Sawyer starts up a jog, and we get lost in our workouts and the thumping bass of his playlist blasting out of the speakers. After a couple of songs, he uses his smartwatch to turn the volume down.

"Is Mattson coming over tonight?"

I eye my brother, shaking my head. Sweat drips down my hair and into my eyes, and I grab a towel to deal with it. "Can't you wait until the offseason to try to fuck my teammate?"

"C'mon, Hay-Hay. Invite him."

"Dude, last time you fucked around with one of my teammates, you ghosted him and he got all weepy and obsessed. Then shit was weird on the ice until I got traded here. It fucked with the team chemistry."

Sawyer rolls his eyes. "That was one time. Besides, Mattson is a big boy. He can handle himself."

I laugh, knowing that Sawyer will get his way eventually, so I might as well save myself the hassle and invite Torin over tonight. "He's also straight." I level my brother with a look, but honestly, he indulges my crazy, so the least I can do is indulge his. "I'll invite him. Don't make me regret it. I want the Cup this year."

Sawyer's grin is smug as fuck as he turns up his music and starts running again.

I shake my head, but I can't help but smile. Asshole knows I'd do anything for him.

Hours later, after a shower and helping Cassidy fill up the

empty half of my closet with her clothes, the game's turned up on the sound system and the rowdy shit talking of my teammates fills my living room.

A cold beer in hand, I lean against the kitchen island, taking it all in. My teammates are sprawled across the sofas, eyes glued to the flatscreen where the Storm are duking it out with the Armada. Sawyer's watching Mattson more than the game and I shake my head at him when he catches my eye from across the room.

We're playing the Storm in our next away series, so we're watching for intel we can use to kick their ass on their home ice.

Cassidy walks into the kitchen and I pull her into my side, kissing her temple and breathing her in. I'm addicted to the smell of her shampoo and can't get enough. It's better than a benzo at calming me the hell down.

She looks up at me with a smile that makes my chest tighten. In my t-shirt and some leggings, she looks like she belongs here. She didn't dress up for the guys and isn't desperate for their attention, which is what I was afraid of when I first invited them over.

I should've known better. She's not like that.

I lean down, pressing my lips to hers in a quick kiss that's more possessive than anything else, with my fingers digging into her jaw enough to tilt her face the way I want. "You good?"

She nods, leaning back against the counter next to me. "They're... intense."

I laugh, taking a swig of my beer before passing her the non-alcoholic mixed drink I poured for her before she walked in here. She's a bartender, chances are she'll notice. Hopefully she just thinks I'm shitty at mixing drinks and pour light because I'm not letting her drink a drop of alcohol tonight. Not when she could be pregnant already. "Yeah, hockey players are like that."

"Gee, I never noticed owning a *hockey bar* and everything." Her grin could level cities with the amount of punch it has. Then she breaks eye contact to look around the room. "It's kind of hot the way they're so... passionate."

Jealousy flares inside of me like a tornado of fire, consuming everything good and rational in its path. "Don't get any ideas," I growl, pulling her back against me.

She laughs and smacks my chest, but I can see the heat in her eyes. She likes it when I'm jealous, likes that I'm so fucking obsessed with her.

"I'm a total idiot for it, but you're the only one I want, Hayden," she says, and it's all I need to hear to calm down.

"How about we clear this shit up right now?" I say, wrapping my arm around Cassidy and steering her into the living room.

"Guys," I call out, voice slicing through the noise. Heads turn, attention snagged by the edge in my tone. "This is Cassidy." I tip my head in her direction and squeeze her tighter to me. "My girlfriend."

The guys nod, murmuring greetings as they look back at the game. But I can see the way their eyes linger on her, the way they size her up. Check her out.

I tighten my grip on her and she side-eyes the fuck out of me for it.

I try to calm down by reminding myself they don't know what she looks like naked or how good she tastes when she comes on my tongue. They don't know how tight her pussy is or how she moans my name when I fuck her so hard she walks funny the next day.

I'm about to make sure it stays that way... unless they find her OnlyFans. Fuck.

"You fuckers touch her and I'll break your fingers," I say, loud enough for everyone to hear while I sink into the couch and pull Cassidy down onto my lap. "Got it?"

There's a chorus of *yeahs* and middle fingers in my direction, but I don't miss the way they eye Cassidy. I can't really blame them. My future wife is hot as fuck.

"Nice to see you again," War says, tipping his beer in salute. Somehow, I forgot that some of these guys probably met her before at the bar, or when she was dating Roman. I try to block that shit from my mind and pretend it never happened.

"Damn, Vaughn. She's out-of-your-league hot." Corbin earns a glare from me that has him raising his hands in surrender. Who the fuck says something like that right in front of me? "I mean, respectfully. In a non-sexual way."

I nod while the guys laugh, taking a swig of beer, refocusing on the game. The Armada's breakout passes are sloppy as hell. We'll feast on turnovers next week.

Mattson gestures at the screen. "Their goalie's a sieve. Five hole all day."

We all watch the screen as the Storm's winger, Bouchard, slides a shot right between the goalie's legs.

"Called it." Sawyer holds out his beer and Torin clinks it with my brother's, grinning at Sawyer and not realizing he's falling straight into his trap.

Cassidy leans forward, her eyes fixed on the TV. She's ignoring all my jackass teammates in favor of the game, the way it should be. "Karlsson's always been weak at blocking the five-hole." She smirks up at me and I grin.

Five hole.

Chuckles ripple through the room. I set my beer down and stretch my arm along the back of the couch, muscles flexing. My other hand's wrapped around Cassidy's thigh.

"Yeah, dude's gonna be seeing pucks flying past his pads in his nightmares after we light him up," I say.

"Shit, the Storm's defense is looking tight tonight," Kingston mutters.

Warren snorts. "Not as tight as your mom was last night."

Kingston flips him off and the rest of us laugh and throw pillows at War.

Cassidy relaxes back into me and I breathe her in. This right here is something I never had with my last team and didn't know I needed until right now.

On screen, the Armada's top scorer, Jensen, weaves through the defense and rips an answering wrist shot top shelf.

"Damn," Gabe mutters from the recliner. "We gotta shut that kid down."

Torin nods, his eyes glued to the game, which is no doubt pissing my brother off. "No doubt. He's got wheels for days."

Cruz nods at the screen. "See that? Armada's defense is sloppy on the transition. We could exploit that."

"Yeah, just like you exploited that 'open net' last game, huh?" Warren grins at him, and Gabe rolls his eyes, smacking War in the face with a pillow.

The guys groan and start chirping about the Armada's shitty defense.

Cassidy reaches for a slice of pizza from the box on the table, but I don't let her get far. I wrap my arms around her waist, pulling her back against my chest as we watch the game. She's comfortable here with my teammates, relaxed and happy. And I'm realizing that she fits in my life just as perfectly as I do in hers.

And if she doesn't like it, well... she's not going anywhere.

"Refill?" I ask, already moving to grab her glass before she can answer, and meeting Sawyer's gaze, telling him with my eyes to keep an eye on her so none of the guys fuck with her while I'm gone. Then, I head to the kitchen and mix up another non-alcoholic fruity drink, handing it back and watching her sip it. Can't have anything messing with what might be growing inside her—my legacy.

Anchor's Aweigh

1 oz navy rum • 1 oz white rum • 1 oz blue curaçao • 2 oz pineapple juice • 1 oz coconut cream • ice
Garnish: pineapple spear and cherry

Blend all ingredients with ice until smooth. Pour into a hurricane glass and garnish with a pineapple spear and cherry.

Cassidy #35

"COME ON, PRINCESS," Hayden coaxes, his voice a low rumble that vibrates through my body as he wraps his arms around my waist from behind. I'm drying my hair after a shower that probably got me dirtier than it did clean, since Hayden can't keep his hands off me. Not that I'm complaining. "You love the Anchors." He presses his lips to my neck and I shiver, meeting his dark eyes in the mirror. "You'll get to see me in action. I'm hot in my uniform."

I bat my eyelashes obnoxiously into the mirror. "You mean what I just experienced in the shower wasn't you in action?"

His grin is devious, his teeth flashing white. "That was just a warmup."

I laugh and shake my head, turning back to the mirror and ignoring the hard dick now pressing against my hip. My boyfriend has crazy stamina, and I can't seem to get enough. "No way am I going to your hockey game without Sawyer."

Hayden's arms tighten around me, and he growls low in his throat. "Why not?"

"Because you'll be on the ice surrounded by thousands of screaming women who'll do anything to get your attention," I say, rolling my eyes. "And I don't want to go to jail for murder." I don't tell him how the team WAGs dropped me like I was less than nothing the second Roman cheated and now that I see them for who they are, I want no part of their little clique.

In other words, I need a shield. Or backup. Whatever.

Hayden spins me around and pins me against the bathroom counter, his eyes blazing with heat and something darker that sends a shiver through my body. "Is my little liar jealous," his voice is rough as he leans down, nipping at my neck, "even though you're the only one I see?" I feel his grin against my skin. "That's hot as fuck."

I shove him back with a laugh, but he doesn't move an inch. "I'm not jealous."

His smirk says he doesn't believe me, but I can't help it. The thought of being in Anchors Arena surrounded by all those screaming women makes me want to stay home and watch the game on TV.

Or stab someone—repeatedly.

But Hayden's been trying to convince me for the last couple of weeks, and I've held out so far.

"I want my girl there cheering me on," he says, tucking a strand of hair behind my ear. His fingers linger, tracing down my jaw. "C'mon, Princess. If I get Sawyer to agree to go, will you be there?"

He sees me wavering and his eyes light up because I'm about to give in. Stupid freaking big-dicked asshole.

A grin tugs at his lips. "Sawyer!" he bellows, walking out of the bathroom into our bedroom in nothing but a pair of black boxers. His ass is legit a work of art.

A few seconds later, his brother pokes his head into the room, hair pulled up in its usual messy bun.

"What's up?" Sawyer asks, looking from Hayden to me and back to his brother.

"You're coming with Cassidy to the game tonight," Hayden tells him, ever the bossy asshole.

Sawyer raises an eyebrow at me, and I shrug. "I need a buffer."

Hayden scoffs, but Sawyer just laughs. "Between...? You and Roman? You gonna pound his face in, Slugger?"

I roll my eyes when Hayden opens his mouth and my moment of weakness falls out. "No, I'll deal with Morozov. She's jealous because half the crowd wants to fuck me."

Sawyer laughs, this dark, raspy chuckle. "We're going to have so much fun, Cass," he says, winking before turning to his brother. "But if I go to jail defending your woman, you're paying my bail."

Hayden nods, looking relieved that I'm giving in. "Obviously, bro."

Sawyer grins and disappears back into his room down the hall.

"You're lucky you're hot and good in bed," I mutter, crossing my arms over my chest.

Hayden's grin is smug as he pulls me into him. "Damn right." He kisses me hard and deep until I forget why I was even mad at him in the first place. "Imagine how wet it'll make you to see me dominating on the ice."

I sigh, knowing he's right. I've seen Hayden play on TV and he's incredible. Fast and agile, with a shot that has me wondering if he's part sniper or something. There's a reason they call him The Hitman. Seeing it in person might just turn me into a puddle like that melting emoji. That'll be me by the end of his game, I just know it.

"Fine, I'll go," I sigh like I'm doing him a huge favor when in reality, I've loved the Anchors since I was a kid and haven't had a chance to see them play in person since things ended with my asshat ex. For a minute there, I thought he might've ruined the team for me and there was something crushing about that I didn't want to examine. When my dad died, the bar and the Anchors were all I had left of him and Roman almost cost me one and I'm not about to let him take the other.

Hayden grins, kissing me again before disappearing into the closet to get dressed before the game. When he steps back out, he's in a tailored suit I'm tempted to rip off.

The man is hot as fuck in joggers and a t-shirt, but in a suit?

Shit, am I drooling?

"Don't look at me like that, Princess," he warns, his voice a low rumble as dangerous as a thunderstorm. A shiver runs down my spine and my nipples tighten in a way I'm sure he can see through the t-shirt I threw on after our shower. "I don't have time to fuck you right now."

Hayden's phone buzzes on top of the dresser and he groans, running a hand down his face. "That's my alarm. I've gotta go."

"Have fun," I say, blowing him a kiss as he walks out the door. "Bash some heads in!" His laugh carries down the hall as he leaves.

I take my time getting ready, knowing I'll need the armor for this. I slip on a skirt over tights since the arena will be cold, then grab an old jersey from the back of the closet. Roman's number 22 is the only one I've got, and an idea starts to form as I look down at it. Hayden's insanely possessive and seeing me in my ex's jersey instead of his is going to push every single one of his buttons.

I can't wait to see what he'll do. I shrug it on, grinning like the Grinch and trying not to cackle as I think about what's going to happen when he sees me in this thing. For the first time, I'm glad I didn't burn it when Roman cheated.

I don't really like makeup, but I dig out the good shit as I cover my face with war paint. By the time I'm done, I'm flawless. There's no way I won't run into some of the bitchy WAGs at the game, and I don't want to face them unless I can go toe to toe. I feel sort of like a clown with the contouring and the fake lashes and everything, but this is the expected uniform.

Gross, I know.

When I finally step out of the bedroom and meet Sawyer by the front door, he whistles as he looks me over. "My brother's going to kill someone tonight," he says with a laugh. "You're gonna be one hell of a distraction." Then his eyes linger on the jersey, and he grins.

"What?" I ask, looking down at myself, playing dumb. I know exactly what I'm doing—playing with fire.

"Nothing," he says, but the look in his eyes, so much like Hayden's, tells me everything I need to know about what's going to happen when Hayden sees me with Roman's name and number on my body.

I blink at him, trying to stay neutral. "Do I need to change?"

He shakes his head. "Nope. Get in," he jerks his chin toward a low slung black sports car that looks like it costs more than my apartment building.

I slide into the passenger seat and his laughter follows me in. Yeah, this is going to be fun.

Blueline Blast

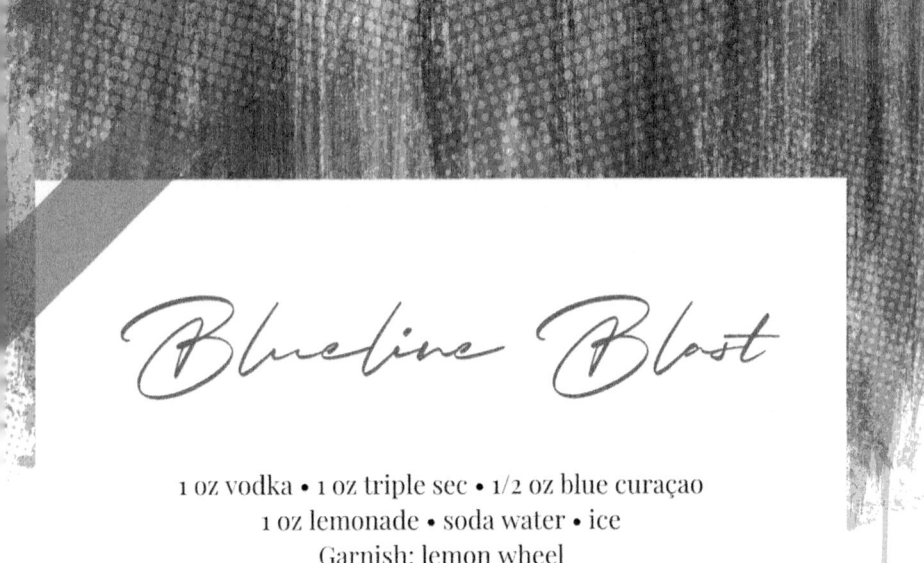

1 oz vodka • 1 oz triple sec • 1/2 oz blue curaçao
1 oz lemonade • soda water • ice
Garnish: lemon wheel

Shake vodka, triple sec, blue curaçao, and lemonade with ice. Strain into a glass filled with ice, top with soda water, and garnish with a lemon wheel.

Cassidy #36

I FORGOT how much I love this.

The smell of freshly carved ice and popcorn fills the air and I inhale until my lungs are full.

I've kept my distance from watching the Anchors live in their arena ever since Roman screwed me over.

I've been hesitant to come back because this was something sacred from my childhood, something I shared with my father. Once he died, I wasn't sure I'd ever step foot back in this place again. Then Roman walked into my bar one night and the rest is history.

Say what you want about the guy, but he can be persuasive at the best of times and downright manipulative at the worst.

I went to my fair share of Anchors games last season. I embraced that whole WAG lifestyle, or at least I tried to as much as they would let me.

It sort of felt like being the new kid in the middle of the year in high school. You walk into the cafeteria and all you see is a sea of cliques who are already well established, and you just don't know where you fit in.

That was me last year as Roman's shiny new girlfriend.

When Hayden mentioned me coming to his game tonight, sure I thought about the environment, the energy of the crowd, getting to see him on the ice, but really, I didn't want to come because I was dreading running into the wives and girlfriends.

Sawyer shoves an enormous tub of popcorn into my arms and snaps me out of my thoughts. He's got his arms loaded with all sorts of junk and I look at him dubiously. "I can't believe you eat this crap and still look like that."

He laughs, ripping open a pack of licorice and shoving one into his mouth. It's not even the red ones. It's the disgusting black kind. "That's why I spend so much time in the gym so I can eat whatever the hell I want on game days." His voice comes out garbled around the half-chewed food inside, and I wrinkle my nose at him as he pats his abs.

"I thought it was so you could fuck anyone and everyone."

"That, too." He gives me a flirty grin, and I shove a piece of his gross licorice up his nose. He chokes and sneezes and spills some of his popcorn on the floor, promising retaliation.

Eventually, we make our way to our seats. I try to keep my head down as we walk toward the glass because you never know where the WAGs might be or if they'll pop up like one of those jump scare videos to give me a heart attack.

We're sitting to the left of the penalty box and I have a pretty good view of the Anchors bench, which means I'll get to thirst over Hayden for the entire game. Honestly? Can't wait.

Sawyer and I sink into the seats, and, yep, we bought too much food. There's really nowhere to keep it. These seats are close together and there's only so much space. I'm just about to tell Sawyer that he better get eating and do it fast because I don't want to have to manage his snacks while trying to pay attention to the game when the Anchors skate onto the ice.

Hayden's the one who set up our seats, so his gaze locks onto me almost immediately. The look in his eyes, under his visor, is so intense I melt into the seat a little. He was right. Seeing him live in person in his element is a whole new level of hot.

Sawyer must have fished an ice cube out of his soda because my attention is ripped away from Hayden by the icy wetness he's just put down the back of my shirt. I squeal as the frozen block slides down the back of my neck and into the jersey that I'm wearing. I jump up and try to shake it out, cussing out Sawyer the whole time.

My boyfriend's brother is laughing his ass off, but someone bangs into the glass in front of us and I jump because it's so loud. I turn back to look at Hayden, standing on the other side. His face is thunderous as he stares at my chest. I bite my cheek to keep from grinning, wishing I could shove some of that popcorn in my mouth, too, while I watch the fireworks as Hayden realizes I'm wearing Roman's jersey.

"You think I pissed him off enough to break through the glass?"

Sawyer eyes me with a new appreciation. "You did this on purpose?" Then he chuckles while he looks back and forth between a fuming Hayden and me.

"What?" I shrug, eyeing Hayden, whose jaw is clenched so tight, I bet his teeth hurt. "Don't act like you don't love a little chaos, too. And honestly, the sex is so hot when he's angry, I'm sort of addicted to pissing him off." Shit, I regret my words immediately, turning back to Sawyer. "Do not tell him I said that."

"No promises," Sawyer somehow manages to get out around a mouthful of snacks. I turn back to my boyfriend, who's glaring at me with eyes so dark they're practically black.

He takes off his glove and crooks his finger for me to come closer to the glass. I lick my lips and ignore the tingles spreading through my body.

I move before I even have time to think about it, stepping down the couple of stairs to get to the glass.

Hayden mouths something at me, but I can't quite make out what he's trying to say. So I yell, "What?"

He points at my jersey, and he says, "Take it the fuck off."

No mistaking it this time.

I shake my head because I have nothing else to wear. And the tank top that I've got on underneath is not even close to warm enough for this arena. Plus, the more I resist, the angrier he'll get. It's like my body's programmed to respond in the horniest way possible to his irritation, and I press my thighs together.

"Now," he repeats.

"I don't have anything else to wear," I yell because I know that he probably can't hear me very well. But he must understand what I say because he immediately drops his other glove onto the ice, unclasps his helmet and drops it, too, and then reaches for the hem of his warm-up jersey. He strips it off, tossing it over the glass at me.

I catch it and gotta be honest, it's damp and smells like sweat and a hint of Hayden's cologne. Not exactly something I want to put on my body, but now people are starting to pay attention to us. I may have wanted his attention, but I don't want everyone else's.

"Your turn," he mouths at me. His coach and his teammates are taking notice of him not doing the warm-ups he should be, and I can feel my cheeks heat.

Instead of fighting with him anymore, I just say fuck it and I strip it off. I've had my fun, and now, when the game's over, I'm sure he'll get his payback. I shiver, and it's not from the cold. He gestures for me to throw it over the glass to him. I do, hurriedly putting on the jersey that he threw at me and trying to ignore that it sticks to my skin.

When he looks back at me, the darkness in his face lightens a shade when he sees me in his jersey, the caveman, and he blows me a kiss before he skates off toward the bench with my Morozov jersey clutched in his fist. He didn't even pick up his gloves or helmet from the ice.

"I think I might love you," Sawyer says, making heart eyes at me as he sips his beer.

I smirk. "I dare you to say that to your brother."

He just laughs and holds out his bottle so I can clink my soda with his beer, and I do. "Hayden's got his hands full with you."

"Maybe it's me who has my hands full with him." Goosebumps ripple down my arms, and this time, it's not from sexual tension. "Hey, do you think there's enough time before the game starts for me to hit the shop? I don't want to wear this sweaty thing for the whole game. It's disgusting."

"Uh," he glances up at the jumbo screen hanging over the ice. "No, but we can go during the first intermission and get you one that's not soaked in Hayden's sweat."

The sound of collective gasps echoes through the arena as Hayden's fist connects with Roman's face, sending him sprawling onto the ice. His teammates rush forward to break it up, but it takes two guys to hold Hayden back while he yells something at Roman that I can't quite make out.

"Holy shit," Sawyer says next to me, his mouth full of popcorn again. How much was in that bucket? "That was fucking epic."

Roman gets to his feet, his nose bloody and a cut on his cheek, but he looks more pissed than anything else. He lunges for Hayden again, but a few of their teammates pull him away. Hayden's coach is on the ice barking orders and Hayden disappears into the locker room.

"I should've known you'd be the cause of a scene like that."

My spine goes straight and my whole body tenses like I'm bracing for battle. Sawyer abandons his popcorn to toss his arm over my shoulder before turning his head to look back at Tatiana Petrovich, wife of the Anchors' fourth line center, Kyle.

Also known as the head bitch in charge of the WAGs.

And the last person I ever wanted to see again.

Stick Save

2 oz gin • 1 oz Aperol • 1 oz grapefruit juice • 1/2 oz lime juice • ice
Garnish: grapefruit slice

Shake gin, Aperol, grapefruit juice, and lime juice with ice. Strain into a chilled cocktail glass and garnish with a grapefruit slice.

Cassidy #37

TATIANA LOOKS me up and down, her eyes lingering on Hayden's jersey, before she finally opens her mouth. "I hear you've found a new player for the season. Good for you." Her voice is cold and patronizing, and I bristle as she looks down her nose at me. She's got a face that looks like it's been through about five different plastic surgeries and she's dressed like she just walked off the cover of Vogue. Maybe she doesn't realize she's at a hockey game.

For some reason, being around her leaves me feeling small, and I hate that.

"Fuck off, Tanya," Sawyer says in a bored tone, and how the hell does he even know her?

"It's Tatiana."

Sawyer ignores her, and she stiffens before flipping her long dark hair over her shoulder. Then, she smiles with all her teeth before turning her attention to me again. "So what? You're going to be one of those girls who hooks herself to players just for the attention? Or maybe it's the money."

Sawyer laughs. "Like you're any different."

Tatiana's eyes flash and I can feel her rage from here. It's like those waves of heat that rise off a desert road. "I'm not a fucking groupie," she snaps, looking back at me. "But I guess you are, huh, Cassidy?"

I don't answer because I know anything I say will just make things worse. She wants a reaction out of me, but I will not give her one. Instead, I just stare at her, my face blank.

"You think you're special because Hayden Vaughn gave you a little attention? You think he'll stick around once he gets bored?" She keeps going, I'm sure hoping to get a rise out of me. What's the point of arguing with her? She means nothing. I don't want to be her friend. In fact, I'd be happy if I never had to think of her again.

I'd be lying if I said her words didn't chip away my insecurities, though. My gaze slides to where Hayden's standing by the bench and I find him already watching me with narrowed eyes. He mouths something that looks like *you okay?* and I nod before turning back to Tatiana.

She's still ranting, but I've tuned her out. She's not worth my time or energy, and Sawyer seems to agree because he's got his phone out and is scrolling through it while she talks.

"Enough, Tamara," he finally says, having enough with her shit talking. "You've got no room to criticize anyone considering you were on your knees for me at Cassidy's bar two weeks ago. Or were you too drunk to remember that? Shittiest blowie I've ever had, by the way, and before you I thought there was no way to fuck it up. So congrats. Now take your ass implants and your fake tits somewhere else. Cass and I want to watch the game." Sawyer looks out over the ice, gaze lingering on Torin Mattson. "Unless you want your husband to know you're using your side pieces to fund your coke habit?"

Tatiana's face goes white and then red as she spins on her heel and stomps away like a child who didn't get her way.

Sawyer turns back to me with a grin, but I just hold up my hand for a high five and laugh. "Damn. That was cold as hell."

He slaps my palm with his. "Yeah, but she deserved it. She's a raging bitch and you don't deserve that shit. Plus she legit tried to get me to buy her some coke after her shitty head like some common prostitute, yet she's here trying to tear you down." He shoves his phone back into his pocket and grabs another handful of popcorn as the lights dim for the national anthem. "Besides, Hayden would kick my ass if I didn't have your back."

After that, the puck drops and we get lost in the game. Sawyer and I cheer for Hayden when he gets an assist, but I keep thinking about what Tatiana said.

What if she's right about him getting bored? Maybe he'll move on to someone else once he's had his fill of me. The thought makes my stomach flip and my heart hurt, but I try to push it away as the game goes on.

Sawyer frowns down at his phone, fingers flying across the screen for probably the tenth time since we sat down. "What's going on?" I finally ask him when he huffs in annoyance beside me before shoving his phone back into his pocket.

"Nothing. Just the senator fucking up my mood with his usual demands."

I sip my Dr. Pepper, thinking about what that could mean. Finally, I decide to just ask. "What demands?"

"You know how you hear stories about people coming out and their parents kick them out?" I nod and he laughs, but it's humorless. "The Senator threw a party."

"Seriously?"

"Yep. One complete with a press conference for the perfect photo op and interview. Also, his rich donor friends. So many assholes with way too much money looking to throw it at a cause that makes them look progressive. Being bisexual makes me his automatic in with my demographic and he takes advantage any time he wears me down enough to give in."

I hear the bitterness in his voice and I can't blame him. It sounds like a nightmare. "I'm sorry."

He shrugs. "It is what it is. Hayden has it worse." Then he turns back to the game and we watch Hayden score on a slapshot that has the crowd on their feet. Sawyer and I jump up too, cheering as he skates around the ice with his arms raised in celebration while his teammates circle him.

"What could be worse than your own father using you?"

"Your father teaching you that the only way he could ever love you is if you're winning. The second you lose, all that love and attention disappear. It's the way he's always been with both of us, but Hayden more than me since he can get something else from me now."

"What do you mean?" I ask, confused.

"Hayden was always the one who had to win. Always had to be the best because it was the only way he got any attention or love from our dad. And when he started playing hockey, it was like a godsend for him. He could channel all that rage and frustration into something productive, and it gave him a way to prove himself to our dad. But it also meant that he never got to be a kid. Never got to have that feeling of unconditional love that all kids deserve."

"Where was your mom?" I ask, thinking about how my own mother showered me with love and affection when I was little. Warmth fills me before twisting into a sharp stab of pain at the loss, even all these years later.

Sawyer sighs. "She left when we were little. She couldn't handle being married to the senator and having to deal with his shit on a daily basis. She just packed up one day and left us with nannies and housekeepers. We didn't see her again until I was sixteen and she showed up at my graduation with a new husband and a new family."

"Wait. You graduated when you were sixteen?"

Sawyer grins, a real one this time, as he points at himself. "Smart as fuck."

I laugh, but then get lost in thoughts about everything Sawyer told me as we watch the Anchors crush the Armada. By the time the final buzzer sounds, the score's 8-2 and I'm horny as hell from watching Hayden in his element.

I wonder if this means I have a competence kink.

"Let's go wait by the locker room," Sawyer says, standing up and tossing the trash. I've got a bag from the gift shop with Hayden's sweaty jersey in it so at least the new one I'm wearing is clean and dry if I have to face the posse of hockey wives and girlfriends again down in the family waiting room.

When we get down by the locker room, I stop before we go into the room for the player's friends and family. "Can we stay out here? I'm not really in the mood for another run-in with Tatiana or her clones."

Sawyer nods, leaning against the wall as he scrolls through his phone again. "No problem. If they start shit, I've got no issue causing a scene."

I bump my shoulder into his as I settle into the spot beside him, crossing one foot over the other. "Thanks."

It doesn't take long before Roman's slamming out of the locker room doors with a brand new black eye and stitches along his chin. He glares at me and then Sawyer before storming off.

"What a douche," Sawyer mutters under his breath, and I can't help but agree.

Hayden comes out a few minutes later, freshly showered and looking hot as hell in his suit. His gaze finds me immediately, and he strides toward me with purpose. He grabs my face between his hands and kisses me hard and deep, making me forget about everything but him. When he pulls back, he looks down at my arm with his number on it and smirks. "I never want to see anyone else's name on your body but mine."

"What, a tattoo of your name isn't enough?" I say, caught in the intensity that's always between us, when I remember Sawyer. He's distracted by Hayden's teammate Torin, who just walked out of the locker room.

"No. It's not."

"And that's my cue to leave. See you at the bar," Sawyer says before pushing off the wall, shoving his hands in his pockets and walking off after Torin.

"Should we go make sure he doesn't do anything stupid?"

Hayden smirks. "Sawyer's a big boy, Princess. He can make his own mistakes." He runs his hand up my outer thigh and under the hem of my skirt before dropping it and grabbing my hand instead. "There's something I've always wanted to do," he murmurs into my ear before pulling back and looking down at me with a predatory glint in his eye. "You game?"

I don't even hesitate. "Hell yes. Show me."

And then he's dragging me into the unknown.

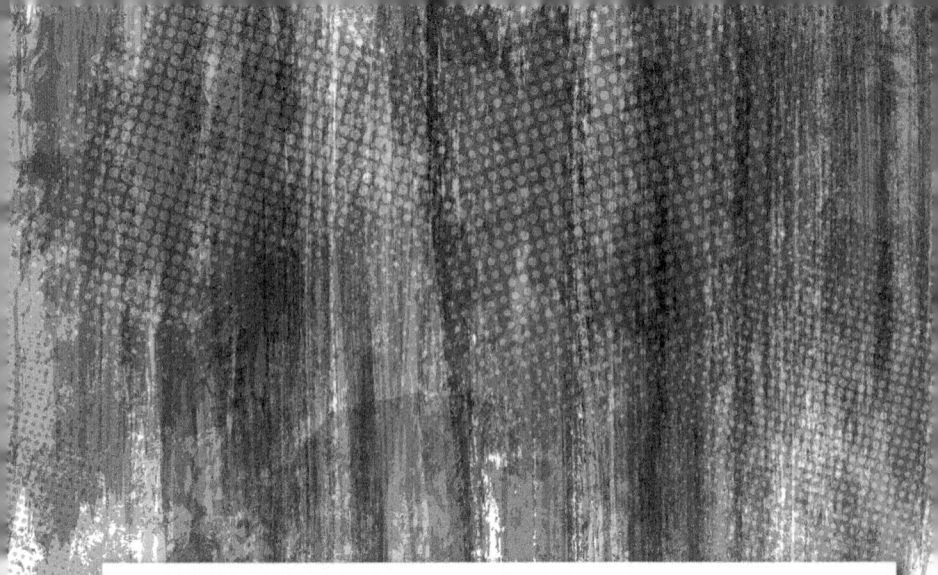

Sassy Pants
@SlapshotSass

I swear Vaughn's got more hits than my Spotify playlist. And they're all metal AF. #BrutalBeatdown

Hayden #38

CASSIDY DOESN'T KNOW IT, but after the game I slipped one of the arena's clean-up crew some cash to stay out of one of the upper sections of seats—all so I can play out a fantasy I've had since I met her.

When she showed up in Morozov's sweater tonight, I almost lost my shit. She knew exactly what that jersey meant and what seeing her in it did to me. But now that we're alone? It's my turn to remind her I own her ass.

That no one else gets to touch her, not in this life. Not in the next.

She's going to get a taste of what it means to wear me on her body, inside and out.

I lead her up the stairs and into the empty section, where I pull her down into one of the seats. Thank fuck she's wearing a skirt. That's going to make this easier.

"What are we doing here?" she asks, looking around at the empty space.

"You'll see," I say, grinning as I pull off my suit jacket and toss it over the back of the seat next to us. Then, I reach for her hips and tug her into my lap so she's straddling me.

"Hayden," she gasps, but I cut her off with a dirty kiss, stealing not just her breath but her will to resist. Her fingers dig into my hair as I fuck her with my tongue, tasting every inch of her mouth until she's grinding on me, her body begging for my dick.

I pull back, panting as I look at her, licking the taste of her off my lips. "I'm going to fuck you right here," I rasp, "so that every time I play in this arena, I get to replay the memory of you screaming my name. Hearing it echo across the ice. I want you to scream it loud enough that you never forget the only name that belongs on your body."

Her eyes widen and her cheeks flush as she looks around again. Every nerve in her body is on high alert, likely anticipating the inevitability of someone discovering us. But I give no fucks. I want to leave our imprint here, a memory that'll never fade.

Let them listen. Let them watch.

I hike her skirt up her hips, but she's wearing some sort of tights underneath. I'm too impatient to pull them down and off, so I rip through the thin material with a growl. She gasps, but then moans when my fingers shove her panties aside and find her clit already slippery. I groan as I slide two fingers inside her. "You feel that, Princess? How your body craves me?"

She nods, biting her bottom lip as she grinds down on my hand.

"Good," I say, pulling my fingers out of her and reaching for my zipper. My dick is already hard and ready for her. It springs free as soon as I get my pants open and my boxers pulled down just enough to let it out. "Now sit on my dick."

She lifts and sinks down onto me, and inch by inch, the

heat of her sucks me in. There's no thought in her head but me. No bullshit reminder to put on a condom.

It's perfect.

I grip her hips with a bruising force and thrust up into her tight, wet pussy until she's bouncing on my lap, her tits bouncing underneath the sweater with my name on it. Her hands grip the back of my seat as she rides me like she was born to do it.

When she comes, it's fucking beautiful. Her head falls back, her hair tumbling down her back as she moans my name loud enough to echo across the ice below us. It's enough to send me over the edge too, and I come inside of her, filling her up with everything I have.

She collapses against me, panting and sweaty, and I wrap my arms around her waist as I catch my breath. My dick's still hard inside of her and when she shifts, I groan. "Don't move yet," I tell her, tightening my grip.

If she's not already pregnant, I want to keep my cum inside of her as long as possible to help it do its job.

She laughs, but then leans back so she can look down at me. Her eyes are soft and warm as she reaches up to brush a strand of hair off my forehead. "You're crazy, Hayden Vaughn."

I grin at her. "I'm straight up insane for you."

She rolls her eyes and then leans forward to kiss me again. This time it's slow and sweet and I lose myself in everything Cassidy. The world disappears, and it's just her and me in this bubble I never want to leave. When she finally pulls back, she looks down between us where we're still joined. "We should probably clean up and get to the bar."

"Probably." I know she's right, but I don't want to take my dick out of her. If I could live inside of her like this, I would. I'd give up everything to make her my home. "But first..." I pull out my phone and open the camera app, handing it to her, needing to preserve this moment so later when I think back on it, I'll be able to look at her messy hair, swollen lips, and relaxed smile and know I did that to her. "Take a picture for me?"

Her cheeks flush as she takes it from me and holds it up, angling it so it gets both of us in the frame. I grunt as her pussy clenches around me when she moves to get the perfect shot. We're framed on the screen with a hint of the ice behind us. She snaps the photo, then hands me back my phone.

I look down at the screen and my stomach drops like I'm on a rollercoaster as I stare at us together. Or maybe those are butterflies. We look damn good, and our kids are going to be pretty as hell. "Perfect," I tell her, dropping a peck onto her lips before lifting her off me and tugging her panties back into place.

I slap her on the ass as I pull down her skirt and then tuck myself back into my pants. "Can't do anything about your tights, Princess. Sorry."

We both know I'm not sorry.

That flash of irritation sparks in her eyes, the one I love so much, and she opens her mouth no doubt to tell me off, but the sound of footsteps coming up the stairs has us both freezing.

"Shit," Cassidy whispers, jumping up from my lap and smoothing down her skirt. She looks around for somewhere to hide, but there's nowhere for either of us to go.

I stand up and grab her hand, pulling her behind me as we make a run for the exit. We get to the top of the stairs before whoever it is reaches the seats where we were just fucking like animals. We're both laughing as we race down the stairs and out into the hallway where we stop to catch our breath. "That was too damn close," Cassidy says, breathing hard but grinning as she leans against me.

"Yeah, but it was worth it." I wrap my arm around her waist and lead her back toward the locker room so I can grab my shit and head out. Knowing my teammates, after a win like tonight, no doubt they're going to be rowdy as fuck at The Sin Bin, and I know she'll want to be there to keep an eye on things.

Me? I just want to celebrate with my girl.

She's the reason I feel like I've won everything.

The Enforcer

2 oz rye whiskey • 1/2 oz sweet vermouth • 1/2 oz dry vermouth • dash of Angostura bitters • ice
Garnish: maraschino cherry

Stir rye, sweet vermouth, dry vermouth, and bitters with ice. Strain into a chilled martini glass and garnish with a cherry.

Cassidy #39

HAYDEN PULLS me into The Sin Bin behind him, his hand wrapped around mine as we make our way through my crowded bar. He hasn't stopped touching me since we left the arena, but it's not like I want him to let me go. I'm still wet between my legs, and can still feel him there imprinted inside of me.

I'm still getting used to this connection I have with him, the intensity of it that makes the world seem gray when he's in full color. Sometimes it's hard to want to do anything but fight and fuck Hayden Vaughn. I still don't know how this is my life now.

He leads me through the throngs of hockey fans and groupies who all cheer for him as he passes. Despite keeping his head down, he nods and waves. He doesn't stop to sign autographs or talk. It's like he's on a mission to get to the back where Sawyer is waiting for us at a table with Torin, Kingston, and Corbin.

"Hey, Cass," Torin Mattson says, standing up to pull out a chair for me to sit down next to him. Hayden scowls at his teammate and drops his big frame into the seat, tugging me onto his lap instead. Then his arm snakes around my waist, locking me in place.

"Hey, Torin," I say, smiling at him as Sawyer rolls his eyes at his brother. "That goal in the second was killer."

His grin widens. "Thanks."

"You guys looked good out there tonight," I tell the guys as Hayden's hand slips under my skirt and up my inner thigh, making me shiver. He plays with the hole he put in my tights, his fingers brushing back and forth over the soft material and my bare skin. Back and forth. Back and forth in a maddening rhythm.

"Thanks," Kingston Beaumont says with a grin. "It's all Hayden though. Say what you want, but his methods work."

Hayden shrugs at his line mate but doesn't disagree. Cocky asshole. His fingers find their way between my legs, teasing me through my wet panties and making me squirm on his lap.

Sawyer groans. "Hayden, stop being a dick." He looks pointedly down at his brother's hand under the table and what he's doing to me.

Hayden just smirks and pulls his hand back, sliding it up around to rest on my stomach.

"I need a drink," I say, needing a moment to catch my breath and get some space from Hayden before I come in front of all his teammates. If I did, I think I'd probably die of embarrassment, which is kind of hilarious to think about considering I make myself come in front of thousands of strangers on my OnlyFans. "Anyone else?"

They all nod and I slide off Hayden's lap and head to the bar. I feel his eyes on me as I walk toward Lila and the new girl, Saylor, who Lila hired a couple of weeks ago to help behind the bar when I can't be here. It wasn't fair for it all to fall on Lila's shoulders, and she seems to be working out. I watch as she tosses her hair and laughs at something one of the hockey fans waiting on her to pour their drink says. Girl's already learned that flirting gets you better tips, so I think she'll do just fine.

I laugh and shake my head as I walk behind the bar. "Hey, Lila," I say, smiling at her as she finishes up a drink for one of the hockey fans decked out in Anchors gear sitting in front of her. She hands it to him with a flirty smile before turning to me.

"Hey, girl. You okay?" She looks me over like she's checking for injuries or something.

I nod, grabbing a tray from under the bar and loading it up with drinks for our table. "Yeah. Just needed a minute."

She grins and leans forward on her elbows, looking over at Hayden, who's watching me with dark eyes. I shiver at the possessive vibes radiating off him. It feels like I shouldn't like it as much as I do. "I bet you do." She winks and then turns back to the next person who approaches her for a drink.

I grab the tray and start loading it up with everything I know Hayden and his teammates like. I'm trying to figure out what I want, when movement over by the table catches my attention. A gorgeous woman with glossy hair and a killer smile framed by red lips leans her huge boobs right down into Hayden's face as she whispers in his ear.

Fire scorches through my veins and my stomach churns as I watch them. Hayden doesn't look happy or anything, but he's not exactly pushing her away either. He just sits there, nodding as she talks to him, her hand on his shoulder like it belongs there.

Like she has any right to be near him when he's *mine*.

Why the *fuck* is he letting her touch her?

I whip around to face the bar, slamming down the last of the drinks with a trembling hand. My stomach plummets with each step I take back to the table, suffocating me until I can barely catch my breath. Rage courses through my body, causing my hands to shake uncontrollably as I make my way across the room with the tray of drinks.

When I get to the table, I slam the tray down so hard, some of the drinks fall over and spill.

I don't give a single shit.

My vision narrows down to a pinpoint, fixated solely on the spot where her hand rests on what belongs to me. She continues to murmur in his ear, but Hayden's gaze burns into mine as I stand there, my chest heaving with rage as I struggle to maintain composure.

Is this another game of his? Testing my limits and provoking me? Seeing how far I'll go if he fuels my jealousy enough?

Well, he's about to find out.

My mind shuts down in a surge of pure instinct. Fury rises inside of me and I lunge forward, grabbing a fistful of the girl's hair with brutal force. I yank her back violently, pulling her away from my man, daring anyone to come between us.

She screeches in pain, and the sound fuels the rage she provoked. *He* provoked. A grin that has to look completely savage twists my mouth up as I tighten my hold. "Don't fucking touch what doesn't belong to you," I snarl at her, pulling her head back so that I can look her right in the eye. She's got mascara-stained tears running down her face and I love it. I want her to *hurt*.

I've never felt this out of control before. Even when Roman cheated on me, I got angry, but it wasn't like this. There wasn't this all-consuming need to *destroy* that's blinding me to anything but my jealousy.

This girl wants to take Hayden from me and I'd rather die—rather kill—than let her.

She's trying to claw at my hand, but she's not going to dislodge my hold no matter how much she tears at my skin. I've got too strong of a grip on her hair.

Hayden stands up, and his eyes are black as a starless night. They're fixated on me with a twisted sort of hunger intense enough that I can feel it sparking across my skin like little pinpricks. His teammates are all laughing and cheering me on as I drag her toward the door, but not him.

No, he stalks after us, silent and predatory in his own way. His eyes gleam with a dangerous intensity as they devour the sight of what he's turned me into. Enjoying every second of my possession of him. She stumbles over her heels, leaving one behind. Sawyer follows behind, not doing anything to stop this train wreck as he picks up her dropped shoe and tosses it outside behind us.

He really is a bad influence

She's still crying and begging me to let her go as I pull her down the sidewalk and around the corner where there's less of a crowd to witness my madness. When we get out of sight, I finally let her go, shoving her away from me. She falls onto her ass on the concrete, looking up at me with wide eyes.

"Stay the fuck away from him." I jab my finger in her face as I tower over her. "And stay the fuck out of my bar. Find somewhere else to bag your athlete meal ticket. Got it?"

She nods frantically, scrambling to her feet and running off down the street without looking back. She didn't even pick up her missing shoe.

"Well, that was hot as fuck," Hayden drawls from behind me in a rough voice that strokes against all the best parts inside of me. His hard body pressing up against the length of mine as he wraps his arm around my waist and tugs me even closer. His other hand comes up and circles my throat in a dominant grip.

"I'm mad at you," I say, even though there's no heat behind it. The anger and jealousy are bleeding out of me as his lips drag along the side of my neck and leave a trail of fire in their wake.

When I say he makes me stupid, this is what I mean. I should be punishing him for what he pulled with that girl. My anger is as much his fault as hers, maybe more. But here I am, melting into him like he deserves to have me.

"I like it when you're mad at me. The sex is so fucking hot," he whispers into my ear before nipping at my earlobe. "But, baby, no need to be jealous. Your name's inked on my body. That means forever. You have to know I didn't do that shit lightly." He spins me in his arms so that we're face to face, his eyes searing into mine as he leans forward and kisses me. It's deep and bruising and makes my head spin.

I melt into him as the tension seeps out of me like poison. He's right, and most importantly, he's not Roman. As hard as it is, I need to trust him.

"Don't act like you weren't waiting to see what I'd do. I saw that look in your eye. You didn't shove her off because you wanted to play with me. To see how riled up you could get me. Admit it."

He raises his eyebrows. "Like you wore Morozov's sweater to my game to piss me off?"

Shit, he's right. "Uh..." I've got nothing.

He chuckles, running his hand through my hair. "You're right. It was a dick move, but I was curious how far you'd go. I wanted to see if you'd fight for me." He grins down at me, his eyes glinting in the streetlight. "And baby, you fucking did like no one ever has. I'm so hard right now, I can barely think straight."

I shake my head, laughing as he tugs me back toward the bar. "You're crazy."

He grins. "I'm yours."

Ice Rink Martini

3 oz vodka • 1 oz dry vermouth • olive brine (to taste) • ice
Garnish: olives

Shake vodka, dry vermouth, and olive brine with ice vigorously. Strain into a chilled martini glass and garnish with olives.

Cassidy #40

THIS HAS GOT to be a dream. Seriously. I'm not lucky enough to have this view in real life.

Hayden's jumping rope in his home gym, his sweaty abs flexing with every movement. He's shirtless, his tattoos glistening with sweat, and I can't look away. I'm transfixed. Hypnotized. His gaze meets mine as he keeps up the steady rhythm of the rope hitting the floor, and he smirks, knowing exactly what he's doing in those fucking gray joggers and backwards black hat.

I don't think he's wearing underwear, either, because things are... bouncing.

My phone's practically burning in my hand with the need to record this, so I do, lifting it up and aiming at just the right angle to capture everything. I didn't think anything could distract me from the show, but then an Instagram notification pops up over the screen. At first it's just a trickle of a few notifications that I try to ignore, but then it turns into a flood.

Huffing out a breath of annoyance, I click into the app and my already queasy stomach flips over. I have to swallow back bile when I see what my shitbag of an ex-boyfriend has done now.

There's a picture of me sitting on Hayden's lap in my bar. It's not a great picture, but it's not terrible, either. No, what makes this nausea-inducing is the caption he's put up with it. "Guess it doesn't matter which teammate she's with as long as he's got the $$$, right @hayv29? #sloppyseconds"

To be honest, I probably should've seen this coming. Roman's an attention whore, and when he's not getting mine, he lashes out. He did it the entire year we were together, and here he is doing it again. He's even tagged my freaking bar. I'm scared to look at the comments.

I'm distantly aware of the ropes thwacking to a stop, and then Hayden's in front of me. He gently pries my phone out of my hand and looks down at it. His face goes dark, and his eyes narrow as he reads the caption before scrolling through the comments that I'm sure are fucking awful.

"Fuck," he mutters, handing my phone back to me as he grabs a towel to wipe the sweat off his face and chest. "I'm sorry."

I'm really trying to keep my shit together. My eyes are stinging, but I don't want him to witness me falling apart. I never cry and I blink hard to keep the tears from falling. I will *not* let Roman make me cry. "It's fine."

He wraps his arms around me, pulling me into his chest so that I can feel the steady beat of his heart against my cheek. He's sweaty and my skin sticks to his, but it's comforting all the same. "It's not fucking fine. I'm going to fix this, and then I'm going to end him for hurting you."

I lean back and look up at him. "Hayden, no."

He frowns down at me, his jaw tight with anger. "Yes. You don't deserve this shit and that's not who you are." He runs his fingers through my hair and then leans forward to kiss me softly. "Let me handle it."

I sigh, knowing he's not going to let this go. He's stubborn as hell, but so am I. So I swipe my phone back from him, take a deep breath, and click into the comments. Yeah, it's probably not smart, but I need to know what I'm dealing with.

It's worse than I thought. There are comments about how I'm a whore and how Hayden should be careful before he catches something or that I'm just using him for his money. Comments dragging me, making shit up and stating it as fact. The nausea hits hard and I have to breathe through my nose to keep from throwing up. I was already feeling queasy this morning, and this just about pushes me over the edge.

I notice a couple of people have tagged my bar, so I click into the account for The Sin Bin and the hate is actually kind of impressive. There are a few positive comments, but mostly it's negative. Laughable if it wasn't hurting my business.

Hayden watches me as I scroll, his face growing darker and darker as he looks down at my phone and sees the shit people are saying about me, him, my business. He takes my phone back and sticks it in his pocket before grabbing my hand and pulling me out of the room. "Where are we going?"

"Shower," he says, not looking back as he drags me down the hall and into his huge bathroom. He turns on the shower and then starts stripping off his clothes before reaching for mine. I'm too numb to stop him as he strips me bare and then pulls us both under the hot spray of the water.

He grabs my shampoo and pours some into his hand before working it through my hair. I groan because it feels amazing.

"Don't do that," Hayden says, his voice rough. "I'm trying to be good here. I want you to understand how much I worship you, Princess. Not just your body—all of you." His fingers brush across my forehead as he tips my head back against his shoulder and the warm water rinses through my hair. "Those comments are bullshit and you know it. You don't deserve it, and Morozov will pay for putting his shit on you like this."

"Maybe I do," I whisper, looking up at him with tears in my eyes. "Deserve it, I mean. Maybe this is what I get for being with someone like Roman."

"The fuck you do," he scoffs, running his fingers through my clean hair to get out the tangles. My tears mix in with the warm water and run down the drain like they were never there. "What you deserve is to be cherished and adored every second of your life, with no exceptions. And when the opportunity presents itself, I'll fucking destroy Roman for what he's done to you."

"Hayden, no. You can't risk your future, everything you've built—"

"Yes. Fuck yes. He doesn't get to treat you like shit and get away with it." He turns off the shower and grabs a couple of towels before wrapping me in one and himself in another. Then he pulls me out of the bathroom and into the bedroom. He sits me on the edge of the bed and then grabs his phone.

"What are you doing?" I ask as he taps at the screen.

After a few seconds of silence, he rotates the screen so that I can see it. He's posted the picture of us in the arena after the game, the one where he's still inside of me, though you can't see it in the shot. He's just captioned it #mine. Then he gives me a lopsided grin that's way too attractive. "Roman's saved us the *when do we go public* conversation. Now I can post about you as much as I want."

I laugh because it's ridiculous, and he looks so proud of himself. And for a second, the despair lifts away. "That won't fix anything."

"I didn't do it to fix anything. I did it for me. For us."

Well, okay then.

Hayden walks across the room and disappears into the closet, coming back out and tossing one of his soft t-shirts at me. I slip it on and decide just to trust him. I'm going all-in with this trust thing. He said he'd fix this. I have no idea how, but Roman's his teammate, so maybe he can get him to do things I can't. It's just past breakfast time and I'm already exhausted. And now that the nausea's gone away, I'm hungry.

I look down at my stomach as it grumbles again. "Breakfast?"

Hayden laughs. His hand slides around to the back of my neck as he pulls me closer. "You got it." Then he drops a kiss on my mouth and pulls back after just a hint of tongue, looking down at me like he wants to eat me instead of food as he drags his thumb along his bottom lip.

"What?" I ask, knowing that look means trouble.

He smirks. "Nothing." But then he grabs my hand and pulls me to the kitchen. I sit and watch the muscles in his back flex under his skin as he cooks me breakfast. By the time he's done, the kitchen island between us is covered with pancakes, bacon, eggs, OJ and the smoothie he makes for me every day. He picks up the glass and hands it to me. "Start with this."

I swear his eyes are predatory as he watches me wrap my lips around the straw and sip.

"You're so bossy," I tell him after I've swallowed. He laughs but doesn't deny it, grabbing his coffee cup off the counter. It says *My Deke is Legendary* on the side and he smirks at me as I eye it.

When was the last time I had my morning coffee? I frown, trying to remember. It smells amazing, and I reach out to try to snag it from him so I can take a sip. He pulls it away at the last second. Damn hockey player reflexes.

"If you're a good girl and finish this first," he says, pushing the smoothie back at me, "then I'll give you a taste."

I laugh, taking another strawberry-banana flavored sip and

then set it down, wondering how he can make one of the worst mornings I've ever had somehow better. "How do you manage to make everything sound so fucking dirty?"

He smirks. "Pure talent."

The air's heavy between us like always, like it's taking so much effort to keep even this amount of space between him and me. I set down my half-finished smoothie, wiping my icy fingers on the t-shirt I've got on as I get lost for a second in him. He's not wearing a shirt and those gray joggers he always wears now that he knows they're my weakness are slung so low on his hips I can see the tattoo of my name.

Fuck, that's hot.

I open my mouth, about to ask him to take me back to bed, when my phone buzzes again. I didn't even know he brought it down here, but there it sits on the counter within arm's reach. I'm tempted to ignore it, especially because it's probably some of the bullshit from Hayden's or Roman's posts, but the spell's broken now, so I reach for it.

Hayden tries to grab for it before I can unlock it, but I dodge out of his way.

I hold it up to scan my face while I take another sip of the damn smoothie that Hayden insists I drink every day. I almost choke on it when I see the alert I set up for new mentions and reviews for my bar. There are dozens—maybe hundreds—of new reviews completely bashing The Sin Bin on one of the major review websites. Our rating's trashed, and the room spins as everything I just drank revolts in my stomach.

"Cassidy?"

When I don't answer, Hayden plucks the phone out of my hand, his eyes scanning the screen as he scrolls through all the hateful comments about me and my bar. All the lies. "Fuck," he says, setting the phone face down on the counter between us. "You need to stop looking at your phone."

I blink, tears burning my eyes *again*. What the fuck is with all this crying? "I can't just pretend this isn't happening, Hayden. I need to figure out a way to make it stop, or fix it, or I don't know." I tug on the ends of my damp hair. "I have no clue what to do, what step to take next. If I don't figure it out, my business is as good as dead. Reviews are everything. The Sin Bin is a fucking one star. No one's going to give us a chance."

I'm starting to wonder if I should just give in to Roman. Just let him win and stop all this fucking fighting all the time. I'm so damn tired.

Hayden wraps his arms around me, knocking over my smoothie but not giving a single fuck about it. "I see that look in your eye, Princess. Like fuck will I let you give up. We're winners in this house, understand? We don't lose and we never, ever fucking quit."

I nod against his chest, letting his words sink in. He promised he'd fix this even though it's not his problem and I have no idea how he'll do it. But I trust him enough to believe him when he says he'll figure something out.

And that's more than I've trusted anyone in a long time.

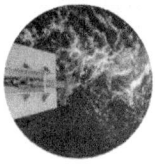

⚓⚓⚓
@AnchorsAsshole

Saw Vaughn at the game tonight, and damn. Opposing team needed a safe word. #Pineapples

Hayden #41

CASSIDY PASSED out right after breakfast. She's been tired as hell lately and I'm trying not to act too interested in it.

After this morning, though, baby or not, I can't blame her for wanting to shut down and forget about the world for a while. Roman's becoming a real problem, not just an annoyance, and I'm going to have to figure out exactly how I want to deal with him.

But first, I have to put out the fires he's already set... one of which Cassidy doesn't even know about, and I hope I can keep it that way.

At the same time he was outing my relationship on his social media, he dropped the link to Cassidy's OnlyFans in the team group chat, and ever since then my phone's been blowing the fuck up.

War and Kingston both texted me on the side to find out what the hell's going on, but King's was more of a warning.

> King: FYI Morozov sent the link to everyone

> King: Management included

Fuck.

I've got practice in forty-five minutes, and my body's shaking with the amount of rage and adrenaline I've got coursing through my veins right now. No doubt once Coach and the other higher ups see those videos, they'll know I'm in them.

The mess keeps getting fucking messier, and Roman? He doesn't have enough blood in his body to pay back the debt of retribution he's wracking up.

Sawyer's in the kitchen, gulping down the last of a protein shake dressed like he's on his way out to the hospital.

"Whoa. Why am I looking at your murder face?" My brother's hand reaches for the knives and he wraps his fingers around the hilt of the biggest one. "Knife or..." he looks around before brightening, "plastic bag?"

My lips twitch, and the violence in my blood cools a degree or two. "Plastic bag?"

Sawyer nods and lets go of the knife, grabbing the grocery bag. "You can do a lot with this." He pulls it over his head to demonstrate. "Asphyxiation, for starters."

I chuckle and then sigh as I lean back against the counter. "Morozov sent the link to Cassidy's OnlyFans to everyone on the team, including Coach and the GM." This is one of those times I appreciate having zero secrets from my brother. I don't have to explain what I'm talking about because he already knows.

Sawyer curses under his breath, dropping the bag back onto the counter. "Shit. That's bad."

"Yeah. It's fucking bad."

"What are you going to do?"

"Go to practice."

Sawyer grabs the plastic bag and then swipes his keys off the counter. "C'mon. I'm driving you."

I follow him out of the house, shoving my phone in my pocket so I don't have to see any more of the messages coming through from the guys. They're all fucking idiots, and if they think I'll stand for them watching my future wife like that, they're dead wrong. My fists ache with the need to hit someone, knowing all of my teammates are watching my girlfriend get herself off.

Watching me fuck her.

Goddamnit, they're all going to know what she looks like when she comes and I don't know how to feel about it.

Sawyer glances at me but his expression is completely serious when he says, "You," he makes air quotes with his right hand while he steers with his left, "'accidentally' break something on Roman's body that sends him to the hospital while you're at practice, and I'll dose him with something that'll fuck him up for a while."

I smirk at my brother. "You know I love you, right? Like, I fucking love you so much."

He grins. "I love you too, asshole."

When we get to the rink, Sawyer drops me off at the door.

"Good luck," he tells me as I slam the car door and head inside.

I don't need luck. I need Roman's blood on my hands.

But first I need to get through practice.

I don't get the chance to even lace up my skates before Coach is on my ass, telling me to follow him upstairs. We're bypassing his office, which is never a good thing.

Fuck, fuck, fuck.

I wipe my sweaty palms on my shorts, disgusted with myself for my nerves. I don't get anxious; I get mad. Determined.

Even.

Roman did this, and even if the team can't prove it's me on

those videos, which one look at my tats and they'll know, he might get his wish of me kicked off this team—maybe out of the league.

He leads me down the hall and into the conference room where the team's management is sitting around the table with their laptops open and their eyes on me as soon as I step into the room.

I definitely should've answered the calls from my agent, but it's too late now.

My stomach clenches and I blow out a slow breath to keep my shit together. It's not going to help my case if I walk into that room looking like I want to rip some throats out.

And I can't even handle thinking about all my teammates and this room full of suits watching my girlfriend—the mother of my future children—get fucked, even if it's me doing the fucking.

Somehow it wasn't so bad when I thought about the people watching her in an abstract way, but now that I have to face them, it's become very real.

Coach turns to me, his expression unreadable as he says, "Sit down, Hayden."

My jaw clenches and my fists ball up at my sides as I look at each of the men in the room one by one. They're all watching me with expressions ranging from disgust to amusement.

I'm going to kill Roman Morozov with my bare hands—and maybe Sawyer's plastic bag.

I sit down in the chair at the end of the table, still holding eye contact with everyone in the room.

The suits ask me questions and I answer honestly. There's no point in lying or covering for myself now. It's all out there and I'm not ashamed of it. Is it ideal? No. But I also wasn't about to let Cassidy put herself out there with anyone but me.

"So you admit that you're the man in the videos?" one of

them asks me, his voice condescending as fuck and I fight to not flip him off.

I nod. Might as well own my shit. "Yes."

"And you knew this could be a problem for the team?"

I shrug, knowing they're trying to trip me up and get me to admit something they can use against me. "It's not a problem for the team unless it affects my ability to play."

One of them snorts, but Coach shoots him a glare that shuts him up.

"Do I need my agent here? Or my lawyer?" I ask, leaning back in my chair and crossing my arms over my chest.

They shake their heads, but I'm not so sure.

"We're still discussing how to handle this," Coach says, his voice gruff as he looks down at his laptop screen, his forehead creased as he shuts it, looking tired as hell. The guy looks fifty instead of thirty-six, like he hasn't slept in weeks. "You'll be suspended until we figure out what to do."

"You know this is bullshit, right?" My voice is quiet and controlled, but there's no hiding my anger. "Morozov sent that link to everyone on the team. He's trying to get me off of it."

Coach Morin nods slowly. "I know. But these aren't private videos, Hayden. Anyone can pay 25 bucks to unlock one and then what happens if the media finds out the man is you? What then?" He shakes his head when I don't answer. "Right now, we have to follow protocol."

I don't say anything else as I stand up and leave the room, heading back downstairs to grab my shit and leave, texting my agent a heads up on the way. This whole thing is a fucking joke. Sticking my dick into my girlfriend on camera has zero to do with what I do on the ice. And it's not like she posted it on public social media.

Until I got here, this team was mediocre at best. Now that we're in the running for the playoffs, they're going to bench me?

Idiots.

I slam the locker room door open and ignore all of my teammates who are still lacing up their skates and grabbing their sticks as I head toward my locker. I grab my bag and rip the zipper open, checking that I've got everything.

Roman's standing by his locker, his phone in his hand as he looks down at it with a smirk on his face. He looks up at me and winks, like he knows what just happened upstairs. "You fucked yourself over, Vaughn. You should've kept your dick in your pants. Now things can go back to the way they should be."

Warren's got a frown on his face as he stares between Morozov and me while I shove shit in my gear bag. "What's going on?" he asks.

"Dickhead over there," I say, nodding toward Roman, "just got me suspended. Indefinitely."

"Bullshit," War says, laughing like this is a joke.

"I'm not kidding."

He tenses up, and Kingston walks over, sensing the energy shift, I guess. "What's going on?"

"Vaughn's suspended."

"The OnlyFans?" Kingston guesses and I nod.

"How long?" King asks, and of everyone affected, he's going to the feel the impact of me not being on the ice with my team the most since he's my line mate and our chemistry is fucking awesome. I know where he is at all times when we're on the ice together without even having to see him, that's how in sync we've gotten.

"Don't know yet." I shove the last of my shit into the bag and zip it up, slinging the strap over my shoulder.

"We're not gonna let them do this," War says, glaring over his shoulder at Morozov, who looks smug as fuck and extra punchable right now.

I shake my head. "It's already done."

"Fuck that," Kingston says, his jaw clenching. "You're one of us. We don't let each other go down without a fight." He nods like he's decided on something and then turns to War. "Spread the word. Get everyone together after practice. We need to make a plan."

"Everyone except that asshole," Mattson says, upnodding toward Roman as he joins our little huddle.

War's jaw tics and he looks more serious than I've ever seen him. "Done."

I laugh, knowing they mean well and that they'll fight for me, but it's not going to change anything. The suits upstairs made their decision, and it's final.

But I appreciate the fuck out of my team right now—well, most of them.

I leave them there to finish getting ready for practice, bailing when they're all huddled together. I rub my chest where there's a knot forming that has nothing to do with the fact that I just got suspended and everything to do with the way Cassidy's going to look at me when she finds out what happened.

She's going to think this is her fault. That she ruined my career.

And fuck if that doesn't make me want to break something even more than I already do.

Slapshot Sour

2 oz Scotch whisky • 3/4 oz lemon juice • 1/2 oz simple syrup • 1/2 oz egg white (optional) • ice
Garnish: dash of bitters

Shake all ingredients (except bitters) with ice hard. Strain into a rocks glass filled with ice. Top with a few dashes of bitters.

Cassidy #42

I JUMP when the door swings open, pressing my hand over my heart to try to hold it inside my body. "Jesus," I mutter, taking a deep breath to calm down. After feeling so freaking vulnerable this morning, having my relationship with Hayden outed on social media without my permission and then my business messed with because of it, I guess I'm jumpier than usual.

Hayden walks into the room, and the energy surrounding him is like an incoming storm. Crackling with destructive electricity, menacing in its ferocity, and frankly, scary as hell. "Aren't you supposed to be at practice right now?"

I'm sitting on the couch in his t-shirt and nothing else, trying to figure out how to fix the shitshow that my asshole ex dropped into my lap this morning, but I set it aside because I can tell Hayden's not okay.

He doesn't answer me, just stalks forward and wraps his

arms around me before pulling me against his chest. He holds me tight like he needs me to breathe, and I let him.

"Hayden," I whisper, running my fingers through his hair as he buries his face in the crook of my neck. "What's going on?"

He pulls back and looks down at me with dark eyes that are full of rage and frustration and a hint of despair that makes my heart ache for him. He shakes his head and then leans down to kiss me softly on the mouth. Then he says, "I'm suspended indefinitely."

I blink up at him, not sure if I heard him right. "What? Why?"

He sighs and lets me go so he can sit down on the couch. I follow him, sitting beside him and taking his hand in mine. He looks down at our fingers intertwined and then up at me. "Morozov sent the link to your OnlyFans to everyone on the team. The entire organization."

I swallow hard, trying not to let the guilt I feel creep up and choke me. This is all my fault. If I had never met Roman or gotten involved with him, Hayden would be at practice right now and not suspended. "Fuck," I whisper, looking down at the floor. "This is all my fault."

Hayden's fingers tighten around mine as he pulls my chin up so I'm looking at him again, his fingers indenting my skin as he presses hard enough for me to get that he's serious. "Don't you dare blame yourself for this shit. You're not responsible for Roman's actions or the team's decision to suspend me. That's on them."

"But..."

He shakes his head and then pulls me onto his lap so that I'm straddling him, my knees on either side of his thighs as he looks up at me with a fire in his eyes that makes me burn. "No. This isn't your fault. Got it? I made the decision to insert myself into your videos, not you."

I nod slowly, even though I don't really believe him. If it

wasn't for me, he wouldn't be in those videos at all. Roman might've found another way to mess with him, but maybe not. I'm still lost in my head when Hayden leans forward and kisses me. It's gentle and so unlike him, all I can do is blink my eyes closed and fall into it. It's like with this kiss, he's trying to reassure me that he doesn't blame me. And okay, I know it's not *all* my fault. If Hayden wasn't jealous as hell, he wouldn't have insisted on being in the videos in the first place. But still, a lot of this is on me.

But Hayden's never lied to me about anything, and despite my dumpster fire of a past, I trust him.

Which is why I decide to tell him what I've been thinking about since this morning, even though it scares the shit out of me. Doing this means I might never be able to pay Hayden back for paying off my debt to Roman. And forget about making The Sin Bin into the family-friendly restaurant my dad dreamed about. "I think I need to shut down my OnlyFans."

Hayden's eyes narrow as he looks at me, his fingers tightening around mine. "No."

"Seriously?" I squirm under the intensity of his glare. "I figured you'd be ecstatic."

"I'm not letting you give up your dreams because of Morozov. Fuck that." He shakes his head and then leans forward to press a kiss on the tip of my nose. "Did I hate the idea of you showing a bunch of horny guys what belongs to me? Yes. Do I still hate it? Also yes. But that doesn't mean I want you to stop doing something you want to do just because some asshole is trying to ruin you."

"Ruin us," I correct.

He shrugs like it's no big deal, and I know he means it. He's not worried about himself at all. It's me he's worried about, and honestly, I don't know if Hayden's ever been selfless like this before. I'm kind of stunned, to be honest.

Hayden's fingers run down my spine and I shiver. "Remember what I said about this house?"

I sigh and lean forward so I can rest my forehead against his, closing my eyes as I let myself breathe him in for a second. I fill my lungs with that delicious smell that's crisp, subtly spicy, and all Hayden, and the storm fades away with each passing second. "We're winners and we don't quit."

"Damn right. So you're going to keep doing what you want to do and fuck everyone else. Understand?"

I dig my fingers into the cotton of his t-shirt, gripping tight while I nod against him. He's right. If I give up now, Roman wins. And I'm not about to let that asshole take anything else from me. Not when I've finally got something worth fighting for.

Hayden leans back against the couch with me still on his lap, looking up at me with dark eyes as he runs his hands up my thighs. "Now I need you to distract me so I don't go find Morozov and break both of his legs so he'll never skate again."

I bite my lip, knowing exactly how I want to distract him. "You know," I say, leaning down to kiss him softly on the mouth as I reach between us and cup his dick through his joggers. He's already hard and I play with his piercings through the layers of soft fabric. I grin against his mouth as he groans. "I think I have an idea or two."

And then I lean down and kiss him hard, letting him taste me and reminding him that no matter what happens with his suspension or anything else, from now on, we're in this together.

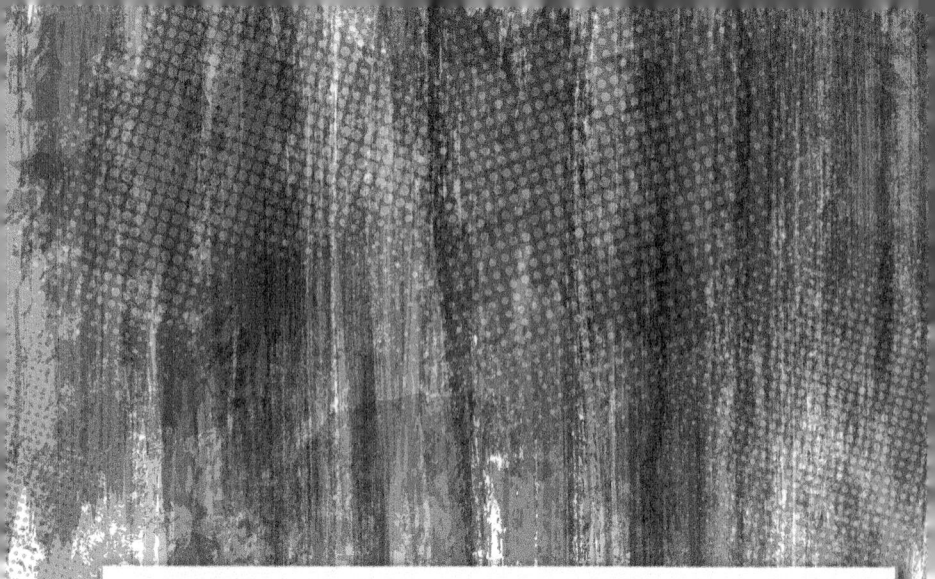

Hamilton
@HockeyHarasser

Hayden Vaughn doesn't just cross the line. He fucking obliterates it. #LineWhatLine

Hayden #43

I DON'T KNOW what time it is when my phone buzzes on the bedside table, but I snatch it up before it can wake Cassidy. She's passed out beside me, her breathing deep and even as she snores softly. Because of the sleeping pill I dissolved in her water before she crawled into bed, she doesn't move. I need to know if she's pregnant and I plan on getting answers tonight.

My phone buzzes again and I don't even have to look to know it's my brother. He's outside in the hall. I can feel it. Still, I look at the message, squinting against the brightness of the screen as I read it.

> Sawyer: Come out here

I sigh and run my hand through my hair before carefully sliding out of bed. I pull on a pair of joggers and a t-shirt from the floor before grabbing my phone and slipping out of the room. Sawyer's leaning against the wall with his arms crossed over his chest like he's been waiting for hours.

"You good?" he asks when I walk up to him.

"Yeah."

"I heard about the suspension."

I raise an eyebrow. Sawyer was at the hospital all day and I hadn't had a chance to talk to him about it yet, or ask him about what I need from him tonight.

"Heard it on the local sports talk radio station on my way home." He pushes off the wall and bends down to grab the bag I'm just now noticing at his feet. When he stands to his full height again, eye to eye with me, he's grinning. He wiggles the bag back and forth a couple of times. "Thought you might want some good news after your shit day."

"What's in there?" I ask, reaching for it, wondering if he's already read my mind.

He pulls it back and out of my reach before I can get my hands on it. "It's not for you." He turns around and starts heading down the hall toward my room.

I follow him, trying not to wake Cassidy up as I follow him inside, stopping a few steps away from the bed. "Are you..."

He kneels beside Cassidy and opens the bag, pulling out all sorts of medical shit. "Drawing her blood to see if you knocked her up? Yep."

"How'd you..."

He gives me a look that can only be interpreted as calling me a fucking moron. I stand over his shoulder while he ties a rubber tube around her upper arm, swabs her inner elbow, and jabs her with the needle. Cassidy doesn't even flinch, and it's over in seconds, the answer I'm dying to have held in the blood in my brother's hand.

He's gentle as he cleans her up and then I'm following him back out into the hall. I'm gonna have to remember to get that bandage off her arm before I fall asleep so she doesn't notice anything in the morning.

"I'll text you as soon as I know," Sawyer tells me with a grin on his face as he walks backward toward the front of the house. I'm assuming he's going to the hospital now when the staff is lighter and no one will question him running this test himself.

"Thanks, bro."

He nods and then disappears out the door. My heart feels like it's going to burst out of my chest. I want this more than I ever thought I could want anything. And if Cassidy's pregnant, I know it's going to be hard as hell to keep my mouth shut about it until I figure out the best way to tell her.

Considering she doesn't know I've been stealthing the fuck out of her since we met and feeding her fertility drugs in her morning shakes, it needs to be a good plan. One that doesn't make her hate me for keeping secrets.

One that ensures she won't be able to run when she finds out everything I've done to keep her.

I climb back into bed, making plans as I wrap myself around my girl. I get lost in my head, and it's a welcome distraction from the clusterfuck that's my career. I've been dodging calls from my agent all day because I'm not ready to face the reality of what my suspension could mean.

I'm so distracted by the time my phone buzzes in my pocket, my muscles ache from being in the same position for so long. I dig it out, surprised that hours have passed. It's a little after three a.m. and I have a single text from my brother.

Sawyer: Congrats, dad

Hayden: Holy shit

Hayden: you're sure?

Sawyer: you doubt me?

Hayden: fuck no

> Hayden: I'm just in shock it actually worked
>
> Sawyer: it's that Vaughn super sperm 💪
>
> Hayden: damn straight
>
> Sawyer: now you gotta tell her lol
>
> Sawyer: RIP your dick when she finds out
>
> Sawyer: 💀🔪🔪

I roll my eyes as my phone continues to vibrate in my hand, tossing it onto the nightstand. Then I blow out a breath and look down at Cassidy who's still passed out, but her hand's curled into my shirt like she doesn't want to let me go even in her sleep.

Fuck, I love this woman so fucking much. I look down at her stomach, and it's such a mindfuck knowing my baby's inside of her right now, growing, getting bigger every day. I run my fingers over her skin, imagining what it'll be like when she starts showing. My dick hardens picturing her stomach swollen with my baby and my mouth waters when I think about all the ways I'm going to enjoy her pregnant body.

And I'm not letting anything or anyone stand in my way, not even her.

Instead of sleeping, I spend the night figuring out how to fix the things I've fucked up in Cassidy's life since I pushed my way into it, and as an idea hits me when the first rays of the new day start to crawl across the ceiling, I grab my phone and fire off a text into the team group chat.

I promised Cassidy I'd fix what I broke, and this idea is step one. Then, I need to figure out how to lock her down so thoroughly that when I tell her about the baby, she won't want to run.

It's gonna take a lot of fucking work, but I've never shied away from doing whatever it takes to get what I want. And right now, all I want is her.

Forever.

Power Forward Punch

1 oz tequila • 1 oz mango liqueur • 2 oz orange juice • 1 oz lime juice • splash of grenadine • ice
Garnish: lime wheel

Shake tequila, mango liqueur, orange juice, and lime juice with ice. Strain into a highball glass filled with ice, add a splash of grenadine, and garnish with a lime wheel.

Cassidy #44

HAYDEN'S ACTING weird this morning. I'm groggy as hell, and he's rushing me through my shower and morning routine. It's making me cranky. I can't deal with his weirdness on top of feeling nauseous and dizzy and somehow still tired after sleeping twelve hours last night.

Ugh. I wonder if I'm getting sick.

He keeps checking his phone, and it's constantly vibrating. I'm trying not to be annoyed. I really am. But I can't take it anymore. "Can you please go deal with that," I flick my hand toward his phone, "somewhere else?"

I'm in the closet picking out what I'm going to wear to work this afternoon and Hayden's hovering behind me, watching me like he can't stand having me out of his sight for the five minutes it'll take me to get dressed. At least when his face isn't buried in the screen of his phone.

Which begs the question... am I irritated he's not giving me any space or that his attention isn't fully on me?

Yeah, I'm not gonna examine the answer to that right now.

Hayden tucks his phone in his pocket right as I'm pulling on a black cropped t-shirt with The Sin Bin written across it in white and a pair of black skinny jeans with rips down the legs. Comfort clothes.

I try to pass by Hayden to get back into the bedroom, but he stops me with a hand around my waist, pulling me back into his hard chest as his fingers go underneath my shirt to splay across the bare skin of my stomach. As always, sparks ignite where his skin touches mine, and a tremor runs through my body. He kisses the side of my neck and I feel his smirk against my skin.

"Don't you have somewhere to be?" I ask, trying to sound irritated but failing miserably. I may even tilt my head to the side and close my eyes while he drags his lips up my neck.

He chuckles and then spins me in his arms so I'm facing him. "I do." He leans down and kisses me hard on the mouth with plenty of tongue before pulling back and looking at me with those intense eyes that make me melt every damn time. "With you."

I raise an eyebrow, wondering what he's up to. "Where?"

"It's a surprise," he tells me with a grin as he grabs my hand and pulls me out of the closet and into the bedroom. "But we gotta go."

"I don't have time for surprises," I say, trying to tug my hand out of his, but he doesn't let me go.

"You do for this one." He opens the drawer beside his bed and pulls out a blindfold before turning to me with a wicked smirk on his face.

Oh, hell no.

I narrow my eyes up at him, knowing I'm going to lose this

battle but still trying to fight it anyway. "I have to work today, Hayden. I can't just take off whenever you want me to."

"You can and you will." He reaches forward and wraps the soft material of the blindfold around my eyes, tying it tight at the back of my head before spinning me around and pushing me toward the door. "Trust me."

"Hayden," I groan as he leads me down the hall and into the garage where his Range Rover's parked. He helps me into the passenger seat and I inhale the familiar smell of leather and Hayden's cologne. The door closes and then the driver's door opens and I'm assuming he climbs into the car. He starts it up and pulls out of the garage so fast I get dizzy and a little motion sick.

Great. Just what I need right now.

He reaches over and takes my hand in his, lacing our fingers together and squeezing gently as he drives. "You okay?"

"Yeah," I lie as my stomach churns and I breathe through my nose and exhale slowly. "Where are we going?"

"Nice try," he says with a chuckle. Then he turns up the radio when I'll Make You Love Me by Kat Leon and Sam Tinnesz starts to play. I love this song and he knows it. I lean back in my seat and try to relax even though I feel like I'm gonna puke any second now and I'm breathing deep and slow through the wave of sickness. After a minute it starts to subside and I let myself get lost in the music and the feel of Hayden's thumb brushing along the side of my hand.

Back and forth. Back and forth.

It's almost hypnotic.

We don't drive for long before he parks and helps me out of the car. My hands are a little sweaty and I wipe them on my jeans. I have no idea what to expect, and surprises aren't my favorite thing. We're in a parking lot from the sounds of it, and there are people around us, but I can't tell how many or who they are.

Hayden takes my hand again and leads me forward, his fingers tightening around mine as he pulls me toward wherever we're going. I hear a door opening and then he's pulling me inside, shutting the door behind us.

The smell is familiar. I'd know the scent of my bar literally blindfolded like I am now. It's the smell of my childhood, days and days spent running around with my twin brother, Callan, causing trouble while my dad built this place from nothing into what it is today.

The blindfold comes off and I blink up at him as I try to get my emotions under control. What the actual fuck? I never cry. I give him a watery smile that probably looks deranged. "Just thinking about my brother. I'm okay."

Hayden studies me and then looks over my shoulder. When he does, it's like whatever spell he casts on me with his hotness is broken because the stillness between us from seconds ago turns into loud laughter, the buzz of conversations, and glasses clinking. Sounds so familiar to me, I hardly notice them anymore.

But after Roman's post and the review bombing of my bar, business has dried up. The regulars still come in, and it's only been a few days, so it might blow over, but I've been trying to avoid thinking about it because I don't know how to fix it.

Hayden promised me he would, but I'm not the type to sit around and do nothing while I wait, but so far I've come up blank on what to do.

Hayden grips my shoulders and turns me so I'm facing into the bar. My mouth falls open and tears prick my eyes again when I take in the group of his teammates in their jerseys taking selfies and signing anything that's shoved in front of them.

There's a massive crowd around them.

I look up at my boyfriend. "You did this?"

He shoves his hands in his pockets and shrugs, looking more uncomfortable than I've probably ever seen him. Yeah, Hayden has a soft side and I don't think even he knew it until right now. "It's not a big deal. The guys saw what the Dickhead did and wanted to help."

I shake my head as I look back at his teammates, who are all here for us, for me. "It *is* a big deal. This could save my business." I turn back to him and wrap my arms around his neck, pulling him down for a kiss that he returns with so much heat I go weak in the knees. "Thank you."

"Anything for you, Princess." He pulls back and takes my hand in his again before leading me toward the bar where Warren and Kingston are posing for a selfie with a fan wearing a Mattson sweater. War's got a lopsided smile he's flashing at the camera, but Kingston Beaumont is wearing his trademark scowl. I don't think I've ever seen the guy crack a grin.

"Hey," War says when he notices us coming over. "Come pose with us." He pulls his phone out of his pocket and gestures Hayden and I over. "The rest of the guys have been posting on their socials that they're here and to come out, but I haven't done mine yet."

Hayden pulls me into his chest, wrapping his arms around my waist from behind as I lean back against him. His teammates squish in on either side of us, but the way Hayden's holding on to me, neither of them touches me at all. I'm sure he planned it that way. His lips brush my ear as he whispers, "I love you so fucking much"

I turn my head and look up at him, wondering if he really just said what I think he did. Sure, he sort of cornered me into kind of admitting that I love him once before and he sort of admitted it back, but he hasn't outright said it until now and even though Warren's snapping pictures, I can't look away from my boyfriend.

He smirks down at me and then kisses me with enough tongue that it hops right the hell over the line for public decency before pulling away and taking his own phone out of his pocket. He takes a couple of his own selfies with me still wrapped up in his arms, but I don't care what he's doing because I'm still reeling from what he just said.

Hayden Vaughn loves me. And I don't know how to deal with all these fucking feelings that are making me want to cry again.

"I got most of the reviews taken down," Hayden says as I blink back more stupid fucking tears. I'm watching Lila and Saylor sling drinks behind the bar and my head snaps up to look at him.

"What? How?"

"Remember that hacker I told you about?"

I nod.

"He got it handled."

About a thousand pounds of tension bleeds out of me and I melt back into Hayden's body. He tightens his grip, holding me up as I whisper, "Thank you."

Holy shit. I might actually be able to save my family's business. For once, Roman might not win.

And it's all thanks to Hayden and his teammates who are all here to help me, even though they don't have to be.

It's overwhelming and I'm not sure how to handle any of it. So I lean back against Hayden and let him hold me up while we spend the rest of the afternoon with his teammates and the fans who come to my bar to see them. The bar fills up and eventually I move behind the counter with Lila and Saylor to keep up with demand, but every time I look up, my gaze finds Hayden who's watching me from across the room like he can't stand being too far away from me for too long.

I can't get over the fact he did this for me. And that he loves me.

It's crazy. Mind blowing, actually.

And it's all mine.

He's all mine.

I don't know what I did to deserve someone as amazing as Hayden Vaughn in my life, but I don't think I want to let him go.

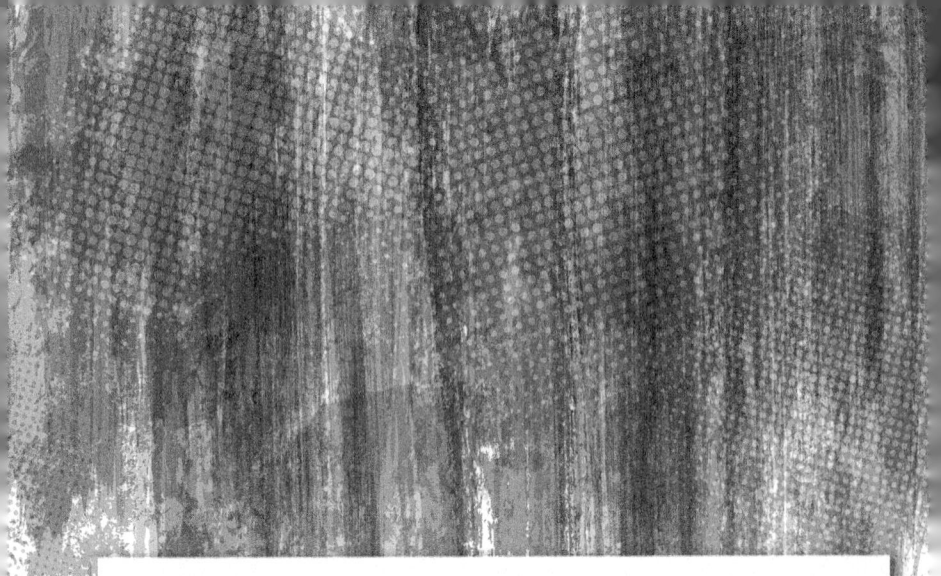

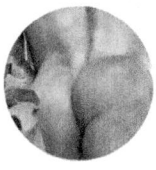

I'd Do Me
@NetNasty

Don't skate too close to 29 unless you've updated your will. #damn

Hayden #45

"WE NEED TO TALK."

I tear my eyes off Cassidy and focus on my teammates. Warren, Kingston, Saint, and Torin stand shoulder to shoulder behind me and I spin on the barstool to face them. "What's up?"

War looks at Mattson and then back at me with a smirk on his face. "We think we came up with a way to get you back on the ice."

Gritting my teeth, I narrow my eyes at them with a mix of fear and desperation. My whole body tenses as I struggle to contain the rising hope within me. I've been focused on fixing Cassidy's bar so I didn't have to stop and think about how my career has gone to shit, but War's words strike me like a bolt of lightning, sending my heart into a chaotic rhythm. "How?"

Saint leans forward and rests his forearms on the bar as he stares at the TV hung behind the bar showing the Knights-Hellcats game. "We're going to refuse to play."

"What?"

Kingston nods once, looking like he wants to kill someone.

But then that's his usual expression. "The four of us will refuse to play unless they reinstate you."

My jaw drops and I look between the four of them in shock. They're serious. And they're willing to risk their own careers for me.

"Maybe some of the other guys, too," Warren says, reaching around me and grabbing a maraschino cherry and popping it into his mouth. "And we're telling Coach we're not skating as long as Morozov's wearing the C, either."

"Holy shit," I whisper as my heart does its best impression of an MMA fighter against my ribs. I can't believe they'd do this for me. And it just might fucking work. "You guys..." I bite my lip and look down at the floor as emotions I don't want to deal with right now threaten to choke me up. "Thank you."

Warren shoves my shoulder with his. "We've got your back, man."

"And we're not about to stand for what Morozov did. Shit stays with the team. He took it outside, he's done," Mattson adds.

I nod, knowing he's right. That's the unofficial teammate code and Roman broke it. I just didn't expect them to come to my defense. I've never been a team player, so knowing these guys have my back is weird as hell, but I appreciate it more than they know.

Kingston nods once like he's decided something and then turns to walk away, Mattson following him. Saint claps me on the shoulder and then goes back to watching the game while Warren spins on his stool and leans against the bar so he can watch Saylor work.

I refocus on Cassidy. She's got a smile on her face and a lightness about her I've missed. She has no idea what just happened, but fuck if it doesn't make me feel like I can breathe again for the first time since I walked out of the Anchors facility thinking my career was over.

"When are you guys going to do it?" I ask War as he grabs another cherry, grinning at Cassidy when she tries to slap his hand away and misses.

"Tomorrow," he tells me, popping the cherry into his mouth, ripping off the stem, and chewing it before swallowing. "We're all going to meet at the arena before practice and tell Coach we won't skate unless you're back on the ice." He sucks the stem back into his mouth, and a few seconds later, he plucks it out tied into a knot.

Saylor laughs as he grins at her where she's cracking the tops off half a dozen beers. "Impressive," she says, shaking her head.

"You know it, babe. Wait until you see what else I can do with my tongue." He winks at her and then turns back to me. "Tomorrow, we got you. Be ready to skate."

We play the Orcas tomorrow night and if the guys' insane plan works, I'll be in that game. And fuck if that doesn't make my blood pump faster through my veins.

Cassidy comes over and leans against the bar beside me, resting her head on my shoulder. I wrap my arm around her waist, my palm splaying across her stomach where my baby is, and kiss the top of her head, breathing her in while Warren talks about some new trick he wants to try on Saylor when they finally hook up.

I tune him out as I look down at Cassidy who's watching him with a small smile on her face, but her eyes are tired and she looks like she's about to fall asleep standing up. It's a good thing so much shit's been going down lately, because otherwise she'd notice how the pregnancy's affecting her and get suspicious. "You okay?" I whisper in her ear.

Her slow nod is laced with a devious glint in her eyes as she looks up at me with a dangerously sweet smile. I couldn't resist her if I tried. This burning desire to taste her sweetness overwhelms me. Without a second thought, I close the space between us and kiss the hell out of her.

I have to take advantage because normally she's two seconds away from tearing into me. I love that fiery side of her, but this soft side is something new and I'm going to eat it up like it's my last meal. "I'm great."

We've been here for hours and the crowd's thinning out as it gets later and later, but there's still a buzz in the air that wasn't there before we showed up. At least for now, Cassidy's bar is saved. And maybe my career, too, if the guys' crazy plan works.

It feels strange as fuck to hope, and it's not really my style. Forcing my will on everyone around me is more my standard, and I can't even hide my grin when I think about how much I've rubbed off on my teammates. Them pulling this protest shit? That's something straight out of my playbook. Force the team and the coaches to listen. Make them see what a piece of shit Morozov is. How toxic he is to this team.

How he's the reason they played like shit before I got here, and how he doesn't deserve a place here. I may play dirty, but he's the fucking worst of us all. I want to win. He wants power.

Cassidy leans into me more heavily and I know it's time to go, no matter what she says. She's exhausted and I've had enough sharing her with people anyway. So I stand up and pull her with me, saying goodbye to the guys and thanking them one last time as they head out with us, making a plan for them to text me the second they walk out tomorrow.

I'm not going to be able to sleep tonight until I know what Coach says. And if he doesn't give in, I don't know what we'll do.

But I'm ready to fight for my place on this team and for Cassidy. It feels fucking great for once. Like maybe I can have something good in my life that isn't just hockey.

And maybe that's what love is supposed to feel like.

Argggh
@PuckPirate

Vaughn hit that guy so hard, his ancestors felt it. #HistoricalImpact

Hayden #46

THE TEXT COMES in around three the next afternoon. I'm on the stationary bike in my home gym, trying to warm up and burn off all my nervous energy when my phone vibrates in my pocket. I shoved it in there so I wasn't checking it every two seconds, especially after the third time my asshole brother texted me because he knows I'm on edge and he loves to fuck with me. But when it buzzes again, I can't stop myself from pulling it out and unlocking it.

> War: We're out

> Hayden: And?

> War: Coach is pissed but he's gonna reinstate you
>
> Mattson: Not like we gave him a choice
>
> King: More than half the team walked
>
> Saint: It was fucking awesome

> Hayden: Holy shit
>
> Hayden: Thank you so fucking much

War: Don't mention it

Mattson: You're one of us

King: And Morozov's done as captain

Saint: He doesn't know it yet, thought you'd want to see the fireworks

> Hayden: Damn
>
> Hayden: You guys are crazy as hell
>
> Hayden: And he's going to lose his shit, should be a fun show

War: That's what we thought too lol

I shake my head as I stare down at the texts, still in awe that they did this for me. I never would've expected it from my teammates, and it means more than I can say.

I finish up on the bike and then head upstairs to shower and get ready for tonight's game against the Orcas. It's going to be a bloodbath and I'm not going to hold back. Not with Morozov out of the way as captain and me back on the ice. Now's the time to show my team that they stepped up for me for a reason, and I intend to bring home the cup this year.

Now that things are falling back into place with the team, it's time I shift my focus to Cassidy and the baby.

If she doesn't like what I did, I don't give a fuck. She's mine and I'm keeping her.

My breath puffs out in front of me as I do a lap. Coach pulled me aside before I took the ice and threatened that if I so much as breathe wrong the rest of the season, I'm off the team. I don't blame him. He had to deal with a mutiny today and it's all because of me.

I wave to some kids who are watching from the glass as I skate past them, but my mind is anywhere but here. It's on Cassidy and how she's going to react when I tell her everything. And then there's Morozov, who's been glaring at me from the other end of the ice since he got here. The team's about to rip that C off his chest, and I smirk at him knowing what's coming.

He deserves it for fucking everything he's done.

When we're leaving the ice after warm-ups and get inside the locker room, that's when shit starts to go down. Kingston takes the lead, walking over to Morozov with War, Mattson, Saint, Cruz, Gabe, and even Akseli, our goalie, behind him. I sit in front of my locker with my forearms on my thighs, bent forward, watching.

Morozov looks up at them with a sneer on his face. "What?"

Saint steps up and grabs the C from his jersey before ripping it off and throwing it to the floor at Morozov's feet. "You're not our captain anymore. You're done."

"What the fuck?" he yells as he looks around at the rest of us, who are nodding in agreement. "It's not up to you." He looks around for Coach Morin, who, for once, is nowhere to be found. Smart man.

"We can't trust you as a teammate, let alone to lead us," Mattson says. "You made Vaughn's personal shit public. You've been trying to bully the rest of us into making sure you get every pass, every shot opportunity out there so you get all the stats while the team loses because you're not good enough to make them count. You're out."

I fight back my grin. I think that's the most I've ever heard Torin say at once. Kingston nods as Warren picks up the C and hands it to me. I take it and look down at it in my hands, knowing this isn't over yet. The team still has to vote for a new captain, but this is symbolic and I'm not about to disappoint them.

Morozov looks around at the rest of the guys, who are nodding in agreement with Mattson and Saint, before his gaze lands on me. "You fucking bastard," he says, pointing at me as he storms toward me. "This is your fault."

I stand up and meet him halfway, shoving him with both hands so he stumbles back a few steps. "No, asshole. It's your fault for being a piece of shit who can't handle losing."

He shakes his head as he glares at me. "You're going to regret this." He turns and stalks out of the locker room, slamming the door behind him as he goes.

"I don't know where he's going. We have to be on the ice in ten minutes," War says, shaking his head, but he's got a wide grin on his face like he enjoyed putting Morozov in his place as much as I enjoyed watching it go down.

"Probably to bitch to management and see if they'll intervene for him like some kindergarten tattle tale," Gabe says with a roll of his eyes.

"Fuck that," Kingston says, looking around the locker room at all of us. "We're not going to let him get away with this shit anymore. We're done letting him run us into the ground. It's time we fight back."

War nods and claps me on the shoulder as he looks up at me. "And Vaughn's gonna lead us to a cup win."

I smirk down at him as I look at my team, my brothers, and realize how lucky I am to have them in my life. They've got my back, and that's something I never thought I'd say about anyone other than Sawyer. But now that Cassidy's in my life and this team is really mine, it's like I can finally breathe again.

"Don't jinx it," I tell them. I look down at the C in my hands and know that this is just the beginning.

It's time to prove myself as a leader and bring this team back from the brink of ruin Morozov pushed them toward. And I'm going to enjoy every fucking second of it.

I look up to find everyone watching me, waiting for me to say something to hype them up before we take the ice—the way a captain would. "Let's go kick some Orca ass."

The group erupts in cheers and shouts, and then we're heading back out on the ice where Morozov's waiting for us with his arms crossed over his chest, still wearing his C like he thinks he has any power left. He must've changed into a new jersey, but King rips it off him again as we pass by and hands it to me. Not one of us addresses the dickhead, no matter how much he yells or tries to get us to fall in line as we march past him through the tunnel and out onto the ice.

The crowd goes wild, more hyped than ever as we get deeper into the season and we're on the brink of making the playoffs. After the national anthems, the puck drops and it's game on.

I take my place in front of Akseli and focus on the game as Morozov skates around yelling shit at me, instead of focusing on his play. I ignore him, knowing he's just trying to get under my skin. In fact, it looks like everyone's ignoring him because he was wide open for a pass that Gabe Maddox passed to War instead, even though War was nowhere near where he should've been to receive it.

It's like they're all playing a different game than Morozov, and it's fucking beautiful to watch them leave him out.

We scored three goals in the first period and I can already feel it in the air that this is our night. We're going to win and we're going to do it with basically four men on the ice every time Morozov is on shift.

By the end of the second, we're up 4-0 and Coach has realized what's happening, that the team's shutting Roman out. Coach pulls him and Roman storms down the tunnel, throwing his helmet against the wall loud enough I heard it on the ice over the crowd.

I smirk as I skate around with my stick raised in the air as the fans chant my name and I feel like I'm exactly where I'm meant to be. This game, this moment, it's all mine. And I'm not letting anyone take it away from me.

We win 5-0 and when we get back to the locker room, everyone's celebrating like we just won a playoff game instead of a regular season one. Everyone except Roman, who storms across the room and gets in my face. "You think you've won? This team is nothing without me."

"I think you need to get your head out of your ass and realize how toxic you are to this team," I tell him, shoving him back again so he stumbles into the wall behind him. "You're done here, asshole. I thought we all made it clear out there that it's over. No one wants you on that ice with us. No one wants you as captain."

He narrows his eyes at me as he pushes off the wall and closes the space between us. "I'm not going anywhere. You can't make me leave."

I shrug as I lean against the locker beside mine, trying to look like I don't have a care in the world when, in reality, I'm ready to beat the shit out of him if he comes any closer. "We'll see about that."

Kingston steps up beside me and crosses his arms over his chest as he stares Morozov down. "We voted. You're done, Morozov."

"You can't—" Roman starts, but Mattson cuts him off.

"We can and we did. You're. Done." He looks around at the rest of the team, who are nodding in agreement before turning back to Roman. "And if you don't get your ass out of here, we'll haul your ass out the door ourselves. We're not playing with someone we can't trust."

Do I think management is just going to let us push him off

the team? Fuck, no. But it feels good to show Morozov that he's not as untouchable as he thought he was.

Roman looks around at all of us and then shakes his head as he backs away. "Fuck all of you. This isn't over." He turns and slams his way out of the locker room, kicking the door behind him like he's trying to make a statement. But I don't give a fuck what he has to say anymore. None of us do.

I don't think I ever realized how bad things were here until this moment, the way they all so readily pushed him out. No one really talked about the shit he'd pull before I showed up, but the impression I got today was all kinds of fucked up.

The guys start celebrating again and I lean back against my locker, feeling lighter than I have in weeks. It's like a weight's been lifted off my shoulders now that Morozov's out of the way. I look down at the C still in my hand and smile before turning to Kingston.

"Thanks for this," I tell him, holding it up.

"You earned it," he says with a nod before turning back to his locker and starting to strip out of his gear like everything's normal. But nothing about this is normal. We just mutinied against our captain and it worked. And now we're going to have to deal with the repercussions of that, but for right now, I'm sure as fuck going to enjoy the moment.

And tomorrow?

It's time for me to lock Cassidy down so tight she won't ever be able to leave.

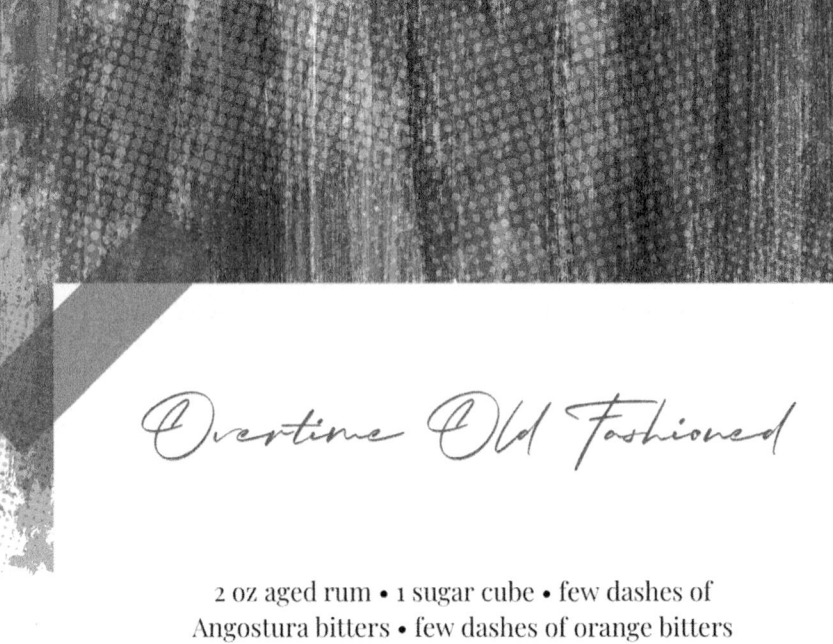

Overtime Old Fashioned

2 oz aged rum • 1 sugar cube • few dashes of Angostura bitters • few dashes of orange bitters • ice
Garnish: orange peel

Muddle the sugar cube and bitters in an old fashioned glass. Add rum and fill with ice. Stir well to combine and chill. Garnish with an orange peel.

Cassidy #47

MY BOYFRIEND'S up to something.

It's been days since he played savior to my bar, and since then he's been busy with games and the team.

But based on the message he just sent me, his focus isn't hockey right now.

I stare down at the picture of tall black iron gates—specifically, the gates to the cemetery where my parents and brother are buried—and then back at the message that says *come find me.*

That's it.

To be fair, I guess those three words *are* pretty self explanatory.

A mischievous grin spreads across my face as I lay down my phone, knowing he's going to make me work for whatever he's up to. But I'm intrigued and, honestly, I need a distraction from everything I've had to deal with these past couple of weeks. I'm ready for whatever game he wants to play, so I grab my keys and head out the door.

It takes me less than ten minutes to get to the cemetery and I spend the entire drive trying to figure out what the hell Hayden could be doing here. Wondering what he's up to and trying to ignore the whirlpool of anxiety in my belly. I've never told him where my family is buried, but somehow he found it anyway because of course he did.

I don't have any answers by the time I pull up to the cemetery and park alongside the road.

I walk toward the gates that Hayden sent me a picture of and find him leaning against them wearing a suit for some reason. It's black on black and for a second I wonder if someone died. Even if they did, it might be worth it to see him like this, depending on who it is. Roman, for example.

I see Hayden in suits all the time before games, but there's something about this combination, with his wavy hair swept back and his dark eyes focused completely on me, not even a hint of stubble on his jaw, that really does things to me.

When I get close, he holds his hand out, still not telling me what we're doing here. I don't even hesitate to slide my palm against his rough one, and he tugs me forward so I'm pressed against his hard body. Then he kisses me hard enough that I forget how to breathe.

"What are you up to?" I ask when he pulls away, looking up at him with narrowed eyes.

He smirks and then turns toward the gates, pushing them open with a loud creak and pulling me through. "You'll see."

I huff out a sound of annoyance because he still doesn't seem to care that I hate surprises. Okay, I can admit I haven't hated any of his yet, but still... he should know this about me. All he does is grip my hand tighter, and I let myself enjoy the way he's holding onto me like he can't stand being physically attached at all times as we walk through the rows of headstones. It's quiet and peaceful here, and I find myself relaxing into Hayden's side as we walk.

The deeper we get into the graveyard, the more tall evergreens sway overhead with the wind. I look up at them, getting lost in how massive they are—how many years they've stood here in this place filled with grief and loss, watching over the souls grieving for their loved ones. I'd like to think they watch over me when I'm here visiting. There's something comforting about that to me, knowing these giants never judge, but their presence is always here.

Hayden stops suddenly and I look down to find us standing in front of two headstones that make my heart crack a little like it always does when I face them. My parents' graves. And beside them is a third one with Callan's name on it. My twin. My other half gone.

My blurry vision clears as I lift my gaze to meet Hayden's, not understanding what he's doing here. What *we're* doing here. "How did you know where they were?"

He shrugs like it's no big deal. Like he didn't just bring me to the place that holds my worst memories, the place that makes me feel like I'm being crushed under the weight of grief every time I come here. But also the place where I feel closest to my family now. The place I come when I need to feel like I'm part of them still, even in the smallest of ways. "It wasn't hard to figure out. Your dad's name was on the records for the bar."

I nod slowly as I stare down at the three graves, still wondering what he's up to—and why he's in a suit. "Why'd you bring me here, Hayden?"

He doesn't answer, and I tear my gaze away from my brother's grave to seek Hayden out. When I find him, he's standing behind me, but he's not alone. His brother stands just off to his left, Lila to his right and his teammate Warren behind him. "What... is this?"

"*This* is our wedding day." Hayden smirks down at me as he

grabs my hand and presses it against his chest. His heart is beating steadily, like he's not at all nervous about my saying no. Asshole.

"Funny. I don't remember you asking." I should probably yank my hand back and really lay into him for being such a dick, but I'm all floaty inside and I'm also still kind of in shock that he's doing this. Seriously... Hayden Vaughn wants to marry... me?

In a graveyard?

How's that math work?

"When have I ever asked for anything when it comes to you?" He reaches into his pocket and plucks out a ring that he slides onto my finger. I stop breathing when the light filtered through the heavy blanket of clouds hits the emerald in the center. Of course, Hayden would never give me something as basic as a diamond.

My eyes snap up to meet his, blurred with tears as I finally see the depth of his love for me. It hits me like a tidal wave, crashing over every wall I've built to keep him out. This man, with darkness swirling in his fierce brown eyes, has laid his heart at my feet in the last place I ever expected. The laugh that comes out of me is tear-soaked and a little hysterical. "You're pathological."

"And you love me anyway." He leans down and kisses me once, twice, three times before pulling back and looking into my eyes. "So what do you say, Princess? You gonna marry me?"

I sigh. "I guess."

He smirks as he pulls me into his arms and spins me around. "Good, because we're doing this here. Now."

Wait... "Here?"

Hayden sets me down and brushes my wild hair back out of my face as the wind whips it around. I fall into his dark eyes as he says, "Here where your family is."

I blink back another wave of tears as I look up at him, realizing how much he gets me. How he knows exactly what I need and when I need it, even when *I* don't know. And how he's willing to give it to me without me having to ask. "Hayden," I whisper, so overwhelmed I can't even find the words to tell him how much this means to me. "Is this really what you want? To get married in a cemetery?"

"Only if we can take lots of pictures to rub in my dad's face. No doubt he'll flip the fuck out." Hayden and Sawyer discuss the strategy of making the most of pissing their father off while I get lost in my head.

I've never been one of those girls who fantasized about my wedding day. I wasn't even sure if I wanted to get married, but if I ever did, I knew the one thing I'd want was my dad to walk me down the aisle. My twin would be my man of honor, and my mom would try to pretend she wasn't crying in the front row.

When I lost them, that future disappeared and I never thought I'd be here, with someone who cares enough about me to make sure my family's with me on this day in the only way they can be. I've been blinking back tears, but one escapes anyway and Hayden brushes it away with his thumb as he stares down at me with so much love and affection it makes my heart ache. When he puts away his asshole side and turns sweet, I almost can't take it.

"You good?" he asks softly.

I nod, even though I'm not sure how true it is. But I want to be. Despite the grief that still sometimes feels so fresh, it's hard to catch my breath, today's supposed to be a happy occasion. I want it to be. "Yeah."

He watches me like he knows exactly what's going through my mind and then pulls me toward Warren, who's got this look on his face like he's about to say something obnoxious. Before he can, Hayden says, "Warren's ordained online so he'll do the ceremony."

I blink up at him as we stop in front of my brother's grave.

My other half and a piece of my soul I'll never get back. I curl my fingers tighter around Hayden's, needing to ground myself. "You're serious?"

"As a goalie during a shootout," War says with a grin as he holds up a piece of paper that looks like it was printed off the internet. "I even have a certificate and everything."

I laugh as I look up at Hayden who's smirking down at me with so much love in his eyes it makes my heart skip a couple of beats. "Well, if he has a certificate, it must be okay."

"Okay?" War asks, looking between us. I don't think he heard the sarcasm in my voice, or maybe he's choosing to ignore it. "It's fucking awesome." He turns to Hayden. "You're still good with me doing this?"

"You're here, aren't you?" Hayden says, gesturing Sawyer and Lila closer. "I need you guys to all sign this before we start." He grabs for a bag Sawyer has slung over his shoulder and digs out a piece of paper already clipped to a clipboard. Sawyer signs, then Lila, who passes it to Warren and finally Hayden has it back in his big hands.

"Once we sign this, the ceremony doesn't really matter. We'll be married," he says, his eyes locked on mine and studying me, I guess to see how I'll react to the idea of being married to him. From one second to the next, going from being single to attached for life is a lot. Like, *a lot*.

Hayden's eyes drop to the paper as he scrawls out his signature. Then he holds it out for me. My fingers tremble as I take the pen from him and stare down at the empty line where I'm supposed to sign. This is it. This is real. And it's happening now.

I look up at Hayden, who gives me this little nod like he knows what's going through my head and he's telling me it's okay. That I can do this. That I want to do this with him. So I take a deep breath and sign my name on the paper before handing it back to Warren, who looks between us and then shoves the clipboard back into Sawyer's bag.

Despite having not said a word, I'm married. To Hayden Vaughn.

Holy *shit*.

Warren claps his hands and rubs them together, grinning like a maniac. He moves so he's standing between my mom and dad's shared headstone and my brother's to their right. "Fair warning, this is going to be weird as fuck, but just go with it. It'll fit the vibe." Warren gestures around as if to remind us that we're standing on top of a whole sea of dead people.

Hayden grips my hand tighter and pulls me to stand in front of his teammate. Sawyer flanks him on one side and Lila moves up beside me on the other. She catches my eye and gives me a wide *I told you so* smile before shoving a bouquet of lavender, baby's breath, and eucalyptus into my arms. It smells incredible and I bury my face in the petals, breathing deep.

We stand here, the most unconventional bridal party ever, the chill of the cemetery biting at our skin. But none of that matters. Because in this moment, it's just me and Hayden, this consuming kind of love we have for each other, our friends, and the ghosts of my family.

I Need a Beer
@LazyWinger

The way Vaughn glared at RoMo just now... If looks could kill, we'd need a new forward. #Anchors #Drama

Hayden #48

MINE. *Mine. Mine.*

The word thrums through my mind, drowning out War's voice as he says some shit comparing love and hockey that I'm sure only makes sense to him.

Cassidy's my wife.

I'm actually impressed I pulled this off and that she went along with it. She didn't even give me shit about her lack of dress or whine about the fact this isn't some fancy princess wedding like a lot of girls dream of.

She didn't try to rip my balls off for assuming she'd marry me.

Instead, she's staring up at me with glitter in her green eyes, looking more beautiful than I've ever seen her in a skirt and t-shirt as she holds onto my hand like she never wants to let go.

I can tell she's trying not to cry and I know she's thinking about her family, but I hope this is making her happy. That *I'm* making her happy. Because that's all I want. To make this woman happy for the rest of our lives together—and the ones after that."

Warren finishes his speech and then looks at me expectantly. "You guys want to do your own vows? Or I can make—"

"No, we're good," I say, focusing on my wife and letting everything I feel for her, the things I've never admitted out loud, push to the surface. "Cassidy..."

She smiles up at me with tears in her eyes and I reach out to brush them away with my thumb before they fall, knowing how much it means to her that she keeps it together. She's strong, my wife. "There's nothing quite like the way you turn me inside out. This obsession I have for you, it's turned into so much more. You're everything, and now you're mine. Officially. Legally. Fucking irrevocably. I promise to protect you, to fight for you, and to never give up on us. You own my body, but I can't give you my soul because it's always been yours. Your name's etched into my skin and now you should know I'll never let you go."

She bites her lip, clearly trying to keep her composure as much as I am. "Hayden... God, you're infuriating," she starts, and there's laughter in her voice that makes my chest tighten and my brother laugh loud enough I side-eye him. "You've bulldozed into my life, turned everything upside down and inside out. And somehow, I've loved every second of it. You make me want things I never thought I would." Her fingers tighten in mine. "I promise to fight for you just as hard as you fight for me. And to never give up on us, either. You're mine now, too, Hayden Vaughn." She jabs her finger into my chest and her eyes narrow up at me. "Don't fucking forget it."

War clears his throat and then looks between us. "Well, that was... intense. Rings?"

I reach into my pocket and pull out the band I picked out for Cassidy, the one that matches the emerald in her engagement ring. I bought a matching one for me, black titanium with a small emerald set into it that matches hers. It's subtle, but is just one more thing that connects her to me.

She holds out her hand and I slide the ring onto her finger as she does the same for me. War's words drift away as I drown in Cassidy's gaze as she stares up at me with so much emotion it's hard to breathe.

When Warren finally gets to the part where he asks if we take each other, I nod without hesitation. "I do."

Cassidy's wicked grin tests the limits of my patience as she draws out her answer, but then she laughs and finally says, "I do, too."

Warren grins like an idiot. "Then by the power vested in me by a random website on the internet, I now pronounce you husband and wife. Time to kiss your bride, Vaughn."

Considering my dick's been half hard since Cassidy showed up, it's not a surprise that the kiss between my wife and I turns dirty right away. I don't kiss her; I *worship* her. Consume her. Brand the taste of her on my soul. I'll never get enough of the way the world disappears like it's just me and her. This all-consuming need to possess every inch of her and even then, it's not enough.

Nothing with her will ever be enough.

We kiss until she yanks herself away with a gasp, like she's been underwater with me until her lungs were on the verge of bursting and she needs the air to survive. But she doesn't go far, her forehead resting against mine as she shares that much-needed air with me.

"Holy shit, after that I need to get laid," Warren says, laughing from somewhere behind us.

I ignore him, brushing Cassidy's hair back behind her ear. It's time to tell her the secret I've been keeping.

She leans into me and I don't even think she's aware she's

doing it. I bite back my grin, whispering, "There's one more thing, Princess," into her ear.

She shivers, but says nothing, waiting for me to confess. "You're pregnant."

I don't know what I expected. Maybe a knee to the balls or a slap across the face? Maybe a whole mouthful of threats to my manhood or promises of retribution? But what I don't expect is the laughter.

My wife laughs so hard she has to pull away from me, clutching at her stomach as she bends over. She's laughing so hard there are tears streaming down her cheeks and she can barely catch her breath.

I stare down at her in shock as she finally starts to calm down, wiping the tears from her eyes as she looks up at me with this grin on her face that makes my heart stop beating for one and then two beats. "You're kidding, right?"

"No," I say, shaking my head as I look down at her stomach where our baby's growing.

Sawyer moves up beside me, his hand dropping onto my shoulder and squeezing. "'Fraid not, Sis. I ran the test myself. Hay-Hay knocked you up."

That fire I'd been waiting for sparks in her eyes then and they shift back and forth between my brother and me. "You... ran the test."

Sawyer nods. "Yep."

Cassidy's gaze cuts back to me, and it's so sharp it could slice me in half. And fuck if that doesn't turn me on even more than when she's all sweet and soft with me. "Tell me what you did." I open my mouth and she cuts me off before I can say anything. "All of it."

"So, I'm just gonna..." Lila interrupts, pointing toward the line of our cars. "I'll see you guys at the bar."

"Yeah, same," War says as he starts backing away.

"I rode here with Hayden so... guess I'm staying for the show." Sawyer moves to lean against Callan's gravestone, folding his arms and not even trying to pretend that he's giving us privacy.

Cassidy ignores them all, still staring up at me, waiting for an explanation.

"I knew you'd never agree to get pregnant without a fight, so I handled it," I admit, not feeling an ounce of guilt for it. She's going to be pissed at first, but then she'll realize how good this is for us.

"You handled it?" Her voice is quiet in a way I've never heard before. Flat. Hollow. I hate it. I want her fire, not whatever this is. "What did you do exactly? And how? We used condoms."

"We did," I confirm. "Until I took them off when you were coming and too fucked out to notice."

"Anything else?" she asks through clenched teeth.

"I may have slipped you a fertility enhancer or two in your morning smoothies."

She stares up at me, her mouth open in shock as she processes what I'm saying. "You... drugged me?"

"It was only a few times and Sawyer said it was safe. He's a doctor, so..." I trail off when her eyes narrow up at me like she wants to rip my dick off with her bare hands.

"You fucking asshole!" She shoves me hard enough that I stumble back a few steps. "You can't just do shit like that! You can't just make decisions about our lives without even talking to me about it!"

I reach for her, but she backs up, so I tuck my hands into my pockets instead. She needs time to come around to this? I'll give her a few minutes, but I'm not going to tolerate her putting distance between us, especially on our wedding day.

"I'd say I'm sorry, but I'm not. I'd do it again and again. In fact, I *will* do it again and again. And now that we're married, no takebacks." I move forward, letting my fingers drift down the bare skin of her arm until our fingers tangle together. I take the fact that she's letting me touch her without hitting me as a good sign. "You promised me forever, Princess, and I intend to collect."

Breakout Booster

2 oz apple vodka • 1 oz green apple schnapps • 2 oz white cranberry juice • ice
Garnish: apple slices

Shake apple vodka, green apple schnapps, and white cranberry juice with ice. Strain into a chilled cocktail glass and garnish with apple slices.

Cassidy #49

THE AUDACITY OF THIS MAN.

My *husband*.

Getting me pregnant on purpose?

Oh, fuck no.

It's like he forgot the girl he married because I've already got ideas spinning through my head about how to get my payback.

I'm not going to walk away, not when the asshole made me love him.

But I am going to fuck with him right back.

First, though... I need to make him think I'm over it. That I'm okay with what he's done. That everything's fine.

So I take a deep breath and lean forward, letting my forehead rest against his chest while I breathe him in. Despite what he's done, he's still mine and I'm still his. And maybe it's crazy, but I don't want anyone else. I want Hayden Vaughn and his stupidly sexy smirk and his sweet side that he only shows me.

And the idea of seeing him as a father? I almost can't handle the way that thought makes tingles spread through my body and center between my thighs.

"You're lucky you're hot," I tell him as I pull back and look up at him as his hand falls to my stomach. It still hasn't sunk in there's a baby in there. "And that I know you only did this because you're as bananas for me as I am for you."

He smirks like he knows he's won, and I bite back my own smile as I let him wrap me up in his arms. "Bananas?"

I scowl. "Really? After what you've done, you're going to tease me?"

Hayden has the decency to look apologetic, and you know, I think I'm going to like having this to hold over his head forever.

Sawyer scoffs from Callan's grave. "That's it? I thought for sure I'd get to see Hayden cry."

Hayden flips him off over his shoulder and I can't help it—I laugh.

"Hope you don't mind that I posted this on my socials," Sawyer says. "I need to see Dad flip out, Hayden. He's going to lose his shit when he sees you got married and he didn't get to use your wedding as a fundraiser or news headline."

Hayden groans. "You couldn't give us a day? Hell, an hour?" Hayden tightens his hold on me, squishing my bouquet between us, and I feel his words rumble in his chest. "You know he's going to be up my ass about what a disappointment I am, and while normally that's the highlight of my day—"

He cuts off as a buzzing starts in his pocket. He curses, reaching his hand inside and pulls out his phone. My gaze snags on the black band on that hand and there's a warm contentment settling in my bones when I see it there. As much as my name on his skin means he's mine, this is for the world to see. There'll be no question who Hayden Vaughn belongs to, and just thinking about it sends a surge of excitement coursing through my veins.

Hayden looks down at the screen and then back up at Sawyer with a smirk on his face. "Speak of the devil."

Sawyer grins as he moves up beside us. "Answer it."

Hayden flips him off again before putting the phone to his ear and answering with a gruff, "What?" He puts the call on speaker and holds the phone out so his brother can listen.

"What the fuck is going on? Why are you marrying that girl without talking to me about it first?"

"Oh, I don't know, because I'm a grown-ass man and don't need your permission to live my life?"

"Now you listen to—"

"Actually, Dad, I have things to do. Gotta go," Hayden says and then taps to end the call.

Sawyer laughs and punches his brother on the arm. "Holy shit, bro. He's definitely showing up now."

"When he shows up at our door with a camera crew, you better make sure you bring me popcorn," I say, glaring at my brother-in-law to show him I mean business. He's still on my shit list, too, for his part in helping Hayden knock me up. Sawyer's got to have broken about a dozen ethical rules for his part in all of this, and I wonder for the first time what kind of doctor he is to go along with Hayden's plan.

But we bonded over our love for drama, and that's not about to stop now. What can I say? I really like the guy.

And side note, but I can still have popcorn, right?

I haven't even begun to process the whole I'm pregnant thing, and holy shit, *I'm pregnant*. I know nothing about what I can and can't do or how to take care of a baby. I should probably be panicking about it honestly, but pressed here in the safety of Hayden's body, it's hard to worry.

My hand finds its way to my belly, and it all makes so much sense now. How tired I've been. The dizziness. The nausea. I thought it was just the stress of Roman harassing me and the break-ins, mixed with all the change lately.

Guess I was really, really wrong.

Hayden's hand slips around to my back, running up and down my spine. I shiver, but it's not from the cold. His touch always does this to me. Everything else fades away. It lights my whole body up, every nerve ending sparking to life with the simplest brush of his skin against mine. Even just a look from his dark eyes with that carnal intensity he's always got when he stares at me can turn me into a desperate mess.

And now we're married.

I'm married to Hayden Vaughn.

Whose hands are still roaming over my back and ass as if he's trying to memorize every curve of my body. As if he hasn't already.

"We need to get out of here," he growls in my ear, sending sparks down my spine. That tone of voice just does things to me. "Now."

Sawyer groans like he's disgusted. Serves him right.

Hayden steps back, gripping the hand that's not holding my bouquet and tugging me toward our cars. "Keys," he says, stopping and holding out his hand. I dig my car key out of my pocket and hand it over. He tosses it to his brother, who catches it out of the air with one hand. "Take her car and we'll meet you at the bar."

Sawyer salutes Hayden before he takes off.

"Wait," I say when Hayden tries to pull me toward his car again. "I need to do something first." He lets me go, but hovers behind me as I turn back toward my family's graves, his hand on my lower back like he can't bear to not be touching me at all times.

I kneel on the damp ground in front of the headstones of my family, bending down to place a piece of the bouquet Lila gave me on each of their graves. "It's been eight years since you've been gone, and I still sometimes think I'm going to walk into the bar and see Dad behind it, mom playing pool and Callan tossing bottles in the air trying to add some sort of adrenaline high to bartending." I let out a watery laugh as Hayden stands over me, close enough I can feel the heat of his body, but he gives me just enough space to do this.

"I know you'd be proud of me keeping The Sin Bin. And you'd love Hayden, too, even if he's a pain in the ass." His low chuckle from behind me is like a sip of hot cocoa, warm and sweet on my insides. "He's my soulmate, the love of my life and everything I didn't know I needed." My hand drifts back to my stomach again, and I know they know. They know everything. "I wish you were here for this. For the wedding. For the... baby."

Hayden kneels down beside me, his hand slipping into mine as he leans forward and kisses my forehead. "They are here," he says as he looks down at the graves. "Can't you feel them?"

I nod, blinking back the tears that want to fall as I stare up at him. I *can* feel them. Their love for me, their pride in me for keeping our family legacy alive. And I know they're happy that I'm happy. That I've found someone who loves me just as much as they did, even if he sometimes drives me to want to punch him sometimes too.

We sit for a few minutes in silence, and I close my eyes, tilting my head up to the shaft of sunlight that's broken through the clouds. It would be a really special moment if Hayden's voice didn't break the spell.

"Not to be a dick, but I need to fuck my wife and if I'm not balls deep inside of you in the next fifteen minutes, I'm going to lose my goddamn mind."

I roll my eyes as I stand up and brush off my knees. "You're always a dick."

He smirks down at me as he takes my hand and starts tugging me toward his car again. "And you love it."

Damn him.

I do.

Nick
@NetNastyNick

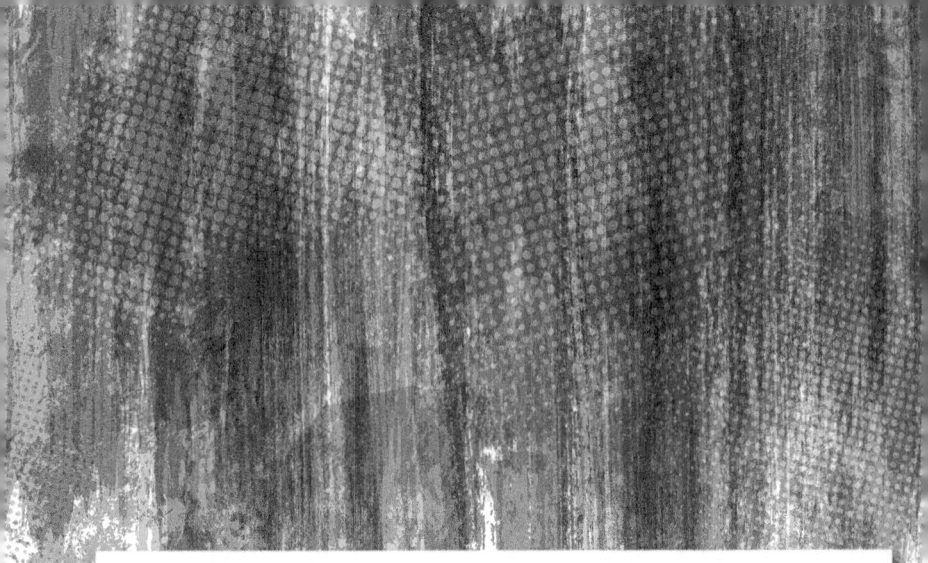

Vaughn's hit list this road trip: 3 Orcas, 2 Pioneers, and a Partridge in a pear tree. The man's a fucking holiday spirit. #SeasonsBeatings

Hayden #50

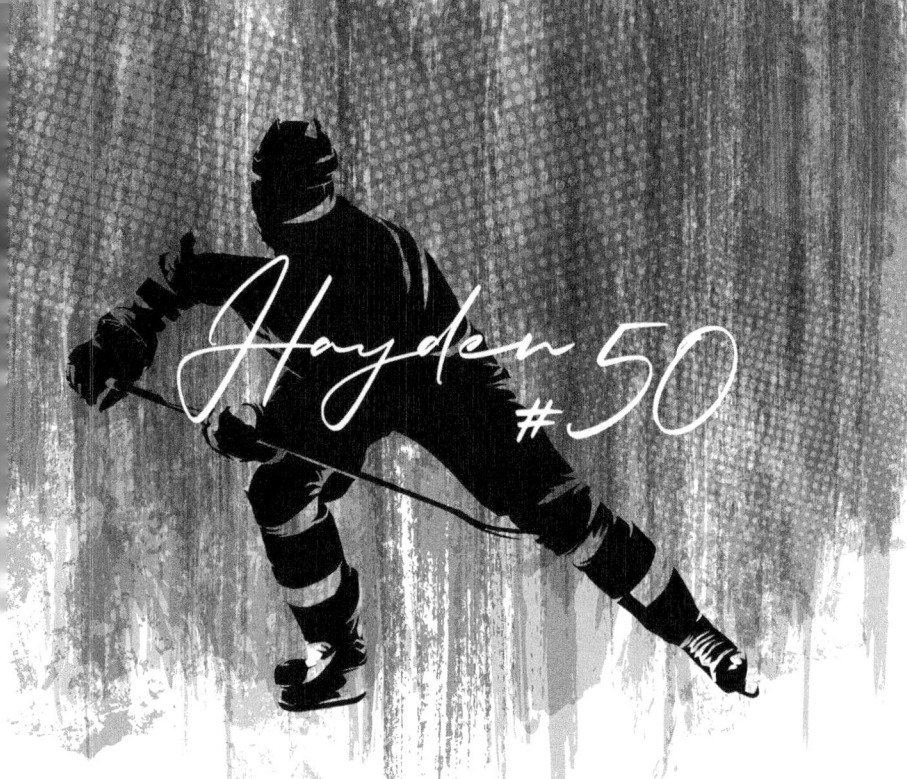

THERE'S something about fucking your wife that hits different.

Her fire might've gone down to cinders when she said her goodbyes to her family, but that anger from earlier is back as we stumble through the front door of our house. She's clawing at my clothes, violent as she bites into my lip and draws blood.

"I'm so mad at you," she bites out, shoving me back against the wall as she yanks my shirt off over my head. She's got this look in her eyes I've never seen before, and fuck if it doesn't make me hard as a rock. "I want to make you hurt for what you did to me."

"Do it," I say, reaching for her, but she slaps my hands away as she unbuttons my pants. Her hands shake and she growls when she can't get them open, ripping the fabric so hard that it tears and then shoves them down my legs. Thank fuck Sawyer listened to me and stayed out because no way are we making it to the bedroom.

At least not for round one.

She shoves me back against the wall again and drops to her knees, taking my dick in her hand and stroking it as she stares up at me with that inferno in her eyes that I'd destroy anyone or anything for. "You think you own me now?" She squeezes me hard enough that it hurts, and I groan as I nod. "I think *I* own *you*." She flicks her tongue against my piercing, and it feels like lightning shoots straight to my balls. Then she licks up the length of me before sucking the tip into her mouth and swirling her tongue around it.

"Christ," I grunt as she takes me deeper, bobbing her head up and down as she pushes me to my limits with her tongue, gagging when I hit the back of her throat. My fingers dig into her hair, gripping it in my fist. Her hands clutch my thighs, nails digging into my skin so hard I think I might be bleeding, but I give no fucks. She wants to hurt me? I'll take every bit of the pain and ask for more.

She pulls off with a pop, spit dripping down her chin and there's nothing better in this world than wrecking my wife with my cock. She stares up at me with those eyes that make me want to fall to my knees for her instead. "Take out your anger on me, wife. I deserve it."

She smirks up at me as she strokes me with one hand while reaching up to tweak my nipple with the other. "You do," she says as she twists it hard enough that it hurts like a bitch.

"Fuck," I hiss and she laughs, licking the spot where her name's tattooed on my abs.

"How hard do you think you have to come for it to hurt?" she asks sweetly, batting her lashes up at me as she bites her lip. She's so fucking sexy when she's like this, trying to be the one in control. I'll let her have it for now.

"Harder than you can take," I tell her with a smirk, knowing she'll rise to the challenge. She always does.

She stands up and shoves me back against the wall before reaching up to wrap her fingers around my throat. It's not tight enough to cut off my air, but my dick jerks as her nails prick my skin. "We'll see about that." She leans up and kisses me hard, biting my lip again before shoving me back and then down onto the floor.

I land on my back and she crawls on top of me, straddling my hips and yanking her panties to the side. Her skirt is shoved up around her hips and right now I want her to do whatever the fuck she wants to me. My wife wraps her fingers around my dick and then rubs it along her slick pussy. Back and forth, back and forth without putting me inside of her. It's maddening and torturous and I buck my hips up to try to force my way into her cunt where I belong.

"No," she says as she tightens her grip on my cock until it aches and she stops sliding across my length. "You don't get to take what you want. Not this time." She leans down, biting my nipple again and I grunt as I reach for her, gripping her hair in my fist as she sucks on it until it hurts. "I'm taking what *I* want." She sits back up, staring down at me with the devil in her eyes as she sinks onto my dick, daring me to move.

I don't even breathe.

She goes slow, so fucking slow that it feels like hours before she's fully impaled, her pussy squeezing the life out of me. She grinds against me, moaning softly as she tilts her head back and closes her eyes. "Hayden..." She says my name like a prayer, and it's all I can do not to flip her over and fuck her into oblivion.

But she wants to be in control. And I want to give it to her.

There is one thing I won't compromise on tonight. I reach up and grip her chin, forcing her to look down at me. "You look at me when you're riding my cock, wife."

Her eyes lock on mine as she bites her lip and rocks back and forth on top of me, using me to get herself off as she takes what she needs from my body. Her fingers dig into my chest as she moves faster and faster, bouncing on top of me with this wild look in her eyes that tempts me to blow my load just to piss her off. But I hold back, gritting my teeth as I let her use me however she wants.

Her pussy tightens around my shaft and she moans out my name as she comes, grinding against me as she rides out her first orgasm. She leans forward, kissing me hard as she keeps moving. "I fucking love you," she whispers against my lips, some of that fury in her eyes cooled.

So orgasms calm her right the fuck down. *Noted.* I'm tucking that shit away to use against her for the rest of our lives.

She starts to move again, riding me faster and faster until I can't take it anymore. She's had her fun, but now it's my turn.

I flip us over, pinning her beneath me against the hardwood floor as I fuck into her with deep strokes that make her scream and claw at my back like she's trying to get away, but she's not going anywhere.

My baby's growing inside of her and my ring's on her finger. She's got my last name and my name's tattooed on her skin. There's no escaping this life with me.

I reach between us and start rubbing her clit, needing her to come again before I lose my mind—or blow my load. Her back bows up into me as she wraps her legs around my waist. "God, Hayden," she chokes out in between moans and gasps.

"That's right, wife. Strangle my dick. Come all over me," I thrust harder, fucking her so hard it feels like I might break her, and for a second I wonder if I'm hurting the baby by being this rough. But then she's tipping her head back and choking the life out of my cock while she comes again, her body trying to pull me in deeper and never let go.

I don't hold back, fucking her through her orgasm and then letting myself come too as I bury myself inside of her and fill her with everything that I am. It feels like my entire being shoots out of my dick and into her. My balls ache when it's over, like a lifetime's worth of cum just left my body, along with a good chunk of my soul.

Cassidy wraps herself around me, holding me close as we both try to catch our breath. "I want you to know," she whispers against my ear. "I'm still mad at you."

"Yeah? Maybe I like you mad."

She laughs, her fingers drifting up to play with my hair as I stay inside of her, on top of her. "You're an asshole."

"Your asshole."

Vancouver Orcas Wave

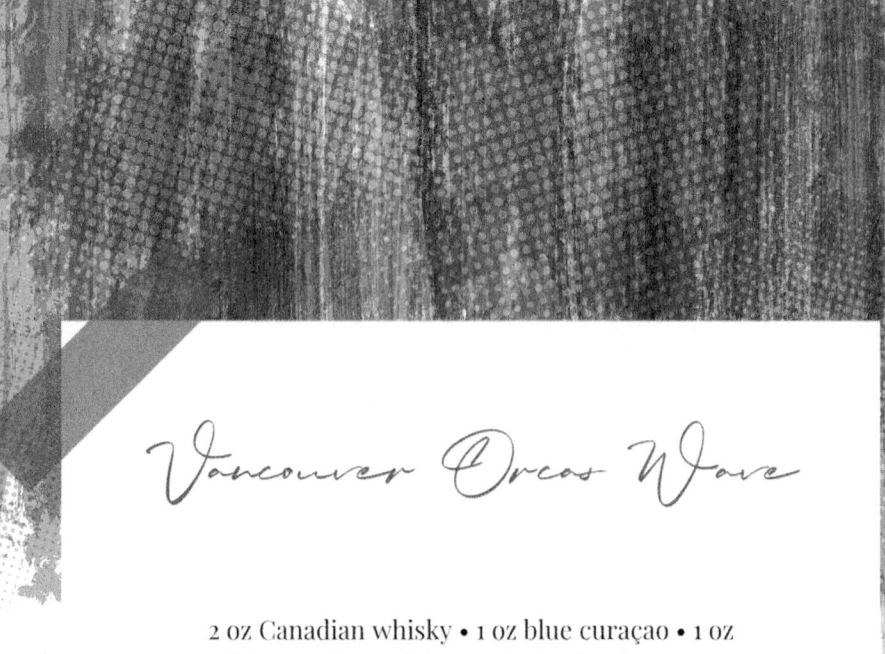

2 oz Canadian whisky • 1 oz blue curaçao • 1 oz white cranberry juice • splash of soda water • ice
Garnish: frozen cranberries

In a shaker, combine Canadian whisky, blue curaçao, and white cranberry juice with ice. Shake well. Strain into a chilled glass and top with a splash of soda water. Garnish with frozen cranberries.

Cassidy #51

TODAY'S the day I get my revenge.

Is it as bad as everything Hayden did to knock me up? Nope.

But did I wait a week so he wouldn't suspect what I'm about to do? Sure did.

I take a sip of my orange juice to hide my grin as I sprinkle the crushed up blue pill into my husband's protein shake and hit the button to turn on the blender. When it's done, I pour it into a glass and turn off the heat on the burner where his egg white and spinach omelet is done.

As I'm plating it up, Hayden walks into the kitchen already dressed in a low-slung pair of black joggers and a hoodie. He's got a baseball hat turned backwards on his head and I snap my mouth closed so I don't drool. I need to keep my out-of-control libido in check today if this plan's gonna work.

"Morning, wife," he says as he comes up behind me and

wraps his arms around my waist, letting his palm splay out across my belly. He's been using that name for me as much as possible in the last week, and every time he does something inside of me swoons like a fairytale princess.

Hayden kisses my neck and my stomach flips like it always does when he touches me. I used to think it was just because this thing between us was new and that's why our reactions to each other were so intense, but now I think it's just always going to be this way. It hasn't faded at all, my reaction to his skin against mine or even being in the same room as him. If anything, it's only gotten stronger.

And I'm not mad about it.

He reaches for the protein shake and I hold my breath as I watch him take a big sip. He doesn't even hesitate. In one go, he drinks it all down and then sets the glass on the counter before grabbing the plate with his breakfast and heading toward the dining room table. "You coming?" he calls over his shoulder.

"Yep," I say as I grab my plate and follow him. I glance at the clock, knowing I've got probably an hour max before the pill in his shake kicks in. Thankfully, he's got practice in forty-five minutes, so the timing should be perfect.

We sit down to eat, Hayden in the seat across from me as he digs into his omelet like it's the last meal he'll ever eat. He's always hungry, and pasta and protein are his two main food groups, so messing with his morning shake was a no-brainer.

"What time is practice today?" I ask casually, like I don't already know, as I take a bite of my toast. Morning sickness is a real bitch, and it's about fifty-fifty on if I'll actually keep it down.

"In," he glances at his phone. "Twenty-five minutes. I've gotta go." He stands up and walks over to me. No, he *saunters* over to me like he knows I'm eating him up with my eyes and he wants to let me have my fill. That infuriating smirk's on his face as he threads his fingers into the hair at the back of my head and grips tight, tilting my face up so he can kiss me.

It's not a gentle kiss. It's hard and possessive and I'm tempted to drag him back upstairs and fuck him until we both can't walk. But I hold back, knowing that this is all part of my plan.

He pulls back, nipping at my bottom lip before he lets me go and heads toward the door. "See you later, Princess," he calls as he slings his bag over his shoulder and then disappears out the front door.

I wait for the sound of his car starting before I stand up and grab my phone from where I left it on the table because I'm going to need it soon.

Sawyer comes downstairs while I'm waiting for the inevitable call or text from my husband when he realizes something's not quite right. He eyes me as I rinse our breakfast dishes and load them into the dishwasher. I'm biting the hell out of my lip to keep from cracking up over what's about to happen.

"What did you do?" he eventually asks while he leans his shoulder against the door frame and folds his inked arms across his chest. He looks like he's been in the gym already with a sweat-soaked t-shirt and messy hair pulled back in a bun.

"I don't know what you're talking about." This time I press my lips together so I won't smile and give myself away.

"You've got that look," Sawyer says as he pushes off the door frame and walks toward me. "The one that means you're up to something."

"I'm always up to something." I shrug, trying to play it off, but Sawyer sees too much and knows me too well.

"You finally gave him the pill, didn't you?" Sawyer's mouth curves up into a wicked grin when I say nothing. "Didn't you?"

My phone buzzes and I glance down at the screen, grinning when I see Hayden's name flashing there. "Oh, look. My husband's calling me. Gotta go." I shove Sawyer out of the way as I head upstairs, answering the call with a sweet, "Hello?"

"You want to tell me why my dick's so hard I can't get it into my cup?" Hayden asks in a gruff voice that makes my toes curl. He sounds like he's in pain and it's all I can do not to laugh.

"Huh. Not sure why you think I'd know the answer to that question, husband. But you should probably go into the bathroom and take care of that."

"You don't think I tried?"

This time I do laugh. I can't help it. Revenge is fun.

A voice yells in the background, and he groans. "There's nothing funny about this. You did something. Everyone's looking at my dick, Cassidy. My inappropriate hard as fuck dick."

"Good thing it's a nice dick," I manage to get out in between wheezes. Honestly, I deserve a damn medal for doing the lord's work here. There should be sculptures of his dick put on pedestals in museums around the world. His teammates get the benefit of basking in its glory while I get my revenge.

Call it a win-win.

Sawyer must've finished his breakfast because he's just come up the stairs, and I think he's on the way to his room when he hears me talking. He stops right outside the doorway, watching me swipe tears from my cheeks as I try to control my laughter. His head tilts to the side like he's trying to interpret why I've got an unhinged smile stretched across my face.

Hayden growls into the phone. "You know you're gonna pay for this, right?"

I lose my battle and crack up. Sawyer's grinning at me now because I think he's catching on that I fucked his brother over and he lives for chaos, even at Hayden's expense. After all, he's the one who helped me do this.

I finally manage to choke out two words and I mean every syllable.

"Can't wait."

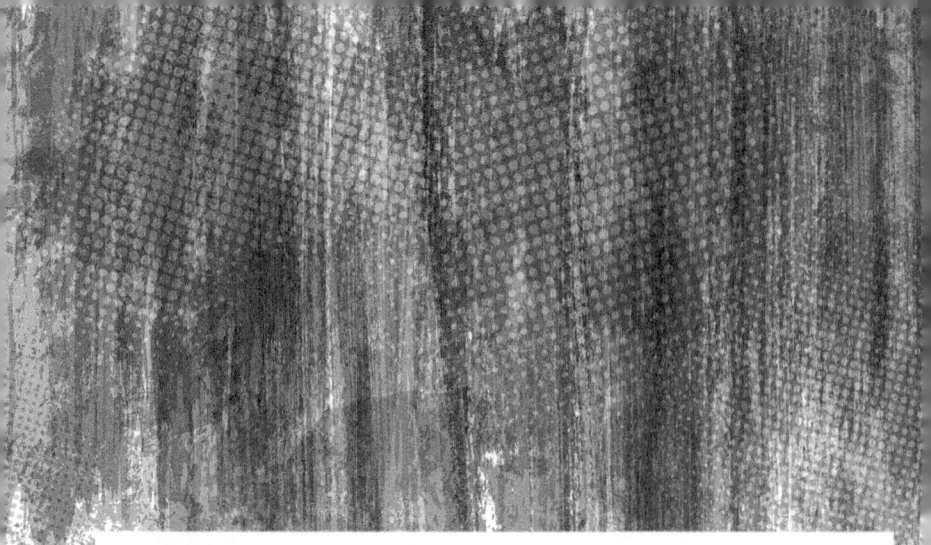

Smitty
@Hellraiser

29's playing style is like bringing a spiked bat to a pillow fight. Overkill but fucking effective. #NoMercy

Hayden #52

MY TEETH GRIT TOGETHER as I shove my shit back into my duffle. My dick brushes against the inside of my sweats and my knees almost buckle. It's so hard, it's pulsing with every beat of my heart, and it's only a matter of time before the guys notice.

And what the hell am I going to tell Coach? "Sorry, I'm too horny to practice today."

He'll kick my ass.

I don't know what the fuck Cassidy did to me, but this shit isn't normal. I can't skate when my dick's a goddamn steel pole between my legs and even the smallest brush of anything against it almost sends me over the edge.

Somehow I know that if I jack off, it's not going to help.

My wife had to have slipped something into my breakfast, and the worst part is I can't even be mad about it. Not after doing the same thing to her.

Warren slings his arm over my shoulders, and I blow out a breath as he jostles me. "Dude, what's wrong?"

"Nothing," I bite out, trying to shove him off me. He's like a fucking barnacle sometimes and him touching me while I'm hard is fucking me up.

He looks down at my dick and then back up at me with a smirk on his face that would drive even the most even-tempered guy to want to knock his teeth out. "Huh. I thought I liked hockey, but I've gotta say, you might be taking it to an unhealthy level. Unless that's for me?"

I shove him away hard enough that he stumbles back while he's laughing his ass off. A couple of the other guys are starting to pay attention to War's bullshit and I want no part of them realizing I'm sporting a massive boner in the locker room.

Let's just say it's not a good look.

Mattson and Kingston huddle around Warren, asking him what's going on as I ignore them all and grab my stuff, heading for the showers. It's not like I can hide it forever, but maybe if I can get some cold water on my dick, it'll go down so I can get out of the building.

It doesn't.

I take a freezing shower, trying to think of anything but my wife and all the ways I'm going to fuck her when I get home as retribution for this, even if I respect the hell out of her for fighting back.

But that only makes it worse.

My cock jerks against my stomach, and I groan as I reach down to stroke it. Yeah, because instead of sticking straight out like normal, I'm so fucking hard the damn thing is standing up.

What. The. Fuck.

The locker room is definitely not the place for this shit. My fingers wrap tighter around my shaft and it's too much and not enough at the same time. My balls are so tight they ache and there's no way I'm getting any relief until Cassidy gives it to me.

I glance behind me as I wonder if I'm really going to do this here. The locker room's the least sexy place I can think of, but my dick doesn't seem to care as it pulses in my hand and I clamp my mouth shut against the groan trying to slip out.

Goddamn it.

I stroke myself once, twice, three times before I come so hard it hurts. My knees buckle as I lean against the shower wall to keep from falling. I don't even know how long it takes for me to recover, but by the time I do, my dick's hard again. Or maybe it's still hard.

"Motherfucker," I mutter as I grab a towel.

How much of this shit did Cassidy give me?

When I get back to my locker, almost everyone's already on the ice, so I pull my clothes on, tugging my hoodie lower so it covers my raging hard on. For fuck's sake. It's like I didn't even come.

"Vaughn," Coach Morin barks when he sees me. "Why the fuck aren't you on the ice?"

I shift on my feet, hoping like hell Coach can't see my boner. My heartbeat echoes in my dick and I'm going to spank the shit out of my wife when I get home before I fuck this out of my system.

"Emergency at home, Coach. I've gotta go," I say, making a wish on every star in the universe he doesn't ask me for specifics. *Oh, sorry Coach, my wife dosed me with something this morning and now I'm too hard to skate.*

He stares at me for a second, weighing my words before he nods. "Go. Get your shit sorted out and be back for practice tomorrow."

"Will do," I say as I grab my bag and head for the door, trying not to walk bowlegged as my cock throbs with every step. It's like it's got a mind of its own, and this is a first for me. Usually, he and I are on the same page.

But not today.

The asshole's gone rogue.

I make it to my car, tossing my bag in the backseat before I get behind the wheel and take off toward home, hoping Cassidy's ready for what's coming her way.

She better be.

I pull up to our house and storm inside, dropping my bag by the door as I stalk through the living room and up the stairs. She's standing at the top waiting for me, leaning against the wall with her arms crossed over her chest and a smirk I'd be proud of if I wasn't so fucking horny and pissed off over what she's done.

I walk right up to her, using my size to back her straight into the wall. She presses her whole palm against my chest to try to stop me but I don't let her, gripping the backs of her thighs and lifting her so she has no choice but to wrap herself around me.

"Hayden, stop. You're not fucking me," she says as she tries to wiggle out of my grip.

I let out a deranged-sounding laugh, feeling so on edge I want to crawl out of my skin. My fingers tighten against her skin and I hope I leave bruises I can trace with my tongue later. "Oh, Princess. After what you did? You're lucky I'm not inside you already."

"Stick your dick inside me right now and you're going to need to tie me down at night so I don't cut it off in your sleep," she threatens, narrowing her eyes into slits and digging her nails into my chest through my hoodie. "Now put. Me. Down."

I let her drop slowly so she has to slide down my body. I don't miss the way she shudders, but she tilts her head up in that stubborn way she has as she shoves me back. This time I let her.

She crosses her arms over her chest again and I want to rip that stupid fucking t-shirt she's wearing off her so bad my fingers twitch with the urge. "What did you give me?" I ask as I reach down and adjust myself in my pants. It's not helping anything, but it feels good when I rub my hand against my cock, even though it's still throbbing like a bitch.

She smirks, and I know I'm going to lose my shit if she doesn't give me what I want soon. "A little something Sawyer got me. If you can use him to mess with me, I don't see why I can't do the same to you."

I groan. Of course my brother had a part in this. "I'm going to kill him."

Cassidy opens her mouth like she's going to say something, but the doorbell rings, interrupting whatever it was. "Better get that," she says, patting me on the chest and slipping out from between me and the wall. "You might want to do something about..." She gestures to the outline of my dick, which is fucking ridiculous in these pants. I can't believe Coach didn't notice—or maybe he just kept his mouth shut.

"I thought that was your job, wife," I say, adjusting myself, but it's useless.

The doorbell rings again, and Sawyer pops out into the hallway. "Are you planning on ignoring that or...?" He trails off as he looks me up and down before smirking. "I see your wife got even."

"No thanks to you, asshole. I thought you were supposed to be on my side." I glare at my brother, but the fucking bell rings again, so I growl and stomp down the stairs, feeling maybe the most out of control I ever have in my life. My blood's pumping so hard it's like I can feel it rushing through my veins.

When I yank the door open, my fucking father stands on the doorstep in the impeccable custom suit he's always got some version of on, salt and pepper hair perfectly slicked back.

Goddamn it.

"I'd ask how you know where I live, but I know better," I say, not bothering to open the door any further, but Satan himself pushes his way in anyway. His bodyguard follows and I swear to fuck if he goes near Cassidy, I'm going to rip his arm off and shove it down his throat.

"Hayden," my father says, looking me up and down with a

sneer on his face. His eyes linger on the black band on my left ring finger. "You look... well."

I fold my arms over my chest, knowing that if I don't keep my hands to myself, I'm going to punch him in the face. And now I have to do battle with my dad with a hard dick and I swear I hear Cassidy's evil laugh from somewhere in the house. "What do you want, Dad?"

He glances around like he's expecting someone else to be here with us before he turns back to me. Maybe he wanted Sawyer as a secondary punching bag, but my brother's smart and staying the hell away. "To make sure you haven't lost your damn mind because you're sure as hell acting like you have."

I grit my teeth, trying not to let his words get under my skin. He's always been good at that. "I don't know what you're talking about."

He tucks his hands into his pocket and looks around the room, his shrewd eyes no doubt judging every bit of it and finding my home lacking. "Did you or did you not give a sex worker thousands of dollars?"

What the actual fuck? There's so much to unpack in his sentence, I don't even know where to start, not that he gives me a chance before he starts in again.

"And did you or did you not marry this sex worker in a goddamn graveyard?"

"First of all, what I do with my money is none of your fucking business." Again, I don't bother asking how he found out about my paying off Morozov for Cassidy, but it looks like I need to fire my accountant. "And she paid me back every cent, not that you deserve to know that."

And she did, transferring me the money a couple of days ago. I tried to tell her I didn't want it, but her glare kept my mouth shut. I knew she needed to do it for herself, so I let her.

He scoffs like he doesn't believe me and I'm tempted to shove him out the door, but then he says the thing that triggers my rage. "We don't play house with the help, Hayden. These are the things we do with our wives, not the girls who service us when we get bored. I thought I taught you better than this, son."

"Yeah, well, I've always been a disappointment to you. Figured I'd see how far I could take it." I shrug like I don't care when really it's all I can do not to punch him in the face. He knows how to push my buttons like no one else. "Now, if you'll excuse me, I don't have time to listen to your bullshit."

I turn to walk away, but his next words stop me dead in my tracks. "You know, Hayden. You're making a mistake with this girl. I brought some papers my lawyer drew up to make this mess disappear. All you have to do is sign."

He holds out his hand and his bodyguard slips a manila envelope into his palm and it hits me like a goddamn freight train. I don't know why I never saw it before, but somehow I know all the winning in the world wouldn't make this man love me. Not the way a parent should love his child.

Not the way I already love mine.

And then I laugh. "You know, my whole life I've been trying to make you proud of me. To win your love. But you know what I just realized?" I step closer to my father, noticing for the first time how he's shorter than me by a couple of inches. Less broad. He's always felt so massive, this presence that's overwhelming. But not anymore. For the first time, I'm seeing him for who and what he really is. "It doesn't matter what I do, because you're not capable. This whole time, you had me convinced the problem was me. That I wasn't worthy. Turns out the problem's been you all along."

And a whole-ass weight lifts off me, like gravity itself is lighter as I stare down at the man who gave me life and then made it hell.

He stares up at me with his jaw clenched and his eyes hard as stone before he shoves the envelope back into his bodyguard's hands when I refuse to touch it. Then he turns to leave.

"You'll regret this decision, Hayden," he calls over his shoulder as he walks out the door.

I don't bother to reply. He's wrong, but I don't need to waste any more energy on him. I'm done letting him control any part of me.

And would you look at that?

All it took was a showdown with my asshole sperm donor and my dick's no longer a problem.

Thank fuck for small miracles.

Philadelphia Phantoms Specter

2 oz rye whiskey • 1 oz Amaro • 1 dash of Angostura bitters • ice
Garnish: flamed orange peel

Stir the rye whiskey, Amaro, and bitters with ice in a mixing glass until well chilled. Strain into a rocks glass filled with ice. Garnish with a flamed orange peel to evoke a ghostly flame.

Cassidy #53

"LOOK who decided to grace us with her presence," Lila drawls as I flip her off and move behind the bar. It feels like it's been too long since I worked back here now that we have Saylor to help cover. But after Hayden's showdown with his dad a couple of days ago, he and Sawyer have been breaking down every minute of their childhoods and I needed to get out of the house. "Though if I was the one getting railed by a hockey god every night, I wouldn't bother showing up either."

I roll my eyes as I tie an apron around my waist and grab a glass to start pouring drinks. I frown down at my stomach, wondering if that's a tiny bump I see. I have no idea how far along I am, and I should definitely get in to see someone to find out. "You're just jealous."

"Damn straight I am," she says as she mixes a drink for one of our regulars. We're busy tonight, but not so busy that I can't keep up with Lila and Saylor. The Sin Bin is my baby, and I'm proud of how well it's doing, even though it's been a lot lately with everything else going on in my life.

"Aren't you gay?" Saylor asks as she walks behind us to grab a fresh bottle of gin. "And have a baby with, like, another girl?"

Lila rolls her eyes at me as she passes the drink she made across the bar. "What, being gay and in love with my girlfriend means I don't have eyes? And can't appreciate good sex? Besides, Cassidy's husband is hot as hell."

Saylor stumbles to a stop, turning wide eyes on me. "Husband? You got married?"

I nod as I finish pouring a beer for someone down the bar and slide it toward them before flashing her my rings. "Yep."

She stares at me for a second before she shakes her head like she's trying to clear it. "Okay, we're going to need details later when it slows down." I bristle a little because I'm protective of my relationship with Hayden and I don't really know Saylor enough to want to share intimate details of my life with her.

Once she's on the other side of the bar and not in hearing range, I move closer to Lila, jerking my head once toward my newest employee. "What's her deal? How's she doing?"

We both look over at her in a totally not cool and not at all stealthy way. Thankfully, Saylor's frowning down at her phone while she types on it so she doesn't see us. "She seems good. A little distracted sometimes, but she gets the drinks out fast and hasn't screwed up too bad yet."

I nod as I grab a rag and wipe down the bar top while we have a second to breathe. My feet are aching and I still don't know how I feel about all the changes happening in both my business and private life, but I'm trying to just roll with it. I'm not really a spontaneous kind of person, but I'm trying. "Okay, that's good."

Lila nudges me with her elbow. "Don't worry about her too much. She's fine."

"I'm not worried," I say, but it comes out sounding defensive and Lila laughs. "I just want to make sure she's not going to, I don't know, burn down my bar or chase off all our regulars or something."

"She's not." Lila laughs. "And if she tries anything, I'll kick her ass for you," Lila says as she makes another drink for someone who just walked in.

"Deal." I watch her work with a happy smile on my face, knowing she's got my back no matter what. I leave her and Saylor to work while I head up to the office. I'm so behind on paperwork, it's depressing. It's been hard to find time with everything else going on, so I've been putting it off. Now that I'm here, I need to get it done so I can focus on other stuff.

I sit down at my desk and groan at how good it feels to sit down. It doesn't take long to pull out the stack of receipts and invoices that are due to be paid and start entering them into my accounting software. It's tedious and boring, but it needs to be done so I don't get any late fees or penalties.

By the time I'm finished, my neck hurts like a bitch, my eyes sting, and my ass is numb. I'm in desperate need of a walk to get some blood flowing back into my legs, and my stomach growls because I'm starving. I check my phone and grin at the message there from Hayden.

> Hayden: You know it's unhealthy for you to be away from me for more than half an hour
>
> Hayden: Doctor's orders

Then he sent a picture of him and Sawyer cheesing for the camera, his brother in his white lab coat. It's ridiculous and I kind of love it. Hayden's possessive, but then so am I. We have that toxic co-dependency vibe going on and honestly, I'm living for it.

> Cassidy: Huh
>
> Cassidy: And here I thought the road worked both ways

> Hayden: Smartass

I send him a picture of me flipping him off with my tongue sticking out and he sends back a heart eyes emoji which is so unlike him I can't help but laugh.

> Hayden: Come home now
>
> Hayden: I've got something I want to give you

> Cassidy: It's your dick, isn't it?

> Hayden: You'll have to come home to find out

> Cassidy: There's this incredible invention called the car
>
> Cassidy: If you want to see me, better figure out how they work
>
> Cassidy: Or learn to be patient because I still have a couple of hours here

> Hayden: We both know if I show up there you're not getting shit done

> Cassidy: True
>
> Cassidy: Guess you'll have to suffer through

> Hayden: Cold

I grin as I slip my phone into my pocket and stand up, stretching my arms over my head as I try to get some feeling back in my body. Lila's off in a few, so I head down to the bar to tell her goodbye. I think I got enough done upstairs that I can spend the rest of tonight with Saylor slinging drinks until closing.

Lila looks up when she sees me walking toward her and rolls her eyes. "I know you didn't finish all that paperwork."

I laugh as she unties her apron and tosses it on the counter before grabbing her purse from behind the bar. "You know what? Paperwork is now a banned word in my bar." I pull her in for a quick hug, noting Saylor's not behind the bar. "Where's Saylor?"

"She's been distracted, so I told her to go take a break and deal with whatever's bugging her. That was about ten minutes ago, so she should be back any second."

"Got it. Give Tavi a kiss for me, k?"

She nods as she waves and heads out the door. I take her place behind the bar and start pouring drinks for the customers who are still here, but it's slowed down a lot.

Eventually, Saylor comes back in with red-rimmed eyes looking like a wreck. I check the clock and it's only about half an hour until closing. "Hey, you can cut out early if you want," I tell her. I'm tired as hell, my feet ache and are no doubt swollen even though I'm not even that pregnant yet, and I'm the kind of hungry where it's walking dangerously close to the line of nausea.

But I also know being emotionally wrung out isn't a good space to be in when you're handling drunk customers.

"Can I ask a favor instead?"

I raise my eyebrows because I kind of thought letting her go home early for personal reasons was the favor, but I bite back my irritation. Snapping on my employee because I'm hangry isn't going to help. "You can ask, but no promises I'll do it."

She nods like she gets that. "Can you give me a ride? My car's in the shop and I don't really have any other way to get home." She sniffles and oh god, if she cries I have no idea what

I'm going to do. I'm not good with tears. "I just found out my boyfriend's been cheating on me and he was supposed to be my ride, but I can't handle seeing him right now."

I groan. "Why are men the worst? I swear they're all trash."

She chokes out a sad laugh as she grabs her stuff and starts untying her apron. "I mean, you married one, so you must not hate them that much."

I shrug because she's not wrong. "Hayden's different." He's still an asshole sometimes, but it's more in a fun way than a dickish one. And he's mine, so it's okay.

"Yeah, well, I wish mine was different," Saylor says as she tosses her apron into the bin with the dirty bar rags. "But thanks for doing this. It means a lot."

After I call a ride for the last customer, we close the place down. Then I wait for her to walk out of the door before I flick off the lights and lock up behind us. "No need to thank me. My ex was a cheating shitbag. I'm actually jealous of all the people who've never met him. That's how horrible he is."

Saylor shifts her weight from one foot to the next, but gives me the faintest smile before falling into step beside me as we head to the parking lot. "I guess we're about to have that in common, then."

I unlock my car and climb in behind the wheel, trying not to think about the awkwardness between us. Saylor's quiet and on her phone, so after connecting my phone to the car, I click on the playlist at the top of my app and Choke by Royal & The Serpent plays while I sing along.

I may or may not also fill the time fantasizing about everything I'm going to eat when I'm done with this. Steak tacos? Lemon chicken? Either way, I'm gonna need a milkshake.

My mouth's full-on watering as Saylor gives me directions to her place. She lives further away than I thought, in a suburb north of the city. As I pull into her driveway, I'm wondering why the hell she works at my bar, considering she lives all the way up here. There must be dozens of bars between mine and her house.

My phone buzzes in the cupholder where I tossed it. No doubt it's Hayden wondering where I am since I forgot to text him, and I go to reach for it when Saylor opens her door to get out. But before I can grab my phone to check, she asks me if I want to come in. Considering she hardly spoke to me the whole way here, the idea of sitting in her house in uncomfortable silence for the next however long is about as appealing as having all the hair on my head plucked out one by one, but then I feel like an asshole when I see her glassy eyes.

I remember what it was like when Roman cheated on me and I felt like I had no one to talk to who understood what that kind of betrayal felt like. I sigh and turn off the car, unbuckling. My stomach churns when I think about it, so as much as all I want to do is go home, curl up in bed with Hayden and eat all the things, I'm going to do my best to be here for her.

And it's not until I'm stepping inside the dark house behind her that I realize two things:

One—I left my phone in the car.

And two—I think I just got played.

Portland Pioneers Trailblazer

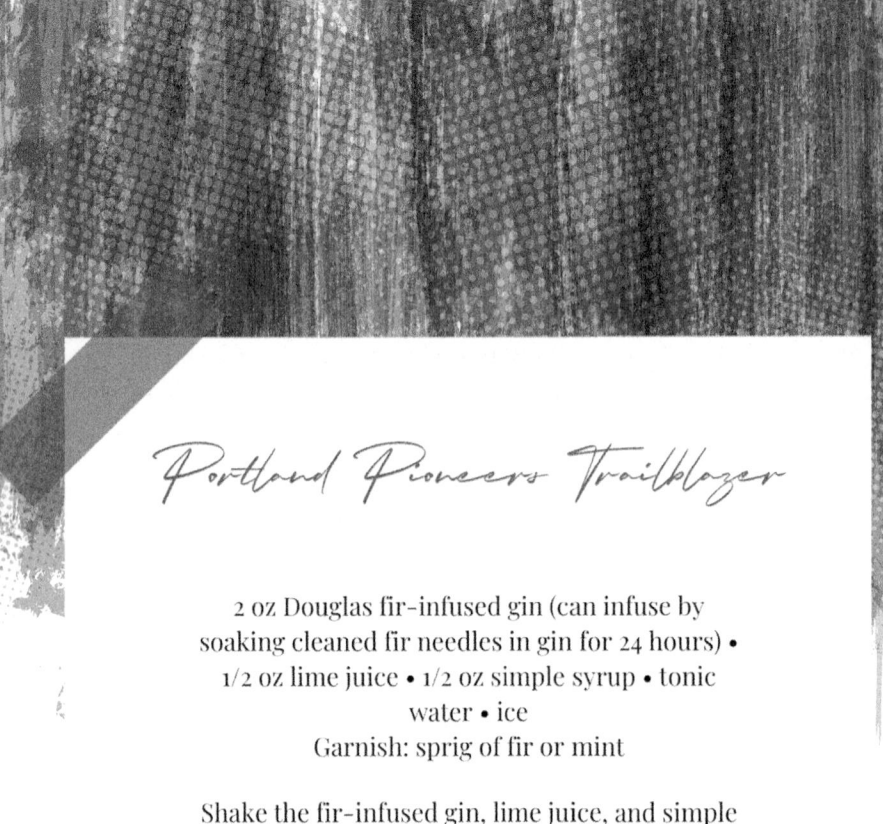

2 oz Douglas fir-infused gin (can infuse by soaking cleaned fir needles in gin for 24 hours) • 1/2 oz lime juice • 1/2 oz simple syrup • tonic water • ice
Garnish: sprig of fir or mint

Shake the fir-infused gin, lime juice, and simple syrup with ice. Strain into a highball glass over fresh ice. Top with tonic water and garnish with a sprig of fir or mint.

Cassidy #54

"WHAT THE HELL IS THIS?" I ask, the fury that ignites inside of me when I see Roman standing in Saylor's living room making my voice shake. "Why are you here?"

Before he can answer, a few things click into place and I laugh. It's a harsh and nasty laugh and he deserves that and so much worse. Shit, I wish I had my phone. "Let me guess." I point at Roman. "The cheating boyfriend?"

Saylor stands up straighter. All her earlier sadness washes away in literally a blink or two of her eyes. I gape at her like an idiot trying to wrap my mind around what exactly this is. Clearly, I'm missing a few pieces of the puzzle.

She smirks at me as she tosses her golden hair back over her shoulder. "You really thought I needed your pity? That I was going to cry on your shoulder about my shitty boyfriend? Please."

Roman hasn't said anything yet, and I honestly think this

might be the longest he's ever been in a room and not tried to direct the conversation to himself. But I should've known it was too good to last, because he opens his mouth, and yep, bullshit falls out. "Do you remember when we were good together? Back before Hayden Vaughn came to town and stole everything from me?"

I roll my eyes so hard I get a little dizzy. "Interesting take on the reality of the situation."

He, of course, ignores me.

"The problem is," he says, taking a step toward me like he's going to touch me or something. I move back until my ass hits the wall and I can't go any further. "You never stopped being mine. This whole time, I knew what you were doing. Playing hard to get, punishing me for messing around. You wanted me to chase you. Wanted to punish me for what I did."

I stare at him like he's lost his damn mind because he has. He really fucking has. "You know what? I need to go." I want to yell at him about how delusional he is, but there's a manic look in his eyes that I don't like. It's making that tiny alarm in my head blare like a damn tornado siren.

I turn to leave, but Roman's hand snaps out and grips my wrist so hard it hurts. "You're not going anywhere."

I try to yank away from him, but he just tightens his hold and I know I'm not strong enough to break free on my own. He's a huge, built professional athlete and just the thought of running is sickening to me. It's not even close, strength-wise. I glance over his shoulder at Saylor, but she's fallen back on the couch with her legs dangling over the arm, kicking back and forth as she scrolls on her phone.

It's like she doesn't even care about the clear assault that's happening right here in her house. She fucking tricked me and she's shooting straight up my shit list to deal with once I get away from Roman.

My heart's beating scary fast as I consider my options.

Kneeing him in the balls sounds like a solid choice. Let's call that plan A. In fact, I don't need a backup because if I drop him, I can make a run for the door. No way will Saylor catch me. I'd like to think I've got adrenaline on my side.

Roman leans in so our foreheads are almost touching. My stomach heaves and I bite back bile when I think he might actually try to kiss me. How did I ever find him attractive? But instead, he says, "I caught you, and now you're going to give me everything you've given up to that loser," he leans closer and drags the tip of his nose along my cheek. "Plus interest."

That's my breaking point. I lift my knee and slam it into his dick as hard as I can. I think he shifts at the last second so it maybe doesn't connect as thoroughly as I wanted it to, but whatever. He drops me so he can cup his junk and I shove him away so hard he falls on his ass. Then I haul ass straight for the door.

A loud click sounds from behind me and Roman's voice, cold and scary and not at all like I just rearranged his balls up into his body with my knee, stops me with my fingers inches from the doorknob. "You always did like doing things the hard way."

I turn to face him and he's got a gun pointed straight at my face. My stomach drops as I realize how bad this just became. *Oh shit, the baby.* My heart rate reaches new, record-breaking levels when I think about the little life inside of me and the danger they're in.

I hold my hands up in front of me like they're going to stop a bullet. There was a time I thought I'd rather die than ask literally anything of this man. My lack of begging suggests I still feel that way. "You don't want to do this."

"Oh, but I do." He grins as he takes a step toward me, then another and another, until he's close enough to press the barrel of the gun against my forehead.

My fear is quickly turning to rage as I stare into this

asshole's eyes. He cheated on me. He's done nothing but harass me, gaslight me, and make me feel bad about myself. And now he thinks he can try to take my life from me? Hayden? Our baby?

Not today, asshole.

"Get that motherfucking gun out of my face, you vile piece of shit," I say through clenched teeth. I'm not going down without a fight, and I'm definitely not letting Roman Morozov be the one to end me or my baby. "If you think I'm going to cower for you, kneel on the floor at your feet and beg you for mercy you might as well shoot me now because it. Will. Never. Happen."

Roman's eyes harden, and his jaw clenches so tight I think his teeth might crack. He's pissed, but so am I. And if this is how it ends, then so be it. I'll die with my head held high, knowing I fought back and didn't let him win.

"As much fun as watching this little showdown is, I'm going to shower and go to bed," Saylor says from somewhere behind Roman like he doesn't have me at fucking gunpoint and it's just another night for her.

Bitch.

"Hey Saylor? You're fucking fired," I call over Roman's shoulder, not taking my eyes off him even though the barrel of the gun still presses against my forehead.

She laughs as she heads up the stairs, leaving me alone with Roman and his fucking gun.

I want so badly to press my hand into my stomach and the tiny swell there because as much as I'm trying to hold myself together, to think rationally and not just lay down and take whatever Roman has planned, that mama bear instinct is already firing off inside of me and I want to tear his face off for daring to threaten my baby. But I don't. I don't want to give away that I'm pregnant if I can help it, though if he doesn't move the gun, I might have to.

Telling him about the baby's a risk and I'm not ready to take it yet.

With the hand not holding his gun, Roman grips the back of my neck and I stumble when he yanks me into his body. The smell of his cologne makes me gag and I'm actually sad I didn't eat tonight so I'd have something in my stomach to vomit all over him.

"Now here's what you're going to do," Roman says, not dropping that damn gun even an inch. "You're going to take off your clothes—"

"Like hell I am," I snarl, raising my knee to hit him in the balls again, but this time he's ready, and he pulls his arm back and slams the gun into my temple.

I crumple to the floor like the dead weight I am as the world goes black.

Fuck my life.

These goddamn hockey players are going to be the death of me.

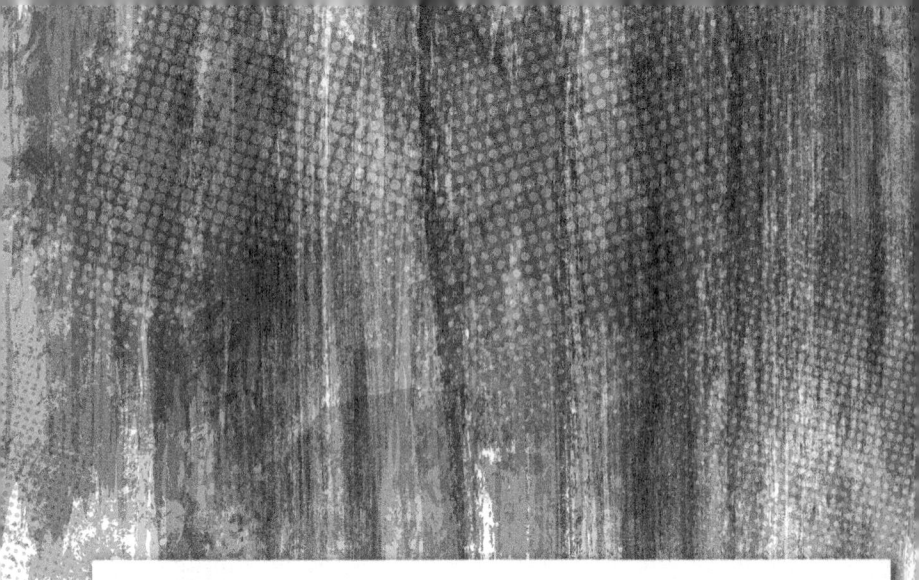

Will
@PenaltyBoxPoet

29 just sent another one to the shadow realm. Who's next? Taking bets now. #SoulCollector

Hayden #55

I'M PACING the halls of my house.

Stalking.

Waiting.

Looking at my useless fucking phone every two seconds just to see nothing's changed. I shattered the screen when I threw it at the wall after she didn't pick up her phone for the fifth time, so I squint my eyes through the spiderweb of cracks in the glass.

She texted me hours ago, but she never came home. She's not answering her phone and I know something's wrong. She doesn't do this shit. She's not irresponsible or forgetful. And I know she loves me, so if she's not here with me, something's happened.

She's the other half of me, and I feel the wrongness of whatever's keeping her away. I feel it right in my gut.

She's in trouble, and she needs me.

Our baby needs me.

If she wasn't so goddamn stubborn and turned off the location tracking on her phone every time I turned it on, I'd know exactly where she is. I'd be there right now, murdering the fuck out of anyone who dared to think they could take her from me.

No one, not even Cassidy, knows the lengths I've gone to in order to make her mine. They have no idea the things I'll keep doing to make sure she stays mine.

My brother leans against the wall, watching me. "We need to think this through, Hay. We don't even know where to start looking."

I glare at him as I shove my phone in my pocket and run a hand through my hair. "You don't think I know that?"

"You can't just go out and kill everyone you think might have her," he says, like he's trying to be reasonable or some shit. "We don't even know if she's in trouble."

I laugh because it's fucking ridiculous. She wouldn't run from me, not now. Not when she's carrying my baby and she's addicted to me the way she is. No, I've woven my soul so thoroughly with hers, you'd have to cut us both into pieces to separate us. Even then, I don't think it'd work.

She'd never walk away on her own.

Something happened, and I need to find her before it's too late. Before whatever fucker who took her tries to take everything from me.

It's got to be Roman. He spied on her, broke into her apartment, tried to blackmail her, and tried to threaten me away. But I already checked his house. He's not there, and neither is Cassidy.

I stalk toward the door and grab my keys from the hook by the front door. Sawyer grabs my arm and I shake him off, but he doesn't let go. "We need a plan."

"Fuck your plan," I say as I shove him away hard enough that his ass hits the wall behind him.

"I get that you're hurting, but I will fuck you up if you shove me again," my brother growls at me.

I shove my fingers into my hair and yank on the ends. "Fuck, I'm sorry."

Sawyer stands up and straightens his clothes but brushes off my assholish behavior. It's not the first time one of us has been a dick to the other and had to call him out on his shit and it won't be the last. "Forgiven. Now, what about that Romeo guy? Think he could help?"

I nod, knowing he's probably my best bet for finding out where Cassidy is. He might be an asshole, but he's got connections and resources I don't have access to. A spark of determination flares in my gut. I will never, ever let Cassidy go and it looks like today's the day I prove it. "Yeah, let me text him."

> Hayden: Need your help

> Romeo: What do you need?

> Hayden: My wife's missing. Need to find her ASAP. Any way you can help with that?

> Romeo: It won't be cheap

> Hayden: No fucking shit

> Hayden: Name your price

> Romeo: That's a dangerous thing to say to me

> Hayden: Just fucking help me find her

He doesn't reply for a few minutes and I'm about to throw my phone at the wall again when he finally texts back.

> Romeo: Give me a couple of hours

I want to rage at him, tell him I can't wait that long. *She* can't wait that long. But Sawyer pries my phone out of my hand before I can send anything else.

"We need to calm down," Sawyer says, looking me in the eye. "You're not going to do her any good if you're too emotional to think straight."

He's right, but that doesn't make it any easier to swallow. "I just need her back here with me where she belongs. I need them back."

"And we'll get her back," he says, clapping me on the shoulder as he leads me into the kitchen. He grabs two glasses and fills them with water before handing me one. I wish it was liquor, but I need to be able to drive the second I know where my wife is.

I take a sip and try to breathe through the panic clawing at my throat. I don't get fucking anxious. I don't panic. But here I am, losing my goddamned mind. Going fucking insane without her. Losing touch with reality as my mind fragments into pieces.

My brother leans against the counter and sips his own water. He's tense and I know he's worried about my wife, too. The connection I share with him, this bond we have no doubt means he's all kinds of twisted up over seeing me like this, too.

"Did you try calling Lila?" he asks. "She might know something."

I shake my head as I pull out my phone and dial her number. She answers on the third ring, sounding half asleep. "Hayden? What's wrong?"

"Cassidy's missing," I say, my voice rough and broken in a way I hate. "Have you heard from her?"

"No, I haven't. She was there until close with Saylor, but I got off earlier."

I go still. "Saylor?"

I haven't been spending as much time at the bar lately, not with Cassidy being home more and taking on more responsibility with the team now that Morozov's been demoted. I knew she had to have hired someone to cover the hours she'd been working, but I didn't think about the new girl.

She wasn't Cassidy, so I wasn't interested in knowing anything about her.

"Uh, the new girl? I swear you've met her at least once or twice." When I don't say anything to confirm because I honestly don't remember, she keeps going. "She's kind of quiet, so I don't know how much help she'll be."

I growl as I pull the phone away from my ear and tap into the text thread between me and Romeo. "Thanks for the info, Lila. Let me know if you hear anything."

She agrees and we hang up as I send Romeo the information about this Saylor person and tell him to track her down, plus give him the heads up about Roman. If she's got anything to do with Cassidy being missing, I need to know.

I call Romeo, but it goes straight to voicemail. Fuck. I need him to hurry the fuck up. I can't sit here and wait while my wife and child are out there somewhere in danger.

Sawyer watches me as I pace the kitchen again like a caged animal. I'm ready to fucking attack, but I rein it in. My brother doesn't need my wrath. I'll save it up for whoever took my wife, because I know someone took her. I feel it in my bones the way old people feel storms coming. "What do we do now?"

"We go out and look for her," I say as I grab my keys again and head for the front door. "We drive around until we find her."

"You don't even know where to look," Sawyer says as he follows me to the door. "She could be anywhere."

"Then we fucking look everywhere."

Atlanta Aces Peach Smash

2 oz bourbon • 1 fresh peach, pitted and quartered • 1/2 oz lemon juice • 1/2 oz honey syrup • mint leaves • ice
Garnish: peach slice and mint sprig

Muddle the peach quarters with lemon juice and honey syrup in a shaker. Add bourbon and mint leaves, then fill with ice. Shake well and strain into a rocks glass filled with crushed ice. Garnish with a peach slice and mint sprig.

Cassidy #56

THERE'S a warm weight at my back when I wake up, and I swear I just had the worst nightmare of my life. A heavy arm's slung over my waist and I take a few seconds to stretch before snuggling back into it. I don't open my eyes, not yet. I don't know what stops me, only that I know I'm not ready. I want a few more blissful seconds with Hayden before I have to face the day.

Except it hits me that the person behind me in this bed isn't my husband.

And that's when my whole body goes cold and my stomach rolls so hard I think I might throw up. My eyes fly open and I dig my nails into Roman's arm hard enough to draw blood as I breathe through my nose and swallow down the burning in the back of my throat.

He groans in his sleep and pulls me closer to his body, but I shove him away and scramble out of the bed. The room's spinning around me, and I can't get enough air into my lungs to keep from passing out.

And for some goddamn reason, I don't have on pants.

Where the fuck are my pants?

Roman sits up and looks at me like he's confused as to why I'm not still in bed with him. "What's wrong?"

"What the fuck is wrong with you?" I ask, my voice shaking so badly it's almost unrecognizable.

"Is this one of those mornings where you wake up so hungry you turn into a massive fucking bitch?" He scrubs his hand through his dark hair and his accent is thicker when he first wakes up.

I hate that I know that about him.

"Yes. Yep, that's it. I didn't eat dinner and I need you to go make me something to eat." I find my jeans halfway under the bed on Roman's side. Knowing he took them off me after he knocked me out—and yes, my head's throbbing like a bitch now that the shock of everything else is fading—makes me want to scrub my skin down to the very last layer to get rid of his touch.

Roman's eyes narrow as I step into one leg of my jeans and he wastes no time whipping out the gun from under his pillow and pointing it at me. "Don't you dare put those on. I've got big plans for you today, so you're going to crawl back into this bed and wait here like a good girl while I go get you food." His icy eyes are locked on me and I really don't like the glint in them.

"Saylor!" he bellows and I hate that I flinch. I hate that he notices more. I loathe that he smirks at me like he knows he's in my head.

She steps into the room with a scowl on her face. "What?"

Roman kicks off the blankets and stands up. I breathe out in relief when I see he's got boxers on. "Watch her while I make breakfast."

Saylor scoffs. "I'm not a babysitter. I'll make breakfast."

Roman chuckles. "So you can poison us all? I don't think so." He gestures toward the bed with the gun and she rolls her eyes, stepping further into the room as he walks out into the hall.

I debate whether or not I should pull on my jeans while Roman's certifiable ass is out of the room, but I've got to play this smart. Pissing him off over something small might hurt my chances of getting away later. And I don't want to push him too much and risk having him hurt the baby by getting physical with me.

"Why are you helping him?" I eventually ask Saylor as I sink down on the floor with my back against the wall and wrap my arms around my knees, ignoring Roman's demand to get back into the bed.

She sighs as she flops down on the bed and starts scrolling through her phone. "He promised me with you out of the way, I could have Hayden."

I can't help it, I laugh. And not quietly. I throw my head back and fucking cackle. This chick actually thinks my husband would just, what, forget about me and hook up with her? I sober when I realize how far I've come with trusting Hayden. The damage that Roman and the guy who killed my family caused has mostly healed over, thanks to my husband and his smothering ways.

Damn, look at me growing as a person.

"What's so funny about that?" Saylor sneers down at me in all her delulu glory. "You think he won't want me once you're out of the picture? I've got so much more to offer him than some trashy bar owner."

"Oh, sweetie," I say, shaking my head like I feel bad for her. And I do. She's got some serious issues if she thinks this is going to work out the way she wants it to. "Hayden will never want you."

She scoffs. "I guess we'll see, won't we? Oh, wait." She mock gasps and covers her mouth. "You won't." She rolls over on the bed so her back's to me and I assume she starts typing on her phone again.

I don't bother arguing with her anymore. She's too far gone and I need to focus on getting out of here before Roman comes back and tries to force feed me whatever shit he's made.

I glance at Saylor again, considering my options. With Roman and his gun out of the room, I think my best bet to get out of this situation is to try to overpower or outsmart her so I can get her phone. Then I can send a message or call Hayden.

Should I call the cops? Probably, but I want Hayden here more. I know he'll fix this in a way no police officer would, and I'm so very tired of having to deal with or think about Roman. If the cops come, it'll only mean facing him in court.

All I want is for this to be done for good.

I briefly consider climbing out the window and making a run for my car, but my keys are missing from the pocket of my jeans and my head's still fuzzy. Sometimes I'm seeing double and driving in the condition I'm in seems like a colossally terrible idea.

I'll do it if I have to, if it means surviving Roman, but it'd be better if I didn't.

I take a deep breath and stand up slowly, hoping she doesn't notice me. She's still scrolling on her phone, so I figure she's distracted enough for me to make my move. I tiptoe toward her, trying not to make any noise on the tile floor.

How the hell am I going to get her phone and send a message without her realizing I've done it?

She must hear me coming, because she sits up and tosses her phone onto the bed before turning to face me with her arms crossed over her chest. It's still unlocked and in a long list of things I need to go my way right now, it's a relief something's going right. "What are you doing?"

"Just getting back in bed," I say as I move toward the

mattress. "My head's killing me." The last thing I want to do is climb back into this bed, but I've got a plan—a bad plan—and I need to see if it'll work. "Could you please get me some Tylenol or something?"

"Ugh," Saylor wrinkles her nose. "I'm not the help."

"Seriously, I might throw up."

"Gross." She jumps off the bed and rushes toward the en suite bathroom. I have probably thirty seconds max to send a message, so I waste no time grabbing the phone she left behind and sending Hayden a text. I've never been more thankful for my dad's paranoia when I was a kid insisting that I memorize all the important phone numbers I might need, something I still do to this day.

> Unknown Number: 🫥

> Unknown Number: I'm at Saylor's house. Roman's here, he has a gun.

> Unknown Number: Hurry

Saylor's slamming things around in the bathroom and I hear the pill bottle shake, so I delete the messages as fast as I can and toss her phone back where it was. My pulse is racing as she comes back into the room with two pills in her hand. She tosses them toward me on the bed and I pretend to swallow them dry. No way in hell am I taking anything these two give me.

I hold my breath when she picks up her phone, but if she notices it's not in exactly the same spot she left it, she doesn't say anything. She just goes back to scrolling like nothing happened.

And that's when Roman decides to come back into the room with a plate of food in one hand and the gun in the other. He flicks his disinterested gaze at Saylor. "Leave."

She stands up and puts her hands on her hips, her phone

clutched in one of them. She looks like she's about to have a full-on tantrum, and I hope she does. I hope they get into it with each other and forget I'm here long enough for Hayden to show up.

But I'm not that lucky.

"You could at least say thank you," Saylor says in a snotty voice and Roman rolls his eyes.

"You're getting what you want just as much as I am. Don't act like it was some hardship to sit here for fifteen minutes doing nothing. Now go away. I've got some things to discuss with my girlfriend." His gaze moves back to me while Saylor heads for the door.

Shit. Shit. Shit.

I do *not* want to be alone with Roman. Nothing good can come of that.

Quebec Armada Iceberg

2 oz Canadian whisky • 1 oz maple syrup • 1 oz lemon juice • ice • sparkling water
Garnish: lemon twist

Shake Canadian whisky, maple syrup, and lemon juice with ice vigorously. Strain into an ice-filled highball glass. Top with sparkling water and garnish with a lemon twist.

Cassidy #57

I CURL my fingers into the blanket and tuck it tighter around me. I'm not stupid enough to think it'll keep Roman out, but it's all I've got. Also, the smell of eggs wafting off the plate my bastard of an ex is holding makes me gag a little. "Where are you going?"

Her face melts into a smug mask as she grins at me. "Your bar. It'll be opening soon and I have to make sure I'm there when my future husband comes in looking for you. He's going to need someone to comfort him."

Roman chuckles as he sets the plate down on the bedside table and sits on the edge of the bed next to me. I scoot away from him, but it's not far enough. "Don't worry about that, babe. He's never going to want you again after what we're about to do."

I don't like the sound of that at all. "What exactly are we doing?"

"First you're going to eat. You're going to need your strength for the plans I've got."

He holds up a fork full of food like he's going to feed me, and I turn my head away. "I'm not hungry."

Roman drops the fork with a loud clang, and when I look over, Saylor's gone.

Damn it.

"Even better. If you don't want to eat, we can move on to the fun part." He tosses the plate onto the nightstand and some of the food flies off it, but he doesn't seem to care. Then, he grabs the blanket in his fist and yanks it off of me so fast I don't have time to hold on. "We're making our own video for your porn account. Just a little something to remind everyone who gives you the best dick."

More like the most selfish dick. I don't think Roman ever actually made me come. But I don't say that out loud. I don't have a death wish.

I'm sprawled out in his bed in nothing but my Sin Bin tank top and a pair of lacy white panties Hayden bought me. I cross my legs, trying to keep them closed while Roman grips one of my thighs and forces them open. His gaze drops between my legs, but his eyes get stormy and fill with fury the longer he looks.

"What the fuck is this?" I slap his hand away when he goes for my panties, but he manages to tug the front of them down enough to reveal the tattoo of Hayden's name. His rage-filled eyes lift to mine. "You fucking slut. You let him mark you?" Every word gets louder and by the last one he's full-on yelling, spit flying from his mouth—the whole thing.

I flinch, hating that I do it, but Jesus, he looks unhinged and not in the fun way Hayden is. He crawls up my body and I kick and bite and scratch at him, but it's like he doesn't even feel me do it. He presses the gun to my temple and settles his weight between my legs. The cold metal stops me mid-fight and the tip of his nose is nearly touching mine as he stares down into my eyes.

"You need to learn what it means to be fucking loyal, Cass," he growls as his fingers dig into my hip hard enough to bruise. Like this asshole has any idea about loyalty. "And before today's over, you're going to regret ever betraying me."

I swallow hard as I try to keep my breathing steady. "You don't want to do this, Roman."

He scoffs as he grinds his disgusting dick against me through our clothes. Yep, he's hard. "Don't tell me what I want or don't want." He leans down and bites my neck so hard I cry out in pain.

Ah, fuck it. I have one last card to play, one last idea to buy time. Admittedly, it's not great. If he's this insane over a tattoo, he might go ballistic when he hears what I'm about to say. But there's a small sliver of hope it'll snap him out of whatever mental break he's having and remind him that I'm a human being and he doesn't actually want to kill me.

"I'm pregnant." He freezes, so I keep going. "I'm pregnant and Hayden is my husband, Roman. That's not just going to go away because you want it to."

He pulls back and stares down at me with a mixture of shock and disgust on his face. "You're lying."

I start to shake my head, but the metal digs into my skin, so I stop. "I'm not."

Roman rolls off me and stalks over to his closet, disappearing inside. I scramble out of the bed, fully ready to make a run for the door, when he appears with a knife in his hand.

I don't know what he plans to do, but I do *not* want to find out.

I bolt for the door, but he's right behind me and grabs me around the waist before I can get away. He slams me back against the wall and presses the tip of the knife against my stomach. "If you're pregnant, then I need to take care of it."

Somehow I doubt he means raise the baby as his own, not that I'd be cool with that either.

My heart pounds so loud in my ears I can hardly hear anything else. My vision tunnels down to just Roman and the knife as he presses it harder into my skin. Where the hell is Hayden?

I'm breathing so hard I'm dizzy, and I'm so freaking afraid as the tip of his knife nicks my skin.

"I knew you were a whore, but I can't believe you took it so far," he growls. "You let another man knock you up and this," he moves the knife slightly, his attention dropping to my stomach before he grabs my hair and yanks my head back. I bite my cheek to keep from reacting to the fear and the sting. "Isn't happening."

"If you do this, I could die," I warn him, glaring at him with every ounce of the hate I feel for this man.

His lip curls. "Better you die than have that asshole's child. The last thing we need is more of his bloodline tainting the planet."

"You're pathetic," I spit, deciding that pissing him off can't possibly make this worse. He's already about to do the worst thing I can imagine. "Such a sad excuse for a man that you have to resort to this to get someone to want you."

He slams me back against the wall again so hard my teeth click together and my head bounces off the drywall. Between him pistol whipping me last night and this, I think I might pass out or have brain damage. My eyesight is blurry and I see stars. It takes me a second to realize he's talking, but when I do, I wish I hadn't heard him at all.

"If you don't shut your fucking mouth, I'm going to cut out your tongue and wear it on a necklace around my neck to remind you of what you are." He leans closer until his face is inches from mine. "And that is nothing."

I swallow hard against the sting in my scalp and the throbbing in my skull. The light feels like a knife stabbing me in the brain and thinking is becoming an issue, but I'm pretty sure I have a concussion. "You're going to ruin your life if you do this."

He laughs, but it's not funny. It's dark and twisted and sends chills down my spine. "Who cares? It's already ruined. Your husband," he spits the word, "made sure of that. Now you're going to help me break Vaughn and I don't give a shit what happens after that."

And I can see it in his eyes—he means those words.

He'll never stop.

His fingers loosen from my hair but grips my throat so tight I can't breathe.

And for the first time, I think he might be about to actually kill me.

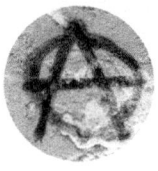

Jo
@ArenaAnarchist

Vaughn's style of defense includes two fists and zero fucks given #Hitman #Anchors

Hayden #58

"YOU'RE NOT GOING to be able to help her if you kill yourself and take us all down with you," Sawyer grits out as he braces himself with one hand on the dashboard and the other on the handle over the door.

Kingston's in the back seat after he showed up when we were about to go drive around looking for my wife. He wanted to know why I'd asked him to stake out Roman's house all night when there was clearly no one there. Now I'm doing ninety up the I-5 freeway, weaving through traffic like a maniac while Kingston barks out directions to Saylor's house from the back seat.

Thank fuck Lila was able to get into Saylor's employee file or I'd be fucked. As it is, it took way too long to get what I needed after that text and I'm climbing out of my skin.

"We'll be fine, but she won't if we don't hurry the fuck up." My voice is rough and raw and Sawyer looks at me like he wants to say something comforting, but knows it won't help.

He's right.

Nothing will until I have Cassidy back in my arms where she belongs.

Kingston leans forward between the seats as I take the offramp so fast we nearly tip over. "Take a left at the light."

I do, and he keeps giving me directions until we pull onto Saylor's street. I slam on the brakes and park in front of her house before jumping out of the car and running toward the front door.

It's unlocked and I shove it open, not caring that it slams against the wall behind it. I can hear Cassidy screaming from somewhere inside, and I run toward the sound. She screams again, but it's muffled and I'm fucking terrified of what that means. I barely notice my brother and Kingston bursting through the door right on my heels.

I tear up the stairs, following my wife's tortured scream and into a bedroom. Roman's got his hand around her throat as he presses her into the wall. She's clawing at him and kicking, but she's not getting anywhere. Her face is red and her eyes are wild with fear and I see fucking red.

I don't know how Roman got a gun since I don't think he's a US citizen, but he has one pressed to her temple and she's fighting like hell to get away.

"Don't fucking move," Roman snarls when he sees us come around the corner. "Or I'll put a bullet in her skull."

Cassidy's eyes meet mine and they're filled with tears. She's shaking and it makes me want to rip Roman apart with my bare hands, which, unless I can get that gun from him, is what I'm going to have to do. I can't let him walk away after this. He's been fucking with her for too long and now that he's hurt her, he needs to fucking die.

I'll deal with the fallout later.

"Let her go, Roman," I say, holding up my hands as Sawyer and King flank me on either side. "She doesn't want you."

Roman laughs as he tightens his grip on Cassidy's throat.

"So? You fucked up, Vaughn. You took everything from me, so now I'm going to take everything from you."

I glance at Cassidy and she's still struggling against him, but it's like he doesn't even notice. Her body's slumping, her eyes fluttering, and I know I only have seconds before she loses consciousness.

"You don't need to do this, man. Just let her go and we can talk about it." I take a step toward him, hoping he'll focus on me instead of my wife. He needs to get his fucking hands off her. "We can figure something out."

He shakes his head as he presses the gun harder into her temple. "I don't want to talk. I don't want to *figure things out*," he mocks. "You made sure of that when you fucked up my life. Now you're going to watch me fuck up yours."

Cassidy's eyes roll back and Roman looks down at her with disgust and I swear to fucking god his finger starts to tighten on the trigger. He's done listening to anything I have to say and I feel Sawyer lunge at the same time I do. Kingston moves, too, and I have to hope that the on-ice chemistry we've built where we react to each other without having to say a word is in play right now as we rush Roman together.

I slam into him so hard he flies back and Cassidy drops to the floor. She's gasping for air and Sawyer drops beside her as Roman tries to scramble away from me. I'm not letting that happen.

I grab his arm and yank it toward me, twisting it until I hear a pop that tells me it's dislocated. He screams like a fucking baby, but he doesn't drop the gun. He slams it into my face instead and my grip loosens on him just enough for him to kick away from me. My jaw hurts like a bitch, but I'm too pissed to let it slow me down. I trust my brother to make sure my wife's okay, so I don't stop to check on her. Instead, I focus on Roman, who's trying to get up off the floor with one good arm.

I grab him by the throat and lift him to his feet before slamming him into the wall behind him. He groans and drops the gun, but I don't let up on his neck. He needs to fucking die for what he did to Cassidy.

"Hayden," Kingston says from somewhere behind me, his voice calm and steady. He presses the gun into my free hand, and then he gives me a grim nod. I know what he's saying, that he'll take whatever happens here to the grave. That it's necessary. That he understands and he's got my back.

I nod back as I raise the gun and press it to Roman's forehead.

He laughs through the pain, blood dripping down his chin from where I must have busted his lip when we collided. "Go ahead and do it, you pussy. You won't be able to live with yourself if you do. I'll haunt you for the rest of your life. You'll never be free of—"

I don't hesitate as I pull the trigger. The sound of the gun going off echoes through the room and Roman's head snaps back before his body slumps to the floor in a heap. He's dead, but I don't feel guilty or sick. Just fucking relieved.

Kingston's heavy hand falls onto my shoulder and he squeezes. "I'm good," I tell him, and I mean it.

I'd do anything for my wife, for the family we're creating together, and this is the ultimate proof.

Maybe murder is my love language. Looks like my fantasy of burying Roman's body in the woods is about to come true.

I turn to Cassidy, who's unconscious on the floor. I drop to my knees beside her, letting the gun fall from my grip. My fingers shake as I brush her tangled hair off her forehead. She's got bruises on her temple and when Sawyer lifts her eyelid, her eyes are red where they should be white. My fingers clench into fists and I want to kill Roman all over again for hurting her.

I should've made him fucking suffer.

"Is she—"

"She's alive, definitely concussed. But I can't tell much more than that until we get her to the hospital," my brother says, his voice steady with that calm doctor demeanor that comes naturally to him after all his training. He presses his fingers against the inside of her wrist. "We need to go."

"We can't just leave him. And wasn't there supposed to be a chick here?" Kingston asks, gesturing at Morozov's corpse as it leaks blood onto the tile. Yeah, that's gonna be a problem.

Fuck.

With every cell in my body, I want to go with my wife. I *need* to go, to hold her hand, to make sure our baby's safe and healthy. But I know I can't, not yet. Not if I don't want to spend the rest of my life in prison.

So I let the one person I trust more than anyone else in this world, outside of Cassidy, take care of the most precious thing in my life. "King's right," I say to my brother. "You take her while we clean up and deal with Saylor." That bitch needs to suffer for her part in hurting my wife. "Text me when you know anything. I'll be there as soon as I can."

"You sure?"

"I'm not going down for killing this asshole. Just make sure she's okay, Sawyer." I know I look deranged when I growl at him, but after an entire night of not sleeping, going insane with worry over what happened to my wife, and killing a now former teammate, I have no fucks left to give.

My brother nods before scooping Cassidy into his arms and carrying her out the front door like she's the most precious thing in the world. She is to me, and I know he understands that.

Kingston steps up beside me, his gaze on Roman. "What do we do with him?"

"We need to get rid of the body."

He nods. "Any idea how to do that?"

I eye him. "Why are you not losing your shit right now?"

He lifts his eyebrows. "Why aren't you?"

Kingston blows out a breath. "This isn't my first ride on this particular crazy train. Let's just say I had an unconventional childhood and leave it at that." He shrugs as he looks down at Roman's body. "But right now, I'm here to help, so let's get to it."

I don't ask him for details because I know he won't give them. We all have secrets, and I respect that. But I'm glad he's here with me now when I need someone to help me clean up this fucking mess. I drag my phone out of my pocket and step out of the room, hitting Romeo's contact. It rings three times before he finally answers.

"You're racking up quite the bill, Vaughn. Let me guess. You need my help?"

I scrub my hand down my face before realizing it's got tiny droplets of Roman's blood on it. I'm too tired to spar back with him, so I just go with the truth. "Yeah, I do."

"What do you need?"

"To get rid of a body."

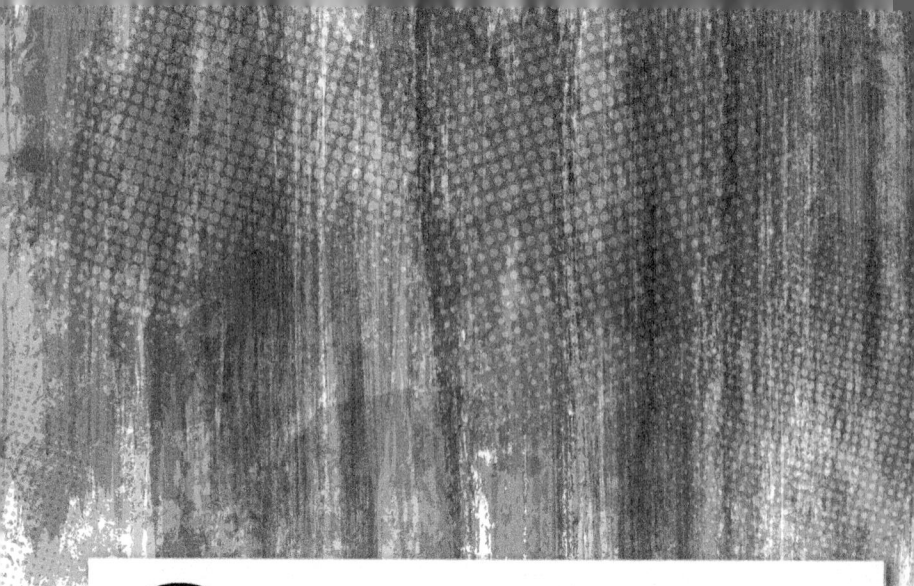

Deke
@DrunkOnDekes

Did anyone else see Vaughn obliterate that Pioneer? Dude's gonna find ice shavings in places he didn't know existed. #IceBurn

Hayden #59

ROMEO CHUCKLES on the other end of the line while I pace the hallway outside the room where I just killed my teammate. "You don't ask for much, do you? Did you kill them, or are they just dead?"

"Does it matter?" My voice is rough as fuck.

"Maybe." He sighs and mutters, "I don't know why I'm the go-to guy for body disposal for all of you assholes." I don't know what he's talking about, so I don't say anything. "How dirty do you want to get your hands in all of this?"

"They're already stained fucking red."

"Fair enough. Have you ever been to Emerald Hills?"

"Why the fuck are you asking me that?"

"Calm down, Killer. It's relevant."

I shake my head before I realize he can't see me. "No, never."

"The woods are beautiful up here. Dense. Private. I'll text coordinates for one of my favorite hikes. You'll want to bring a shovel, unless you want my guy to go hiking for you. Which will cost you extra."

His speaking in code is obnoxious considering we've already talked all about the dead body in the other room, but I get the impression that he just likes fucking with me.

"I don't have the time for a hike tonight, so hook me up with your guy." The last thing I need tonight is to spend hours digging a hole deep in the woods to toss Roman's corpse into. No fucking thank you. It's already killing me not to be at the hospital with Cassidy right now, making sure she and our baby are okay after everything Roman and Saylor put her through.

"You got it. Text me when you get to the address. I'll have him meet you there."

Romeo ends the call and I walk back into the room to find Kingston's already found a tarp from somewhere and he's spreading it out onto the ground. "Smart. We've got a plan. We need to get him into the car."

"What car? Didn't your brother take yours?" he asks as he kneels down by Roman.

I sink down beside him, and we shove Roman's body onto the tarp before wrapping him up. There's some rope King must've grabbed, too, so we tie everything securely so the blood and other things don't leak out while we move him. It's already a big enough mess in here. "Yes, but Cassidy's is outside. We'll take that. We just need to find the keys."

The two of us scour the house and eventually come up with my wife's keys hidden in a drawer in the kitchen, which just makes the fury I've managed to wrangle under control flare up again. I wish I could resurrect Roman and kill him again for even thinking of taking Cassidy from me, let alone hurting her.

Kingston props open the back door and we haul Roman's body outside before loading it into the back of Cassidy's SUV. It's the middle of the day, so the worst possible timing to move a body, but we can't leave it here. I don't bother looking around to see if anyone's watching. At this point it won't matter, they've already seen us and checking our surroundings is only going to make us look more suspicious.

Kingston jumps into the passenger seat, and I slide behind the wheel. "Hope you don't mind, but we've got a stop to make on the way."

He glances back into the back briefly, and I can only imagine what he's thinking. We're in a car with a dead body. The longer we're in the city with Roman's corpse in the car with us, the more at risk we are of being caught.

But I don't have a choice. I'm compelled by my insane protective instinct to do this. "It'll only take a minute."

Finally, King nods. "I trust you." He looks back at Roman again before adding, "And I owe you one for saving me having to spend one more second breathing the same air as that douchebag."

I know what he means, but there's really nothing to say. We've got shit to do, and time is of the essence. I pull out of Saylor's driveway and head toward The Sin Bin.

Saylor needs to suffer for her part in this. She might not have physically hurt Cassidy, but she sure as fuck helped Roman do it.

I park down the street from the bar and Kingston eyes me warily. "What are we doing here?"

"Tying up loose ends. Wait here." I don't have to tell him that he needs to be ready to move in case anyone comes sniffing around the car.

I tuck my hands in my pockets as I walk down the sidewalk toward my wife's bar, getting ready to put on the performance of my life. Saylor needs to believe I think Cassidy blew me off and that I'm here looking to tell her off for it. Then I need to act like I'm open to her flirtation, even if it'll make me want to puke, to get her out of the bar so she can take a little trip into the woods with us.

I push open the door to The Sin Bin and step inside. It's

early afternoon, so the place isn't technically open yet. The girl I assume is Saylor is behind the bar and she looks up as I approach, a smug smile curling her lips. "Hayden, what a surprise. What can I do for you?"

She seems awfully fucking familiar with me, considering I barely know who she is. I don't like that shit at all.

"Is Cassidy here?" I ask, not even having to act to sound pissed off. Looking at this bitch and thinking about what she did is making my tone authentic.

She shakes her head, her eyes glittering with something that prompts violence to flood my veins. "No, I haven't seen her."

"She was supposed to come home last night and didn't show. I thought maybe she'd be here." I look around like I expect to see her hiding in the corner or something.

"I'm sorry she stood you up," Saylor says, leaning forward on the bar so her cleavage is practically spilling out of her shirt. "Can I get you a drink while you wait?"

I let my gaze drift down her body, holding back the sneer I want to unleash on her. The words I want to use to cut her down before I do it for real. I'm still undecided on if I want to kill her for what she's done, and if I don't, I need something that's equally horrible to punish her with. "No, I'm good." I tuck my hands in my pockets again when her eyes find my wedding ring. "You want to get out of here?"

She grins at me like she thinks she's won. "Yeah, let's go."

I add the fact that she's so willing to abandon my wife's bar and her responsibility to it to her list of crimes. "After you lock up," I say, gesturing toward the door.

Saylor rolls her eyes but walks around the bar and grabs a set of keys off a hook before heading toward the front door and locking up behind us. She turns to me with a flirty smile on her lips. "What are we doing?"

I don't answer as I lead her down the sidewalk back toward

Cassidy's SUV. Kingston's got his phone in his hand, pretending to be scrolling social media, but I know he's keeping an eye out. When we get close, he glances up and nods once before climbing out of the car and walking around to the back seat and climbing in.

We're on the same page. No way in hell can we stick Saylor in the back seat and risk her asking questions about the body-shaped cargo in the back. I open the passenger door for Saylor and she slides into the car, brushing her body against mine while she does it. I lean in and she sucks in a breath while her pupils blow wide. "I didn't realize you were bringing a friend."

I just give her my meanest smile while I pluck her phone off of her lap. She doesn't even notice. She also must not notice that I'm driving Cassidy's car, the same one that took her home last night and was likely parked in her driveway this morning when she left to come here.

What an idiot.

When I straighten, I close the door before she can say anything else and power her phone off while I walk around the front of the car. Then I tuck it into my pocket and start the drive east to Emerald Hills. Now that I've got Saylor in my grasp, my thoughts spin out about my wife. It's been more than an hour since my brother took her to the hospital. Why the fuck haven't I heard anything about how she is?

I'm so up in my head, I don't realize how hard I'm gripping the wheel and my fingers ache.

Saylor's too busy trying to seduce both Kingston and me, so she doesn't even realize or care where I'm taking her.

"Where are we going?" she finally asks when we hit the on-ramp for I-90.

"Emerald Hills," I answer, glancing over at her as I weave through traffic. "I want to show you something."

She smiles and reaches over to run her hand up my arm. "I bet you do."

I shake off her touch, trying not to be as much of an asshole as I want to. She pouts but pulls back, leaning into Kingston instead. He looks like he's about to lose his shit with her, but he holds it together while we make our way out of the city.

The drive takes us nearly an hour, and by the time we reach the hiking trail Romeo sent me coordinates for, Saylor's getting antsy. She keeps asking what we're doing here and where we are. I've distracted her every time she starts to look for her phone, but I'm on edge like a motherfucker because I still haven't heard from Sawyer.

Just as I'm about to get out of the car, my phone buzzes and I grab it so fast, I fumble it into the backseat. Kingston chuckles but hands it back, getting out of the car with Saylor on his heels. I owe him so fucking big for all of this.

> Sawyer: She's okay
>
> Sawyer: They're okay

Two simple words that mean the whole fucking world.

My head falls back and my eyes close for a second while I let myself bask in the relief of knowing my wife is safe and she's alive. Our baby survived.

Fuck.

I glance outside, knowing now I need to focus. The rest of the world needs to fall away because there's one last thing to take care of before I can go be with them.

And with that in mind, I send the text that's going to wrap this all up, grab a bag of supplies from the back seat, and climb out of the car.

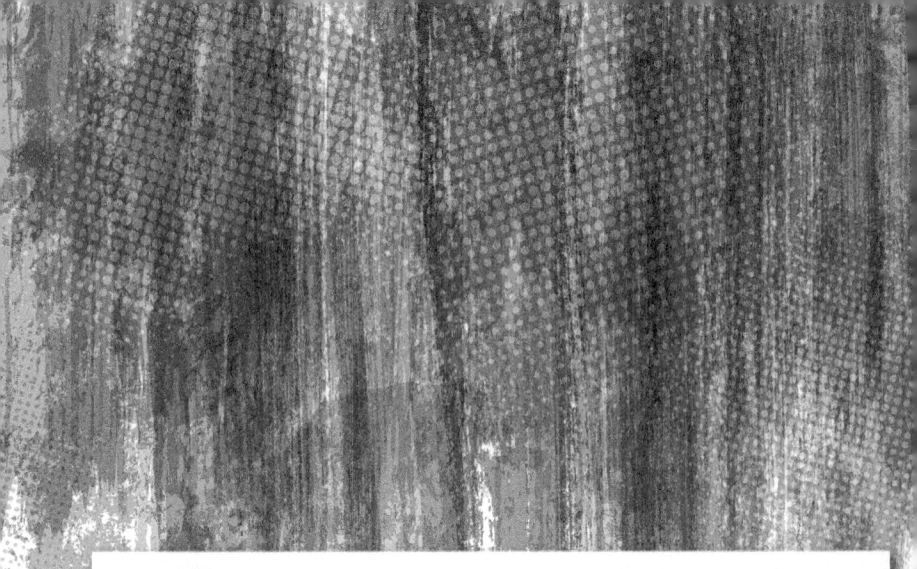

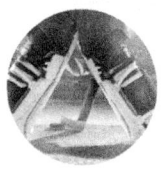

get it
@InTheFiveHole

Every pass between 29 and 22 is less 'here, have the puck' and more 'fuck you, asshole' #PassiveAggressivePassing

Hayden #60

AFTER TRIPLE CHECKING the car's locked, we head into the woods feeding Saylor some crap about wanting to hike to my cabin. Saylor's whining about not having the right shoes or some bullshit, but neither Kingston nor I are giving her the attention she wants.

About ten minutes in, she stomps her foot like a child and crosses her arms. "I'm not going another step. You seriously couldn't get us a, like, a hotel or something? Take me back."

I move closer to her and lean down into her space. "Aw, what's wrong, baby? Thought you could handle a couple of elite athletes in bed, but you can't hack it on a little hike?" I smirk at her as I straighten back up. "You're going to keep walking until we get to where we're going. And then you're going to do exactly what I say or I'm going to kill you."

Her eyes widen, and she takes a step back. "What?" She looks at Kingston like he'll save her, but he just shrugs.

"You heard him."

She glances between us and must realize we're not fucking

around because instead of doing what I told her to do, she screams and turns to run. I sigh and then two steps later, I've got my hand slapped over her mouth and my arm around her waist. "The last in a long line of bad decisions."

Then I turn to King. "Can you grab the tape out of the backpack?"

He steps up and digs around in the bag on my back before reading my mind and tearing off a piece of duct tape and slapping it over Saylor's mouth when I take my hand away.

"Thank fuck," he mutters. "If I had to listen to any more of her bullshit, I was gonna slit her throat myself."

She's got mascara tracks down her cheeks as the tears flow, but I feel nothing. I'm empty inside. Well, that's not really true—I'm fucking seething, but her suffering gives me satisfaction and what I suspect is an insatiable hunger for more.

After she stumbles and falls to her hands and knees with a muffled cry, I get tired of how slow she's walking and throw her over my shoulder. I figured she'd have more fight in her, but then she's not my Princess. My little liar. *My wife.*

After today, I doubt I'll ever think of Saylor again.

Eventually, we go off trail and walk into the woods deep enough that it feels like we're miles away from anyone or anything. That's when I toss Saylor at the base of a huge fir. "Strip," I tell her, digging the gun I used to kill Roman out of the backpack and aiming at her when she refuses to move.

Kingston says nothing, just stands nearby watching to see what I'll do, ready to step in if necessary to subdue Saylor or help with whatever. He really is going above and beyond with this teammate thing.

Saylor's shaking her head frantically, her arms wrapped around herself as her wide eyes dart around like she's going to find someone to help get her out of this. But there's no one here but me and Kingston, and neither of us are going to save her.

"You want me to do it for you?" I ask as I hand King the gun.

I pull a switchblade out of the backpack and pop it open. She shakes her head again and starts yanking off her clothes until she's standing in front of us naked, shivering in the cool air.

I don't even look at her body, keeping my eyes locked on her face. I won't betray my wife that way, but Saylor being naked is a critical part of the plan. Not only is the ground littered with sharp pine needles, but it's cold and wet as fuck up here in January in the mountains. I don't want her to have any kind of protection from the elements.

"Sit down," I order, reaching back into my bag and pulling out some spectra rope. I toss the backpack aside after slipping the blade back inside and then I approach Saylor, kneeling down in front of her and waiting until she meets my eyes. "Do you know why I'm doing this?"

She shakes her head as tears continue to flood her face. She looks wrecked with a red nose, mascara smeared under her eyes, swollen skin from her crying, and messy hair.

"Because you fucked with my wife." I clench my teeth. "You put my baby at risk. I can't risk you fucking up everything I've taken for myself, the things I've done to have her." I glance back at Kingston, nodding at him to start wrapping the rope around Saylor, tying her to the tree. The spectra rope is notoriously hard to cut, so even if she finds something to try to saw through it with, it won't work. "I want you to know that you're probably going to die here in these woods, all alone, with only your regrets."

Her eyes widen as she shakes her head frantically again. She's trying to say something, but it's muffled by the duct tape over her mouth. I don't care what she has to say anyway, so I stand up and help Kingston wrap the rope around her again and again. When we're done, we knot everything tight and test the strength of it all, making sure it's impossible to escape without someone stumbling on her and the odds of that are minuscule all the way out here, away from any trails.

When we're done, I squat down in front of her again, my elbows on my thighs. "You're only alive right now because I want this to be slow. I want you to spend your last moments suffering. And if by some miracle you manage to get free, you need to run and never look back. Should you come for me, or worse, for my wife, I'll tell the world about that little scheme you were running before your move to Seattle."

I didn't think it was possible, but Saylor somehow gets paler and I grin, enjoying the way this is all coming together. Whatever Romeo charges me for his digging still won't be enough for everything he's done to help me with this. Last night when I had him dig into Saylor, I never expected he'd find a scam she ran on people from her small town, convincing them to donate thousands to a fund for a made up sickness before they caught on and she had to change her name and flee to the big city.

"What do you think the people of Wallace would think if they found out you bailed with their money, changed your looks, invented a whole new persona and have been living it up with their money?" I stand to my full height. "I won't hesitate to ruin you if I find out you survived. So if you do, I suggest you don't draw my attention to you because I will stop at fucking nothing to make my wife happy. Your existence is a threat to her happiness, and that cannot stand."

She's sobbing as I turn away from her, nearly hysterical with the way she's losing her shit. I chuckle as I slip the backpack onto my back and Kingston side-eyes me. "What?"

He shakes his head as we start walking back toward the car. "Nothing."

"Don't judge me," I mutter, shoving my hands in my pockets.

He laughs. "I'm not judging you. You're just intense as fuck, man." He looks over his shoulder before adding, "And maybe a little crazy."

"You ever been in love?"

King doesn't hesitate. "No."

I smirk at him. "Just wait. I bet you'll be worse than I am." We walk back the way we came, through the woods, checking to make sure as we go that we can't see or hear Saylor.

He laughs. "Fuck, I hope not."

By the time we get back to the car, I'm feeling lighter than I have in days. But then I notice the guy leaning against it. Surprisingly, he's younger than me. He's got messy hair, light eyes that are somehow darker than anything I've ever seen, and a gives no fucks vibe about him. He's in a leather jacket and worn jeans as he pushes off. He upnods the two of us. "Romeo sent me." He jerks his thumb back at the car. "Said you needed my brand of expertise."

I eye King, wondering if he knows what this guy's deal is, but he looks just as confused. "What brand is that?"

The guy shrugs. "My name's Grave. Do with that what you will."

Kingston whistles low as he walks around the back of the car. "How does someone get into your line of work?"

The guy laughs, running a tattooed hand through his hair. "It's as fucked up a story as you're probably imagining."

"Do we want to know?" I ask, pulling Cassidy's keys out of my pocket and unlocking the SUV.

He shrugs again. "Probably not." He pulls open the hatch and looks inside, then he grins at us. "Good call with the tarp. I hate it when they leak on me."

I glance at Kingston, who just shakes his head like he can't believe this is happening. I don't blame him. It's been a fucking wild twenty-four hours. "So, what now?"

The guy closes the hatch and turns back toward us. "I deal with our friend here and we never see each other again. Unless you need me again."

"Actually, I was hoping you could deal with getting rid of the car and the mess we left behind at the house. I don't even know where to start," I say, twirling the keys around my finger. I hate that we're going to have to drive the corpse mobile back to civilization, but we don't really have a choice, and this burning itch under my skin of needing to get back to Cassidy is becoming unbearable.

He nods. "Sure, that's doable. But it's going to cost you extra."

I huff out a laugh. "Of course it is."

He walks over to the classic matte black Mustang parked beside Cassidy's SUV and pops the trunk before pulling out a shovel and some other supplies and dropping them at his feet. "You guys can go. I'll get the address from Rome and one of us will text when it's done."

King and I exchange a look before we both nod at the guy and climb into the car. He starts whistling as he walks toward the woods, dragging Roman's body and his stuff behind him.

"What the fuck just happened?" Kingston asks as I start driving back toward Seattle.

We bump over the unpaved makeshift road back toward the highway. "I don't know, but I'm not going to ask questions about it."

"Agreed." King leans back in his seat and closes his eyes, looking like he's about to pass out. I don't blame him. It's been an insane couple of days for all of us. At least we're on the All Star break, so we don't have to be at practice. Most of our teammates are on vacation somewhere warm, so as far as murders of a teammate go, we couldn't have timed this shit better.

"Hey," I say, and he cracks an eye open. "If you ever need anything, you know I'm there, right? You got blood on your hands for me, and I'll happily do the same for you. No questions asked."

He nods and closes his eye again. "We're brothers now."

I smile at that, liking the sound of it.

Brothers in blood.

blue
@UnderTheIce

If @hayv29's illegal checks were a drinking game, we'd all be blackout drunk by the first period. #AlreadyBuzzed

Hayden #61

BY THE TIME we make it back to the city, I'm ready to collapse from exhaustion, but I need to see Cassidy before I can even think about doing that.

I drop King off at his place and head home to shower off the blood and burn my clothes. I do it as fast as I can and I'm sure it's a half-assed job, but it's all I can handle at the moment. The second I'm done, I make sure the fire's out in the fireplace and get back in Cassidy's SUV, driving it over to Saylor's house.

I back it into the driveway, leave the backpack with the gun inside and then walk a mile down the road before calling a ride to take me to the hospital where my brother works and where he took Cassidy.

When I get there, I run through the halls until I find Sawyer standing outside a room with a chart in his hand. He looks up when he hears me coming and grins. I walk straight into his arms and he hugs me tight, holding me together and taking on some of the weight of everything that's happened so that I can be strong for my wife when I walk through that door.

"Everything good?" he asks, letting me go.

I nod. "Yeah, it's taken care of."

He looks down at his watch and nods. "It's been hours. I was starting to worry you'd gotten caught or something."

"Nope, all good." I glance at the door he's standing in front of and he steps aside.

"She's okay," my brother reminds me, his hand clasping me on the shoulder and squeezing. "I was actually getting ready to do an ultrasound to check on the baby. Go in and get the shit I don't want to see out of the way and I'll be back with the machine."

I nod and take a deep breath before pushing open the door and stepping into the room. Cassidy's asleep, her face bruised and swollen from Roman's attack, but she's alive. She's safe.

And I'll make sure she's so fucking happy, she doesn't have a chance to sink into her trauma from what Roman and Saylor did to her.

I pull up a chair beside her bed and grab her hand, kissing her bruised knuckles before holding it against my cheek, just needing to feel her skin pressed against mine. She stirs, her eyes fluttering open as she looks around before settling on my face. Her lips curve up into a smile that puts light in my world again. "Hi," she says, her voice hoarse and raw.

"Hi, Princess." I lean forward and brush my lips over hers gently, but there's that spark between us and she deepens the kiss before I have a chance to. She whimpers when our tongues collide and I swallow it down. She still tastes like mine and I shudder at the thought I could've lost her and never had this again.

When we finally break apart, it's only because my brother wheels a machine into the room and I force myself to pull away. I grin when her lips chase mine, and even with all the bruises on her face, she's so fucking gorgeous I rub my chest because it hurts to look at her. She's smiling up at me, and it makes me want to cry from how fucking happy I am that she's okay. That we're okay.

My brother stops the machine beside Cassidy's bed and starts setting it up as I lean over and kiss her forehead. "Sawyer said he wanted to check on the baby."

She nods, looking nervous but excited as my brother lifts her hospital gown and squeezes some cold gel onto her stomach. She jumps and Sawyer chuckles. "Sorry, should've warned you."

He presses a wand against her skin and moves it around until he finds what he's looking for. I know everything about my brother, all his little tells, which is why I notice it when he tenses before he forces himself to relax.

"What?" I bite out, knowing I'm being a dick but having zero filter after almost forty-eight hours without sleep, killing Roman, kidnapping and likely killing Saylor, and thinking I lost my wife and baby. I can't handle any more bad news.

Cassidy starts to panic and tries to sit up, but winces and gasps from the pain as her eyes get glassy. "Is something wrong with the baby?"

"No, not wrong," Sawyer says slowly, and I can tell he's trying to figure out how to say what he needs to. I'm so fucking over this day. I brace harder, and I want to lash out at him, even though I know whatever's about to come out of his mouth isn't his fault. "It's, uh." He coughs out a word, but I can't tell what he's trying to say.

"What?"

"Twins. It's twins, brother." He looks over at me, his eyes wide, like he can't believe it. "We should've known. You never do anything without doing it all the damn way."

Cassidy bursts into laughter and I startle, surprised she's taking the news this way. I should've known she would after the way she reacted when I told her she was pregnant.

When she calms and wipes the tears from her cheeks, she

points at me. "This is karma for giving me fertility pills in my smoothies, asshole. Did you forget I'm a twin? They run in my family. Add in to the mix making me extra fertile and you're lucky it's not a whole litter."

I chuckle, shaking my head as I lean down and press my forehead to hers as Sawyer finishes up the ultrasound. This moment feels like a miracle, like something I've had to walk through fire to get to, and I take a breath, cementing it into my memory. "You're amazing, Princess. You know that?"

She nods, her eyes glinting. The bruise on the side of her face shadows her happiness, and I again wish I'd made Roman suffer before I killed him. I hope he's burning in hell right now. "I know." She smirks at me before adding, "But you can keep telling me anyway."

My brother wipes off her stomach and puts the machine away. "I'll give you two a minute," he says as he walks out of the room.

Cassidy reaches for me and I lean down, kissing her again because it's all I want to do for the rest of my fucking life. But we're interrupted by the door swinging open and two police officers walking into the room.

"Sorry for the interruption," the first one through the door says, "but we've got some questions about what brought you in, ma'am."

Both men move to stand at the end of the bed and Cassidy and I lock eyes for one heartbeat, before she blinks at them like she's confused. "I, um." She squints her eyes like it's hard to remember. "I don't really remember. I think I was out for a walk, maybe?" She flutters her hand like it doesn't matter. "Anyway, I'm pretty sure I tripped and hit my face on a rock wall in someone's front yard. Totally clumsy and not at all something we need you guys for. Sorry to have wasted your time, though."

The second cop's taking notes and the first one's gaze slides to me. But then his eyes widen. "Holy shit, you're Hayden Vaughn."

His partner's head snaps up, and a wide grin splits his face. "No way. The Hitman," he holds up his fist for a bump and I tap it. "That goal last week against the Orcas was insane!"

The two cops start talking hockey and asking me for autographs. At some point, my brother comes back into the room and ends up taking a bunch of pictures for the guys with their phones. I'll happily do a thousand of these if it means they don't ask any more questions about what happened to my wife.

And now I'm even happier I stopped to shower and change before coming here because I'd have looked like I murdered someone if I hadn't... which I did.

But that's a secret I'll take to my grave.

For her.

For us.

For our family.

I don't know how long it takes, but eventually the cops leave and Sawyer closes the door behind them. "That was unsettling as fuck, huh? At least they were fans. Who knew your mediocre celebrity would come in handy?"

I flip him off as he laughs and Cassidy rolls her eyes before cringing. "Crap, don't make me roll my eyes. It hurts. And why does sound make me feel like my brain is splitting in half and melting out of my ears?"

Sawyer moves toward her with a frown, fully back in doctor mode again. "Your concussion. You need to be monitored for at least another twenty-four hours." He looks at me with a raised brow. "I'll take you home when my shift is over."

I nod, squeezing myself onto the bed next to Cassidy. She sighs happily and then curls herself into my side. I run my fingers through her tangled hair as Sawyer turns off the dim lights and leaves. I tighten my hold on her when I think about how I almost lost her. Them.

Fuck, *twins*.

The amount of shit I have to process would be overwhelming if I let it, but I just shove that shit down deep inside to deal with later.

When I close my eyes, I crash with my hand on Cassidy's stomach, imagining our future together.

I don't know what's going to happen, but I do know it's going to be fucking beautiful.

Houston Hellcats Blaze

2 oz tequila • 1/2 oz lime juice • 1/2 oz agave nectar • 2 slices jalapeño • 3-4 blackberries • ice

Garnish: blackberry skewer and jalapeño slice

Muddle jalapeño slices and blackberries in a shaker. Add tequila, lime juice, and agave nectar. Fill with ice and shake until chilled. Strain into a rocks glass filled with fresh ice. Garnish with a skewer of blackberries and a slice of jalapeño.

Cassidy

epilogue

Six months later...

HAYDEN SCOWLS at me as he walks through the door of my bar, and I shiver, hiding my grin. He narrows his eyes and clenches his jaw so hard that I'm surprised he has any molars left, honestly. He's been like this for months, ever since my ex boyfriend tried to kill me and our babies. Secretly, I love that he's so overprotective, but I wouldn't be me if I didn't make him crazy on purpose.

Besides, he loves it.

He's so hot when he's angry. I smirk at him before turning to pour a beer for one of the regulars and passing it across the bar. My belly brushes against the counter and I rub it when one of our little ones kicks—hard. The boys one hundred percent take after their father if the pummeling my ribs, organs, and especially bladder take on a daily basis is any indication.

"Princess, what the hell are you doing here? You're supposed to be staying off of your feet."

"I'm fine," I say, waving him off as I waddle around the bar to go collect empty glasses from the tables. "I'm pregnant, not broken."

Hayden growls as he follows me, grabbing my elbow and pulling me back toward him. "You need to sit down before you fall. You're looking a little pale. Sawyer said you need to stay in bed."

"Sawyer needs to mind his own damn business." I glare at Hayden as he smirks at me. He loves that we fight about this shit because he knows I'm going to give in eventually. "And staying in bed all day is boring. I have too much to do with the restaurant opening next week."

Yep, I finally did it. Hayden convincing me to continue with my OnlyFans the last six months meant I got all the weirdos who have a pregnancy kink flooding to my channel and enough money to expand The Sin Bin into a restaurant and bar the way my dad dreamed. There's something so satisfying about being able to fulfill his dreams and see them come true, knowing he'd be proud of me.

He probably wouldn't love the way I did it, but hey, we're not thinking about that.

The point is, I did it and the chef I hired is finalizing the menu, so mostly all I need to do now is taste test all the things.

It's a hardship, truly.

I run my fingers down the middle of Hayden's muscular chest, trying not to drool while I look up at him. "Unless you want to entertain me."

After the season ended in round two of the playoffs, Hayden's had nothing to do but work out and hover over me constantly. It's been fun. I'm surprised I got away from him this long today before he tracked me down.

His eyes darken as he grabs my wrist and pulls me toward

him. "You know I always want to entertain you." He gives me the kind of dirty kiss that makes my toes curl and one of the regulars whistle at us.

Okay, so I guess I don't actually need to be here. Lila's got it covered and my back is killing me. My feet are swollen, and I'd kill for some grilled chicken and veggies. Yeah, other women get fun pregnancy cravings like ice cream and mac and cheese, but all my babies want is veggies and lean protein like freakin' animals.

"Take me home?"

Hayden yells over to Lila that we're leaving as he scoops me up into his arms, giant belly and all, and carries me out the door like I weigh nothing. Not gonna lie, it's super hot. But eight months pregnant with twins, his dick isn't going anywhere near me.

Lucky for me, my man is the giving type, so despite the lack of penetration, we still find ways to enjoy each other.

And that's how I find myself, half an hour later, spread out naked in our bed with his head between my thighs and a camera recording it all. My fingers grip his hair as his wicked tongue does things to my clit that make me scream. He's got two fingers inside me, curling them against my g-spot while he licks and sucks until my legs shake and my eyes roll back in my head.

I've lost count of how many times he's made me come.

He finally pulls away when I'm panting and sweaty, his face glistening because it's coated in me, and he licks his lips before hovering over my body and licking one of my nipples. "I can't wait until your milk comes in."

"Hayden," I moan, arching into him as he teases me with his tongue. His hard dick presses against my thigh, but I know he won't push me when I'm this uncomfortable and it's all his fault. "You're going to kill me."

He grins as he kisses his way up my chest and then nips at

my jaw. "You're not allowed to die, and you're definitely not allowed to die before you bring our sons into the world."

He falls beside me, pulling me against him so I'm the little spoon while his hand rests on my belly. I sigh, living for these moments. Soon, our lives are going to be complete chaos, so I'm relishing the quiet while I can. "What do you think they'll be like?"

"Hopefully nothing like me," he says with a chuckle.

"Hey," I say, twisting as much as I can to glare at him over my shoulder. It doesn't go well. "Don't talk about my husband like that. I wouldn't procreate with anyone who's less than incredible."

He chuckles. "I didn't exactly give you a choice, wifey. Next time—"

I scoff. "*Excuse* me? Next time? What makes you think there's going to be a next time? I'm never doing this again." Okay, so maybe I'm lying. I've loved being pregnant, mostly. Sleeping sucks and my back hurts twenty-four-seven, but feeling my babies roll and kick? Best thing ever.

He laughs as he kisses the back of my neck. "Whatever you say."

"Hayden..."

"It's happening, even if you won't know when or how. Better get used to the idea now. I want at least five."

"I will spike the hell out of one of your drinks and pay a doctor to give you a vasectomy."

He laughs again, his hand moving down between my legs and rubbing slow circles over my clit. "You can try."

I moan as he works me up to another orgasm, knowing I'm going to be too tired to fight with him about this later. I think that's his ultimate plan, keep me too high on him to say no. But it's okay because we both know I'm going to give in eventually. He's too damn convincing and I'm too damn gone for him.

And maybe I want more babies with him. Maybe I want to

see him hold our little ones and watch him fall in love with them the way he did with me.

But it wouldn't be us if it wasn't a fight.

He's not above playing dirty to get what he wants, but then, neither am I.

In the end, I think we'll both win.

I guess we'll just have to wait and see.

The End

Watch for Kingston's story, coming soon in Cheap Shot, book 2 in the Cold-Hearted Players series...

Stalk me

(scan for links)

About the Author

Heather Ashley writes dark & steamy forbidden stories with toxic, obsessive heroes. She's a PNW girl through and through and lives for foggy mornings among the evergreens.

Printed in Great Britain
by Amazon